ISLANDS
of
TIME

A Novel

Barbara Kent Lawrence

Library of Congress Number: 2012953331

Lawrence, Barbara Kent
Islands of Time: A Novel/Barbara Kent Lawrence
p. 240
1. Fiction—General

I. Title.

Soft cover: ISBN: 978-1-934949-66-5
Kindle: ISBN: 978-1-934949-74-0
Smashwords: 978-1-934949-67-2

Published by

JWB
Just Write Books

Topsham, Maine 04086
207-729-3600 • jstwrite@jstwrite.com
Printed in the United States of America

For my brother Des, who led me back to Maine.

With fond memories of Captain Wilfred A. Bunker.

What people are saying about Islands of Time

Islands of Time: I really like it. The story about a girl from away falling in love with a year-round kid from Maine, then coming back as an adult to reclaim her self, resonates with me. It's also a love song to the people and landscape of Maine.

—Linda Greenlaw, *New York Times* best-selling author and swordfishing captain. Her most recent book: *Seaworthy.*

Penned by Barbara Kent Lawrence, a former Maine resident who treasures the state and its people, *Islands of Time* is a multilayered love story, rich in emotion and introspection...Lawrence moves effortlessly between the 1950s and the present day as Becky's memories surface...people of all ages can relate to Becky's journey — her struggle to understand how past events, tragic and wonderful, have shaped her life, and how to move forward in the best way possible.

—Aislinn Sarnacki in the *The Bangor Daily News*

Barbara Kent Lawrence has written a page turner of a novel about first love, its loss and the near hopeless pursuit of recapturing that for which one was unprepared.

Rebecca Granger returns us to a time that is past but an emotion that lives on. Hers is a character so deftly drawn that you will sympathize, empathize and possibly fall in love with her.

Prepare for a day or night of non-stop reading because you won't put *Islands of Time* down.

—Barbara Lazear Ascher, Author most recently of *Dancing in the Dark; Romance, Yearning,* and *A Search for the Sublime.*

Islands of Time is a deeply sensitive and revealing work...I read it...in three furious days—I couldn't put it down! It is masterful the way Lawrence has woven the narrative so that it moves throughout time with such fluidity, while still pulling us forward into a better place.

—Caitlin Fitzgerald, Actress: *It's Complicated, Like the Water, Masters of Sex.*

Barbara Kent Lawrence draws us into a steadily deepening engagement with a passionate, self-demanding character who is determined to create a new existence out of a broken past. The reader shares her growing freedom and empathy as she returns to a Maine island to revisit the site of a passionate encounter that has colored her whole existence. Over the course of the novel her errors and vulnerabilities become a source of strength. Her brave encounters with solitude and uncertainty take her beyond herself into unknown emotional territory. *Islands of Time* provides an amazing insight into the long standing cultural divisions of the Maine coast and the possibility of transcending them through human compassion and understanding.

—William Carpenter, author, *The Keeper of Sheep, Speaking Fire at Stones, Rain,* and *The Wooden Nickel.*

Other Books by Barbara Kent Lawrence:

Working Memory: The Influence of Culture on Aspirations, (a Case Study of Mount Desert Island, Maine). Dissertation, Boston University: UMI, Ann Arbor, MI, 1998.

Bitter Ice: a memoir of love, food, and obsession, Rob Weisbach: Wm. Morrow Inc., NY, 1999.

The Hermit Crab Solution: Creative Alternatives for Improving Rural School Facilities & Keeping Them Close to Home, AEL, Charleston, WV. 2004

Dollars and Sense: The Cost-Effectiveness of Small Schools, Lawrence, Barbara Kent *et al.,* KnowledgeWorks, Concordia, Inc. and The Rural School and Community Trust, Cincinnati, OH and Washington DC, 2002.

Dollars & Sense II: Lessons from Good, Cost Effective Small Schools, Lawrence, Barbara Kent *et al.,* KnowledgeWorks Foundation, Cincinnati, 2005.

The Hungry i: a workbook for partners of men with eating disorders, Greene Bark Press, Allentown, PA., 2010.

Acknowledgements

Howard Wells has been much more than an editor, though his work in that role has been invaluable. He has been midwife to this story and my ability to tell it: coaching, cajoling, encouraging, but always able to tell me when I needed to reconsider, cut, or breathe deeply to understand the story more fully myself. I would not have been able to write this book without him.

Publisher Nancy E. Randolph welcomed *Islands of Time* and me with enormous energy and enthusiasm. Her warmth and generosity of spirit are unbounded and provided the strength and skill necessary to make this book a reality.

I love the cover painting by artist Scott Baltz, and thank him for his support and kindness in letting us use it. He captures the mystery of islands and I feel the images and colors of his painting pulling me inside *Islands of Time* every time I look at it.

My partner Bob has helped me find my own safe haven, from which I have learned that I love to write. This is an enormous gift that I appreciate every day.

Wonderful friends and relatives helped immeasurably in the telling of this story by reading drafts, commenting, and encouraging me. I'm grateful to each of them for their questions, insights, and patience. I hope I haven't inadvertently omitted anyone, and I apologize if I have. They are in alphabetical order: Paula Bartlett, Barbara Fernald, Caitlin FitzGerald, Des FitzGerald, Connie Gourdeau, Katherine Hathaway, Faith Howland, Tim Lemire, Jennifer Lenichek, Sheila MacDonald, Judy Mansfield, Abigail Mellen, Sally Merchant, Tad Meyer, Nina Moriarty, Nan Newton, Diantha Nype, Gerda Paumgarten, Charlie Taylor, Joanne Thormann, Elizabeth Train, Michael Train, Betti Trapp, and Rob Weisbach. I also appreciate the help of Jan Dempsey, Director of the Hamilton-Wenham Library, her extraordinary staff and The Icehouse Writers.

My thanks to all the people I have known, even in passing, who contributed to this book. Many of the places exist, but none of the characters do, though I have drawn some of them from people I've met or aspects of myself.

Introduction

I never loved my husbands. I loved Ben. I was fourteen when I fell in love with Ben Bunker. It happened when I heard his voice. It wasn't that he said anything special, but his voice reverberated through me. Instantly. I was so close I could smell the salt on his clothes. I looked up into his eyes—blues of the sea and sky flecked with sunlight—and I was drawn into them. It was just a moment, but so powerful it still lives in me.

I did what I always did when an emotion threatened me. I froze. I was used to guarding against pain. I couldn't trust love, trust myself or even the idea of love. My sister's death and then later my father dying, too soon, too young. How can you trust yourself when everyone you love leaves and you know it was your fault?

I wasn't very likeable then, even to myself. Perhaps particularly to myself. Too shy and awkward to fit easily anywhere; too wounded to be comfortable in my own skin, in some ways too smart to be a woman. It was a strange time—hard to understand now. Women like my mother, Anne, were trained to be dependent, to keep a good house or houses, to look beautiful and give good parties. Too bad if you wanted to do something different. I didn't know what I wanted, I just knew I didn't want to be my mother.

Ben was my Romeo and I was his Juliet. I loved him, submerged myself in him, or tried to. But I was so broken I destroyed what I most loved.

ISLANDS *of* TIME

There be three things which are too wonderful for me, yes four which I know not;

The way of an eagle in the air; the way of a serpent upon a rock; the way of a ship in the midst of the sea; and the way of a man with a maid.

Proverbs 30:18

Chapter One

I knew the room would still be dark if I opened my eyes, the curtains and shades blocking all light. Thoughts and memories drifted back and forth like a gentle tide, past and present blurring, so that I could at first not recognize where I was or why. Like an animal coming out of hibernation, I lay in the bed feeling the shape of my body against its warm folds. Stretching, I breathed deeply and remembered I had left my life in Boston and come back to Maine.

I didn't want to look yet at the two rooms I'd rented for the summer, though I had barely seen them when I arrived late last night. I wanted to postpone confronting my new reality by listening to the sounds of the morning as the street came alive. I could hear the faint rumbling of trucks and imagined they were bringing food to the market and that the soft closing of doors signaled people were leaving their homes and setting off for work. I heard the scrabbling of gulls over the garbage cans and occasionally dogs barking, first on one side of the village, then others answering back. I stayed in bed, luxuriating in the soft down-covered mattress and comforter, enjoying the darkness of the room and wondering why I was there.

I wondered if I would know anyone in the village. My mother, Anne, had sold our land many years before. My stepfather Taylor didn't like it, and she didn't want to go back by herself. Instead they went to Nantucket and Hobe Sound and, after he retired, they traveled more, and I saw them less. My brother Robbie didn't like it much either, but then he was too young to remember being here. When he went to Stanford I worried that he would marry someone from California and stay there—which is what he did. Now we're more like cousins than sister and brother.

I lay in the unfamiliar bed, wondering if the village would be as I'd left it three decades earlier, preserved like an elaborately costumed doll in a glass case. Finally I dressed in black wool slacks and a purple sweater and went downstairs to talk with my landlady, who ran the stationery store below the elegantly refurbished suites on the second floor. "Good morning, Mrs. Jacobs," I said to the wiry woman.

Mrs. Jacobs pushed a wisp of gray hair back from her forehead and replied, "Good morning, Mrs. Evans, I hope you slept well."

"I did. You've made the room so comfortable and the feather bed over the mattress is incredible. I slept like a tired puppy."

"Glad to hear it. I hoped those rooms would rent to people who didn't want the big houses anymore but appreciated being comfortable and in the village. Now, I suppose you'd like some breakfast?"

"Yes, I thought I'd go to the pharmacy to eat and read the paper."

Mrs. Jacobs frowned and said, "I'm afraid you won't find it. The building is there, of course, but Frank couldn't keep the pharmacy going, so he sold it to a man who has a gift store. They sell fancy things for fancy prices, but you can get breakfast at The Lobster Pot across the street. It opened last summer and did real well. Now it's open again after winter, but they'll keep the prices low for a few more weeks until summer starts. Good country cooking. Remember, my kitchen's open to you, but you'll need to buy your own food."

"Thank you. I'll go to the market later. I guess some things have to change, but I'm sorry about the pharmacy. Where do people go now for medicine?"

"Oh, up to Ellsworth. "There's not so many living in the village year-round now. Too expensive."

"And ice cream cones?" I added, remembering the towers of black raspberry and vanilla ice cream my father and I got at the pharmacy when we returned from a picnic, and licked furiously, hoping to catch the melting ice cream before it oozed onto our hands.

"You can get ice cream. There's three places," Mrs. Jacobs said, gesturing to different parts of the little street, "The Old Cow, The Dugout and the Lobster Pot."

"And can I still get a newspaper in your store?"

"Sure—and lots besides—candy, calendars, balsam pillows and even videos."

I walked across the street to the Lobster Pot and sat at a table covered with red-checked gingham. The small restaurant smelled of grease, potatoes, sausages, and maple syrup. It was a warm, enveloping smell that took me back to the mornings my father and I ate French toast while he read the day late *New York Times* and I half-looked at a book.

"Good morning, Ma'am," the waitress said, holding a pot of coffee aloft ready to pour. "My name's Crystal. Would you like coffee?"

"I'd rather have tea, if you have it."

"Sure. Get you a pot right away," Crystal said, turning to the counter behind her. "Earl Grey or English Breakfast?"

"English," I replied, startled to have the choice.

When Crystal came back, she put the teapot on the table and asked if I was ready to order.

"I'd like the French toast with blueberry syrup, just for old time's sake. I used to get that with my father across the street at the pharmacy, when I was a child."

"Oh, so you're coming back then? My aunt owns this place, but her mother used to work behind the counter at the pharmacy. Aunt Molly learned how to cook from her mother. She just went to get some things from the market."

"I was here with my family in 1959."

"Well, enjoy," Crystal suggested, and I did. The French toast was thick and sweet, cut from homemade bread, and as I poured the thick blueberry syrup, I knew I was feeding more than my stomach.

It was our first summer in Maine. My parents rented a white-shingled cottage near the clubs, but only a short walk to the village. It didn't have a view of the water, but I could see the harbor from a window in the attic. There was a turret on one side of the house, which created a circular extension off the living room on the first floor and the master bedroom on the second. My mother loved to lie on the chaise longue in their bedroom and read, and Daddy liked the spacious porch where he could sit and talk with anyone walking past. The wallpaper in my room had a design of butterflies and bees hovering over flowers, which made me feel as if I was outside even on a day when fog shrouded the house. What I loved most was the smell—a combination of salt, flowers and old plaster in a house closed up for most of the year.

Whenever he was up for the weekend from New York, Daddy would take me with him early to the village stationery store to get the New York Times. *My mother ate breakfast in bed. At home in Manhattan, Sheila, the cook, made breakfast, Mildred served, and Isabel took care of Robbie. But in Maine we just had Tracy, a local girl who cared for Robbie, and Mrs. Swanson who came to do the shopping, cleaning and cooking.*

Sometimes Daddy took me out for breakfast at the pharmacy—pancakes with blueberry sauce and side orders of sausage. We sat at the marble counter. I sipped hot chocolate and Daddy and the local men drank mugs of coffee. At first I thought the men were starting their day of work, but after a while I realized they were taking a mid-day break, and they'd been up since before dawn. I loved sitting on the green vinyl stool, listening to them talking together, or sometimes with Daddy. Their voices changed when they turned to him. They were much more formal, though they seemed to like him.

There was a rhythm to the village. At ten, the street dance began in earnest. Everyone had to come to the post office because there was no mail delivery in town. Of course, Daddy explained, some people could send their butler or maid, but then they missed the fun of gossiping while they waited for the postmistress to sort the mail. There were older summer ladies with elegantly coiffed blue-tinted hair, and women from the village with their hair in pink plastic rollers, little boys in frayed jeans or Brooks Brothers shorts, little girls in Liberty dresses with smocking, little girls in cheap nylon skirts from stores in Ellsworth, men in tightly woven straw hats with madras bands and men in sweat-grimed caps. I loved watching them.

The summer people bowed and waved, shook hands, brushed against each other's cheeks—air-kissing Daddy called it—I knew they would congratulate themselves later about how easily they mixed with the locals.

❧

A short and very round woman with huge blue eyes and red cheeks holding a large brown paper bag came bustling through the screen door, smiling at everyone. "They had some mangoes and kiwis I thought we could put in the fruit cups. That should jazz things up," she said, looking around at her customers. There were eight of us, four men at a table in the back who looked like retired fishermen, their faces weathered like dried cod, a middle-aged couple whose cameras suggested they were tourists, me, and a bearded man wearing a Greek fisherman's cap. He looked familiar and I tried to subtract thirty years from him. When I stripped away the layers of flesh and years, I thought I saw the librarian, Bob.

As he left, he stopped at my table. "I think I know you, but I can't place you. Have you been here before?"

"Yes," I replied. "I used to come to the library all the time—sometimes with my father, mostly by myself, but just for two summers a long time ago. My name then was Becky Granger."

"Becky. I should have known. The Lone Granger's back in town! You weren't here but that one whole summer, and a little bit of the next—still, I remember how much you loved books. I'm Bob—at the library," he said as he stretched out his hand. "When you came back, that was such a short time," and then he looked at me, his eyes twinkling, and said, "Besides, you were too busy to come to the library as much the second summer."

I stood up and shook his hand, flattered he recalled the nickname he gave me the first summer when I was in the library so often, apprehensive about what he might remember of the second summer. "Do you still work at the library?" I asked to deflect him, and myself, from thinking about what had happened.

"I do. Been there thirty-eight years—each year is my last one. You have to come see it. You won't recognize it. We've added lots of space and books and finished the new media center," he said, taking his Briarwood pipe from his shirt pocket, rubbing the shining dark brown burl, and rolling the stem between his thumb and forefinger.

"It seems lots has changed," I said, unable to think of anything else to say. "I rented a little suite for the summer from Mrs. Jacobs. I wanted to be in the village. I'm thinking about trying to write and I wanted to come back here, to where I was a child," I added, trying to understand my own words.

"Yes, Dot worked hard on that all winter. Glad you like it there. Well there's no better place than this village, and there's no better work than writing," he replied, standing by the door, lighting a match, and sucking the flame into the tobacco. "Let me know if we can help you get settled, and come to the library soon. You can work there too. We have lots of room. And welcome back," he added, walking through the door and taking a big puff on the pipe, the smoke trailing a wake behind him.

As I walked through the town, stopping at places I had known, I tried to separate what I thought Bob might remember of me, and then of Ben and me—two teenagers in a summer love. He couldn't know what had happened, I thought, but then remembered how everyone in this small community seemed to take pride in knowing what everyone else was doing. My God, I shouldn't have come back, I thought, but the memory was too painful to allow in for long. The first sweetness of love, love that had buffered the sadness and loss then was lost itself because of me.

I continued walking down the street, focusing on the changes in the town. The movie theater was a bank now, but the clothing store still offered handsome tweed jackets and well-chosen ties that had changed little even in thirty years. I walked farther down the street and into The Village Shop, where I admired the chintz pillows, the colorful French Luneville plates and an array of table mats displayed like colors on an artist's palette around a large round wooden table. I looked at the Steiff bears and handmade Raggedy Ann and Andy dolls in the children's section. Then I saw the boats arranged on a shelf with the toys—lobster boats, rowboats and white sailing dinghies with blue or red oars. I picked up a little sailing dingy with red oars like the boat Ben had made for me and held it in my cupped hands until finally I turned it over and read: "Made in Islesford, Maine: Arthur Bunker & Sons," and my heart jumped. "Ben. Ben Bunker. He's the reason you came back." I winced and said angrily back to myself,

"No, please no," but tears reddened my eyelids. I fought it, but a feeling lingered nearer the surface than I had allowed it to come in a very long time, an unexpected feeling of being safe.

❧

Late that afternoon, after the shops were closed, I walked back through town along the village street, letting myself be pulled past the last store on Main Street, then past the parking lot for the Yacht Club, and down to the Club House where I spent so many miserable hours that first summer. When I looked at the small gray Cape in the fog, it seemed diminished, and it was hard to imagine that walking into the swirling mass of children and grownups with sail bags over their shoulders had made me feel so lost. I peered through the small panes of glass into the room and saw them all there—Mr. Craft, Ginny and Jon Thomas, and Sarah. I heard them teasing each other after a race, saw the salt crusting on their hair, and felt ashamed as the rope slipped through my fingers and the rowboat smacked the water.

I didn't want to go to sailing class, but my mother said everyone went. The first time Daddy and I walked into the Fleet headquarters, I looked up at the loft where bleached gray canvas bags lined the perimeter. "Those are sail bags," Daddy said. "Each boat in the fleet has a peg for its sails."

Children and older kids milled around, some talking loudly, showing off. There were only a few other parents, one of whom Daddy knew, but I didn't know anyone.

"They call this place 'Philadelphia on the Rocks,'" Daddy told me. "Lots of new friends for you. You'll get to know them." But I knew I wouldn't. When I looked around the room, I realized that only the little children were wearing shorts like mine—people my age were wearing long khaki pants and striped T-shirts and a few had colorful Shetland sweaters tied around their shoulders. I could feel a zit on my nose pulsing and I felt hot, but I tried to smile as I imagined myself sinking into the oiled wooden floor.

A tall man in khaki pants wearing a navy sailor's hat over his curly red hair walked into the middle of the room and said, "Good morning. I'm Mr. Craft. Good to have you all here for another summer." He smiled at the children and teenagers and then told everyone in rowing class to go to the side of the room where two older girls were standing. The little children in their orange life preservers walked over to the girls, some holding their mother's or father's hand, some running over and giving the instructors a hug. "Oh," one of them said to a little boy in blue shorts, "you've grown into such a big boy. You aren't going to have any problem making a dock landing this summer," then she swept him up into her arms and hugged him as she twirled around in a circle.

The smaller children filed out of the room towards the nearest dock while Mr. Craft turned back and said, "Is there anyone new this summer, anyone who hasn't passed the rowing test?" I looked around the room, praying there would be someone, but no one raised a hand. Then Daddy said, "My daughter Becky is new. She needs to learn to row." I could feel everyone's eyes on me, feel them looking at my boring brown hair and my red shorts, knobby knees and thick legs. One of the girls cupped her hands and said something to a friend that made them both giggle.

"That's fine, Becky," said Mr. Craft. "We all start sometime, and I'm sure in a few days there will be other people your age. Summer is just beginning, and some families won't get here for a week or so. By then you will be rowing all over the harbor and tying square knots. Now come here next to me and wait while I get everyone else started."

I looked up at Daddy and he nodded. I knew I had to stay, but I wanted to leave with him. As he walked out of the room, I thought, he just wants to play golf, but just before he passed through the large wooden sliding door, he turned and blew me a kiss.

After dismissing the sailing class and their instructors, Mr. Craft said to me, "We're a little short-staffed today, so could you go with the other rowers?" and seeing disappointment shadow my face, he added, "just for today."

"You mean the little kids?" I asked, my stomach tensing.

"Yes, but you are learning to row just like they are," he pointed out needlessly. "You'll like the instructors. Maybe they'll give you your own boat. Now, just run over to the dock, and tell Jen I said you're joining them for today."

"I'm fourteen" I thought, "I'm going to feel like a dinosaur," but my feet carried me obediently towards the dock and near an instructor who was waiting for two children to get into a rowboat.

When she saw me she asked, "Oh, hi, did Mr. Craft send you for the attendance?"

"No, I'm sorry," I replied. I towered over the older girl. "Are you Jen? I don't know how to row, I'm sorry. I'm new, and he didn't know what else to do with me, so he sent me here."

"Yes, I'm Jen. Well, hey, let's see. Oh, I know. Why don't you take the Sea Slug out? It's a good boat to start on. Stay close to us and you'll hear what

to do," she said, her eyes looking around at the children in twos and threes pushing their dinghies off the dock.

"All right," I mumbled, feeling trapped and embarrassed.

"Okay, now slide it into the water and get in," Jen said, looking at me and then at the dirty white boat. I followed her eyes to the Sea Slug, seeing only the rust smudges staining the sides from the oarlocks and seagull droppings splattered on the bottom.

I tripped over a rope as I tried to slide the heavy wooden rowboat off the float. As I pushed, the boat picked up momentum and its weight snatched the rope from my hands. As it bellied into the water, Jen looked back at me and yelled, "Be careful. You don't want to hit someone. Wait. I'll get it for you." Jen got into her dinghy, rowed out to capture the Sea Slug, then nudged it over to the dock. "Try again," she commanded, but I was still looking numbly at the Sea Slug, shocked by how heavy the boat was and how quickly it had slipped away. Now, I thought, even the little kids will think I'm an idiot.

"You don't have to wear your life preserver if you don't want to," Jen said. "You can swim, right?

"Umm. Well, I'm learning," I replied, raising my hand to chew on my thumbnail, then catching myself and shoving it into the pocket of my shorts.

"Leave it on then," Jen ordered, looking me up and down, her eyebrows twisting as she sized me up.

I tried to imagine how Jen saw me—a tall skinny girl with big legs, a pimple the size of Everest on her nose, and eight years on anyone else in rowing class. She must think I'm retarded, I realized, and blushed. Sometimes I felt so hopeless, clumsy and inept. I could see what I wanted to do, or should do, but something short-circuited. The effort to do something perfectly made perfection even less likely, and I would stumble or trip or drop the plate. When my mother got angry it seemed that her words were coated in ice. "There, you've done it again, haven't you? Well, pick up the pieces. It's Herend, you know. Or was."

I was glad rowing class got out before the kids my age came back from sailing. I looked out over the harbor and saw the Bullseyes racing between the islands, darting back and forth like seagulls and didn't think I would ever make friends with the sailors. I didn't want to tell my parents that I hated rowing class and didn't want to go back, but when I got to the cottage, my father looked at me and I couldn't raise my eyes to meet his. I could feel my chin starting to wobble and tears watering my eyes. I tried to walk past him, but he caught me by the hand and said, "Pumpkin, what's wrong?"

"I hate it. I hate it, Daddy," I blurted. "I can't swim and I can't row, and all the kids my age went sailing while I went with the little kids. I felt so stupid, Daddy. I don't want to go back."

"So what do you want to do with the rest of this day?"

"Me?"

"Yes," he nodded.

"I want to go out to our land and sit on my rock and read," I answered, sucking on my lower lip, then sneaking my hand to my mouth to chew on a hangnail.

"So that's what we will do," Daddy said as he drew my hand from my face and held it. "But tomorrow you must try again to learn to row. And when you do, you will row me around the harbor. I know you can do it." I wanted to live up to what he expected of me and for me but I didn't have his easy confidence with people or my mother's beauty, and I was pinioned by my fear of disappointing them both.

❦

I thought I would never fit into the group of summer kids. I guess I was just too shy, and they all knew each other, or I thought they did. And, of course, I never met any of the children of the people who lived in the village year-round. They almost didn't exist for me, though I remember hearing kids playing on the fields around the elementary school in town, and I wanted to join them because they sounded happy. I knew I couldn't. Perhaps that's what made joining them seem like fun—my mother wouldn't approve. She made it clear that people like us only went to the Episcopal Church and that the small Catholic Church in town was just for the help. But then I met Ben.

If I closed my eyes I could see him. He was tall, taller than I was and I was always too tall for a girl. His skin, at least what I could see of it then, was bronzed from the summer sun. I can taste the salt on his neck, feel his arms around me. His eyes electrified me. I felt sometimes as if I was sinking into a warm safe place when I was with him. Before I ruined everything.

I lay on the rock overlooking the sound and there was nowhere I wanted to be more than this place, this island. I lay cradled by an indentation, staring at the granite's molded fall to the water, almost hypnotized by the ceaseless wash of the waves against the pink stone. I looked down the sound framed by the mountains—Brown, Sargent and my favorite, Dog, which really did look like a gray-muzzled Lab lying next to its bowl. My father had told me glaciers scalped the earth to form the sound, the only fjord on the East Coast.

As I watched, I saw a speck on the horizon, a speck I could not identify, square against the sky, pushing towards me.

While I lay there, an eagle skimmed over my head, and hovered, screeching, over the water until he plunged, dug in his talons and scooped out a fish. Shocked, I wondered what it would feel like to be the fish. When the eagle flew off with its writhing prize, I shifted slightly to press against the rock, settling again into its warmth. My fingers lazily traced the infinite fractures in the stone. Looking at my hand against the pink rock, blue-gray veins coursing through flesh and granite, I could not separate myself from the land and water, rocks and trees, sounds and smells surrounding me.

The speck was larger now, a boat, though not an ordinary boat. "It's here!" I shouted as I jumped from my rock couch and ran through the underbrush, scratching my legs against the rhodora and sweet fern, the clean smell of broken leaves a trail behind me. "The float. I can see it!" My mother was putting the picnic plates into a leather-handled rattan basket, while my father played with my little brother Robbie on our new red and blue plaid picnic blanket.

"There, out past that pine tree with the long twisting branch." My mother looked in the direction of my outstretched hand and then we followed my father down the path to the car and out to the open space overlooking the water. It was the only flat grassy place on our land, a spot where we could run and fly kites that we called "the Green Place." I loved to sit under the knuckled branches of a gnarled apple tree by myself, away from my parents, reading or watching the gulls circle over the water as they followed the lobster boats.

My father said the broker told him that this property had once been part of a granite quarry and that schooners had tied up to a dock at the Green Place, where the land had been built up and flattened for the wagons and trucks that hauled the blocks of stone to the edge of the bank. All that remained of the old dock were heavy, gray barnacle-encrusted timbers and giant blocks of granite rising through the water. On the ledge above was a huge metal staple punched into the rock, pocked and rusted by air and salt.

As we walked out onto the grass, the wind caught our hair and shirts, billowing them into sails. When I looked down the sound, I could see the boat clearly. It was a white lobster boat with red trim and a little red triangular sail flying at the back, and it was towing a float and a skiff. Two men in yellow slickers stood in the back and a third stood in the wheelhouse.

The lobster boat pulled its load into the little cove, coming so close I thought it must crash against the rocks. "How can they come so near?" I asked.

"The water is very deep here; it just goes straight down," my father replied. "That's why you have to wear your life preserver when you play near the water." His voice growing firm, almost stern, he added, "When you learn how to swim, you won't have to wear it." I felt my face grow hot with shame that I could not swim although I was almost fifteen.

The boat stopped, and the man in the stern threw out an anchor whose heavy chain clanked out of a metal channel on the side of the boat until it stopped with a shudder.

"Afternoon," the captain called up. "We got her here for you—little later than I'd hoped; tide's runnin' ha'd today."

"That's fine," my father replied. "Good to see you, Captain Bunker. Mr. Stephens said you'd take good care of us."

"We'll put her near the old pins where the granite ships used to tie up," Captain Bunker called, talking loudly across the water, his hand loose on the wheel.

"That's fine," my father said putting his arm around my shoulders. "Mind if we watch? Becky, my daughter, is going to learn to dive and fish off this float."

"Finest kind," Captain Bunker responded, his voice clipping the words so I wasn't sure I understood what he'd said. "This is my grandson," he added, putting his arm around a boy who'd moved from the back of the boat to stand next to him. "He's here to watch too—goin' to learn how to do it himself some day."

"Does he want to come up here with us?" My father asked. "He could see better."

Oh no, daddy. Don't say that, I thought. Though he was still far away, I could see the boy standing in the bow of the boat, his yellow slicker pants bulging out over his legs and a bleached blue baseball cap snug on his head.

"What am I going to say to him, Daddy?" I asked, but he ignored my question and turned back to the boat.

"Good idea, Mr. Granger," Captain Bunker called up. "Chummy'll take the skiff over to the ledges. Be up there in a minute to catch the rope for us."

The boy looked at his grandfather, and he seemed to be as uncomfortable as I was.

Chummy, I thought. What a funny name. Like friend? I watched as he walked to the stern, uncleated a rope attached to a blue dinghy riding behind the boat, stepped lightly into it and rowed quickly towards the shore.

One of the men loosened the ropes on the long ramp in order to skid it out over the float. I pretended to watch, but my eyes followed the blue skiff as the boy pulled on the oars. My stomach tensed, as it did at dancing school in New York when the dancing master said the boys could pick their partners from the girls sitting on the red and gold velvet chairs lined against the wall, twisting the fingers of their white-gloved hands, crossing their legs as they'd been instructed. I hated wondering if someone would choose me, not wanting to be chosen, but not wanting to be left on the chair. Still the boy rowed toward me, and with a strange apprehension turning my stomach, I felt him pulling closer to me.

The boy rowed the skiff to the wide rocks of the tide pools that ran flat into the ocean below, faced the bow into the shore, waited for a wave, and pulling hard against the water, shot the boat onto the ledge. Before the next wave, he hopped out, grabbed the coil of rope, then pulled his boat from the water and tied it to the gray hulk of a dead tree cast up on the rock. I saw him walk over to a tide pool, and slowly kneel beside it, but I turned away to watch the men, scared he would think I was interested in him or in what he was doing.

Captain Bunker looked over towards his grandson and muttered, "He's about as useful as a hole in snow," and he and the other man grinned.

"You want me to catch the rope, Captain Bunker?" my father volunteered.

"Much obliged, Mr. Granger, Chummy's lost himself in another tide pool. Hold fast to that spar, and don't lean too far out," he instructed. "If you miss it the first time, we'll do it again."

I tensed as the man threw the line, but it unfurled like a lasso right into my father's outstretched hand.

"Good job, Mr. Granger," Captain Bunker called up to him.

To the far right I could still see the boy as he knelt on the shiny rock, poised above the pool of water. I watched as he darted his hand in the tide pool to bring up something wriggling in his palm and then let the creature run up and down his arm and along the rock before he placed it gently back in the water. I watched as he looked over towards where I was standing, spat over his shoulder into the water, shrugged, and then started to walk towards us.

I turned away and watched as the man who was setting the end of the ramp next to the pins in the rock connected them with a metal bar that ran through openings in the ramp. My father called out, "Captain, can we try it out now?"

"Go ahead, Mr. Granger, just hold onto the railing. The sea is a little rough, and you're going to get a jump from it."

Daddy turned to me and said, "Get your life preserver; it's in the car."

"Oh, Daddy," I moaned. "It's so stupid."

"Becky, there's no one here to see, and you'll feel really stupid if you fall off the dock and can't swim."

I lowered my eyes, my face reddening, and walked towards the car. I was looking at the ground, but I took only a few steps before I stumbled against the boy. All I could see were his torn sneakers with a different colored lace in each shoe. But I heard him say, "I'm sorry, Miss, I didn't see you." It was enough. In that fraction of a second I felt time stop. I smelled the sweet clean salt and felt the warmth of his breath. I felt terrified and safe simultaneously, but shocked—frozen like a tiny rabbit, crouching in fear. When I looked up and into his eyes, I was mesmerized. They were blue like the sea, the colors changing in the light of the sun. He put out his hand and touched my shoulder to balance us both, then backed away quickly, lowering his hand to his side.

"I'm sorry. I didn't see you," he repeated and then stepped aside and almost ran to the top of the ramp before I could answer.

My breath caught in my throat, and I could feel my heart pounding. I thought it was so loud everyone would hear it. I could still trace his hand on my shoulder as I walked slowly to the car, got the orange life jacket, and turned to walk back to the dock. My father called out, "Hurry up, we're waiting for you," as I tied the straps around my waist and felt the bulky, cold preserver sticking out around me like a fat sausage.

"Here she comes—Mae West," my father laughed, and then so did the other men. I blushed and tried to hide my face, but he took my hand and said, "You go first."

I walked down the ramp, the rhythm of the water bouncing against me until I let it lead me as I had learned to do when riding a pony in Central Park, still feeling the boy's hand on my shoulder.

"Well done, deah," Captain Bunker said when I reached the float. "You've got good sea legs already, I can tell."

I smiled to thank him and then walked around the float as my parents came down the ramp with Robbie. I knew the boy was still at the top of the ramp, and I hoped he would stay there. When I got to the side of the float near the shore, I noticed shells growing against the sides of the old granite foundation a few feet away, some with feathers flowing in the current.

"Wow!" I said, fascination overcoming my self-consciousness as I squatted down at the side of the float. "They have little feathers growing out of them!"

"Barnacles. Them's barnacles," I heard him say. I turned my head and saw his sneakers next to mine. With boys my age at home I would never have

had the courage to ask, but now his grammatical mistake disarmed me, and gave me a little more confidence. Even though my heart was still pounding, I pointed at the water and said, "What're they doing?"

"They're eating," he explained. "They stick those feathery things out and let the water run through them." Then, pointing with his index finger, he explained, "See there, that one. Just watch it for a while and you'll see it pull it back and then stick it out again. Those are its feet," he explained," but now I was thinking about how dirty his fingers were, the grime dark brown under the nails, and the faint smell of fish and gasoline coming from his clothes, trying to argue myself out of the extraordinary attraction I felt for him.

I hid from him by letting myself be drawn in by the little creatures before I said, "They're like people in apartment buildings. They're living so close together, all doing the same thing at the same time; now they're out shopping for food," but then I wondered if he had ever seen an apartment building, and I felt myself distancing myself again, talking the way my mother did with servants.

I could feel myself pulling back into my own shell, but I slowly and consciously moved my foot closer to his and looked at our shoes against the bleached silver gray wood of the dock—mine were barely scuffed, expensive Top-Siders, and his were worn dirty high top sneakers. Something was making me want to touch him, to have him touch me—and perhaps because it was so unlikely, impossible really—I wasn't scared as I was with other boys, boys from my world, and I wanted him to like me.

"What are those bigger shells?" I asked.

"Oysters," he replied. "There aren't many of them left here in the sound any more. You're lucky to have them. They taste some good—better than mussels." Then he pointed to a fat green tube floating just below the surface, "That's a sea cucumber."

"That's what it looks like," and the thought made me laugh. "Or a blimp, like the Goodyear blimp over Yankee Stadium," and that seemed ridiculous too because he probably didn't know what I meant.

"Ayuh. I saw a picture of that once," he replied. "Sea cucumber looks like a vegetable, but it's an animal. Know what it does when it's frightened?"

"No."

"It throws its guts at you," he answered, triumphant when I looked startled.

"What?" I said, pursing my mouth in disgust.

"It throws its stomach at a predator to confuse it. Some day you'll see it."

"Well, I don't want to scare it," I said firmly, and he turned and smiled at me, his eyes laughing.

"It don't hurt the sea cucumber; it just grows another stomach."

"Time to go," Captain Bunker announced. "Come on, Chummy, I told your mother I'd have you home for supper and it's almost three-thirty now. You move like a toad in a tar bucket."

I wanted to ask Chummy what his name meant and why there weren't many oysters left in the sound, and where he lived, but he got up and walked back towards the tide pools. Captain Bunker revved the engine, while I read the name The Sea Princess on the stern in royal blue letters and the name of her home port, Islesford, Maine.

"Captain Bunker," my father said, "Mr. Stephens said you take people to the outer islands for picnics. Would you take us sometime?"

"Of course, Mr. Granger," Captain Bunker called back. "You'd like Baker Island. Good day-trip. Let me know when you want to go."

The boat pulled away, hesitating only as it gathered up Chummy and the dinghy, and then The Sea Princess gained the open water, picking up speed. I didn't want them to go, but I was also relieved. The fascination I felt for him was too compelling, almost exhausting. If he turns then he'll be my friend, I thought, but then I realized, our parents would never let us be friends. Just before the gray-blue of the fading light enveloped them, at the last moment I could have distinguished their slickers, Chummy turned, as did the other men, and waved and I waved back.

Chapter Two

As I came back to the present, jarred by the wooden bench biting into my thigh, I smiled at the memory. It was so gentle when we met. So sweet and unlikely. I trusted him immediately. Something about him put me at ease, gave me confidence I never felt with other people. That made me want to be with him even more than the extraordinary attraction. As I played the memories back, I relived my relief when I passed the rowing test right after Ben taught me how to make a dock landing, heard his voice in my ear, pictured him sitting in the stern of the rowboat telling me what to do. I started sailing class the next day. I was good at reading the charts and watching the wind mark the waves, which told me how to trim the sails. A few days later, when Jon Thomas was the skipper, I was even able to tell him I thought he had miscalculated a reading. He looked as if I'd slapped him, but another boy said, "I think she's right. If we go that way we might ground on Sheep's Ledge," and someone else said, "Navigator, that's what we'll call you: 'The Navigator.'" After that, the other kids started calling me, "Gator." My mother bought me some long pants and two Shetland sweaters. She'd been trying so hard to keep me as a little girl, but more than that she wanted me to fit in with the summer kids.

As I walked past the gray Yacht Club and onto the narrow wooden trestle to the deserted docks, I said to the shadows, "I did learn to row, Daddy. Ben taught me. Do you remember?" The wood trembled, and as I walked I remembered how I too had trembled, scared of the water far below, scared of falling in, scared of disappointing, scared of being scared. The mist gathered around me, and I saw the rowboats lined up on the distant floats just as they had been when I went to rowing class. I walked down the ramp, feeling the metal railing cold and damp in my hand, to the dock, sat on a wooden bench and looked out over the graying harbor. The gulls were circling directly over me, wheeling with the wind, gliding in and out of the fog like ballet dancers floating in and out of the wings.

I stood up, walked over to the smallest dinghy and hauled it from its place, catching the line in my hand as the boat slid into the dark green water. Then I stepped in carefully, sat down, placed the oars in their locks, pulled the faded orange life-jacket stored in the bottom of the boat over my head, tied the straps, and pulled away from the dock in short even strokes until I was rowing between the sailboats at anchor. I rowed past the old wooden Bullseyes we'd used in sailing class, and the sleeker new fiberglass sailboats, then farther out beyond the larger Luders and Internationals, and finally even past the largest yachts that lined the outer harbor. I'd been rowing with the outgoing tide for half an hour when the choppy waves and wind in the channel startled me. Only then did I raise my head to the shore and see the dimmed lights of the shingled cottages along the shore in the fog. "Oh God, this is dumb," I said out loud, suddenly feeling the cold.

I stopped rowing, pulled hard on one oar and pushed with the other to turn the little boat, now fighting the tide and the waves, feeling my strength ebb and my fear rise. I wondered if someone would find me, or if a party of the few summer people already in town might be in a power boat coming back late from a day of picnicking and exploring the outer islands. I saw their boat rushing past me and imagined foundering in its wake. It was harder now to row against the tide. My hands hurt, and blisters on my thumbs and forefingers were raw and oozing, but I pulled against the oars and thought, you taught me well, Ben.

Finally, I rowed back into the inner harbor, pulled the boat up on the dock, untied the straps of my damp life preserver, and sat on the bench looking at the darkness. I wiped my face with a dark blue bandanna, wrapped my arms around myself and stared at the water thinking about my father—my father in the canoe with my sister Rachel and me when we were children. "God damn it. God damn it," I cried out. "Why didn't you have life jackets on us?" And then more slowly, "We were just little kids, Daddy." I could see him trying to haul the canoe around. Why didn't you jump in the water and swim after Rachel? I thought. I wondered if he was scared, or knew he couldn't swim fast enough to catch Rachel, or didn't want to abandon me in the canoe, or if he just froze. Whenever I had tried to learn to swim I felt the water dragging me down. I saw one of those monsters in Grimm's fairy tales, reaching up to claw at me and pull me under. I could feel myself swallowing the pool water and gagging as chlorine burned my eyes and throat. I imagined myself turning blue like Rachel, my mother screaming, my father crying.

It happened so quickly. Daddy was paddling. Rachel was six, I was almost nine. I wanted to see where the loons nested on a little island near the dam. My father said we couldn't go too near the nest or we would bother the birds, but we could paddle past it and turn back to hover off the shore. When we got near the nest, Rachel stood up and called out to the loons and Daddy told her to be quiet. She sat back down, but while Daddy and I watched for the loons, Rachel leaned out to play with the water and tumbled in. She screamed, but the canoe was facing away from the current, and while Daddy tried to turn the canoe, the water caught Rachel and pulled her from us. I can still see her being taken by the flow of water towards the dam. Time stopped. My father was yelling, Rachel's blond curls floating on the water. She was screaming and waving her arms, bobbing in the water, and getting farther and farther from us as the current carried her quickly out of sight. Daddy struggled to turn the canoe, while I paddled desperately with my hands. Afterwards the doctor told my parents that Rachel had hit her head hard on a rock when she plunged over the dam.

When we found Rachel, her skin was blue gray and my father picked her from the rock and held her upside down against him the way he held her when she had croup, pounding on her back to make her spit up the water. The blood from her cut was running into the water, and she hung against him limp as her Raggedy Ann doll. Daddy cried, the only time I ever saw him cry, and when we reached the dock my mother screamed and fainted.

I've tried so hard to stop that moment from happening. I've imagined telling my father I didn't want to see the loons, or jumping out of the canoe and swimming to save Rachel. In the nightmares and daydreams, I've tried to stop it from happening, but when the dreams end I know my sister's death was my fault. Why didn't we have life jackets? I asked again plaintively.

❦

That evening, after supper, I sat in the tiny living room next to the bedroom of my suite, sipped a glass of chardonnay, and let my mind wander back to the time before Ben taught me to row. When Ginny and Jon arrived at the dock for the picnic. They were total snots. For the first time since I watched Ben walk away so long ago, I let myself rewind the story, consciously, frame by frame.

One Saturday Daddy said that on Sunday after church we would go with the Johnsons and Thomases and their children, Ginny and Jonathan, to Baker Island just off the main island. I knew Ginny and Jon from sailing class, but I was scared to spend the day with them, scared because they didn't like me, and they were the kind of people my mother would like me to have for friends, or more accurately, to be. I was standing near them one morning before we divided into the rowers and sailors. Ginny said, "You're still stuck in rowing, so it's..." but Jon interrupted, "Not like we're all in the same boat."

That day the Johnsons drove up with their two small children and Mr. Johnson's mother, who was ancient and frail with a cloud of white hair. Then Mrs. Thomas's mother, Mrs. Saunders, arrived on the arm of Nathaniel her chauffeur, who was a portly black man with Louis Armstrong cheeks. She was thin and elegant, her white hair cast with violet. She was wearing a white linen dress, white tennis shoes, and a broad-brimmed white straw hat with two fresh, red-streaked white roses pinned to the red band.

Mr. Thomas told me to wait with Ginny and Jon and, to make conversation, I asked Ginny if they had a powerboat. "Yes," she replied, "of course, but it isn't big enough for all these people. Our parents charter a boat," then she turned to the harbor and added, "There it is now, The Sea Princess." His boat. My heart skipped a beat, like a flat stone over water.

As Captain Bunker eased the large lobster boat next to the dock, I scanned the boat, and when I didn't see Chummy I felt disappointed, but also relieved. A few seconds later, though, I saw him straighten up inside the boat, his arms full of canvas cushions. I felt a tingling in my stomach and the rising flush that always betrayed me. I could see him surveying the crowd of people on the dock so I ducked behind Jon and his father so I could watch him. I saw him run his eyes over the people in the boat then get back to putting the cushions on the bare wood seats around the boat, and I hoped he felt disappointed.

Mr. Thomas called out,"Okay. Everyone in. Watch your step. Margie, don't forget the cooler under the tarp. Nathaniel, bring Mrs. Saunders to the side of the boat, and Captain Bunker and I'll get her settled. Are you coming with us?"

"No Sah, Mrs. Saunders said just to go back to the house and then come back 'n wait for you'all," he replied, and he gave Mrs. Saunders's arm to her son-in-law with his white-gloved hand.

I followed behind the others lining up to mount the narrow steps set on the dock at the edge of the boat. When it was my turn, I stepped up and saw the back of Chummy's head as he was reaching down over the far side of the boat. I looked for a place to sit, but there wasn't one. Daddy said, "Just go up with Ginny and Jonathan on the bow," but I didn't want to. Big relief when Mr. Johnson's mother said, "Now dear, there's lots of room next to me." Just as I started walking over to her, Chummy turned around. He was holding a wet line in his arm, beginning to coil it, and when he first saw me, he fumbled slightly with the rope, and dropped a coil. "Hello," I said, bravely, feeling simultaneously sorry to have embarrassed him, but also a delightful twinge of power.

"Hello, Miss," he answered and then turned to stow the rope under the gunwale. Mrs. Johnson smiled at me, her blue eyes pale as sea glass with a frosted rim, and said, "Well, isn't he a handsome young man. Where do you know him from, dear?"

"I don't really know him, Mrs. Johnson. I met him when they brought our float to our dock." I listened to his steps as he moved around the boat doing his work and pretended I didn't care where he was.

"That's nice, dear," Mrs. Johnson answered, and I was relieved when Captain Bunker called out, "Cast off," and moved the boat into the channel, the engine roaring so I couldn't hear Mrs. Johnson and didn't have to talk with her.

I turned to watch the houses disappearing and the island shrinking, but I knew exactly where Chummy was in the stern. I could see him at the edge of my vision, but I wished I had sunglasses so I could watch him without people knowing, particularly him. Then I saw a black fin roll out of the water and, as quickly, back in. "Oh look, Pumpkin," Daddy called, "see the porpoise?"

Captain Bunker turned to me and said loudly over the engine, "They like to follow the boats, deah. Pretty soon we'll be near the ledge and you can see seals sunbathing on the rocks...just like movie stahs."

I got the binoculars Daddy gave me for Christmas from my daypack and then focused on the water ahead of where I saw the porpoise. Again, the fins rolled out of the water, larger now in the binoculars. "Daddy, I see them! They're so beautiful," I said. I scanned with the binoculars back to the island and looked at the houses and little people on the docks, then towards the ocean and the islands, and then around the boat until suddenly I saw Chummy's face right next to mine, looking at me cross-eyed, enormous through the binoculars. I put down the glasses quickly, and he smiled at me. I knew then we were even, and I blushed, excitement and embarrassment fusing.

A little later, he walked near Mrs. Johnson, who said to him, "Hello, Becky was telling me that you brought their float out to them." I wanted to dive overboard.

"Yup, brought it down the sound," Chummy replied, and when I looked at him I felt my heart beat harder and I tried to smile. My throat closed up and I didn't think I could speak, so I looked down at my hands. "What's the name of your friend, Becky?" Mrs. Johnson asked.

"Oh," I said,"It's Chu..."

"Ben," he interjected, "My name is Ben," and then he asked, "Do you know the names of the islands?"

"No," I answered softly, my heart thumping so hard my chest hurt, "not yet."

"Well," he replied, pointing with his hand towards a low, dark green island, "that there is Suttons. Not many people there, no roads." And then, sweeping his arm to the other side of the boat, he added, "over there is Greenings. Just summer houses there too."

"I know Bear Island Light because we studied it on the charts at rowing class," I said, and I felt as if I was going to faint.

"Rowing class? Now that's foolish! Classes for rowing!" he exclaimed, but then quickly looked at Mrs. Johnson to see if she thought he had been rude. "I mean," he continued, "you don't need to go to school to learn to row. I can teach you that in a minute."

"I'm not good at it," I admitted. I was surprised I could tell him something that worried me and surprised he didn't seem to care.

"I can teach you. Anyone can learn to row," he replied confidently. "My Grammie taught me 'cause my Dad was busy fishing and working with Grampie, and Mumma had the little kids. I'll teach you," he repeated.

In the distance we could see a low swell of rock shimmering against the horizon that, as we got closer, resolved into a ledge covered by seals lolling in the sun. Then a couple of the seals bobbed their heads up near the boat, popping like dark corks from the water, their whiskers glistening and dripping, and Ben said, "See, they're looking at us. They're just as curious about us as we are about them." I laughed, this time out loud, delighting in the seals and in the fact that Ben loved watching them too.

Captain Bunker slowed the boat as we approached an island with a wide skirt of pink granite softened by the sea and guided it into a cove with a circling beach of flat rocks and pink sand. Then he stopped the engine even though we were far from shore. Bradley threw the anchor into the water and, as the boat swung back on the chain, Ben grabbed the line secured to the dinghies that trailed behind us to pull them alongside The Sea Princess. *"Okay Mr. Granger, Mr. Johnson," Captain Bunker called out. "This is as far in as we can go. Time to get in the rowboats. It'll take two trips, so some of you will have to wait.*

The men helped the ladies into the boat and then asked who wanted to be next. Ginny and Jon got up with their knapsacks, and I was relieved when

Daddy said his family would wait because that meant I wouldn't have to be in the rowboat with them. Captain Bunker told Ben and Bradley they would take Mr. and Mrs. Granger and Robbie and himself on the next trip, which left just me and the rest of the picnic equipment and food.

I watched Ben row back towards The Princess, and wondered if his grandfather and Daddy were conspiring to put me alone in the boat with Ben, but I decided no, it was more likely that no one even thought about us being together, about the possibility of an attraction between us that was already working overtime in me. When he got back to The Sea Princess, Ben smiled up at me from the rowboat. I walked to the edge of the boat and stood looking at him, not knowing what to do. I was drawn to him so strongly that I could not take my eyes off him, so finally I just closed them.

"I can show you some tricks to rowing. Just get in the boat," he said and held his hand out to me. His hand was dry and strong, the fingers gripping mine not tightly, but firmly. I wanted him to pull me against him and I blushed at the thought.

"Okay, now what's hard about rowing?" Ben asked, pulling on one oar to swing the bow towards the shore and looking at me. There was something about the way he looked at me that I trusted, that told me I didn't have to pretend to be someone I wasn't because he wasn't judging me or finding me wanting.

"So what do you need to know?" he asked.

I took a deep breath, lowered my eyes to my hands, and said too fast, "I don't know where I'm going, so I go around in circles. I pull on one oar and I'm too far one way and then I try to correct myself and I'm going too far the other way. I make myself dizzy and I feel so stupid." My words spilled out even faster, "Because I'm in this class with kids in first grade. But I was never in sailing before and the instructor has to worry about the little kids, so she doesn't think about me." Ben looked at me and then out to the water behind my head, but he didn't say anything, so I continued. "She's nice enough, but I can't hear what she's saying half the time, and when I can hear her I don't know what she means." Then I lowered my voice and said, "I don't want Daddy to know how much I hate it because he's trying so hard to make my mother happy and give her a good summer."

When I looked up Ben was looking at me—directly but with kindness in his eyes. I felt myself balancing on the edge of a stony cliff, wondering if I could trust him or not. He looked at me so evenly, and so deeply, that I took a deep breath and said, "Well, she gets upset easily since my little sister died."

I watched his face, ready to close back up like the barnacles, but I saw his eyes get softer and deeper and he said, "I'm sorry, " and he asked, "How?"

All I could say was, "She drowned."

"I'm sorry," Ben said, but he didn't ask anything more and I felt my hands relax and realized I'd been clenching them so tightly that now they ached.

When I took a deep breath and looked at him again, he said gently, "You aren't born knowing everything. Even a seal pup has to learn how to swim."

I stared at him and I felt the ache in my throat that always preceded tears. I could feel my own hand still in his and the strength of his arm as he guided me to the seat in the dinghy.

"Even a seal pup has to learn," I thought. He had made me feel accepted in a way I'd never felt before, and it seemed like I was going to a tiny safe and secret island. I think I fell in love with him in that moment.

"When you're rowing, yes, you're going backwards," he continued, "but you just fix your eye on a point and steer by that point. Right now what do you think I'm using for the point?" he asked me. I'd watched him carefully, so I said, "The Sea Princess?"

"Yes, good," he replied. "It's not the best marker, because she swings around. Better if you have something fixed and steady, but this is a short trip, so she's fine. We can practice later, if you want to. What else don't you know?" He looked right at me, and it made me shiver a bit, but I answered him.

"I don't know why your grandfather always calls me 'dear,' and I don't know how to land. I always crash into the dock."

"Don't take it personal 'cause that's what he calls everyone. And I crashed into the dock too—once. Grammie said I was just rushing and fussing about what people thought of me. She said I had to forget that and go with the water." He laughed and added, "She also said I was numb'r than a pounded thumb."

"If I can't do a dock landing, then I'll never get out of rowing class," I replied. "I feel so big and dumb sometimes. I'll be rowing around the harbor until I'm an old lady."

"No, I won't let that happen. I'm going to teach you so you can go in one of those foolish little sailboats and get in the way of the fishermen."

When we got to shore, he rowed hard to beach the boat. His grandfather caught the bow and pulled us in, and Ben told me when to jump out. Daddy called out, "Come on, Pumpkin, we're over here. Do you want to find sticks for marshmallows?"

"Yes, Daddy," I answered obediently, turning my back on Ben, forcing my mind back to the picnic.

I sat on the rocks as the grown-ups drank Bloody Marys. Mrs. Johnson gave Ginny, Jon, and me Cokes and hamburgers and told us to sit together to eat. I trailed behind them as they talked about the sailboat race the day before. There was nothing I could add, and they hardly noticed I was there. After a few minutes comparing their performance on the spinnaker run, Jonathan said to Ginny, "Did you notice he's got black junk under his nails!" When she said mockingly, "Oh I think he's cute," he replied harshly, "Cute! He smells like bait, and he probably left school when he was ten."

I sat quietly, feeling my neck grow hot and pulled a book from my satchel so I could pretend to ignore them, and they could ignore me. I pulled my hat over my head so I could watch Ben sitting with his grandfather and Bradley, taking food from metal lunch pails, and I thought how easily he went back to his world. I wanted to go to sit with him, but I couldn't think of any excuse, so after a while I went to look for a special spot where I could lay in the sun and read and no one would bother me. My parents were so busy talking that they didn't notice, and I walked quickly until I got around the curve of the shore where they couldn't see me and walked down the rocky beach.

I was standing on a flat ledge of rock, looking back to the mountains of Mount Desert Island with a few white clouds dancing above the peaks. The ledge, still shining from the last tide, held pools of water and there were enormous slabs of pink rock set as if by a giant hand—randomly balanced at intervals along it. I wondered if I could jump from one of these rocks to another, and how far I could go in this jumbled landscape before again touching the ledge. I started hopping from rock to rock, trying to jump as far and fast as I could, holding my book in one hand, stretching out the other arm for balance. I found a rock large and flat as a dance floor, and I started dancing. I don't know what possessed me, but I heard the music in my mind and I was alone, facing the ocean and hearing music in the waves, I danced, lost in the rhythm.

"Well, you sure are some dancer," he said from behind me.

"Oh no! Oh," I exclaimed. "You snuck up on me." I turned to face him, my face burning with sun and embarrassment.

"Hard not to when you don't pay attention to anything," he replied. "I called to you, but you didn't turn around."

I watched him as he watched me on my pedestal and I wondered what he thought when he looked at me. "Here," he said, "let me help you off that rock." I wanted his help so much that I refused.

"I got up myself. I can get down," I replied.

"Suit yourself," he said, then stood back and folded his arms in front of his chest as I walked over to the edge and teetered on the side. The rock was higher than I'd thought, and when I jumped my knees hurt from the impact.

"Grammie would say you're independent as a hog on ice," he said.

"What's that supposed to mean?"

"Well, you ever seen a pig on ice?" he replied, grinning. When I imagined the animal slipping and sliding I had to laugh at myself too, which let me relax a little.

"You want to look for crabs in the tide pools?" he asked, so we walked along the shore towards the end of a point.

"Where do you live?"

"Over there," he said, "on Little Cranberry. You can't see my house because it's on the other side of that point."

"Where do you go to school?"

"Went to the Islesford School, but now I go to the high school on the mainland. And you?" he asked me.

"Mainland?" I asked, thinking he meant Ellsworth or Bangor, but he explained that to him and people on Islesford, "mainland" meant Mount Desert Island, and Great Cranberry was the "big island."

I told him I went to school in New York, but I was going away to a new school, Wilton Academy, where my father had gone to school. Ben asked if that was a military school and I told him it was a boarding school.

"Seems funny to leave your family," he said. "But when the weather's bad and I can't get home from school I stay over with Mumma's sister, so that's sort of like boarding."

We walked to a pool left by the retreated tide. "If we scooch down and move quietly to the edge, they won't see us," he said. Again I felt as if I was being drawn into him, and I watched as he knelt, the sun tracing his shadow on the rock, and eased himself flat to the edge of the pool. He lay there while I copied him until we were lying next to each other, but not touching, though I was totally aware of his body and of being so close to him.

"Look," he said softly, "There's bubbles over on the far side, probably a clam in the mud. Now over on the other side, under that rock that looks like an Indian, with the piece of kelp caught on it, do you see the crab?"

"No, I don't know where you mean," I answered quietly.

"Can't point or they'll see me move," he whispered. "They're fierce careful."

"You could use the clock like Daddy does when we go bird watching," I suggested.

"What?"

"You just pretend what you are looking at is a clock and then you say, 'Blue Jay at four o'clock, Yellow-bellied Sapsucker at two o'clock,'" I told him, imitating Daddy in my deepest voice.

He grinned again, and said, "Okay, crab at two-thirty, periwinkles round the clock." We both laughed softly, and when I looked down at my arm lying next to his I saw that the hair on both our arms was standing up. I felt the heat of his arms, chest, and legs along my own body and I wanted to touch him, but then I was overwhelmed with embarrassment, and it seemed he felt it too, because we both moved away from each other at the same time.

We watched crabs scuttling around the rock pools, and Ben opened a mussel to show me how the creature sucked water through its gills. In the center of the shell was a small, iridescent, irregularly shaped pearl, which he picked out, washed in the pool and gave to me. "Get enough of these you can make a necklace," he said. I took it and looked at the tiny pearl shining in my hand and said "thank you" as I felt it with my finger, then I put it carefully into the pocket of my shorts. I could feel it burning there—and I kept thinking—he gave me a present, something I will always have of him.

"Look over there," he said, pointing towards a small purple starfish, suctioned onto a rock in the water. "When they get big they can pull a scallop apart. The starfish moves over to the scallop, but the scallop jumps away like a jet engine." Before I could respond, he added, "If you want, I'll take you out in the rowboat—give you a rowing lesson."

My stomach knotted. I looked down at the little world of the tide pool and wanted to lose myself in it, but Ben seemed to understand and said, "You might as well learn to row from me. I bet I'm a much better teacher than any of those summer kids." And then he looked at me oddly and added, "I'm sorry. I forgot you're one of them. I mean you don't seem so stuck up. They don't seem to notice there's anyone here except them."

"I have to ask my father," I said, and then I admitted, "I can't swim."

"So what," Ben replied. "Most of the fishermen can't swim. Say they'd rather drown fast than slow." I felt sick when he said the word "drown," but he was walking ahead of me and didn't notice. I felt accepted—it was all right not to be able to swim. "I learned," he continued, "'cause Dad said I had to. But you have to wear a life-jacket—that's what Grampie would say. There's no wind now, so it'll be just like being in the harbor."

We walked over to the adults and I said to Daddy, "Ben says he can teach me to row. Is that okay, I mean if we go just in the cove? He says it's safe, and I'll wear a life preserver."

Daddy looked at Ben carefully, and said, "If his grandfather says it's all right, then it's fine with me."

Ben walked over to his grandfather, and Captain Bunker looked over at me and nodded, and Ben returned and said, "Grampie says it's okay, as long as I keep you between the shore and The Princess."

Captain Bunker called out, "Take the Mabel Ann, she's smaller and handles easy."

"Okay," Ben said, checking that there were life jackets in the dinghy, handing me one, and then pushing the rowboat into the shallow water.

"Just don't go barmy 'cause you're in a hen frigate," Captain Bunker called out, laughing.

Ben looked stunned, then blushed and turned from his grandfather, waving at him backhanded, while I could see Captain Bunker and the other man laughing.

"What did he say?" I asked.

"Nope, not telling," Ben said, smiling, but looking awkward.

"But I don't understand what he says sometimes."

"Good. Now when I say to, you get in and sit on the middle seat while I push off," he instructed.

I started to protest, but he added, "Look, we can't change seats in the middle of the ocean, and you'll be fine. I'm going to be sitting in the stern. If you mess up, I can row us in sitting there almost as easy as in the middle."

He pushed the rowboat half into the water and said, "Now, jump in," so I did and sat down. "Okay, put the oars in the oarlocks. Did they teach you that?"

"Yes," I said, making a face at him, "I know how to do that."

When I had lifted the oars into their cradles, he said, "Good, now hang on to the oars, lift them out and hold them up so they don't scrape on the rocks. Grampie paid Uncle Clem to make them oars, and I don't want to get 'em scratched." I swung the oars out so fast I almost hit him as he pushed off.

"Oh Christ, jeezum crow!" he exclaimed. "You like to swat me with one of them things? Sorry, didn't mean to swear. But you surprised me. No matter."

I felt too embarrassed to say anything except, "I'm really sorry."

"It's okay," he replied. "Put the oars in slow. Just dip them in. The tide is going out, so you don't have to work to get away from the shore, but you'll

have to work to get back here." He settled himself back into the stern and asked, "How are you going to figure where you're going?"

"I just fix a point and steer straight," I said surprised by my own confidence.

"That's good," he smiled at me proudly, "bet you're good in school."

"Yeah, I guess. Pretty good," I replied, grinning at him, feeling a little more comfortable with him and myself.

"I bet you like to read a lot," he said, adding, "like Grampie."

"Yes. Yes I do. Sometimes I think that's what I like best of all..."

"Grampie was a sea captain and he read books all the time he was at sea. He has a big library," Ben said, and I told him I would love to see it.

"Pay attention now," Ben said, looking straight at me. "I want you to put the oars in together and pull against them as even as you can—same depth. Now look on the shore. What's your steering point?"

"The tree with its crown broken off," I answered quickly.

"Good. Now let's get going and you keep your eye on the tree."

He made it seem so simple. I pulled the oars, trying to keep the pressure even, the depth even, and to keep the top of the broken tree in the same place. Before long I had pulled the boat close to The Sea Princess and he said, "Well done. You're pretty strong," and then as an afterthought, "for a girl," grinning at me. "Can you turn the boat back to shore?"

I looked back at the shore, surprised it seemed far away, surprised how close we were to The Princess, proud of myself. It seemed so easy when there weren't people expecting anything from me.

"How are you going to turn the boat?" he asked.

"I think I just pull on one oar until the boat comes around."

"Okay," he said, "try it and see what happens," his face betraying no clue.

When I looked doubtfully at him, he added, "Hey, I'm right here and nothing's going to happen even if you make a mistake. Heck, you could go around in circles all afternoon if you wanted to, I'd just lay back and watch the seagulls catchin' dinner," and he reached into the sleeve of his T-shirt, took out a pack of Camels and cupped his hands to light a match before he lay back against the stern with an exaggerated sigh. Putting one hand behind his head, he raised his face to the sun and blew smoke rings through his mouth in a long slow stream and I watched the muscles of his arm moving in the sun.

"I didn't know you smoked," I said, surprised that he was old enough and that his parents allowed him to.

"Have been since I was eleven," he replied, "Mumma says it smells up the house awful, but me and Dad don't care." I pulled on one oar and the boat began to swing around. After several tugs, we were facing the shore again and Ben said, "See, no big deal. Now try it again, but do it in reverse." And when I had succeeded he said, "Now, I'll show you how to land against The Princess."

"Oh, no, Ben," I said, immediately scared again, "what if I slam into your grandfather's boat?"

"I'm not going to let you do that. Besides, that's why we have bumpers for you to slam up against," and again he laughed. I liked seeing him laugh—his mouth turned up and his eyes crinkled and it made me happy that he seemed to enjoy being with me.

"Now row straight for The Princess," he said, and watched approvingly as I chose my checkpoint on shore.

It made me happy to see him smile at me, to see he liked me and being with me, but I felt pulled apart. I was so scared of saying or doing something wrong. It was hard to be with him because it was so wonderful. He was like a glorious magical creature, something alien and powerful in ways I wasn't. Funny and handsome. So handsome. Sexy, though I didn't know what that meant then. Kind in ways no one else except my father was.

As I rowed towards the boat, Ben asked me what I knew about a dock landing. "Well, I go fast and then at the last moment I push one oar the other way, and then glide in and take it out of the water, but I'm always too far out, or too close in. I feel so obtuse."

"What?" Ben replied.

"Obtuse," I repeated, "like really thick. Sorry."

"You mean like numb—numb'r than a hake."

"I guess so," I replied.

"Well, it's sort of like parking a car," Ben responded, "but you have to figure in the water moving," and he moved his hands together and then forwards and back, as if he were parking.

"You know how to drive?"

"Course. Grampie taught me on his old truck," he told me, "I took my license last year in Ellsworth."

"How old are you?" I asked, worried that he was a lot older and wouldn't want to talk to me anymore.

"Sixteen next month," he answered, unconsciously drawing in his breath to inflate his chest and sitting as straight as he could, "and I'm almost six feet tall."

"I can't get a license for years in New York."

"Too bad for you," he replied. "Okay, let's dock now."

"Promise you won't let me bash into The Princess?" I asked, looking him in the eye.

"No, I won't let you. I wouldn't want to put up with Grampie if I did. He'd be madder than a wet skunk," he answered, laughing at the thought.

I concentrated very hard, thinking how I would watch the current and then swing into The Princess softly, just barely slipping along until the dinghy came gently to rest. The first time I tried it I turned way too early and Ben couldn't lean far enough out to catch The Princess.

"Okay. You see what you did wrong?"

"Yes, I turned too early, but I don't know how to judge it."

"Try it again."

I pulled away from the larger boat and turned again, pulling on the oar to face the bow towards The Princess, determined to do it right this time, but again, though I tried, I didn't wait long enough to turn.

"This time I'm going to make you turn at the right time so you get the feel of it. Bring her back out again," he told me, a fierce look on his face.

I rowed the little boat out about ten yards from The Sea Princess and swung it back, so the bow pointed right at it. I rowed hard, but I was getting tired, and my back and arms ached. As I headed for The Princess, Ben reached forward and put his hands over mine, holding them against the oars. I could feel the warmth of his hands and the strength in his arms and I lost all sense of where I was, or the boat, or anything except the feel of his hands over mine and I closed my eyes. I could feel his breath on my mouth, and when I opened my eyes his face was very close, his eyes were closed, and I felt a shudder pass through his hands to mine.

"Bonk!" We slammed into The Princess.

"Oh, jeezum," he exclaimed. "Well," he paused, and then turning quickly back to the shore, looked to see if his grandfather and the other men were watching. "Hope they didn't see that one. That was nasty." He took his cap off and twirled the strand of hair just behind his ear again before replacing the hat.

"You're going to get a bald spot there," I told him, trying to disguise my embarrassment for knocking into his grandfather's boat.

"Oh, not you too. Don't you get on me like Grampie and the rest of them. It's just somethin' I do is all," as his smile faded and he looked at me like a sour little boy.

"Well, sorry," I replied, surprised by his petulance.

I was blushing, and he seemed flushed as well, as if he were standing in the light of a sunset. "Do you want to try again?"

"Not really," I replied sheepishly, "but I guess I should do it one more time and try to get it right, like getting back on a horse when you fall off."

"Okay, once more. I'm going to tell you when to turn," Ben said.

I took a deep breath, settled my shoulders into the oars, and again rowed towards the larger boat; just before I thought we would crash again, he said, "Now, turn," and then urgently, "Now!" And I did. We glided parallel to The Princess and drifted along her hull. Ben put out his hand to grab one of the bumpers and said, "That was well done. I couldn't have done it better."

"I couldn't have done it at all if you hadn't told me when," I answered him, feeling proud and happy, basking in his pride in my success.

"Ayuh, finest kind," he said.

"What's that mean?" I asked.

"That's the best, best there is," he answered slowly, looking straight into my eyes, making me quiver, and giving me the odd feeling again that he could look right into me. "Now, do it again so you're sure you got it." And I did.

As I rowed back, I asked him, "What does Chummy mean?"

"Oh, that's something Grampie calls me. Mumma don't like it, but I do. It means bait. Chum is cut up fish to bait the lobster traps. If you come to my island sometime, you can come to the wharf and we'll see if you can stand the smell." He laughed again and looked up at the sky, a soft smile around his mouth. When we reached the shore, he said, "Now row really hard when the wave comes, hard as you can to beach her, and I'll jump out." I waited for the next wave then pulled against the oars. The boat crunched against the pebbles and Ben jumped out, grabbed the line in the bow and, using the power of another wave, pulled the boat, with me in it, away from the water.

"Wouldn't want my best student to get her feet wet," he teased.

I stepped out of the boat, and we walked over to where Captain Bunker and Bradley were sitting, smoking pipes. When we got close Captain Bunker said, "Look's like you worked ha'd, Miss. You can take Ben's job any day now."

I looked up at Ben, who was smiling at his grandfather, enjoying his teasing. "Oh, Grampie, you'd have to pay her more than me," he laughed, "and you wouldn't want to do that!"

"Couldn't say, not knowin'," Captain Bunker answered, pulling on his pipe and winking at us. "So what did you learn, deah?" Captain Bunker asked me.

"I learned how to steer, and to have a check point, and I almost learned how to do a landing," I answered seriously.

I learned something about love too. The magical joy of looking at him, having him look at me. Flirting. Where do we learn that? As little girls? Does it just bubble up? Turn your head, flutter your eyes, smile. I'd never wanted to spend any time with a boy before. Before I met Ben.

"Good for you," Captain Bunker exclaimed, smiling at me, "landing is some ha'd," he added, stressing the last word and winking again at Ben so I knew he had seen us crash against The Princess, and again I blushed.

I heard Daddy calling and turned towards where he was sitting on the beach with Robbie, my mother and the other adults. "Guess I've got to go now. Thank you, Captain Bunker for letting us use the dinghy. Ben, do you want to come to the picnic and cook marshmallows with us?" I asked, tentatively.

He looked up the beach at all the people sitting together in little groups, and said, "'Spect not. I'll just stay here until you need us to take you home," and he reached for the pack of cigarettes and turned away.

I covered my disappointment by turning away from him, and when I turned back to wave goodbye, he looked different. His shoulders seemed to have fallen and his face was flatter. As he pulled his blue baseball cap over his eyes, I realized we'd created our own world in the rowboat but that now I was retreating back to mine as he was sinking into his.

"All right," I said. "Thank you for helping me learn to row. I really enjoyed the lesson and now I think I'll do much better in class. Thank you very much, Ben."

Chapter Three

I can hear my voice. It was the voice my mother might have used to thank the laundress for ironing our clothes or the gardener for mowing the grass. It didn't end well, did it? How could I have been so stupid? Stupid, I said again softly to myself. We made our own island and I destroyed it. There was no excuse, and I walked back slowly to the rented rooms, and drank two glasses of chardonnay too quickly.

Later as I sat on the couch trying to read, I tried to answer my own question. Part of it was losing Rachel and being the one who should have died. I saw the minister praying over Rachel's little casket, a mahogany box my father and the other men had carried down the long aisle at the church. "The good die young," the minister said, and I wondered if that meant I was bad for living. Later he added, "God only calls his special children to him," and I knew that I wasn't one of them.

My mother had a gift for making me feel like a second-class citizen. I was so proud of having learned to row with Ben, and all she could see was that my shorts were dirty. Somehow, I always did the wrong thing. Thank God for Daddy. I can see him beaming at me, looking at my mother, both of us hoping she would be pleased. She was sitting with Robbie, blond hair crimped around her face, wearing plaid wool pants and a blue shirt, clean sneakers, with a freshly pressed red bandanna tied around her hair. "Oh, Rebecca, you look a fright. Just look at you! Your shorts are filthy, and you're sweaty and dirty and you've got, what is this—pitch pine or tar on your shorts? That won't come out. You know that!" I can still hear my mother's voice high and tight and feel the same tension I felt so long ago.

I hung my head so I didn't have to look at her and tried to let the words roll off. My father, his eyes darkening and sad said, "Now, Anne, don't be so tough on her. Becky's just trying to learn to row so she can be in sailing class, and it's hard work."

"I know, Sam, but I just wish she could be more, more ladylike. She's almost fifteen. I just wish she could be more like Rach..." but she caught

herself. I froze. There it was again, I thought, my mother wishing that I had died and Rachel had lived or that I was the perfect little lady Rachel would have been. We were silent for a few seconds; suspended in a thick liquid that held us motionless. I could see Rachel, her blonde curls bouncing around her face, her eyes blue like the deepest sapphires, shining up at our mother. I could see them playing on the swing-set, going for walks with their hands swinging together, Rachel looking adorable in her favorite dress, the soft blue one with the little yellow ducks parading across the smocked breast. Rachel on the carousel, Rachel always good, always pretty, eating ice cream on a cone and never letting it drip.

"I'm sorry," I said, my voice catching, and again "I'm sorry." I looked at my father, and he quickly looked down at the beach and then away from me. I could see the little muscles twinging in his neck.

He said to my mother, "Honey, let's go for a walk, Becky will watch Robbie. Just down the beach and back." He turned to me and said, "Wait here, Becky," then he stood up, walked over to Mrs. Thompson, and gestured back at us.

Mrs. Thompson came over, and said, "Anne, let me take Robbie. You'll enjoy the view at the end of the beach. Becky will help me. Now scoot you, two."

I took Robbie's hand and we followed Mrs. Thompson to where she had been sitting. I looked back towards my parents and watched them as they walked together along the beach. My father had his arm around my mother's waist and she was holding onto his shoulder, and I wished he had his arm around me too.

Mrs. Thomas's mother, Mrs. Saunders said, "Now dear, come sit here with us." I walked over obediently and sat next to her as Mrs. Thomas added, "tell us about your adventure at sea." The ladies laughed, their voices like chiming bells.

"Well, Ben told me he could teach me to row and..."

"Ben?" Mrs. Thomas asked, her eyebrows arching, "Do you mean the boat boy?"

"I guess so. His name is Ben."

"Well, we don't want to be too familiar, now do we?" Mrs. Thomas replied, adding, "Though it is good of him, more than he gets paid to do… still you need to be careful."

"Oh, but he...," I started to say, and my voice trailed off. I couldn't think of anything more to say. I was glad he hadn't come with me to roast

marshmallows, so I told the women what they wanted to hear, that I could pass the rowing test and join the sailing class.

"Now, that will be good for you," Mrs. Saunders said. "You'll love that. There are races and all sorts of young people your age. You'll make lots of friends. They all come from good families. What about tennis and swimming? Have you been taking tennis lessons?"

"Yes, Mrs. Saunders," I answered primly. I could see the woman looking at me, and through their eyes I saw my own dirty pants, my bruised and scratched legs, my straight brown hair and mud brown eyes. I wondered how Mrs. Saunders could stay absolutely clean—her dress as white as when she'd boarded the boat, every hair in place, the white and red tea roses still fresh in the band of her white straw hat.

Robbie had been playing with pebbles, but he was getting restless, for which I was grateful. I stood up and said, "I think I'll take Robbie for a little walk down the beach. We'll stay right at the edge and we won't go far."

"All right, dear," Mrs. Thomas said. I took Robbie's hand and, as we walked away from the adults, I heard Mrs. Saunders say to her daughter, "She's a nice child really, but terribly shy. Sad isn't it about her sister, such a loss for her parents—something you never get over really. They say she would have been a great beauty."

I wasn't going to be a great beauty—that's for sure. But then I didn't want to be. I didn't want to be like my mother.

❦

The next morning I went to the library. I whispered good morning to the assistant librarian who was sitting behind the large oak desk and walked over to the periodicals, scanned *Down East* magazine, and then sat in front of a computer looking out into the library, but not knowing what I was looking for. I watched as children and their mothers came in and walked over to the children's wing. Two older men went to the section on marine history, and an elderly woman went to the gardening section. "Everything in its place, and all in their places," I thought. But me, I added sadly. What AM I doing here? I asked myself again.

I heard steps to my left and looked up to see Bob towering over me. "Good morning," he said softly. I remembered being surprised when I was there before by how such a large man could make his voice so small and I smiled at him and at the memory.

"Good morning. It's good to be back here, though I hardly recognize it."

"Yes, we've expanded a bit," he said and he looked proudly around the room and down the corridors. "May I take you on a tour?"

"I'd love that," I answered, relieved to be pulled away.

He showed me the new rooms, one with books about the history of the island and of Maine. "We have quite a few very rare books here and rare maps—gifts." He pointed to large leather-bound books in glass-paneled cases saying, "We keep them in climate-controlled cases," and then led me into the next room, a light-filled space for children with low bookcases and large bright rugs on the floor.

"So tell me what you're doing," he asked as we walked into the hall and he turned into his office. "Come, have a seat," and I sat across from him in the snug office. It smelled of smoke and my eyes wandered around the room until I found the pipe collection arrayed along two shelves.

"I don't really know," I said, and paused. I hoped he would fill in the blank or talk about himself, but he did neither and finally I continued. "I went back to school. Did my doctorate on Jane Austen." He nodded, stroked his beard and sat back in his chair looking at me. I felt self-conscious and wondered what he was thinking. "I wrote a dissertation about her work," I continued, "and ways in which it presages feminism. I guess people liked it. My professor told me to get it published, but I didn't know how." I thought of the first reader for my dissertation—a tough woman with hair like Brillo, silver wire spectacles and dark piercing eyes, who encouraged me to think of Austen as an early commentator on the role of women and their powerlessness in a man's world. "Actually, I was going to teach but instead, well, I got divorced—well, I'm sort of sick of the whole thing," I said abruptly. I stopped and looked at him again. He was smiling in an odd way, and I didn't understand.

"What are you thinking?"

"Oh, just that's something I always wanted to do. To go back to school and study someone I loved reading. Like Melville or Tolstoy. That's a good read for a long winter."

"And?"

"And," he added, "it's just too much. Too expensive. I'm lucky to have a job doing something I love, but I can't just up and leave it and go back to school. Even now that the kids are grown. But you did. That's great. How did that happen?"

"Me? I'm like an Austen heroine. I married well. Well, in some ways. At least I married rich, but we didn't love each other, at least not for very long. I left, but it took me a long time. And then I did the same thing again, though for security not money." There was a hardness to my voice that was self-mocking and caught me off guard.

"Why?" he asked evenly.

"I couldn't think of anything else to do. I know that sounds pathetic, but that's what women did where I came from. They married well, or they didn't." And then I added bitterly, "and they gave parties, and did volunteer work, and that was about it, but you know that living in a summer *colony*." I paused and we were silent. "It doesn't fit for me, but I'm not sure what does fit or even where I fit," I admitted to us both.

"Well, that's something to write about," he said, and I looked up at him in alarm.

"I can't do that!"

It was his turn to look surprised, and then for both of us to be embarrassed by the pain in my response.

"Would you like a cup of tea?" he asked. "I brew a mean pot of Irish breakfast."

"Yes," I laughed, relieved. As we sat and drank our tea, my mind wandered back to Austen, asking why I described myself as an Austen character, and which of Austen's women I felt closest to.

He broke into my reverie saying, "Where do you go when you write?"

"What do you mean?" I asked, confused.

"In your mind. Do you have a safe place you think about before you write about difficult things so you can come back to it?"

"No, I never thought about that."

"When you try again to go into those dark places, think about a place you love. Your mind can play tricks on you, but you can also play tricks on your mind. Think about a place that feels safe; leave it to write, but then come back. It will be easier."

"Thank you," I said, smiling politely when I got up to leave a few minutes later, feeling puzzled and slightly embarrassed by his advice.

❧

During the day, I went to the library or wrote in my journal in my room, and when the Swim Club opened in late June, I went for lunch, eating at one of the rough wood tables under the green and white striped awning. The old pool had been just an enclosure of the ocean's cold salt water, but the new, bright aqua pool was warmed both by the sun and an electric heater. The sounds of children playing with their huge plastic toys, a garish armada of pink and green palm trees, gnashing crocodiles and even a Tyrannosaurus Rex, made me think of my own children, Stephen and Katherine. I could see newborn Stephen tucked in his antique wicker bassinet with blue velvet ribbons and lace netting, curled into a little ball I could hold in one hand. Was I too protective of them because of Rachel?

I listened to the women talking about their tennis and golf games, or about their charity work and husbands. To and fro the women go, I thought. My mother was like that—beautiful, but cold, like a painting of a Medici princess, fine-boned, blonde, and elegant, so different from my father. But am I so different? What am I doing for anyone else? I felt no more interesting or compassionate than she, and the thought was discouraging. The only time my mother needed me was after Daddy died, but just in that year before she met Taylor and then married him the next spring. Strange she found him just as I lost Ben. I wanted so much to see him even though he hadn't written me. Just that one letter after Daddy died. I wonder if I would have wanted that if I'd known how being with him was going to change my life so terribly. When my mother asked me what I wanted to do that summer, I didn't know what to say. There was nothing I wanted to do, no one I wanted to see.

"I don't know," I answered. "What do you and Robbie want to do?"

"Well, Carla and Allen have asked me to go to Newport with them for a few weeks," she replied. "I thought maybe you would like to go to camp. Lavinia told me about a lovely camp for girls in Vermont, and then we could go to Maine for a little while. That's the hardest."

"Why do you want to go there?" I asked, surprised that she wanted to return.

"I don't really—but there are some things I have to do there, about the land." I could feel a steel rod running through her even though on the surface she looked vulnerable and drained. When I didn't say anything, she added, "We'll go for just a week or two at the end of the summer. You were getting to know people and made some friends there. It will be good for us, you'll see."

I said, "I love Daddy's land, but I don't want to be there without him."

My mother shuddered; I could feel how hard it was for her to think about that land, and suddenly she blurted out, "We were so happy there. He wasn't worried about work, and we didn't have to cope with all his relatives like we did at the lake. There were just the four of us. I was trying so hard..." She started crying. Instantly, I was crying too. How strange it was that we were so close in some ways, yet so far apart.

When I went back to school, my mother telephoned every Sunday before Chapel. I tried to tell her about school, but it was a foreign world to her, and it never felt as though she were listening to me. I'd try to talk to her about reading Edmund Burke and Coleridge, then she would tell me about how she was helping plan a charity dinner dance at the Gratwicks' house on 72nd Street, which she said was a great coup because everyone wanted to see their

Monets. She was excited, but it was a shallow excitement. Once she told me how hard it was to come home alone to the empty apartment. Even worse she said was the time around six or seven in the evening when she still expected Daddy to come walking through the door and toss his hat on the hat stand from as far away as he could. She said Robbie kept asking when daddy was coming back, and that it broke her heart again and again.

I wasn't much help. I could never think of anything to say or do to make her happy or ease the agony in her voice. She only made my own sadness more real, and I drummed my fingers so hard on the wood shelf below the phone when we talked that afterwards they ached.

I sat by the pool watching the women, picked up my white goggles and walked over to a chaise longue facing the diving board, wondering how I could for so long have been frightened of the water. I watched as the young boys paraded up to the diving board for their moment of glory, cheered on by mothers and girls, and then ran down the board in an explosion of joy and defiance, hurtling themselves into space, crashing into the water, vying with each other to make the most outrageous splash.

I looked at the pool, but suddenly could see only Rachel. I could feel sobs gathering in my throat, trying to push their way out. "No," I whispered, forcing them back. I had learned over the years to push memories so deep that they couldn't hurt me. Now I wondered why they were clawing again up through the debris I had layered over them. Memories of Rachel, and memories of Ben. What connected them?

❦

The next day Mary Barlow, a cheerful blonde divorcee who was renting another suite from Mrs. Jacobs, suggested we go to Bar Harbor. The changes in the town amazed me. The main street was full of stores, most selling T-shirts and plastic lobsters, but there were new boutiques that lured more affluent tourists. We walked along Cottage Street until I found myself in front of the Rock Shop. I imagined stepping inside with my father, going past the shelves with wood and plastic souvenirs, silver jewelry and displays of chunks of malachite, turquoise, jasper, and lapis to the vitrine in the back of the store that held the glowing gold jewelry they made with semi-precious stones. As I stood there, Mary said, "What's wrong Becky? You look as if you've seen a ghost."

"I have," I answered, rubbing my hands together, feeling the emptiness, "but he's a good ghost. My father brought me here years ago to shop for something for my mother."

"Do you want to go in?"

"No, not now, not yet."

I'd taken off the ring from the Rock Shop that my father gave my on my birthday in Maine when my first husband, Jordie, insisted I didn't wear it because he was jealous. My father's ring had been a talisman, but I hid it in my jewelry box, and later it disappeared. It would have been my thirty-second anniversary with Jordie in August and my eleventh with Richard this July. Maybe I should give myself a ring. No, I answered myself, not yet. Not now, not yet.

I looked at my reflection in the shop window, but I saw myself as a child walking past the same window with my father.

We walked into the store and past shelves of plastic trinkets and ugly plaster statues until we reached a glass case displaying jewelry. A thin, red-haired, freckled man who looked as if someone had sifted cinnamon over him came out of a back room, and my father said, "Good morning, Mr. Willis. I'm Mr. Granger. I bought my wife a bracelet here last fall and she loved it."

"I remember," Mr. Willis replied, blinking in the bright light of the shop, his loupe perched over his left eye. "Tourmaline and aquamarine bracelet. Reminds me of the sea and the islands. "

"Yes," I burst out, "that's what I thought of when I was looking at Somes Sound."

When my father said he wanted to get a pair of earrings to match the bracelet, Mr. Willis reached behind him and pulled cardboard boxes off the shelf full of stones: tourmalines green as the woods, light shining through them like the sun through fir trees, and aquamarines in all shades of light blue, rounded like beach glass.

Daddy dipped his hands into the box of aquamarines, and together we let the stones run through our hands. I began to see the variations—the pale aqua of thick ice, the soft blues of a cloud-filled sky. "Pumpkin, you pick your six favorites from that box and I'll pick mine from this one," he said.

Mr. Willis put two black velvet pads on the glass counter. Carefully, my father and I sorted through the stones until we found the six we liked best for the range of their colors, for their gentle curves, and how they fit into a cluster.

Mr. Willis took a third pad from under the counter and we saw two earrings form in front of us, matched for size of stone and depth of color, but varied by subtle differences in the light they caught and defracted. "You picked some beauties, and these match well. What do you think?" he asked, pushing the velvet across the counter and turning it so that the earrings faced us.

"I love them," I said aloud.

"What?" Mary asked.

"Oh," I replied, startled into the present. "The earrings my father gave my mother. And helping him choose them. Just being with him."

As we walked down Cottage Street, I thought about the rings I had owned, or had owned me. At first I was proud of the ring Jordie gave me, with its huge emerald surrounded by diamonds. As casually as I could, I displayed it, moving my fingers to catch the light whenever I felt vulnerable with people, feeling as if he was there by my side, his sword at the ready, his stallion snorting its steamy breath into the cold air, ready to sweep me to safety if the need arose. But he never did, and I began to see him as a pathetic drunk, a mean and lazy aging child, and the ring felt heavy. I thought I was living in a fairy tale with a rich prince, but Jordie thought everything and everyone was tiresome and silly.

That night, as I made supper for myself in Mrs. Jacob's kitchen, I thought about the Christmas after my father died when my mother found the boxes of jewelry he bought for us before we left Maine at the end of the summer.

❧

Christmas vacation without Daddy seemed very long, and I felt as if a black cloud had settled over me, shutting me off from everything and everyone. Best, and worst, was that on Christmas Eve my mother gave me a package and took one out for herself as we sat together on the couch. I knew when I saw the present that it was from my father, from the Rock Shop. I tried to hold myself rigid, contracting my chest muscles, trying not to cry. We sat on the couch and slowly untied the ribbons on our packages. "I found these in his jewelry box," my mother explained, her hand quivering like her voice.

I was crying deeply now, the sobs coming fast and hard; trying to stop them, I felt as if I were choking. "I'm sorry, I'm sorry, I'm trying not to cry, but I miss him. I can't stand this! I really can't stand it!" I screamed. "Why did he die? He didn't have to die! It's so mean of him," but I knew that made no sense. My mother put her arms around me, and we sat close together on the couch. I could feel her heart pounding, but then I saw her lie against the couch, her head drooping backwards, and my heart stopped because I could see my mother when Rachel died, fainting against my father's arms. Daddy slapped her cheek to bring her back, but I knew I couldn't do that. Instead I put my arms around her and said, "I love you, I love you," and in a minute she was breathing more evenly and said, "We miss him so much, don't we, Becky."

We opened our presents, and in my box there was a pair of earrings, small and delicate, in the same stones as my ring: tourmaline, aquamarine, and rose quartz; in my mother's, a large pair of earrings and a bracelet in the colors of sunset, orange and purple, pink and gold, the stones glowing against the velvet in the gray box. "Fred is right," I said.

"Who? What do you mean?" my mother asked, turning her head so I could see her eyes, rimmed with red.

"Fred, the doorman says whenever we think of Daddy he'll be here with us," I said slowly.

"Maybe that's true," she said, pausing to look at the jewelry in her hand. I pictured my father with his hands in the boxes of stones on the glass counter in Mr. Willis's shop, sorting through them to find the ones he liked best. "I'd like to think it was true," my mother added. "I need him here! I need him...." the words exploded out of her so forcefully I felt as if I'd been struck, and I reached my hand out to hold her wrist. We sat silently for several minutes until she said, "I'm sorry. I'm just so sorry."

When I was leaving for school, I stood in the hall facing my mother and Robbie, who were standing in front of the huge, ornate gold-framed mirror my father inherited from his grandfather. I watched their backs as my mother talked and felt as if I could see through them. My mother said she would be all right, that she had lots of friends who would look out for her, that her parents would help, and that she was blessed because she had Robbie to look after. She was hugging Robbie, her hands wrapped so hard the knuckles were white around the red and blue rubber ball he'd been playing with. She told me to concentrate on my studies and that soon it would be spring vacation, but I knew it was another speech she had rehearsed. Then a little tremor shuddered down my mother's back, and I wondered if it was a warning or an aftershock.

❧

One afternoon I decided to go to the Village Dock and sit on a bench looking at the harbor, as I had done so many times when I was a young girl. Gulls squawked while they harvested mussels exposed by the retreating water, dropping them onto flat gray ledges of rock daubed with offal and broken shells. I loved watching the seagulls and the people, the boats rocking at anchor, and the lines of rowboats stuck on the dock like limpets. The breeze smelled of a hint of fuel oil.

There were a few working boats with gear for fishing and scalloping, the gray barge used for hauling supplies to the outer islands, and many more power boats outfitted for the occasional picnic, and yachts with fine lines and elegant gold lines scrolling along their bows. I sat on the green bench overlooking the water until my eyes caught on the familiar lines of *The Sea Princess* chugging slowly into the harbor. I gasped and an image flooded over me—of sitting on the same bench that first summer when Ben walked over from the boat to stand next to me as I sat frozen in silence from the longing, desperate to have him love me. I was so incredibly shy when I saw him after the picnic on Baker Island.

Some days I went down to the harbor and sat on one of the green benches there reading. I knew I could see The Sea Princess *entering the harbor, but I could leave before it docked. For a few minutes I could stare at* The Princess *through my binoculars and sometimes pick Ben out on the deck among the passengers and bags. I'd watch him for a moment, then tuck the glasses and book into my bag, walk quickly to my bike, and pedal up the hill, away from the harbor into the village, my heart hammering in my chest until it hurt.*

A few weeks after he taught me to row I was re-reading Gone With the Wind, *and the story of Rhett and Scarlett so absorbed me that I didn't see* The Princess *as it chugged into the harbor, or even when one of the crew jumped onto the dock to single up the lines, walked up the ramp and passed me on his way to the men's room. When he came out, he said, "Good day, Miss, nice morning," and I almost choked. I didn't have time to say anything before he walked away; I watched him walk halfway down the ramp and start gesturing to someone with his arm and I realized he was signaling to Ben.*

I stared at my book, the words blurring. Rhett and Scarlett, Rhett and Scarlett. What would Scarlett do? I stared at my book until I saw his shoes again standing in front of me. Only then could I look up. "Must be some interesting book," he said.

"It is," I said flatly, staring back at him, my stomach so tense it hurt.

He tried again, "I can't stay long. Bradley said you were sitting here."

"Yes," I answered, looking down, not knowing what to do with him standing there in front of me.

"How've you been?" he said more tentatively.

"Fine," I said, looking back at the book. I wanted so much to look at him and smile, for him to sit next to me and hold my hand, but all the scripts I had written in my mind dried up and blew away. All the wonderful things I had said to him when he wasn't with me caught in my throat and I said nothing.

We were both quiet for what seemed a long time. I could feel my pulse throbbing in my wrist, in time with the throb of the boat's motor as it idled by the dock. "You angry at me?" he asked finally, looking at me sideways, his back half turned.

"No," I replied softly.

"Well, you sure seem it," he said. "I've got to get back to the boat. Sorry I bothered you," he added gruffly before turning towards The Sea Princess.

"Don't go," I whispered behind him, but he didn't hear, and I watched him walk away. I knew Scarlett would have run to him and flirted so he'd fall in love with her. But I wasn't Scarlett, and all I could do was sit on the green bench and watch The Sea Princess leave the dock, turn, and head for the outer harbor, weaving a path between the sailboats and powerboats. When it was almost past the arms of the land, I walked to the railing and waved, knowing he wouldn't see me. I was crying with frustration at my own cowardice and stupidity; because he hadn't swept me up in his arms the way Rhett would, no matter how silly Scarlett was; because I wasn't Scarlett and he wasn't Rhett.

As I walked back to the bike stand, rubbing my nose against the sleeve of my sweater, I passed a fisherman who tipped his cap to me and said, "Now, Miss, don't take it so ha'd," and I ran to my bike, flung my leg over the seat and pedaled up the hill as fast as I could.

I stared now at the boat, feeling its relentless drive toward me until I realized my tired middle-age eyes had created it out of the image of something quite different—a large powerboat with elaborate fishing rigs. How stupid I was, I thought.

❧

As I had done when I was a girl, I joined the choir, lured by the chance to sing and be drawn into my web of memories. Though there was a new organ, a new choir director and a new minister, much was the same, and the sweet musty smell swelled around me as I walked into the choir room. At the break, Suzannah, who had a soaring soprano voice, said "Don't I know you?"

"Yes, I think so," I replied, remembering her voice but not her name. After we had put new names on faces from long ago, Suzannah asked me to a cocktail party later that week.

When I got there, the door of the one-story house was open; inside, people were standing in the hall and living room talking, laughing, holding their drinks in one hand and *hors d'oeuvres* in the other. A light breeze swept through the rooms, and I smelled roasting hot dogs and steak. I could hear more conversation from below the house coming up over the rock ledges, so I walked to the edge of the deck until I was looking at the flat pink rocks and a scattering of people. Smoke from the grills wafted over them as I looked over the sound and in my mind's eye I saw a lobster boat towing a dock towards our land.

I winced slightly and shook the image out of my mind just as Susannah walked up to me. "Now I'm going to introduce you to all the most interesting handsome bachelors, or wanna be bachelors, at the party so you will have lots of beaux this summer." She guided me over to a tall man in a rust colored sweater that matched his reddish gray hair and said, "Randy, I want you to meet Becky. She's here for the summer, and I know you will add her to your list of possibilities."

I recoiled as the man turned, surveyed me slowly from head to toe, and said with a slow drawl, "Why absolutely. Delighted to meet you. Can I get you a drink?"

"Thanks," I replied, tempted to look him over slowly too, but instead facing him and answering, "That's very kind, but Susannah has other people she wants me to meet. Perhaps later."

Susannah looked at me and said, airily, "Okay, see you honey. Not your type? Well, you're right," she whispered as she guided me into a circle of three women and two men. "I collect old cars. Cord L-29s. I only buy them in pairs so I can use one for parts," one man said thickly. Two of the women were platinum blondes, their blue eyes shadowed in shiny blue eye makeup, their thin bodies as angular as the rocks behind them. They gestured and smiled in response to the man as babies do when adults speak, following the rhythm of the words even when they don't comprehend the meaning. Susannah dropped me between the two men like a parcel, much to the irritation of the women, and I moved away when I recognized a man who was in the choir.

"Hi," I said as I drew near him. "I think you're in the choir too. My name's Becky Evans and I'm just coming back for the first time in many, many years."

But I watched him as he retreated like a barnacle into its shell. "Oh yes, rather," he managed, before walking in the opposite direction.

Mary walked over to me and said, "Not much pickings is it?"

I smiled weakly at her, "Well, I'm not picky—or picking really—I just wanted to talk to someone and I thought, well I just thought we could talk about the choir or something."

"You'll get used to it," she said. "How long have you been divorced?"

"Not long—this time—about three months," I answered. "I guess I'd forgotten what it's like. I feel like a pariah or an old horse. I wish the men could just act normal and be friends."

"Let's go for a hike tomorrow or play tennis," Mary suggested.

I walked down the winding granite steps to the water, where there were more people standing on the rock ledges, eating and drinking. I wandered from group to group, not recognizing anyone until I saw a woman about my age, heavily made up, with long dyed black hair turned up at the ends. I went up to the woman, noticed her hands glowing with rings like Tiffany lamps, and said tentatively, "Monica? Are you Monica Lowe?"

"Darling, how are you?" the woman said exuberantly, then looked puzzled and asked, "*Who* are you?" she laughed, though not in an unfriendly way.

"Becky Granger," I replied.

"Oh my GAWD!" Monica exploded. "My God, I don't believe it!" She grabbed me in a bear hug and turned to her companions, saying, "This is my friend from years ago, we were absolutely best friends, lied for each other, covered for each other. I mean, BEST friends. Where have you been the last...well however many years it's been?"

"It's been thirty or forty years. It's a long story."

Monica said, "Well, you'll have to tell me all. I'm just thrilled, thrilled to see you," and she gave my hand a squeeze, and said, "I just got here last night in time for the party, so we'll have to meet at the club and have lunch." Then, seeing my slight look of surprise, she said, "Oh yes, I got in. I married Porky Dearborn. His father owned the colossus next to the yacht club; then he died and we got it; then Porky died and I got it. Guess that makes me a member." And she winked as she smiled at me.

"I'd love that."

I could see sexy fifteen-year-old Monica wearing bubble-gum pink short shorts and a low-cut halter, pausing on the steps of the Yacht Club to get everyone's attention (later she told me she learned that trick in charm school), then sashaying through the crowd of stunned teenagers. The girls giggled behind their cupped hands; boys just stared, some coughing to cover their excitement. Monica's father had made a lot of money in plumbing, and they were visiting friends from Greenwich for two weeks. I loved her immediately, drawn by our differences and my admiration for someone who didn't fit in but didn't seem to care.

Chapter Four

Three days later Monica asked me for lunch. "Not at the club. Come here," she said. "I want you to come here to the house so we can catch up in private."

Her house was an enormous shingled cottage with a circular tower at one end and eyebrow windows peeking through the roof. A wide porch, overflowing with pots of cascading begonias and bright blue lobelia, circled the house. A maid answered the door, and I followed her through a grand entrance hall with a view of the water, through a double living room with cheerful blue and red chintz-covered antique wicker chairs and sofas, antique oriental rugs and more flowers. There was a portrait of Monica over the fireplace, and another across the room of a man I knew must be Porky Dearborn. He was dressed in a tweed vest and camel colored jacket, but there was a twinkle in his eye that told me Monica hadn't married him only for his money.

The maid knocked on a thick wooden door and I heard Monica inside say, "You're here! I'm so glad." The maid pulled back the door to reveal Monica standing in a small room filled with so many objects I couldn't at first take them in. "Come in, come in. This is my private joke room, my retreat. I don't bring just anyone in here," Monica said, holding out an arm as she turned to survey the room. "Only my extra special friends get to come in here. This is the room that kept me and Porky sane. Here's where we stored all our most precious treasures."

The furniture was ordinary, but the pillows in the shapes of flamingoes and black flies, the photographs of signs and people dressed in silly clothes, started me giggling. "What's this one?" I asked, standing in front of a photograph.

"We collected funny misspelled signs, or took pictures when we couldn't have the sign, like this one," she said, handing me the photograph of a sign that advertised "pissa for sale." She took another from the mantel and said, "That's one of the best. We found it in front of a house where the woman must have had a beauty parlor. It read 'Perms for sale,' and she'd put a dollar sign at the front, but she'd forgotten the vertical lines! And flamingoes and black flies are the Maine state birds—so we have lots of them."

"Do you miss him, Monica?" I asked.

"Yes, Becky, I do. I really do. People thought I married him for his money and his class—and that helped—but I loved him. We had a lot of fun together and we both laughed at the same things. Yes, I miss him. Would you like some wine?" Before I could answer, Monica handed me a glass of white wine, poured one for herself, and then held it in front of her towards a photograph of her and her husband dressed in cowboy costumes and said, "Here's to you, Pork."

"So enough, enough about me. How are you?" and she looked at me so directly that I could feel a door opening inside me to everything I had tried to keep hidden even, or perhaps particularly, from myself.

"Oh, Monica, there's so much to fill in. There's so many reasons not to think about any of it. It makes me sad."

Monica sat down and patted the seat next to her. "And?" she said.

"And, I married a man named Jordie, but it didn't last. And later, I married again, but it was a total joke. I never loved Richard, but then he didn't love me either, so I guess it was fair."

"And children?" Monica asked.

"Yes, I have two children, Katherine and Stephen, and that makes it all right really. I mean, you can't regret being divorced if you have children because you wouldn't have them if you hadn't married their father."

"We never had children," Monica replied. "I'm sorry about that. But we didn't." We sat silently for a minute before Monica continued, "So how did you meet Jordie? What was he like?"

"I met him the summer after I graduated from Wilton. I had an awful year. I didn't get into any colleges I wanted to go to. I was pretty depressed, but I never figured that out then. I guess young ladies weren't supposed to get depressed in those days, so nobody else figured it out either." Monica nodded. "And then I met Jordie and he was such a little bad boy, and so rich. My mother and stepfather liked him, which made it easier for me. I saw him for a while, but then I stopped, or he did."

"Where did you meet him?" Monica asked.

"A coming out party. I hated the idea, but it was what my mother and her new husband Taylor expected. At first the idea curdled in my stomach, but then I realized I could be away from them for most of the summer, so I agreed. So I went to parties up and down the East Coast and only came back to Washington to get clean clothes and money. Sometimes I had to stay with my mother and Taylor in Nantucket, but Sadie and Lemuel, who took care of the house, were in Washington, so most of the time I went there."

"Sounds like fun, Monica said. "I wasn't upper crusty enough to go through that."

"Be grateful. When I saw my mother and Taylor, I had to tell them about the dresses and important people. I got very good at lying and not telling them about the real stuff that went on—drinking, smoking, and making out."

"And Jordie?" Monica asked.

"I was invited to a party in Philadelphia that everyone knew was going to be extraordinary because the family giving it was so wealthy. I stayed with one of Taylor's friends whose daughter was a debutante." I laughed, remembering how we walked from her father's blue Mercedes up the long flight of granite steps to the front door of the eighteenth century manor house where there was going to be a dinner before the dance. I envied her thick, wavy blond hair, and breasts rising like muffins from her low-cut peach taffeta bodice.

"The moment we girls entered the house, boys puffed up their chests like pigeons. I didn't think I'd know anyone, but Roger, a boy from St. Mark's, was seated on my right at dinner. I'd met him and his girlfriend in New York, but the place next to me was empty. I picked up the place card and read the name 'Jordan Dyerman.' "Do you know this guy?" I asked. Roger said immediately, "He's a real prick—no wonder," so I was disappointed, but prepared to spend dinner pretending it didn't matter that I didn't have a partner. Finally, when I was sure he wasn't coming, Jordie arrived. He was very tall and angular, but handsome in a slightly malevolent way. As he sat down he said—I remember this perfectly. 'So you're the lucky one. Sorry to keep you waiting.' His arrogance really pissed me off, so I said, 'Maybe I'm lucky I had to wait,' and then I turned to Roger, who was smirking.

"'That's telling him off,' he whispered. During the next course I ignored Jordie as long as I could until I thought I was being rude to Roger and the girl on his right by barging into their conversation. I sat looking straight ahead for a few seconds; I was thinking I wanted to be anywhere else, but that I had to play the game. So finally I turned to Jordie, and said, 'All right, why are you worth waiting for?'

"'Haven't you heard about me?' he asked. 'I'm the answer to every girl's dreams.'

"'You may be someone's nightmare.'

"'Oh, you're cute,' he replied, 'You're cute. Well, you are sort of cute.'"

"He sounds a like a loser," Monica said.

"His laugh was so cold and hard, but somehow that's what drew me in. I think I needed to be hard and cold myself then. So much had happened. I remember looking him up and down slowly, you know, the way boys do, and then saying, 'Well, you're sort of cute yourself, in a forlorn way, like Brando without a motorcycle.' I thought this is too weird and later I realized he liked it when I was putting him down. He laughed too loudly, pushed his chair back from the table, and turned to face me. 'I'm Jordie,' he said. I had the distinct feeling of being a butterfly fluttering towards a net." I remembered the hot tension I felt as he reached out his hands and put them over mine in my lap, but he was really feeling my thighs. "I should have yelled at him and stood up," I said to Monica, remembering that my body was tingling and his hands were warm and that he had moved our joined hands up and down my thighs until they were resting again on my lap, and then pressed his fingers between my legs.

"I really should have slapped him," I said. "Later I was sorry I didn't because it would have ended there and that might have been better."

I wondered what Monica was thinking, and if she had had love affairs that went sour before she married Porky Dearborn. I was about to ask when Monica said, "So what happened next? Did you see him more that night?"

"Yes, he asked if he could take me to the dance after the dinner, and I accepted. I sort of hoped he would try to kiss me so I could slap him; but he didn't. He drove a dark gray Jaguar, very cool though it stank of cigarettes and pot. I thought it was his parents' car because it was so nice—red leather seats and walnut paneling—but he said it was his and that his father told him he could pick any car he liked because he was too busy to go with him to buy it. Jordie told me he got it when he turned eighteen and then he said, "See, it's lasted a whole month," which made me realize previous cars probably hadn't. He drove so fast we didn't talk. I was scared."

"At the entrance to the estate—and it really was an estate—there were two gigantic granite pillars, and a man in a white dinner jacket waved us ahead. I guess he knew Jordie, or at least the car. The house looked like a medieval castle lit with candles in all the windows. It was preposterous. There were even men in green jerkins and green caps, like Robin Hood's merry men, holding flaming torches by the front door. 'It looks like Sheraton Tara,' Jordie said disdainfully, and he was right. We both laughed. He put his arm around my waist and I was proud we looked like a couple. It was an amazing place really. I could see an enormous pink-and-green striped tent off the large tiled terrace behind the house. There was a dais for the band at one end and dozens of circular tables at the other with white linen coverings and centerpieces of incredible orchids.

"What surprised me most was the spired, multi-colored tent village that spread across a field, down to larger tents circled on a wide terrace around a series of pools. In one tent where there was a fortune teller; in another an artist was making pastel drawings of guests, and in yet another a chef in tall white cap—who had been brought over from Paris for the night—was making crepes and omelets. There was even a tent with a phone so you could call anywhere in the world, and another in which a valet dispensed bow-ties or studs—anything the guests had forgotten or mislaid. They'd thought of everything. I was totally amazed, but Jordie was bored and disdainful. I didn't see him after that for months until I was back home after..."

"Did you want to," asked Monica.

"No," but my parents did. They figured out he was Jordan Dyerman the Fourth and his parents were really rich. They weren't Main Line, but they had so much money it didn't seem to matter that they were pretty gauche."

"Like my parents!" said Monica laughing. So did you get back together?"

"I went to college first, and things got worse."

"How do you mean?" Monica asked.

I let out a huge sigh, "I got involved with one of my professors. I was just dumb."

"So how did you end up with Jordie?"

"He called me at the end of that summer, and by then he looked really good. My mother thought he'd be a great catch, but he was so bad that I felt like I was getting away with something. He could put people down without them ever really understanding what he was doing." I paused and then said, "How could I fall for that?" I remembered the excitement I'd felt being with someone who seemed confident and so ready to throw barbs at everything and everyone. I wish I'd seen then what it would feel like to have them sticking in me.

"You were pretty pissed off," Monica noted.

"Yes, yes, I guess I was."

"About your father?"

"I don't know, really. But, I guess I was mad my mother married again so soon, a year and a half after Daddy died. Taylor, Taylor Briarwood. I was mad Daddy died and she was the only one to get mad at. Jordie called one night. I was alone in the house in Washington with Lemuel and Sadie. Jordie said he was driving to Washington and wanted to see me the next day. There was something dangerous about him. I liked that, and I liked that my mother and Taylor didn't have a clue. They just saw the money, so I said yes. We went out for a few weeks and, and one thing led to another, and he asked me to marry him. He wanted me to drop out of college. "I can teach you whatever you need to know," he told me. I remember thinking, 'Not to go back to college,' and how wonderful it would be to be Mrs. Jordan Dyerman IV and not have to do what my mother or Taylor, or my professors or anyone except Jordie told me to do ever again."

"And now?" Monica asked. "Why did you come back here?"

"I don't know, Monica. I just knew I wanted to come back. Maybe just to see what it was like as an adult. To start again." I paused and then said sadly, "In some ways I think I stopped growing when Daddy died."

"And Ben. Is he part of it?"

"Oh no!" I said, laughing with embarrassment. "My true love, the lobsterman."

"Well, you were really attracted to each other. You know chemistry is half the battle. If you've got the chemistry, you can make the rest work. Just look at Porky and me," Monica said. "I'm not exactly from the Main Line either, and Porky's friends were horrified, but after a while they understood that he loved me and was happy. The ones that were hopeless kind of drifted away, and the rest of them turned out to be pretty good people. "What do you know about Ben's life now?"

"I don't know anything. I suppose he's fishing, and he's married and they have six kids. Maybe he's running the Mail Boat and putting out floats."

"Seems to me," Monica observed, "that you should find out or get over him."

"There's nothing to get over," I replied as lightly as I could.

"That's what I was thinking. I just don't think that's what you're thinking," Monica noted, "So, when are you going to call him up?"

"No, Monica. It ended very badly. I have to leave it where it ended."

"But you'd like to," Monica said," or you wouldn't be blushing and talking so fast."

"No, Monica, really I don't. It ended, and that's it."

What do you mean by badly?" Monica asked, leaning forward.

"Just badly. Just not a good memory is all."

Monica looked anxious and then asked, "Did something happen that upset you?"

"Yes," I said, hoping that would be enough.

"Men can be such pigs," Monica replied, and I stared at my clenched hands and didn't say anything, letting her extend what I knew was a lie.

To change the subject I said, "So how's your love life? Here you are telling me what to do and I don't see you going out with anyone special."

Monica's face dropped, and I regretted what I'd said, but she replied, "It is very lonely sometimes. But I know Porky loved me, and that helps. Sometimes I pretend he's here and we're laughing together at things I tell him about." Monica paused, sat back in her chair, raised her glass to Porky's portrait and said again, "Here's to you Pork. And thank you."

"I'm glad you loved him and he loved you. It makes it seem possible," I said quietly.

"Well, the best therapy is living well," Monica said with a laugh. "So, let's think of some fun things to do. I guess we don't have the bodies to display at the swim club anymore, but we can still go out and have fun. You have to meet Dottie. She's always finding ways to have fun."

❦

That night as I ate alone in a little restaurant, I thought about Ben and Jordie. Ben was my first love, but Jordie was the first I was allowed even though I didn't love him. What a disaster. Ben, I don't know what it could have been, but I ruined it. You were my best friend. How precious that seems now.

When I walked from the restaurant back to my suite, I stopped in front of The Village Shop, because the window display was new—an oceanfront scene complete with a small wooden dock, sand, and many small wooden boats arranged on a blue painted surface. Again, I saw the little white boat with the red sail and oars. Ben's present to me for my fifteenth birthday. The memories came too hard and powerful now to block, and I saw us together standing next to the water in the cove where he taught me to swim the summer after my father died.

In the evenings Monica and I went down to the harbor. We met Ben and a boy Monica had flirted with who was entranced by her. Most nights we went to the movie theater, where at first we sat in the front row of the balcony eating popcorn, sometimes putting it carefully into each other's mouths, like wedding cake. Sometimes we threw the popcorn out as far as we could and watched it drift down on people below, sitting back quickly before our victims looked up. But on our third date, after we had seen the movie twice, Ben and I sat in the back row with his arm around me and my head against his shoulder, holding our hands against each other's bodies, feeling the warmth through our clothes, and I felt as if I was drinking him in, willing him to be a part of me.

Two nights before I had go home to New York, Ben asked if I would meet him the next evening at the town dock and go to Frenchman's Cove across the sound. He said he would have a little motorboat and we could take a picnic to a place he knew. I asked him if he would take me back to my father's land instead. "My mother won't go there, and I can't go by myself. I'd love just to sit on the rocks with you and watch the sun set over the sound."

"Yes, we can do that," he said, and I could feel him calculating the extra distance and the time it would take. "But bring warm clothes; it may be cold on the way back. What are you going to tell your mother?"

"I'll tell her Monica and her family are going on a picnic," I answered confidently, though I was scared of getting caught.

My mother seemed pleased I was spending my last evening with a friend, even if it was just Monica, because she was going to have dinner with the Johnsons and a friend they were bringing who had recently been divorced. Ben was waiting for me at the dock. As we headed out the harbor, I watched the lights from the houses lining the shores, blinking through the dull mist. I felt as if I was watching a television show—the black-and-white images flickering as the boat left the arms of the land. When we left the harbor, Ben turned to go up the sound and said, "Sit back. We can go faster here and we have a ways to go. As we picked up speed, Ben bent down close to me and said, "Just ahead, two dolphin," and I could see the curl of their backs and tails as they swished through the churning water.

"When we come back it'll be dark, and you can track them by the light in the water. We catch fish by watching that fire. It's phosphorescence, from the plankton," he explained. As I looked over the water in the sound, I imagined flashes of fire sparkling like Christmas lights strung over the water. The surge of shining light sprayed out behind the dolphin like children running through the summer night with sparklers. He gunned the motor and I sat back, letting the spray splash my face when we hit a wave, wondering how he avoided the lobster pots.

When we reached my father's land, I felt my heart sinking because there was no float and no gangway. I wondered if the land felt as empty as I did. Ben said we would anchor in the cove and that he would use the dinghy we were towing behind the powerboat to row to the tide pools. "Mumma made us a picnic," he said as he swung a large wooden basket into the dinghy and grabbed a blanket and flashlight.

When we reached the tide pools, he rowed hard to beach the dinghy then jumped out and pulled it onto the flat rock. He lifted the basket out and put it on the rocks, then flicked on the flashlight and took my hand. We walked across the rocks shimmering in the fog and up to the Green Place. I found my secret path hidden behind the rugosa rose, and we walked single file through the woods to the opening in the trees and then down to the flat rocks along the shore. The rock fireplace was still there, as well as the long driftwood spar my family had used as a bench while picnicking. I led the way as we walked to the places I loved, down the path with the sweet fern and tangled roots, out to the spoon-shaped dip in the granite ledge I called my nest, up to the clearing where we spread the blanket for picnics, and the hemlock grove where my father hung jungle hammocks for Robbie to nap and where I could read.

Ben and I didn't speak as we walked, but when we finished, when I had watched the pictures in my mind of my parents, my brother, and myself gathered around the fire eating marshmallows, my father holding my mother and looking down the sound, when I had played them back and forth, I turned to Ben, saying, "Thank you, I'm ready now."

"You were a bit like a dog making his rounds," he observed.

"Ben!" I said, pretending to be shocked. "But you're right, I had to see my favorite places."

We sat on the blanket on the rock while he smoked another cigarette. While we were eating the fried chicken and biscuits, still warm in their aluminum foil, and drinking cider, we watched the sun setting over the sound, the red, salmon, purple, and peach colors suffusing the water. Later, we walked along the rocks, eating chocolate brownies, skipping rocks into the water, and talking about school and home. I told Ben I was worried about doing well in school and didn't want to let down my father, and then I told him, "I never learned to swim. I wish I'd learned to swim for Daddy. He wanted me to so much."

"Is it 'cause of your sister?" Ben asked.

"I think so. I just freeze up when I go in the water. I can see her and I get so scared." I could see myself reflected in his eyes and wondered what he thought.

"Makes sense," he said. "You were there when she drowned?"

"Yes, Daddy and I and Rachel. We went to look at the loon's nest and she fell over the side of the canoe and we couldn't get her."

"Didn't she have a life jacket?" he asked.

"No, I don't think we ever used them then. We do now. But not then. I don't know why."

"I can teach you to swim," Ben said. "It's easy. You just have to believe you can do it."

"There's no time, Ben. I have to go home tomorrow."

"I can teach you now if you want," he said. "We can go over to the cove. There's no one there, and it's shallow. The tide's full, and the water's warmer over there."

"How do you know?"

"We come over when you summer people aren't here," he replied, grinning at me.

"I don't have a bathing suit."

"That's fine with me," he teased, grinning again. "Becky, you can wear your underwear. It's almost dark now; no one will see you but the owls."

"Well, all right, but you mustn't laugh at me," I said feeling excited about the thought of him seeing me in something like Monica's bikini, but adding, "I feel dumb, Ben."

"I know that, Becky, that's why I'm going to teach you, so you won't feel dumb with the summer boys," he said, laughing again.

"You won't tell anyone will you?"

"Now who have I got to tell?" he replied. "It's not like I'm going to talk to the guys in their dinky white shorts at the tennis club."

We walked to the cove through the dark trees. I could hear rustling of scurrying animals in the leaves, and once we heard an owl calling near us. When we reached the water, Ben said, "Go over behind the tree, and I'll go over there. Then go get in the water, not too deep, and call me."

I slowly peeled off my khaki pants and T-shirt. I wondered what my body would look like in the faint moonlight—probably a sickly greenish white. My arms are hairy and my legs are fat. I felt a shower of excitement and self-consciousness come over me, but I crept out of the woods and started walking to the beach, my feet pressing into the damp moss and then crunching the pebbles on the shore.

I remembered walking in the cove with my father when the tide was out and digging for clams, the muck in the channel so deep it sucked my sneaker away. He held my hands while I tugged my foot from the ooze, and later my mother said if I had tied my sneakers properly, I wouldn't have lost one. My mother pursed her lips when she looked at us, gray mud drying on our legs like finger paint, and I wondered what she would think if she could see me now. The thought plucked me so quickly from past to present that I stopped suddenly and wanted to run like a fawn back into the woods.

"Ready or not?" Ben called out.

I moved cautiously into the water, pulled in deeper to avoid his eyes; held back because I was scared of being dragged under.

"Ready," I said, not feeling ready.

I watched Ben as he walked from the woods. I could see the whiteness of his upper body and his legs, and the brown of his arms and neck where they had faced the sun all summer. He wasn't wearing boxer shorts like my father, but white cotton underpants that clung to his body and I looked away, feeling scared and almost sick.

When he walked towards me, I knew he was looking at me closely, and I wanted to sink out of his sight, but he waded towards me, the ripples in the water shining in circles around him, and then he stood next to me and said, "Take my hand. We're going to walk just a little farther in. I'm glad the water's warm." And when the water was above our waists he added, "Dad taught me to swim by floating first, so lay on your back and I'm going to put my hands under you."

I sank into the water, welcoming the darkness, but I was stiff, and he said, "Come on, just lean back. I'm not going to let you sink." I laid back, and when I could feel his hands under my back, I lifted my feet up and sank into him. "Close your eyes and just pretend you're lying down in your favorite place," he said.

I lay against his hands and the water, thinking about laying my head against my father's shoulder while he carried me home from church. I opened my eyes and saw Ben looking at me. In the dim light I could see my breasts floating and the nipples poking up through the wet cloth of my cotton bra. I started to sink so he couldn't look at me, but he said, "You've got to relax," and somehow I did, sinking into his hands, trusting him to be there. Then Ben said, "See, you're doing it. You're floating," and I realized he had taken his hands away. "Now don't fluster. Just relax again," he said calmly, and so I let myself soften against his hands and the water and realized I could float if I gave in to it.

"Turn over and try it face down," he commanded. He put his hands around my waist and turned me so my face was in the water. Again, I felt my body tighten up and I started to panic, but he pulled my face up gently with his hand and said, "You don't have to drown yourself, you know." And then he stopped, took a breath and said, "I'm sorry. I didn't mean to say that."

"I know, I'll try again." I took a deep breath and lay on his hands as they cradled my waist.

"Now," he said, "take another deep breath and float." Suddenly it all seemed so simple. I wondered why swimming had been so terrifying, why I had fought the water, flailing, crying, telling my father I was going to drown, crying while I lay in bed at night in a half daze feeling the water pushing me down and filling my lungs and body, pulling me to the bottom, holding my breath until my heart broke and I woke up, sometimes confusing the sweat on my face and chest with water from the lake.

"You're floating again. See, it's easy," Ben said. "Now kick slowly and evenly with your whole leg. I've got you. And lift your head up sideways when you want to breathe," he added. I tried and I could feel his hands holding me as my kicking propelled me forward. "Good," he told me, "now use your arms, like a dog if you want to or the way ladies swim like frogs."

"You mean the breast stroke?"

"Yup, whatever. Just use your arms."

I tried to remember the women at the pool swimming laps before they had lunch on the porch. I'd watched them moving slowly through the water, their heads lifted so they wouldn't get their hair wet even though it was protected by tight rubber swimming caps, and the diamonds and emeralds in their rings casting refractions across the water. Now I mimicked them, first pointing my hands together, then pushing them through the water, and finally separating and pulling them back.

"You can always put your feet down if you want to, but try kicking again and doing that thing with your arms. I'm going to let you go a little," he said, loosening his hands around my waist.

I sucked in my breath, and when I kicked hard and pushed my arms through the water, I felt my body slide across his hands and away, and then I was moving into the darkness, kicking and pushing water furiously, angry again that what had seemed so hard when I was a child had really been so simple, angry for all the times I had let myself be ashamed. Ben called out, "Stop, you're going too far. Come back now."

I stopped kicking and sank down to touch my feet to the bottom, but I couldn't reach the sand and rocks. I was over my head and I panicked. "Ben, Ben, help," I screamed, "I can't reach the bottom."

"Becky Granger, you take a deep breath and swim back to me," he called out in a firm, even voice. "There's no need to yell," he added, "I can swim out and get you."

I felt the outgoing tide against my legs and the coldness of the water, but I looked at Ben, took a deep breath, and started kicking and pushing my hands in an awkward dog paddle. I was swimming to Ben, and when I reached him he held out his hands and said, "You did it. You really did it."

My teeth were chattering, my body covered with the little hills of chicken skin, but I knew I had done it. "I did, didn't I? I really did," I answered, and looked at him like a child, excitement pulling me out of my shyness. He was grinning in the moonlight, the light playing on his wet hair and reflecting into his eyes, and I threw my arms around him and hugged him hard. "Thank you Ben, thank you so much," I said, though I wanted to add, "I love you, Ben."

"Come out now, it's cold. You're a blue blood, but you aren't supposed to be blue," he said grinning. 'We'll wrap you in the blanket and then go home."

"Thank you for being my friend, Ben. Please always be my friend," I said trying to hold onto the strength he gave me. I lifted my head and kissed the small place just above his collarbone where I had seen my mother kiss my father. Ben took my chin in his hand, bent his head towards me as I raised my mouth to his, and he kissed me on the lips, a full, deep kiss, his mouth pressing into mine. I expected the taste of tobacco, was used to it now, and I felt my body soften as I curved against him and felt his heart beating against my chest.

He ran both hands up and down my body and I tried to imagine what my skin felt like to him. My eyes closed; he held me by the waist, and then slowly moved his hands down until he held the curves of my body against him. He swayed our hips together until I felt the still unfamiliar pulling in my groin, my knees buckled and he slid me gently onto the blanket he had spread over the soft pine needles. I heard him pull in his breath as he looked at me, felt him put his hand on my chest and slowly draw it over my breasts, splayed so that the nipples passed between his fingers. He started stroking me, slowly running one hand in a widening circle across my breasts and then my stomach.

When he touched my groin I was startled, but I followed his hands as they moved up and down my body, and felt the strange tingling sensation that made me wish he would touch me there again. The delicious tension spread throughout my body, exciting and soothing me and he murmured against my ear, "I love you Becky. I love you."

Gentling into his touch and words, I answered, "I love you too; I love you so much," and again I kissed him. He slid one bra strap down my shoulder and he kissed the rise of my breast and whispered, "You are so beautiful." I wanted to stop him because I knew I should, but more than that, I wanted his hands and mouth on me. I felt the warmth of his breath on my breast and then his hands, softly caressing me while he slid the other strap down my arm and eased me onto my side, lying against him as he unhooked the bra and it fell away. I wanted first to pull my arms away and cover myself, but then he put his hands on my breasts and I strained against his touch, wanting to turn and twist so they fit his hands perfectly and he would love me. He began to moan softly, and then he pulled my breasts against his face and began to nuzzle me.

The joy of delighting and being delighted, the strange sensations that ran over and through my body like fireflies and, the wanting, wanting, wanting him so much took over and I moved against him, loving that he was loving me. I hardly noticed when he slid off my underpants, put his hands on the roundness of my hips and drew me against him.

His voice was swirling in my mind and I felt only him, was oblivious to what was happening, wanting only him, but then he fumbled with his underpants, and his hesitation broke the moment and I buried my head against his shoulder. He used his other hand to push the pants down his legs, and yank them away with one foot before I realized that we were both naked and the thought both terrified and excited me.

Again he gentled me like a trainer with a filly, speaking softly and soothing me, then playing with my breasts and sliding his fingers into me so I only wanted to push against them. He moved on top of me, nudging his knees between my legs and lay over me, pushing against my groin. "I love you, I love you," he said again.

He pushed against me again, but then he said, "I can't do this, can't do this. No," his words jerking out of his mouth until suddenly he let out a terrible sigh, all the tension left his body, and he turned away from me.

He sat on the edge of the blanket, staring at his hands, and saying, "I can't do this to you."

I reached over to him and ran my hands up and down his arm, coming back down myself from the extraordinary cloud that had carried me, and then edged closer and lay back against him. He took my hand and kissed it, and then he moved his hands to my neck and held it, his fingers gently pressing against me as he stared at me, and stroking me again, said, "I'm sorry. I didn't mean it to go this far." As he stroked my neck, I felt a surge of emotion too powerful to understand, a combination of love and loss, triggered by his vulnerability and tenderness, growing inside me as if all of the energy, tension and loss in my life were gathering in an enormous roiling storm. It was a palpable feeling tearing inside me, but like so many others of that night, one

I did not understand. Combining anger and vulnerability, frustration and sadness, and the terrible emptiness since my father's death, it overwhelmed me and made me pull Ben against me in anguish I could not control.

I clutched at him, pulled his hands across my breasts and held them there, closed my eyes wanting to submerge myself in him, to shut out everything else. I could feel only him, see only him, and think only of wanting him to take me over and erase the loneliness, and I swayed against him as he held me. And when he pulled away, I turned and held him even closer, wanting him so desperately to fill the void that I willed him inside me. I twisted against him urging him into me, and when he pulled away again I touched him so low he moaned and then I was straining against him, pulling him into me until he pushed into me again, deeper and deeper, his breath hard against my ear, then moaning and holding me so hard the pain delighted me because it told me he needed me.

A shudder passed through his body into mine and then he broke into me and I screamed, an animal scream of pain and shock, and raked his back with my nails. As he started to pull away from me, I bit him hard on the neck. It was a bite of agony and ecstasy—release from an emotion too guttural and intense, too painful and deep, too powerful to comprehend. I had forced him to fill the emptiness inside me, but now the sheltering mist that had enveloped us disappeared, and I could only look at him in shock.

I was crying deeply, sobs overwhelming me, then clawing at the pine needles, dry heaves convulsing me. A wave of shame overcame me and a sense of separation and ugliness burned my skin so that I flushed even in the cool air, conflicting sensations crushing my body and numbing my mind.

He covered my naked body with the blanket, then sat on his haunches next to me, silent. My uncontrollable shaking slowed and I curled into a ball under the blanket. He got up and I could hear him walking into the woods, getting his clothes, pulling on his pants, closing the zipper, and then swatting at mosquitoes that now swarmed about us. "I'm going to get some water," he said as he came nearer and then walked away again.

I uncurled and sat up, pulled my wet underwear back on to cover myself before he came back, and wrapped the blanket tight around me. I sat huddled next to a tree, my arms encircling my legs, rocking back and forth under the blanket. My groin ached, and I listened to the buzzing mosquitoes and felt the cold taking over my body.

The memories like shards of glass cut through me and I stood transfixed in front of the shop window. From what seemed a great distance, I heard a voice behind me saying, "It's really a good display, isn't it? Makes me want to buy one of those boats for our grandson." I turned to see an older couple I didn't know standing next to me, and I muttered, "Yes, it's wonderful," before turning to walk as quickly as I could to the stationery store, then running up the stairs to my rooms. Quivering and exhausted, I sat in the armchair, seeing only myself and Ben so many years ago.

I wanted to hide from him, but also to have him hold me so I couldn't get away. I wanted to bury myself in the darkness, but also to have him wrap his arms around me and stroke my hair, saying gently, "it's all right, Pumpkin." I almost heard my father's voice, and I shuddered and moaned in sadness. I wanted Ben to protect me, to be my friend, to love me, but I was so ashamed of what we had done—what I had done—so shocked by what it felt like to have him growing in my hand and then pushing him into me—that I could feel myself shriveling into a tiny knotted lump, raw and bruised.

I heard him walking back towards me, the dry brush cracking beneath his feet, and he hunched down near me. He pulled out a handkerchief, dipped it into a cup of water and started washing my face. I sat motionless huddled under the blanket until he turned away from me so fast that the motion created a cold breeze behind him like a whirlpool.

"I don't know what happened," I whispered, but he didn't hear me.

He stood apart from me and didn't say anything, just stared at his hands as if they didn't belong to him. "I have to get you warm, and I have to take you home now," he said slowly, talking to himself. I was trembling and I wanted to run both to him and from him, but he turned again and walked towards the boat. I got up, and dragging the blanket behind me, stopped to get my pants and shirt, and then stumbled after him, afraid that he would leave me.

"Take my extra shirt and dry off," he said firmly. He turned away, and after I put on my khakis and shirt, we walked quickly through the woods to the boat. "Stay here," he ordered after making a seat for me with the boat cushions and wrapping two blankets over me, "I'm going to get the rest of our stuff." I couldn't tell what he was thinking, and so I thought it must be what I was thinking, that now he hated me, that I disgusted him and he could never love me.

I waited in the boat, shivering, feeling the spine of the hull against my own, wishing he were back, repeating to myself again and again, "It's all right, Pumpkin, it's all right," but I knew it wasn't. I knew I had destroyed something beautiful, though I couldn't define it then. I felt dirty and I scratched my hands against the rough place on the oarlock, feeling the pain somehow a release. I knew no one could ever love me now. I was dirty and I had defiled everything I'd been taught about what made me valuable.

I watched numbly as he pushed the skiff into the water, eased into it, rowed us to the motorboat, cleated the bow rope to the stern of the larger boat and transferred the picnic equipment. I wondered what he was thinking, but I couldn't bear to ask, and so I watched him and was silent. I remembered biting him, and felt sick to my stomach. I looked at the back of his neck, and was relieved not to see a mark, but when he pulled down the collar of his shirt to rub his neck, I saw it, even in the moonlight, a dark blotch under his ear.

We rode in silence down the sound, and then to the dock at The Inn. He walked down the path past The Inn, and he stopped when we could see the light on my house. "I'm sorry," he said, his voice hard and flat, and I heard myself parroting, "Sorry." Numb, too scared to talk, I wanted to tell him I needed him more than anyone in the world, but I thought only how I must disgust him now. I turned and ran to the front door. I turned again before I reached the steps, but he was gone, and I kissed my hand and held it toward where he had been standing.

Chapter Five

I remember walking into the house, I thought, quivering with the memory. I could see someone sitting in front of the fireplace. I was scared it was my mother, but it was Kurt, who was helping us that summer.

He looked at my wet hair and asked, "What were they playing, Moby Dick, or the Old Man in the Sea?" When I didn't answer, he asked what I was doing with my townie boyfriend, and then I was terrified my mother knew. I tried to pretend but he said, "Becky, don't be so dumb, everyone knows you're going out with a townie. But it's okay. I'm a townie back home, so I'm not going to tell. And your mother's oblivious. Besides, now she's met a man she likes." I must have looked surprised because Kurt told me, "The Johnsons' friend. The guy who's getting divorced. She called after dinner to say he'd invited her to the dance afterward." I was stunned and instantly furious. So soon after Daddy died, how could she? I went up to my bedroom and cried and rocked myself against the wall.

Tears overcame me again. There was no one to hear, no one to care. I cried until my chest heaved in sobs that were so violent they scared me, until exhausted I lay back against the chair and said out loud, "Why?" It was a question I had asked many times before, though not in expectation of finding an answer. I asked it only to punish myself, the question itself cutting into my flesh and chastising me. Now, however, I began to see myself as a fragile child and to think about my vulnerability—the pain of being the sister who survived and the child who lost her father. And about Ben who had saved me, at least then.

❧

Loving Ben started so gently. So softly. Again, as I had so many times to ease pain, I thought about Ben, about the first summer when he gave me a present, and I knew he liked me.

My parents' anniversary fell just a few days before my own birthday in the middle of August. I didn't like having a summer birthday because we were never at home and I couldn't invite any friends, though at least at the lake I'd had my cousins. Now, when my mother asked if I would like to have a party, I didn't know what to say. "You could have a little dinner," she suggested. "We could combine your party and our anniversary party, and you could ask some of your friends."

"I'd like to do something with you and Daddy," I told her, thinking that would be easier than having a party of my own.

"We were thinking of an evening picnic. We could charter a boat to bring some people. Others could come by car or their own boat," my mother said. She seemed happiest when lost in the details of planning a party. Somehow, even in her sadness about Rachel, she was still able to think about how to make people feel at ease, to organize everything so everyone would enjoy being together.

"I would love that," I lied to make her happy. Some of the parents of kids at tennis and sailing were friends of my parents—so I knew I could suggest them, and my mother would think I had more friends. I wished Monica were still there. I could imagine my mother's friends looking horrified as Monica pranced and jiggled around in her short shorts and halter top. I started listing the people I knew, "Well, I could ask Sarah, her parents are the Stewarts."

"Oh, yes, wonderful. How many people do you think we can invite?" she asked, and then answered her own question, "I think we could have about thirty easily. You make your list, and I'll make mine. If you have four or five little friends, that would be lovely. But we'd better get invitations out because everyone's so busy with parties at the end of summer."

I didn't want to ask my parents if they might charter The Sea Princess *for their picnic and betray my interest in seeing Ben again, but one day, as we were all having lunch on the rocks, my father said to my mother, "Captain Bunker said he'll pick people up at the dock in town and bring them here."*

"Oh, good," I blurted, caught off guard.

My parents were surprised, but I added, "It's such a nice boat. People will have fun coming down the sound."

The weather was fair and cool the afternoon of the party, and everything seemed perfect. The morning of the party, Mrs. Thomas called to say that Ginny and Jon couldn't come and I was relieved that Sarah would be the only person my age there. My mother was thrilled, however, that so many people had accepted the invitation and said she was sure it was a sign that our family was being accepted socially.

Just before we left for the picnic my father said, "Anne, Becky, I'd like to give you my presents here with just the four of us. Robbie, you come sit next to me and we'll give the women we love their presents." We sat on the flowered blue chintz couch and he brought two little boxes out of his pocket, one wrapped in silver paper with a silver ribbon, the other in teal blue, with a green bow, my favorite colors, so I knew it was for me.

"Anne, I love you with all my heart, and you have made my life complete. Here's to you and our family," my father said, smiling and raising his glass towards her. She smiled back at him, and I could see little tears forming at the edges of her eyes.

"Thank you, Sam," she said quietly. "Thank you." I could sense a current so strong between them that I felt as if I could touch it. They each got up and stood together, their arms around each other, while my mother buried her face against my father's chest then kissed his neck, and he patted her back softly. When they dropped their arms and stood back from each other, I could imagine them before they'd married, before they had children, before they'd lost Rachel, before the edginess came into my mother's voice and before I ever heard them arguing in their bedroom. My mother unwrapped the silver paper and then opened the gray velvet box and pulled out the earrings. "Oh, Sam, they're beautiful. They go with my bracelet. Oh, Sam," and I wondered if she would cry.

"Okay, Pumpkin, your turn," my father said lightly as he held out the little blue box.

"Thank you, Daddy," I said. "I love it already because you wrapped it in my favorite colors."

"Well, actually, Dot at the newspaper store wrapped it for me because you know I'm not good at that. But you're right, I chose the colors."

I pulled the bright green ribbon and then slipped my finger under the tape holding the teal colored paper. Inside was a gray velvet box, like the one he had given my mother, though smaller. When I flipped up the top, strong against its hinge, I saw a ring inside from the Rock Shop with three stones, an aquamarine, a green tourmaline and a pink one, set side by side. "Oh Daddy, that's so beautiful. Daddy, I love it," I exclaimed, my heart jumping. "I love it."

I rushed over to him and hugged him as he bent down to hug me back. I pulled the ring over my finger—it fit perfectly—and went over to show my mother. "Becky, it's beautiful. It is a lovely ring," she said slowly. "Now, stop biting your nails and it will look wonderful."

"Oh, Anne, I think it looks beautiful now," my father said. I looked at my mother, knowing that Rachel never would have bitten her nails and that

the ring would have looked perfect on her hand. But I also knew that if I ever felt lonely, I could look at my ring and know my father loved me.

"Yes, of course, I'm sorry Becky, it's a lovely ring," my mother said.

We drove to our land two hours before any guests would arrive, got the fires going for cooking, and set the lanterns and lights along paths. Some people drove, but others were coming by boat. When I saw The Sea Princess coming down the sound, I felt my stomach turn and a sense of dread and longing pulled at me. I went down to the float, pretending to help the guests, and, as I looked around the boat I found Ben. He smiled at me. "Hello," he said, and the sound of his voice hummed through me again.

"Hello," I replied, my voice catching in my throat even on two syllables. As I stood next to the boat, he helped one of the older women, and when he handed her up over the gunwale, I took the woman's arm and Ben's hand touched my own. His touch spiraled up my arm and through my body, coursing through me like water released from a dam, though I stood there looking as if I had been frozen. I felt myself trembling and quickly withdrew my hand. I was careful not to touch him again, but when all the guests were off the boat, we stood next to each other. Pulled by the force of two magnets—fight or flight—attraction and terror, I stood immobilized, and finally looked up at him. He smiled at me and I was able to mumble, "I'm sorry about the other day at the dock."

"I know," he said cheerfully, and grinned at me with a merry twinkle in his eyes.

"At the town dock," I added unnecessarily.

"I know," he repeated. "Scotty told me, saw you wave to me. Said you were some upset. So happy birthday."

"Thank you," I said, finally raising my head to look at him.

"I brought you a present. Would you like it now?" he asked, standing so close I felt my knees tremble again.

"Oh, a present," I said quickly, stepping back into myself. "This is so exciting. Look what Daddy gave me," I added self-consciously, showing him the ring.

"Oh, mine isn't anything fancy like that. It's just something I made for you."

"You made for me?" I asked. "That's even better. That's the best! Yes, I want it right now!" my joy lifting me out of shyness.

Then Ben looked a little embarrassed. His grandfather and the other man were watching us, but Ben picked something off the bench behind him and then turned back to me. He was holding a little white sailing dingy with red trim, sail and oars. On the bow, in neat black letters, was my name, "Becky."

I looked at him, then at the boat cradled like a little bird in his hands, and I could feel tears coming to my eyes.

"For me?" I asked quietly. "You made that for me?"

"Well, my uncle helped. He makes them to sell at The Village Shop. But we put your name on this one." And looking at my tears he asked, "Don't you like it?"

"Oh, Ben, I love it," I said my voice hushed and coming from deep in my chest, happiness sweeping through me again.

I wanted to hug him, but I saw Captain Bunker and the other man looking at us, so I put out my arms and Ben gently nestled the little boat in my outstretched hands.

"Thank you," I whispered. "Thank you, Ben." I looked at him, smiled, and said, "Will you come with me to my birthday picnic? Please."

"Maybe later," he answered. "I have to help Grampie now. Maybe later."

"Please," I said. "I'll save some steak for you. Thank you for my present. I've never had such nice presents on my birthday—or ever," and I turned and walked up the gangplank back to the party, my heart thumping wildly.

I walked the long way down the road back to where our car was parked because I didn't want to trip in the dusk on the roots intruding over the shore path. I carefully pushed the boat underneath the back of my mother's seat where I knew it would be safe and my parents wouldn't see it.

I could hear the people at the party laughing and talking as I followed the line of lanterns along the path. Their steady glow against the trees moving in the slight wind made the branches seem like stately dancers in a black and white film. I stopped on the path, hearing the people, but listening for the sounds of the forest around me—the rustle of animals and birds settling in for the night and the hoot of an owl in the darkness.

As I approached the edge of the rocks, I saw my parents talking with some of their friends. When I got closer to them, my mother said, "Oh, here you are, our Birthday Girl," and she stretched out her arm to encircle me while her friends smiled approvingly. While I stood next to her, a man said, "Oh, I can see someone went to the Rock Shop." I smiled and showed him my ring, and my mother moved her head back and forth so the light of the fire caught her earrings.

Sarah and her parents arrived late, so I hadn't seen her before, but now she was standing near the fire, so I walked over to her. Sarah asked, "Where were you? I missed you."

"I was helping people off the boat," I replied. Seeing my flushed face and the excitement in my eyes, she said, "Happy Birthday. You seem really happy. Did you get some cool presents?"

"Yes," I said in a hushed voice that made Sarah look at me quizzically. "Yes, I got this ring from my father," and I held out my hand.

"Oh, that's really pretty."

"And, Ben gave me a sailing dingy with my name on it!"

"Ben? The boy you met from here?"

"Yes," I said holding my breath and wondering what Sarah would say.

Sarah took my hand and seemed to suppress a little squeal. "Oh that's so romantic. Where's the boat?"

"I put it in our car. I hid it under the seat so my parents won't see. They don't want me to be friends with him."

"That's smart. Your mom would hate him. Can I see it?"

"Not now—but maybe tomorrow, if you come over."

"Are you going to see him again?" Sarah asked.

"I think so. I asked him to come for supper, but he said he wouldn't."

"So, you should take supper to him," Sarah suggested.

"You think?" I replied uncertainly.

"Of course, I'll help you get some food and cover for you when you take it."

Sarah and I took extra food on our plates and then put together a plate of hors d'oeuvres with a slice of steak and a big piece of maple cake with walnuts and lots of icing. I walked carefully down the path to where Ben was sitting on the float while Captain Bunker and Bradley sat in the boat talking and smoking pipes. When Ben heard me, he turned. "You didn't come to my party, so I brought the party to you," I said, trying to cover my shaky nerves with humor, the way my mother did.

He was drinking a Coke, and I stood next to him and put the plate down on the wood. He couldn't see it clearly in the dark, but he picked up a curried crab on endive and bit into it tentatively. "Jeezum!" he exclaimed, spitting it into his hand.

"Sorry—it's crab with curry."

"Gurry?" he asked, twisting his mouth.

"No, curry. Guess you don't like it. What's gurry?"

"Fish guts."

"Try the cheese puffs. They aren't too puffed now, but maybe you'll like them," I suggested, turning the plate so he could see the them more easily and then letting myself slip down until I was sitting next to him. I could feel the heat of his body on mine, even in the cool August air and I wanted to move even closer to him, wanted to touch him. I leaned closer, until I could feel the edge of his shirt touch mine, but not his shoulder beneath it. I wanted so much to lean into him, but I was too scared and I sat back.

He picked over some of the food but ate the steak and then the cake. "Good cake," he pronounced. "Bet Mrs. Wharton made this cake. She makes the cakes for us too."

"Yes, she did," I answered, happy we shared something we both liked.

"I can't stay long," I said. "My mother will miss me."

"Wouldn't want you consorting with island people now, would we?" he replied, smiling at me, a bit of cake stuck on his upper lip.

"Consorting?"

"Yep. Look it up," he said, looking down his nose at me in a superior way and laughing at the same time.

"I know what it means, but I don't think that's fair."

"So ask her if you can come to my birthday party and see what she says," he said, looking into me with his startling blue eyes.

"All right, I'll do that, and if she says yes, then you'll have to let me come," I retorted, responding to his challenge. "So when is it?" I asked in a softer voice.

"We're having a clambake on the island next Saturday. You can come over on the mail boat at two o'clock. I'll get a ride over and meet you on the town dock." He answered so quickly and clearly that I knew he had been planning to ask me, and a wave of excitement flowed over me.

I looked at Ben again and realized that for the first time in my life I'd been asked on a date. I froze, wanting to disappear.

"Just tell her you need another rowing lesson," he laughed, enjoying my confusion. "And tell your father I'll bring you back on the evening boat and I'll walk you home. Uncle Clem will hold the boat a couple of minutes extra so's I can get back."

"Okay," I said finally, my voice unfamiliar, a throaty purr deep inside me. "All right," I said, worried that my mother wouldn't let me go. "I have to go now," I added, almost panicking.

I didn't know how to ask my parents if I could go out with Ben. I thought maybe I could say Ben was taking me rowing, but that didn't make sense. I saw my mother walking towards where Sarah was standing by herself folding a blanket. So I walked towards them and heard Sarah saying, "Oh, she just left a few minutes ago to go to the ladies' room.

When my mother saw me she said, "Where have you been? We missed you."

"I just went to use the bathroom," I lied and grabbed two corners of the blanket.

"I'm glad you're back," Sarah whispered after my mother left us. "I was worried they'd miss you. Did you see him?"

"Yes. He asked me to his birthday."

"That's cool," Sarah said, looking happy. "Do you think they'll let you go?"

"Would your parents?"

"Sure. They're a lot more open than yours, and besides they're busy writing their books."

"So how would you ask them?" I asked.

"I'd just say I wanted to go and he was nice and it would be interesting."

"We have to get things cleaned up to go now," my mother called over to us. "Here girls, take the big flashlights and lead people down the path to the float so Captain Bunker can take them home."

The guests followed the beams of our lights through the trees from the picnic rocks to the clearing where the gangplank led down to the float. The roots of the trees looked like black snakes running over the ground, but I wasn't scared and I liked leading people along the path I knew so well. I could see Ben with Captain Bunker, but I thought about the comments about the dirt under his fingernails and that he probably couldn't read or write—that he was just the boat boy, not even worthy of being called by his own name. I thought about my mother's pretension and what my parents' friends thought of Ben, and I didn't want him to see me with them. Again, I wondered why I felt more at home in his world than in my own as I walked silently back to the picnic place and found that almost everyone had left. Robbie had fallen asleep on my mother's shoulder, and my father said, "Let's go home now. We can come back tomorrow and finish cleaning up when it's light." When I said good night, Sarah, whispered "Good luck."

Nestled in the back of the car, packed in with presents, bags of leftover food, and bottles, with the smells of pine, marshmallows, wine and beer mingling together, I listened to my parents discussing the party. They were excited because so many people had been there, pleased people had appreciated the fine wine and the food. My father said he was relieved the lanterns had worked so well, no one had stumbled over the roots or rocks, and the light breeze had kept the mosquitoes away. My mother was thrilled by comments from the Johnsons and the Phillips about what an elegant party it was. I nodded off, dreaming of rowing my boat with Ben and when I awoke, we were home. I hid my boat under my sweater and disguised the bulge by carrying a bag of garbage in front of me to the basement and then taking the back stairs to my room.

❧

I often thought of Ben while I was married, first to Jordie and then to Richard, tucking the thoughts into the far crevices of my mind. But as water flows under ice, they traveled beneath the surface, emerging unexpectedly when my marriages froze and I conjured up fantasies to fill my loneliness. Sometimes the dreams and daydreams seemed more real than reality, and always more welcome. When I saw a boy in the line at the market smiling at the girl behind the checkout counter, the creases at the edge of his mouth reminded me of Ben, or at least the version that blended my father and Ben into the perfect and always available lover.

When I drove past the entrance to our land for the first time, I thought of my last night with Ben. After that, I avoided the road that passed the driveway. Now the memories brought tears to my eyes and cramped my throat. As I faded into sleep after seeing Monica, he came into my dreams again. It was an old dream, one I had refined over the years. Each time it appeared, I felt guilty, but each time I was also grateful because it filled the emptiness. In the few seconds afterwards and before I was fully conscious, the sweetness played over my body warming my cold loneliness but leaving me sadder when I was finally awake and realized the pleasure of being loved was just a dream. Towards the end of my marriage to Jordie, the dream of Ben was all I had.

This night the dream was so compelling that I awoke in a sweat. In the thin light of dawn I lay in bed and the remnants of the dream floated around me. I had been in a tunnel, walking slowly, feeling cobbled stones with my bare feet and, with my outstretched hands, slimy walls dripping humidity and mold. I moved slowly through the tunnel, hearing the motion of slithering animals and squishing small crawling insects beneath my feet. I walked through the tunnel towards a faint light and, as I approached it, I saw a torch held by a man in shining green cloth and I knew as I walked closer that the man was Ben.

I put my arms around his neck. He threw the torch in the tunnel, where it sputtered in the ooze, and then he put his hands around my waist, and his fingers crept down my back so they encircled me and held me close to him. I could feel him growing into me, feel my blood and his rushing through our bodies. He moved his hand slowly up my spine, and then he tipped my head back and kissed me—harder than he had kissed me when we were young—passionate and almost desperate, pushing his tongue into my mouth, hard enough to hurt, until I relaxed and answered him, and then we were pulling at each other and he whispered, "Oh God, Becky, how I love you." I answered, "Ben, you're the only man I ever loved." He kissed me again and carried me to moss under a willow tree, laid his cape on the moss and the willow branches sweeping to the ground formed a curtain around us.

Slowly he stroked my breasts until the nipples were hard and I ached for him to touch me. He undid the buttons on my dress and slipped my arms out of the sleeves. I felt as natural with him as a child, and as beautiful. I saw myself sitting in the filtered moonlight while he undid my bra and slipped that off onto the moss, and then he cupped my breasts in his hands and bent to kiss me. He lay in my lap while I stroked his hair and he sucked me until I could stand the aching in my groin no longer and rushed at his clothes. He laughed and helped me until I could see his chest, the black hair twining and I put my hands in it and found his nipples. He moaned and then he put his hands around my hips and drew my dress up, slipped it off, and told me again that he loved me. Then he kissed the little hill below my waist, and I could feel the ache growing and the wetness, and I wanted him inside me more than I could stand. I could feel the passion flowing through me, and then his tongue reached into me turning lightly then hard, finding pleasure spots I had never known existed. I moaned in a voice I had never heard; I pushed myself against him, urging him into me, and then he pulled my body against him, kissing my stomach and breasts again before he slid into me, and we rocked with an explosion of lust and love that overwhelmed me.

We lay back against the moss and explored each other's bodies in silence and I caressed his arms and back, and then as I watched him in the moonlight he started to disappear, his body turning to dust and floating away. Oh, my God, I thought as I woke fully. What have I let myself think? and I tried to push the thoughts of him away. I got up from my bed though it was only four-thirty, and, as the unexpected waves of passion receded, I began to laugh. You horny old woman, I sighed. You poor lonely horny old woman. The dream made me more uncomfortable than it had before, not only because it was so vivid, but because I was in Maine, closer to Ben physically than I had been in thirty-five years. Why did you come back? It seemed now a terrible idea, but I began to see the ways I had used memories of him over the years for succor.

I walked to the desk, sat in front of my typewriter and wrote a poem.

STASIS

There is a bridge in Somesville,
Not the wood one that arches over the stream,
But the bridge between ocean and marsh,
an ordinary overpass passing over
sea turning to land,
salt water to fresh.
Twice each day
the ocean
changes its
direction,
reversing slowly,
building momentum
until it forces itself upon the land.
The land receives first in grudging defiance,
an old virgin fending off a lover,
until he patiently and gently
slides along her shores,
showing her how it can feel
to have water rushing through the channel;
then cautiously opening and laying back to welcome;
mingling for hours until, in exhaustion,
the ocean retreats,
the marsh
oozing and sucking,
holding him as long as she can.

There is a long moment
When the sea and land balance,
When the waters rest,
When it is impossible to know
Which way they flow.

Reading it to myself, I could at last acknowledge the deep longing I had felt all my life to love and be loved, and sense that I had been too scared to act or to be vulnerable.

Ben, I trusted him so quickly, so completely. He was so unlike the other boys I knew then—or the men I know now. I don't know why I trusted him. I hardly knew anything about him, but he didn't judge me. I didn't feel so self-conscious with him—until that day on the dock. That was so pathetically adolescent, but I was just that—a pathetically unsure fourteen-year-old. Monica saw me for the emotional cripple I was, or am? When I saw her the next summer, after daddy died, she knew that Ben was my touchstone. She knew I needed him. And then he forced me out of my fantasies about him by actually showing up.

The summer after Daddy died, we came back to Maine and I was standing outside The Village Shop when Monica rode by on her bike and stopped in front of MacKnight's to pick up the paper for her father. When she saw me, she slammed on her brakes, dropped the bike, which crashed to the pavement, and ran to me. Monica wrapped her arms around me in a tight hug and said, "I heard, I heard. I'm so sorry. I don't know what I'd do if Daddy died." And then she pushed me away to arm's length and added, "You look like crap." I laughed, the first laugh in months, and we stood facing each other outside the store laughing, crying and then hugged again.

"You're right. I feel like crap, and I look like crap."

"Well, I'm going to buy you a present. Let's go in here and see what there is." I hesitated, but Monica grabbed my arm and pulled me to face the store windows. There were flowered vases and boxes of fancy soap, some antique silver bracelets and an amber brooch, but then I saw a boat like the one Ben had given me on a shelf on the wall behind the window. I stared at the boat, until Monica asked, "What are you looking at?"

"Last summer," I answered, my voice trembling, "At the end of last summer, Ben, the boy on the lobster boat. He made one of these for me," I said, putting my hand out towards the boat.

"Oh?"

"I went out with him once, but then my parents wouldn't let me go again," I explained.

"Well, I can't buy you a fisherman, but you could go get him yourself," Monica said with excitement.

"No! I can't do that. He wrote me, after Daddy died I mean, and I wrote him back, but he never wrote me back again."

"You could figure out how to bump into him," Monica suggested. "Do you still think about him?" and then she grabbed my arm again and said, "Let's go get ice cream."

We ordered ice cream cones at the drugstore and sat on a green wooden bench in the park near the harbor. For the first time since my father died, I was able to talk. Talk about my father, my mother, Ben, and how scared I was. "Daddy just died, Monica. It was so quick. I didn't get to say good-bye really 'cause I thought I'd see him again in a few weeks. He just died." I stopped and twisted the hem of my shorts while Monica sat silently next to me. "Everyone else has a father and I don't know why I'm....I feel alone a lot." Monica nodded, and sometimes she let out a little sigh, or patted my arm, but mostly she listened. "My mother is so sad. I hate being around her. She's so sad and I don't know what to do to make her happy. No one talks to me. They just tell me I have to be strong. Everyone says I have to be strong for my mother so she doesn't get upset." I stopped again, then blurted out, "I don't feel strong, Monica. I don't feel strong at all. I feel like... I feel like I'm walking around in a movie, and everything's flat and phony."

Monica took my hand, and we sat together silently on the bench. Finally Monica said gently, "So let's have fun while you're here. Let's just go do dumb fun things. You have to stop looking like hell, so that means we have to go, I mean, we just have to go to the pool and get a tan. Right?" She looked at me and smiled. "Have you got a sexy suit? Let's go get our sexiest suits and we can go to the club, right?"

We met at the pool in half an hour, and Monica strutted around in her flamingo pink bikini. The old men peered up over their newspapers and horn-rimmed sunglasses, while their wives frowned and Monica and I giggled. My one-piece suit wasn't very revealing, but Monica showed me how to stuff paper in the cups to push my breasts up, and we sat together basting ourselves with coconut oil. When I told my mother I had seen Monica she said, "Be careful. She's just using you to get into the club because she can't go any other way. I'm surprised they're here on their own," but she also seemed relieved that I had someone to spend time with.

I remember kicking back the stand on my bike and swinging my leg over the seat like a boy—my mother hated that—and pedaling down to the town dock, like Monica suggested, letting the bike run free down the hill. Ben hadn't written me back, and I'd tried so hard not to think about him, but my dreams betrayed me. Sometimes when I woke up, in that uneasy space between wake and sleep, I thought he was there and cared about me and all the longing came back. I could feel him sitting next to me and smell the salt on his hair again. I imagined him holding my hand and the warmth of his arm as we sat on a rock looking at Somes Sound. It's still so vivid, and it still hurts. I was so lonely after Daddy died. Monica made it feel almost right to think about Ben, to miss him. I was so scared I wouldn't see him in the short time we were there that second summer. I went down to the harbor the next time I could get away from my mother and sat on the green bench for hours.

As I looked out into the fog, I heard a beating rhythm, soft as a bird's wings, coming from outside the harbor. As it resolved into the steady chug of a motor, the bow of The Sea Princess *parted the fog, pushing slowly towards me through the central channel of the harbor, and I felt like a butterfly pinned on a piece of balsa wood. I wanted to run and I wanted to stay right there; I wanted the fog to cloak me so that I could watch what would happen and not be seen. There was no one waiting for the boat—no one but me standing on the dock, and I realized if Ben were on the boat, he would be more likely to see me if I moved. I was frightened he would, and terrified he would not.*

As the fog swirled around me and the boat eased against the dock, I strained to see who was on The Sea Princess. *I saw the forms of an older woman and her daughter, a man carrying a small blue suitcase, and two men in slickers. Then one of them turned around and our eyes locked. "Ben," I said out loud. And there he was. I saw him looking at me and I knew he could see me clearly. He waved, pointed to the lines on deck, and called out to me, "Wait there, I'll be up in a minute. Just have to stow this stuff."*

I watched as he strode quickly up the gangplank, and then he was right next to me and I was looking into his incredible eyes. His voice was deeper, and he was taller than I remembered; when he spoke, I felt currents pulsating through me from my chest to my legs. I was afraid I'd faint. I felt my stomach get tight, as it had when I'd first met him. He looked almost sternly at me and then put out his hands. "Ben," I said, taking his hands, and then I bowed my head because I could feel the tears rushing up. He drew me against his chest, and I buried my head against his shoulder as he held me very tightly.

"It's all right, Becky," he said. "It's all right, it's all right to cry." He led me over to the rocks that separated the shore from the land, and we sat together on a flat piece of driftwood someone had set between chunks of granite, hidden from the docks by a hedge of rugosa roses and the curtain of fog. He had his arm around me, and I sat next to him feeling the pain of the last year ebbing away. He gave me a blue bandanna to wipe my nose and said, "Becky, "I'm sorry. I'm sorry I didn't write back to you. I thought about you at your fancy school, with all your fancy friends. I looked at that elegant paper you wrote me on and I thought there was no way I could be your friend and I didn't know

what to say. I'm sorry, Becky."

"I missed you, Ben," I answered. "I really missed you. I didn't know how much I'd missed you until I saw you."

We could hardly bear being apart. When we stood next to each other our fingers touched and we brushed against each other savoring the touch and smell of the other's hair and skin. I could almost define the circle around us that held us in its warmth, and I began to feel the awful loneliness of the months since my father died fill with laughter and the delight of loving and being loved. We spent every moment of the next days together that we could, but those were moments stolen after his work and when my mother was with her friends, or when I lied and told her I was going to the movies with Monica.

Chapter Six

A week after I visited Monica, she called me and said, "You have to come for tea. I have something to tell you." When we were seated and Monica had poured dark brown Darjeeling from the silver teapot, she said, "I did something maybe I shouldn't have, and I'm sort of sorry I did. But I thought you would never get around to it." She stopped and looked over at me, and I could see us sitting at the picnic tables at the pool talking about boys so many years ago. "I talked to Bob at the library," Monica said gently.

I felt a ball of fear growing in my stomach, and I couldn't think of anything to say except, "I see him all the time."

"I pretended I was looking for a Harlequin Romance and I couldn't remember the title. I told him the story was sort of like you and Ben Bunker."

I wanted to say, "How dare you," but the earnestness on Monica's face and my own curiosity stopped me.

"It was really quite a natural, casual sort of conversation. Bob said he remembered you two that summer and was glad you were back and came to the library so often. He couldn't place the book—well, that's not a surprise because I don't think it exists, but he said he remembered you and Ben. And then I asked him what Ben was doing."

I could tell from Monica's eyes that she didn't want to tell me what she had found out.

"He's married, with six kids, right?"

"No, only two," Monica answered. But that was enough. I took a deep breath and tried to calm my heart. It was beating hard and I knew a blush was racing up my face.

"I'm sorry," Monica said. "I'm sorry to have to tell you he's married. He lives on Little Cranberry with his wife, Abby. They've been married a long time."

"It's all right. Really it is. I don't know why I hadn't asked Bob before, it would have been the simplest way to find out, but I never thought about doing that." We sat there holding our teacups, until I continued. "It's better really, isn't it? I'm happy for him. He's been married a long time. What does he do; do you know?"

"He fishes, but Bob said he got a Masters in Marine Biology and he also does research on the fisheries."

The thought of Ben as a researcher made me uneasy. Later I realized that it was easier to dismiss him if he was "just" a fisherman. That he had gone to college, gone to graduate school was unsettling.

All these years, you could have written him, I thought angrily. You just didn't want to know. "I'm glad you did that," I said to Monica, though it wasn't true. It had been so easy to keep Ben in my fantasies and conjure him up whenever I felt sad or lonely and scared, now he was off limits in a way he had not been before I knew he was married. As the sadness settled around me, I felt afraid of the loneliness without him.

Right after it happened, I started to say to myself as I drove home, but stopped. Right after I…I don't even know what to call it. Rape? It's a horrible thing to think I actually pushed someone into having sex with me. I was so desperate then, like a child on a slide that's too high, but no one noticed. No one put out an arm to catch me as I fell, and I couldn't catch myself. Daddy might have noticed, but he wasn't there, and my mother was too sad herself. Until, of course, she met Taylor, and again a twinge of anger pinched me.

When I went back to school I was even more deeply depressed than the year before because I couldn't tell anyone, couldn't even admit to myself at first what I'd done. I didn't expect Ben to call or write, and when he didn't, it confirmed that I'd defiled myself, and him. When we read The Scarlet Letter *in American Literature, I knew I was like Hester Prynne, only my Scarlet Letter wasn't an A. Instead, I thought it's W—for Whore. The word tormented me. I said it again and again, and one day I even cut out a W from red construction paper and each day I pinned it to my bra. A few weeks later when we were changing for gym class, another girl noticed it and said, "You're sweet on someone whose name starts with W. Right?"*

What I'd done shamed me so deeply I could only push the shame deeper. In biology class, when the teacher talked about sex and the other girls squirmed and tittered in their seats, I thought I was marked and they knew I was no longer a virgin. I thought of myself as a slut, a person no man would ever want to marry, a person no man could ever love. I knew I would have disappointed Daddy and I was terrified I might be pregnant. When I missed my period for two weeks, I was certain I would have to leave school. I lay awake at night staring at the ceiling and imagining being exiled to a home for unwed mothers, so scared no one I knew would speak to me. When I finally got my period, I was still scared because of the biology teacher's offhand remark about spotting in early pregnancy.

Every time I overheard girls talking about boys, I was sure they knew what I'd done, and so I avoided them, staying in study hall, though I didn't do any work. I hid in bathrooms and my room whenever and for as long as I could, coiling deeper and deeper into myself until I couldn't get along with anyone. I got so cold and brittle I saw a slight in anything anyone said. People began to move to the other side of the hall and lower their eyes when I walked past them, and that seemed good to me.

Ben had been my salvation, I thought as I walked up the steps to my rented suite. We were so young and from such different worlds. His family was so different from mine, but also from what I thought it would be, and certainly from what my mother thought. Daddy was right, when Ben asked me to visit him on "his" island that first summer, he gave me a chance to see how they lived, but no one I knew would have believed it. He asked me to his birthday party, which was right after mine.

Every day, all day, I thought about how to ask my mother if I could go to Ben's party; I knew I should ask when my father was back from the city. Sarah agreed. "It's not like your Dad's a snob, but your Mom. Well, moms are like that, I guess. My mom wouldn't be worried, but I know a lot of parents wouldn't want their daughters to go out with someone who wasn't from the Main Line. They aren't so worried about their daughters; they're just worried about what their friends would think."

The night my father came home from New York, before dinner, I stood in front of my mirror and practiced asking. "Guess what, Captain Bunker is having a lobster picnic and he wants me to come. Ben wants to teach me how to land the dinghy against The Sea Princess.*" I tried pitching my voice high and then low, saying my speech fast and slow. I imagined their questions and tried out answers.*

After dinner, when we were sitting in the library, I took a deep breath and said very fast, "Captain Bunker wants me to have a lobster feed."

"What?" my father asked.

I forced myself to slow down, took another deep breath, and said, "I mean Captain Bunker thinks I should have a good lobster before we go back to New York. He asked me to dinner."

"That's nice, does he think we don't feed you enough?" my father said laughing. "Would you like to go?"

"Oh yes, Daddy," I replied, a little too earnestly. "It's Ben's birthday, and all his relatives will be there."

"Oh, I see," my father said slowly, a little grin coming over his face.

He looked over at my mother, who was working on a needlepoint cushion, moving the pink yarn through the canvas and staring at the needle in her hand.

"How would you get there?"

"Ben said he would come over on the mail boat and pick me up around noon and then bring me back on the last boat at nine o'clock. He said to tell you that he would walk me home."

"That's considerate of him," my father said. "He seems like a very nice young man. Anne, what do you think?"

"Well, it isn't as if it is a date. It's not like a young man asking her to dinner in New York. It's not as if we have to worry about anyone seeing them," and her voice trailed off. "I don't know. It seems harmless," she finally replied. "Besides, we're going on a picnic with the Robinsons and they don't have children, so maybe…"

"Hmm, Pumpkin, well if you want to go, I guess you can. We know them. They'll take good care of you, and I bet you'll have a very interesting time."

I let out my clenched breath slowly.

"I don't know anyone else who's been invited to something with the locals," my father continued. "It's quite an honor really. You'll see how the other half lives." He laughed, but then said, "You're sort like an anthropologist going off to investigate another culture."

I called the Beal and Bunker Ferry the next morning and asked for Ben. The man said Ben wasn't there, but that I could leave a message. "This is Becky Granger calling," I replied. "I just wanted to tell him I'll be at the Town Dock on Saturday at noon."

"Yes Miss Granger," the man said, "I'll tell Chum...I mean young Ben for ya."

Saturday morning I washed my hair and used Clairol conditioner, as my mother had told me to do so many times. I'd never wanted to do it before, but I was glad I did because my hair was soft and shining. I thought for a long time about what to wear before choosing khaki pants and sneakers because I was going to a picnic on the rocks, and then a striped blue and white boat neck T-shirt my mother had bought in the village, and a navy blue Shetland sweater. I asked my parents if I could charge a present for Ben at the bookstore, and when they agreed, I bought him Andersonville, because I liked it and there were stories in it about men from Maine. With money from my allowance, I bought him a knife from the hardware store, the kind that fit into a sheath. It had a cord of leather tightly wrapped around the handle shellacked like the one Jon Thomas flaunted, and I thought it was very cool.

When I came down the stairs, my parents were sitting in the library, so I walked in to say good-bye. Daddy looked at me and his eyes opened wider just for a second. "Pumpkin," he said, "You look very pretty. I like your hair like that."

"You look lovely, dear," my mother said, but she added, "and you dressed just right. You don't want to overdo it." I didn't understand until she said, "You don't want to make the island people self-conscious. You come from a very different world and you don't want to make them feel badly about theirs. Just be sure you are polite, not effusive, but polite, and don't expect things to be the way they are here." Then she paused. "Sam," she said, suddenly looking worried, "I'm not sure we're doing the right thing."

"Nonsense, darling," he replied. "They'll take very good care of her, and she'll have a very interesting time and have lots to report back to us."

I could feel the roots of my hair getting hotter, but I mumbled, "Thank you," as Daddy asked if I had any money and knew the cottage phone number. "Yes, but I have to go to catch the ferry," I answered.

"Do you want a lift?" he asked, but I said, "No, I'll just take my bike," because I was eager to get away and wanted to keep them and Ben apart.

When I got to the dock, the mail boat was coming into the harbor, and I pushed my bike into the stand and walked slowly to meet the boat. I tried to walk nonchalantly, hoping to look like Lauren Bacall or Katherine Hepburn. By the time I reached the dock, the mail boat was just touching the wooden float, nestling gently against the canvas bumpers. I searched for Ben on the deck and when I saw him, I felt a burst of delight and wanted to run to him, to hug him and feel his arms around me.

It was an extraordinary attraction—I can treasure that. Why do we forget as adults that summer love, first love, puppy love, is overpowering as it plays itself through us. It's so easy to lose those feelings—Wordsworth's *Clouds of Glory*—in the relentless ordinariness of living. Oh God, how I loved him—and maybe I always will—or at least who he was then to me. I saw him as he jumped off the boat and walked to me.

He smiled and looked me up and down. He seemed pleased with what he saw, which made me happy I'd tried to look nice for him. "Hey, got your message," he said. "I'm glad you could come. Mumma says she's glad to meet you, and..." Suddenly I was scared and I must have looked it. I thought about what I was doing—going to spend the day with a family I didn't know at all, and I didn't even really know Ben. He stepped back and said, "We don't bite, you know."

"I know, Ben, but I just saw all the people at the party in my head, and I won't know anyone and I just suddenly felt, I don't know, I just felt a little, you know, sort of...Well Daddy said I could be an anthropologist and check out..." I wanted to bite my tongue because he looked at me with a strange hardness.

"An anthropologist?"

"Yes, someone who studies, I think he meant, well, I'm not," I stammered.

"Did you bring your pencil and notebook?"

"No."

"Or a pith helmet?"

"No," I repeated.

"Guess the natives might get restless and put you in the pot with the lobstas," he suggested, emphasizing the last word.

"Ben, stop," I pleaded.

"All right, but if I see you taking notes I'm going to tell everyone we have to boil up a bigger pot," he said sternly, his eyebrows knotting together, and then he laughed at me. It made me feel better to laugh with him, but I wondered if his family would find me a bit strange, though I didn't have the courage to ask him. When we got on the boat and stood next to each other in the bow, he turned and said, "You know I was surprised you said you'd come."

"It was sort of a dare," I said, "I didn't know if I...."

"Me too," he interrupted. "Jason, at the beginning of the summer he dared me ..."

"What do you mean?" I felt a weight crushing against my stomach. "Just a dare?"

"Oh nuthin', nuthin', never mind," he said quickly. "You don't have to go. You can get off the boat right now and go back if you don't want to." He looked at The Sea Princess and out to the islands as if measuring the distance, and then he turned back and said gently, "It started as a dare, but now I want you to come to my island."

I shoved what he'd said into the depth of my mind because I didn't want to think about it. I sensed I would be hurt, so I did what I did so often, I let the words slip into me and disappear. It had been a dare for me to accept his invitation, but just with myself, so I told him I wanted to go, and then confessed, "it's just that I'm a little scared." I was surprised I said it, but it was true, and it was a relief to admit. And then he said, "Know what, I'm scared too," and that made it all right. "Mumma said she was some surprised I'd asked you," and even more surprised you said yes. I know they're all going to check you out, but don't worry, you look great, even if you are wearing pants, and they'll like you."

"Shouldn't I wear pants to a picnic?" I asked, panicking again.

"Yes, you should because we're going sit on the rocks the way you did at your party, but they'll all sit in front of the house on chairs and the women will wear dresses. But don't worry about it. I like the way you look." But, of course, I did worry. We sat close together on the ride over, and again the warmth of his body next to mine seemed to create a place of safety around me.

We were almost at the island and, as the boat moved into the harbor, Ben pointed out different buildings: the fish wharf, the museum, his uncle's restaurant on the fishing wharf, and the lobster pound. "You can't see Grampie's house from here because it's around the point, but it's only a short walk."

We got off the ferry and walked through the little harbor, past a gas station and wharves with piles of lobster traps and brightly painted wooden buoys. One man who was working on his traps called out to Ben, "Hey Chummy, Miss. Happy Birthday, hope you get enough cake this year."

"Thanks, Normie," Ben called back, waving.

"What did he mean about the cake?"

"Oh, when I was real little, my first birthday, I stuck my whole face in the cake," he laughed, making a face like a little boy with cake in his eyes and nose. "But it was some good."

I'd thought Ben's grandparents' house might be like one of the small houses in the village with a dirty pink plastic flamingo in the yard, or worse, like ones I'd seen on the way to Bar Harbor with broken cars and old pieces of metal rusting on unmowed grass, or sometimes a broken toilet filled with flowers, or deer antlers tacked over a listing garage door. I didn't know what I expected, but it wasn't what I found when we walked around the point. It was a sea captain's house, white with a gray shingle roof and dark green shutters, a Cape added to over the generations, spread along the shore, with intricate and graceful carved trim outlining the eaves. The house stretched along the grass like a cat in the sun, and beyond it the view of the ocean and the mountains of Mount Desert filled the horizon. I was so surprised I stopped walking and just stared. Ben looked over at me and again he smiled. "Ben, that's the most beautiful house I ever saw," I told him.

"It's been there a while," he answered. "Grampie's great-great-something-grandfather built the first part of it in 1789, and then his great-great-grandfather built that wing over there, and his great-grandfather built the rest. Great-grampie built two more houses for his sons. When we had to fix that part over there last summer," he said, sweeping his arm over the field to the furthest wing of the white house, "we found someone'd used birch bark for a vapor barrier, and it was fresh as if you'd just peeled it off the tree."

"Where do you live, Ben?"

"Over there past the little clearing against the woods and up the road a bit," he said, pointing to the edge of the field. "That was Grampie's house when he was growing up and then when he married Grammie."

"You have a family compound," I told him, "just like the Johnsons and Thompsons."

"Oh, yes'm, just like that," Ben answered, and I knew he was mocking me again.

We walked towards the house and then onto the front stoop, where we stood for a moment and looked at a carving over the door. Ben said, "Grampie says that's called Gingerwork because the ships that went on the China Trade brought back ginger and the sailors spent their free time carving decorations for their houses." He led me into a large hallway with wide board floors and a built-in hutch with beautiful old blue-and-white porcelain plates. Everywhere I looked there were antiques, some I could identify, but more I couldn't. "Ben, where are these from?"

"China mostly, and other places around there," he replied, turning around the room and pointing to plates with intricately painted figures, a little carved jade jar with a gold spoon, and an ivory carving of a man with a fish at the end of a pole. "Grampie's great-grandpa was a ship's captain and he went all over the world. His daddy did too, and then he was in the shipping business to the south, the Caribbean and the southern states. They'd take pogey oil or pine down to the south and bring back cypress for the trim in the fancy houses here. But then the war stopped it all, the Civil War."

"What's pogey?" I asked.

"A fish, a really oily little fish, you could dry it and put a wick right in it and burn it like a candle, so they used it for oil, and people here mixed pogey oil with ochre in a barrel and made paint."

As we walked through the house, I thought my eyes couldn't get any wider, but Ben said, "I'll take you to my favorite room. It's Grampie's library." He led me through the dining room to a room paneled in a deep wood that glowed with the polish generations of women had worked into it with cloths, buffing it until their backs ached. Three sides of the large room were lined with books, most of them bound in leather, and there was a wood and brass library ladder on one side. It looked very old, and when I looked at Ben he said, "That's great-great-grandfather's. He saw one somewhere in a library and he copied it." Ben pushed it gently with his hand to set it rolling around the shelves on its brass and glass casters towards me. I stopped it with my hand, and felt the heat in the wood where he had held it, and felt him holding me instead. "See, it follows the track, and you can move it around the library when you want to reach something high up. I used to come here when I was very little, and Grampie let me climb up to my books. He put them on a shelf for me over there. But now I can read anything I want to."

I walked over to the shelves and read the authors' names: Sophocles, Browning, Wordsworth and Poe. I pulled out a book that was bound in red leather with gold along the edges and when I opened it I saw it was in a language I couldn't read.

"That's Greek," Ben said. "I can't read it, but Grampie can. His father taught him when they were on the ships together." I stood looking at the books on the shelves and at the book in my hand. I wanted to tell him about the summer kids who thought he must be illiterate, but I just stared at the books.

I heard a door open and footsteps, and then Ben's grandfather walked through the door and said, "Hello there, deah. I thought I heard you two."

"This is the most beautiful place I've ever been, Captain Bunker," I said quietly.

He smiled at me and replied, "Thank you, I have to agree with you—and I'm glad you like it. Do you like books?"

"Yes, Captain Bunker," I answered, and then, because I felt safe with him I said, "Sometimes I think they're my best friends," and he nodded in agreement.

"Here, I'll show you one of my favorites," and he pulled a book off the shelf. The small book was bound in red leather with gold-edged pages. He opened the book and then spread the pages like a magician fanning his cards to reveal a scene of a tiny New England village with a church whose spire pierced the clouds. "It's called side painting," he said, "something they liked to do in the 1800s.

He led me along the rows of leather-bound books, pointing out some that were special to him and telling me their stories, then letting me hold them. The pages were soft and the books didn't crack when I opened them like the ones in the house we rented for the summer.

"What's a hen frigate?" I asked him. He looked at Ben and replied, "Some Maine men loved their families so much they took them to sea, and the ships with women and children on them were called hen frigates. 'Course maybe they just loved the cooking and wanted someone to do the sewing." Then it was my turn to feel embarrassed and when I looked at Ben I saw him studying his shoe while he twisted it back and forth on the shining floor.

"But now come meet everyone," Captain Bunker continued. It's time to get the lobsters cooking, and I want you to taste Ben's mother's chowder."

He gestured towards the living room and then led me to a door that opened to a wide terrace. I hesitated on the sill, looking at the view of Mount Desert, my eyes drinking in the beauty of the island and its mountains set against the water. It was the most extraordinary view of the island I'd seen—far enough to give a shimmer of distance, but close enough to see the docks and cottages that lined the shore like pearls on a necklace. Suddenly I realized Ben was waiting behind me, that all his relatives were looking at me, and that I could not have made a more dramatic entrance had I tried. I blushed even deeper, and said, "It's so beautiful, it took my breath away." I knew I sounded trite, but that's how I felt.

Captain Bunker smiled and led me over to a stout, red-faced woman with curling gray hair who was presiding over a large table covered with a red-and-white plaid cloth. "This is my wife, Mrs. Bunker," he said. She wiped her hands on her apron and smiled. "I'm Maude. You must be Becky. Ben's told me lots about you, but he didn't tell me how pretty you are." I felt my face start to burn again, and when I turned to Ben, I saw he was blushing too. I looked around and saw about forty people of all ages sitting at wooden picnic tables or standing on a lawn that sloped gently to the beach. On the beach others were grouped around three fire pits built of gray granite blocks on which there were huge black pots surrounded by swirling steam.

Mrs. Bunker introduced me to an ancient woman wrapped in a red, white and blue quilt who was sitting in a rocker on the lawn. "This is Grammie Bunker," she said. "She's Ben's great-grammie. Speak up because she can't hear too well." I put out my hand, and the old lady laid her pale white hand on top of it. I could see blue veins swelling along the top of her hand. It was thin and cold, and I could feel the bones through the skin in her light grasp. But her eyes were a startling bright blue, like Ben's.

Next, Mrs. Bunker took me down to the beach and introduced me to a woman wearing a blue calico dress and white apron and standing next to a huge pot of boiling water. Her face was red from the steam, and she brushed away a bead of sweat before drying her hands on her apron and offering me a limp, damp hand. "This is Ben's mother, Saree," Mrs. Bunker said.

"Hello, Mrs. Bunker," I replied. "Thank you for letting me come to Ben's party."

"Thank you, Miss. We are so pleased to have you here," she said softly, lowering her eyes. She looked down at the ground as she was talking, and I wished she would look up at me. It was embarrassing that she called me Miss. I couldn't think what to do to make Ben's mother stop feeling so nervous, to stop treating me like a summer person. I wanted to jump out and tell her no, that's not who I am, but all I could think to say was, "Thank you, Mrs. Bunker. Please call me Becky." I felt relieved when she smiled back at me. "You have such a beautiful place here. The view is just extraordinary," I said. Again, I could hear my mother's voice echoing through my own, and it made me self-conscious, but I was glad that Ben's mother seemed to appreciate the compliment.

Then Captain Bunker's wife introduced me to his cousins, aunts, Ben's Uncle Ben, and his father, Elmer. I'm glad his parents didn't name him Elmer, I thought and tried not to giggle. Saree gave me a cup of chowder, full of clams and potatoes, thick and rich with onions, fragrant with thyme, and a delicate salt taste. I told her it was the best I'd ever eaten, she smiled and said shyly, "Can you guess the secret ingredient?" I could name the basics, but not the secret, so finally she said, "Sea water, you put in just a little sea water and the salt gives it a taste of the sea."

I ate a whole lobster. Ben sat on one side of me at the picnic table, and his father on the other. Ben's younger cousins were across the table, and everyone gave me tips on how to break open the legs and poke under the lifted shell. I dunked the small pieces in melted butter. I'd never eaten such sweet clams, and when I asked why they were so good, Ben said his youngest uncle, Curly, a large, bald man with thick muscular arms and a beard, set the clams in sea water and cornmeal so the clams ate the meal until their guts were clean.

When we finished eating, I felt as if I'd swollen up like a tick, and my face and hands were smeared with melted butter and lobster juice. The younger cousins started to clear the tables, but they wouldn't let me help. Ben's mother brought out baskets of steaming towels that smelled like lemons and mint, and we each took one to wash our hands and face. Ben's father and Uncle Clem walked out the front door, each holding one side of a tray with an enormous cake and singing Happy Birthday. Everyone stood up except Ben, while we sang to him. His mother and sisters brought out presents they had hidden under a basket at the side of the house, and then his aunts brought out bowls of ice cream. I didn't think I could find more room for food, but I couldn't resist the fresh blueberries and vanilla ice cream and Mrs. Wharton's maple cake.

As Ben opened his presents, I tried to sneak mine into the pile, but he saw me and saved them until last. When he unwrapped the knife, Ben passed it proudly to his grandfather so he and the other men could admire it, and when Captain Bunker pronounced it "some elegant," I knew I'd chosen well. When Ben opened the book, his Grandfather said, "Oh, it's a fine book, Becky, a fine book. There's lots of history in that about people from here. Yes, my girl, lots of history," and he looked sad and distant for a couple of seconds.

Ben thanked me and I said, "I'm sorry I couldn't make anything so nice for you as the boat, but I hope you like these."

"I do," Ben replied quietly, "I really do," and he reached for my hand. I froze, and looked up at him awkwardly, simultaneously feeling the warmth of his hand on mine, and as if I was floating above us both, disengaged. I stared at our hands, and he held mine for what became a long moment.

Someone brought out a guitar, and Ben's Uncle Clem pulled a banjo from under the table and they started singing. I knew some of the songs, and I could harmonize with the ones I didn't know. One time when I was doing that Ben looked at me and whispered, "You've got a great voice." His grandfather looked over at me and grinned as he waved his arms up and down like a conductor, so I know he heard me.

Most times I would have just shut up if someone noticed me singing, but with Ben and his family it was different. I was singing without any self-consciousness for the first time in my life. I used to go back over and over that moment when the sadness caught me. I'd felt so free, so safe with them. A feeling I never recaptured.

When it was time to go, Ben said we had better hurry or we would miss the boat, and everyone laughed and said they thought probably not because Uncle Clem wouldn't leave without us and the boat couldn't leave without him. As I said goodbye to Ben's family I felt warm, happy and very full. I wondered though why Ben's mother had seemed so deferential, and as we left the house I asked Ben why.

Ben laughed and said, "Oh, she's that way. Her mother worked for summer people and she's always saying they're different than we are. Dad just laughs and tells her she's lucky she's not still living there having to play the dumb native." I looked at him with such surprise that he made another silly face like a goofy hick and put his arm around my shoulder for an instant. I was ready this time, so I relaxed against his arm and wished he would keep it there. "It's not as easy as it looks to play dumb you know," he said. "But you should see Uncle Clem do an imitation of Mr. Randolph. He captains for him sometimes. The money's good, but the guy's dumber than a stick. Can't find his way out of the harbor without clipping another boat. Just has the boat for show. Stubborn too. Stove his boat up good a couple of years ago. Drunk." I listened to this soliloquy and thought again how odd it was that the summer people thought the local people were dumb, but the locals thought the same thing about summer people.

We boarded the boat, and when we docked back in Northeast Harbor, Ben walked me home. We stood under the light on the front porch of the cottage, and I imagined touching him or having him hug me, and I felt my head, heart and body pulling in different directions. I didn't know what to do, and Ben didn't seem to either. So we just stood and stared, and finally I said, "I had a really good time, Ben. I like your family very much."

"I had a really good time too, and I know they liked you," he answered earnestly. Then he seemed puzzled and stared at his shoes. Finally he looked up and said, "Would you like to go to the movies this week?"

I was glad he was shy. It made me feel almost protective. I said, "Yes." When he smiled, and started to put out his arm to me, I was scared, but I let him touch me. I wanted so much to feel him against me, my body literally ached to have him hold me.

"Great," he repeated, "we have a date then. Friday? I can get off work and come get you just before the movie, or we could go first and get some ice cream."

"That would be very nice," I said primly, wanting to jump up and down and hug him hard.

"Six-thirty?" he replied. "Here, Friday?"

"Yes," I said again, looking him straight in the eye.

I watched him go down the little path to the street, turn and wave, and then walk towards the harbor. I stood there hugging myself, my arms wrapped around my shoulders, as I had imagined his would be, and thought, "Wow! I've got a real date. And with Ben!"

As I drove home from Monica's house, I thought about how excited and happy I'd been about being asked on a real date by Ben but so scared to ask my parents for permission.

I waited until Daddy was home from New York and asked him when we were at dinner. I tried to be casual, but he saw right through me. "Oh, Ben wants to go to the movies with me tomorrow evening. The Red Shoes *is playing in the village and we thought we would have an ice cream cone." My mother frowned and rolled her bottom lip into her mouth, which was always a bad sign, but Daddy said, "I think that would be all right, dear. He's a nice boy, and Becky had a great time with his family." But then it came out—what she thought of Maine people.*

"What would people think? People like the Johnsons and the Robinsons. Think about it, Sam," she said. "The first boy who asks her out is the son of a fisherman! You know what they'd say."

I wanted to scream, "The Johnsons are so stuck-up, they're awful. Why do you care about such stupid people," but I swallowed the words. Daddy said, "We'll talk about it tonight and I'll let you know tomorrow morning." At breakfast, he looked so stern, so unlike himself that I knew immediately what the answer was. He said, "Your mother and I have talked, and we decided that it wouldn't be right for you to go out with Ben. It is fine to be friends with local people, but not to…" It made me so angry that he capitulated to her.

I called Ben but I couldn't reach him because he was working on the mailboat. Late in the afternoon I asked Daddy again, but all he could say was that my mother got upset easily now and he had to do what she wanted him to. But then, I crossed the unmarked line. I said, "Daddy, why can't I ever do what I want? Why do I always have to do what my mother wants me to do? I'm not Rachel. It's like living with a ghost!" I knew I had really hurt him because his face went white and then gray before he turned away. "I'm sorry, Daddy," I said, "I'm sorry. I'm sorry," and I was. Then he told me we were going to The Inn for dinner with the Johnsons and I should get dressed.

I stomped around my room and thought about cutting off all my hair. I held the little boat Ben gave me and cried, and then I got dressed very carefully. I took the blue dress I'd worn to the summer dances when I wished Ben was there. But, of course, that would never have been allowed. I lined it all up on my bed, the silky white half-slip, a pair of flowered underpants with lace, a new bra, the white shoes with heels, the little pearl earrings my parents gave me when I turned thirteen and my birthday ring. I felt like a bullfighter getting ready for the ring. When I looked up in the mirror, I saw a prim and proper young lady, but I didn't like her.

The doorbell rang and my heart jumped. Mrs. Swanson called up the stairs, "Miss Becky, your friend is here to see you," and I walked out onto the landing. When Ben looked at me he sucked in his breath and his eyes got wide. I walked down the staircase, step by step, feeling so embarrassed and sad, and all I could say to him was, "Ben, I can't go."

"But why didn't you tell me—I've come over from…" I knew he'd taken a lot of care getting ready. I pictured his mother ironing his shirt and khaki pants, and I saw him standing in front of his mirror combing his hair, and again I wanted to put my arms around him and cry, but instead I said, "My mother says I can't go to the movies with you."

"Why?" he asked, and his voice grew distant and hard.

"Because," I said, but I couldn't think of a way to say anything that made any sense. "Because she doesn't want me to go to the movies with you," I said again.

"I get it," he said so quickly that I realized the thought was always lying just under the surface, always a lurking distrust of me and people like me. "She doesn't want her precious daughter walking around in public with an island kid. We backsiders just aren't good enough; that's it, isn't it?"

"It isn't what I think, Ben," I said, the tears rising in my throat. "Come outside with me, please," I begged.

"Of course, Miss, of course, I'm going," he replied.

"No, Ben, not like that," I answered hoping he wouldn't leave me. And then he told me the truth.

"I'm going. Jason dared me to ask out a summer girl," he said, a wild storm in his eyes. "That's all it was, a dare. He warned me too, so I should have known."

Oh God, that hurt. It hurt so much I didn't crumble and run to my room; I followed him out the front door and shut it behind us. We were standing under the light of the front porch. I remember watching as the moths circled the light in the green lantern, some of them rushing into the bulb and then fluttering down slowly as their wings singed.

"Please sit with me on the bench," I pleaded.

"No, I don't want to be here anymore, I'm leaving," he said, turning back to face me.

"Just a dare," I said. I must have looked so wounded that he softened and said, "At first."

And then I reached over to him and pulled him towards me so I could put my hands around his shoulders and hold him close. I couldn't believe what I was doing. I'd thought so often about kissing him, but I never thought I would do it. I could feel his heart beating, and his body was tense and hard, but then he put his hand on my neck and I leaned my head back and he kissed me. It was a soft kiss. I can feel his mouth on my lips and the warmth of his mouth and his body against mine. I felt dizzy and so weak that when he pulled away from me, I sat down hard on the bench. He sat down just as hard next to me and took my hand. We sat there not saying anything, just breathing in rhythm together, and then he said, "It's all right, it's all right, I understand. It was just a dare, at first, but not now, not now."

We heard a door shut inside the house and my parents walking into the front hall so I said, "I have to go." We let our hands drop, and he stood up, put out his hand to pull me to my feet, and held it just a moment, and I whispered, "Write me." Then he walked down the steps and along the path to the street and didn't turn back. I stood on the porch watching his back and feeling as if I was running after him, but my feet were chained to the granite steps.

When I was calmer, I opened the front door, walked into the house and stared at my parents defiantly. My mother said, "You'll understand better later, dear." I clamped my jaws together as tight as I could so I wouldn't scream at her.

"I hope not, Mother," I said fiercely between clenched teeth. Daddy tried to put his arm around me, but I pulled away and dropped behind them as we walked down the path to the hotel.

I pulled the blanket around me and tried to read, but my eyes saw only the end of that evening—a pull between such happiness that he had kissed me, and sadness. I thought I loved him, but I knew I would not see him again perhaps forever, and certainly not until the following summer.

I followed my parents into the huge dining room at The Inn, and we sat with Mr. and Mrs. Johnson. I toyed with the silver, watched the light sparkle off the crystal glasses, and looked at the waiters with their short, white jackets and white gloves. The ladies in pastel chiffon or organza dresses looked like beautiful butterflies. The buffet table was almost grotesque, loaded with haunches of roast beef, Yorkshire pudding, whole salmon stretched on platters, gravy boats of fresh Hollandaise sauce, and little dishes with chopped dill, capers, and wedges of lemon crimped as if they had been cut with pinking shears. It all seemed like the plastic food some restaurants and delicatessens put in their windows to entice patrons, beautiful, but inedible. I felt as if I weren't even in the room and that I was stuck there, like the wallpaper.

"We are so proud of her," I heard Daddy saying. "She's gotten into Wilton and she'll be starting just after Labor Day.

"That's a terrific school," Mr. Johnson said, "You must be very bright, Rebecca. Sam, you must be very proud of her," and I could see Mr. Johnson looking at me as if I was a promising filly.

"You'll meet lots of suitable young men at such a good school, Becky," Mrs. Johnson added.

Later, while I was pretending to listen to Daddy and Mr. Johnson talking about golf and his race horses, I overheard my mother tell Mrs. Johnson about my trip to meet Ben's family. Mrs. Johnson's face puckered and she said, "Anne, you've got to be careful. It's risky. Germs, you know, of course, they don't wash." My mother looked worried and Mrs. Johnson said, "there's the problem of drinking and worse. The drinking, that's what they do all winter, that and, you know." My mother asked what she meant and then Mrs, Johnson whispered, "Well, they just breed. On an island…." I was so shocked I stared at them and Mrs. Johnson announced that she was going to the ladies room and asked my mother if she wanted to go. I was furious and I wanted them to know Ben's family as I knew them, but that wasn't possible.

We drove home the next day. When we crossed the causeway to the mainland, Daddy said, "Okay, everyone, now let out your biggest, loudest moans and next summer when we get to the bridge we'll yell out how happy we are to be back. Ready?" and we did. I felt a cord stretching inside my chest, pulling me back to the island, back to Ben. I sat in the car for hours silent as Daddy drove. At first Daddy tried to make conversation with me, but when he gave up, I settled into my gallery of images, seeing the special moments with Ben, turning them around and around in my mind. I had no idea then how important they would be for me.

It was a sweet sad memory, and I lay against the pillows on the sofa replaying it until finally I fell asleep.

Chapter Seven

I made some new friends, women who were lonely but not sour, and I saw Monica many times. I learned to avoid the divorced women who were bitter. At first I welcomed them, but soon they seemed like squawking crows who hated men because they were scared of being hurt yet wanted someone to pay the bills. I didn't want to be one of them—so vulnerable they had to feign toughness, veneered to protect the soft wood underneath.

When I was walking to the tennis club one morning in mid-July, a car stopped beside me and a woman leaned out of the window and said, "Becky? Becky Granger? I'm Sarah, Sarah Stewart. I heard you were back."

"Oh, this is wonderful. I wondered if you might be here, but I didn't see your name on the club list and I didn't know how to find you."

"My last name's Porter now. Do you want to have lunch later?"

"Sure, are you free today? I'm just going to hit against the backboard for a while and I'm not doing anything after that."

When we met for lunch, Sarah seemed relaxed and pleased to see me. She was wearing a sage green Shetland sweater and a pair of blue jeans and I noticed her left hand had a plain gold band.

"So you're married?"

"Yes, I'm married with two kids. I married Jeff when we were just out of college. He was a teaching assistant when I was in my senior year at the University of Michigan. We fell in love over American Lit."

"And you've lived happily ever after?"

"Actually, yes. That surprises me, but it's true. We've had some times that were tougher than others, but overall, I'd say we've been happy and lucky."

"Where do you live?"

"Lincoln, Nebraska. Who would have thought? Jeff teaches at the university and I work part-time there. We have an old farm just outside the city. I love it," she said. "And you?"

"Well, I live in Boston. I've been married twice and I have two children. I wish..." I stopped and stared at my club sandwich. I could see my archeology professor and the thought made me shiver. "I wish I'd met someone in college, but I didn't. In fact, I dropped out and got married. I'm happy for you," I said looking at Sarah. "You make me think it's possible. The happily ever after part, I mean."

We sat quietly for several seconds before I said, "I'm sorry I didn't write back after my father died. You were very kind to write, but I didn't know what to say. I just drifted after that. I'm sorry now, and grateful that you tried."

"I can't even imagine what it must have been like for you. My father and mother are so good to me. They've helped with the kids so much, even coming out for months to live in a little cottage we have on the farm. I don't know how I could have grown up without my father. I don't know who I would have been without him always there to help me and give me advice."

I could feel the tears coming, and I stared at my empty plate. The blue flowers in the design blurred and I took a deep breath. "Thank you for saying that. Sometimes I feel so weak and stupid. I think I've missed him more than I dared admit—all these years. I went into an angry vulnerable place. I lost myself..."

"You talk about that as if it's in the past," Sarah noted.

"I wish it were. I know it's time, past time, to get it behind me. I feel as if I have something dragging at me, as if I'm swimming through some viscous liquid." I paused and then added, "You know how the Eskimo—the Inuit—blow up seal bladders like little balloons and tie them onto the harpoons they throw into whales?"

Sarah shook her head, laughing as she exclaimed, "No!"

"I was at the Natural History Museum with my father when I was a child and we looked at a diorama of the Inuit whaling. I asked Daddy about the little balloons behind the whale as it tried to escape the men in their boats—the *umiaks*. He told me they were seal bladders used to wear the whale down as it swam. I feel as if I have a whole lot of seal bladders trailing after me. Most people call it baggage." I laughed, which gave Sarah permission to do so again.

"So why did you come back here?"

"To snip some lines; get rid of those seal bladders, I think. I'm not sure I understand myself. It just seemed right to start back where I last knew my father and see if I could. I know that's not all of it, but it's a start."

"I think it's quite wonderful that you have even that much idea of what you need to do," Sarah observed. "It sounds like a combination of good thinking and going with your gut. You trust your instincts and something good will come of that."

The following week Sarah asked me to supper with Jeff and her children. The children were friendly and fun to be with, and I enjoyed talking with Jeff and Sarah about books, gardens and what it was like to teach in a university. As we got to be friends again during the two weeks Sarah and her family were there, they showed me what it was like to care about each other, their children and themselves.

I wish I'd found someone like Jeff at college, I thought as I was getting ready to go to dinner the next evening, not Jim. I could have been happy with someone like Jeff. I was too wounded to resist Jim.

The required freshman courses at Boston University seemed easy and boring because I'd read most of the assigned texts when I was at Wilton. The one class that interested me was archeology taught by visiting professor Dr. James Blanderson. He was a short balding man with a little potbelly and black hair growing out of his ears. One night, when I was in the departmental office, working on a paper for his class, he came in, said hello, sat at the next desk, and asked me about the paper. His voice was calm and steady and I liked listening to it. He told me stories about dinner plate butterflies, Blue Morphos, glowing as they flapped through the rain forest in Costa Rica like birds, so valuable the natives caught them to sell so they could feed their families. He told me about Howler monkeys defecating on his team so they wore large hats and other secrets of academia that made me feel like an initiate.

A few days later after class he asked me to go with him to the college museum to see some of the carved Inca jades he had collected that were on display. I felt flattered and special. There were no other visitors, and as we looked at the glowing gold ornaments and carved jade, he drew me to him and kissed me, and later I let him make love to me. Though I was aware of pleasant physical sensations, and his skill in making me feel excited, most compelling were the feelings of being loved, of living on the far edge of respectability, and of rebelling against my mother and stepfather Taylor. I liked thinking how disappointed they would be if they knew.

I spent much of that semester swaying in a hammock Jim had brought back from Peru, listening to him tapping on the typewriter in his garden apartment. I was surprised that he didn't have a bigger apartment and more personal things there, but he explained that he was just a visiting professor taking over classes for someone on sabbatical. He didn't talk often about the university where he taught full-time, but I became convinced that he had a conflict with one of the senior professors, and when the man retired the next spring, Jim would return to take over the department. Occasionally, when we were making love, he said he loved me. I began to imagine being a professor's wife and moving to the small town in upstate New York where we would live, I would finish my degree, and we would have children.

I spent so much of my time in Jim's apartment that I didn't make friends at BU, and when my roommate told other girls what I was doing, they avoided me. I liked to sit near Jim while he was reading, but most of all I liked having him read to me. I would sit on "my" side of his bed and feel as if I was drifting into a dream, way back in my mind, a dream from a far place I couldn't identify, and that his voice was a long golden cord binding us together. He had a beautiful voice, and when I closed my eyes I thought of him as tall and blond, with a little dimple in his cheeks, looking out over the ocean. When he held me, and I closed my eyes, I could feel the strength of his hands, and the way he stroked me made me feel calm and comforted.

Sometimes he told me that I was his petite enfant or, if I made him particularly happy in bed, his enfant terrible. I spent most of my freshman year with Jim and as spring approached, I was sure he would ask me to move in with him for the summer, but he didn't. Instead, one night as we lay on his bed, me naked, the way he liked me to be when he read to me or was working, he turned to me, "We've had a wonderful time this year. You really have given me a wonderful year. I could never have imagined how lovely this would be, getting away from home, from the university." I smiled at him, and he continued, "I'm sorry it has to end, really I am."

"What?" I asked, trying not to understand what he had said. "What do you mean?"

"Well, I have to go home, you know. I have to get back to my real job, and I guess we could keep seeing each other, but it would be much less convenient and just once in a while, when I came to Boston, but if that's okay with you, that's fine with me."

"I thought I would… I thought I would go with you."

"But how could you do that?" he asked. "You have your studies here and your friends. You wouldn't want to give that up."

"I'd transfer. I could live with you there and study and take care of you," I added coyly, trying to distract him.

"No, no, enfant, no, it wouldn't work," he said, smiling, as if explaining something to a child. "You wouldn't want to live in Oneonta. It's really a very dreary city."

"But we could be together and that would make it all fine," I pleaded. "I love you, and you said you loved me," I added, as if it were evidence.

I could tell he was getting irritated because his ears were turning red. He was quiet for several moments, and I felt my skin getting colder, the air over my breasts and thighs a draft now instead of a light breeze. I reached for the sheet and tried to pull it up, but he was lying on it and it wouldn't move. He turned back to me, his voice harsh, a voice I almost didn't recognize, "You think just because I liked to play with you here that I want to take you home? That wouldn't work, that really just wouldn't work," he said sternly.

"Why?" I asked in a soft, querulous voice.

"Why?" he bellowed. "Why? You stupid, little girl. How could you think I was… Of course I loved you, loved you every night for one term and a semester, and sometimes twice. Just like when I was your age. You're a great fuck, really," he said, looking at me in an appreciative way that made me want to throw up, "but I can't take you home."

I was crying now and pulling hard on the sheet, but still it wouldn't budge. "Didn't you ever get it? I thought you got it." He pulled the photograph of a woman and two children off the bureau and shoved it in my face. "I don't think my wife and children would like to have you living in the house."

"You said that was your sister and her family," I said through my tears.

"I didn't think you believed me," he yelled. "How can you be so smart about everything else and so stupid about this?"

I got up out of the bed and walked into the bathroom. As I pulled my green wool sweater roughly over my head, I tried to remember the things I had in the apartment, but there was so little—a toothbrush and a comb, some make-up, three books, a few clothes I didn't mind leaving, and the lucky rabbit he bought for me at an auction. It was a porcelain rabbit, about life-sized, sitting up on its haunches, chewing a bright orange carrot. I'd loved it immediately, but now I picked it up from the bathroom shelf. As I walked out his front door, I smashed it against the marble tiles of the hall floor then quietly closed the door and walked down the red brick path to the street and back to my room. I felt like a raw wound, and for the few weeks before the term ended, I hardly spoke to anyone.

It all seems so obvious and pathetic now. I was so lonely, so lost without Daddy. When I got home after my first year of college, my mother and Taylor left me alone, but now I wish they hadn't. I needed someone to reach out, but they couldn't, and I couldn't do anything but sink further out of sight. That's why Jordie seemed such a good alternative. And Ben. Where was he then, and why had I wanted to come back to Maine? Was I kidding myself that I wanted to start again to grow after my father's death and shame about Ben. Do I want the real Ben or the make-believe Ben I crafted so carefully over the years to rescue me again? But Daddy's dead and Ben's married, I said to myself. And that leaves me.

In Boston, no one invited an extra woman to a party unless she was paired with an extra man, and they were more rare than peacocks. Though I hadn't been asked to dinner parties since my divorce, I was invited to cocktails, for which I was grateful. I told myself I had to go, if just for forty-five minutes, and that each time I had to try to meet one new person. In Maine, other women asked me to play tennis and golf or to take walks, and sometimes couples asked me to a picnic, and I began to enjoy myself and my new friends. Then Monica introduced me to Dottie, who seemed oblivious to the requirement for pairs that made single women superfluous at dinner parties. Dottie was a charming woman of indeterminate age from New Orleans, buttressed by corsets and money, her blond wig always slightly skewed, her perfume a little bold, and her mascara a little heavy. She knew from years as a widow what it was like to spend too many evenings at home alone. She had inherited more money than she needed from her series of doting husbands and she loved to fix up houses.

When I went in the front door of Dottie's current house, I felt as if I was in a garden. There were vases of flowers on all the tables, wallpaper with flower patterns in every room, and chintz with ebullient flowers in pinks and peach covering the furniture. Standing in the front hall surrounded by an effusive design of large peach and white peonies with leaves unfurling across the walls, I looked down the corridors and counted eight different patterns. Of course, I thought, we are like our houses. Dottie's was totally feminine, filled with light and warmth, but canny. "I love bringin' these houses back to life. Sometimes they seem so sad, like the life's been sucked out of them," Dottie explained. "Besides," she added, "I've made more money doin' this than anything else. 'Cept getting married, of course."

Dottie asked me to dinner at The Inn and I wondered if it would smell as it had when I was a girl. I wondered if the wicker chairs would still be there, or the ladies with pearls cascading down their bosoms, or the waiters in their uniforms, little smirks in their eyes but not their smiles, as they ingratiated themselves into a large tip from the regulars at the end of the summer. And it was all there, just as I had remembered.

The man behind the desk said, "Good evening, Ma'am. Are you here for Mrs. Parker's dinner party?"

"Yes," I answered, disappointed that I was so obviously one of Dottie's guests, no longer young, no longer there for a little romance.

"They're in the Greenhouse Room," he added, pointing to his left.

"Becky, deah," Dottie called across the room, "A'm just so glad you are heah with us. Don't you look divine! " She tottered across the room in her very high heels, chiffon wafting around her like wings. I leaned over to kiss her cheek as Dottie took my hand. Monica walked over, kissed me and whispered, "Strut your stuff, sister," and wiggled her upper torso just slightly, which made a tall thin man in a tight suit put his hand to his throat in an involuntary and ineffectual attempt to loosen his tie. While we made small talk and ate hors d'oeuvres, Dottie said quite loudly, "You know we thought we'd go to the dance latah. I do so love to dance." Then Dottie giggled like a teenager and winked at me.

"What dance?" I asked Monica, "Are they having a dance here tonight?"

"No—just wait," Monica replied. "It's fun."

"Oh, no, honey," Dottie called over to us, "we're going to go crash the kids' dance over at the Golf Club—we won't stay long, but we'll show them a thing or two!" Dottie giggled again and I laughed. Only Dottie would think of crashing the dance for summer kids and actually enjoying herself. The parents I'd heard talking about the dances seemed to dread being chaperones and worried about whether or not someone else's child—or worse, their own—had spiked the punch or was making out in the woods behind the clubhouse.

I watched Dottie during dinner and marveled at her ability to enjoy other people and herself. She was constantly tending to her guests, asking them leading questions. "Now darhlin'," she said turning to Paul who was seated across the table from her. "Ah know you love playin' classical and that's what they pay you for, but your real love, besides Emily, of course, it's jazz? Am I right?" Paul nodded shyly and Dottie added, "Tell me about that CD you're thinkin' about making. What was the name of the otha man you were gonna get to play?"

"Rick Doughboy Jones," Paul replied softly.

"Now how did you know him?"

"My grandfather," he replied, still very softly.

"Your grandfather. Now he was a wonderful musician," Dottie said, "One of New Orleans finest, and that's fine. If he thought Doughboy was worth introducing you to, then he must be."

An older man with a goatee leaned forward, and his wife, who was sitting next to Paul, turned to Paul, and said, "You must tell me all about your CD and your friend Mr. Doughboy," and I knew this was all part of

Dottie's plan to connect Paul with a backer.

I watched Dottie's joy in people, her ability to bring them together, her delight in how they grew, like her flowers, and thought, she's a gardener of people. She nurtures them like her houses and her gardens, and they bloom. It was a talent I wished I could find in myself, that and the expectation that life could be fun.

❦

As summer ended, I worried about whether or not I should go back to Boston, but I decided to stay in Maine for a few weeks after Labor Day. Friends told me the season went now from Memorial Day to Columbus Day, so I thought I wouldn't be lonely, at least for a while. I knew I had spent too much time walking on the mountain trails, talking with Monica, going to parties, and enjoying the freedom to plan my own time, but now it was time to work, at least to try to work. I wanted more space than I had in my suite above the stationery store, so I went to the real estate office through which my father had bought our land. The broker was a gray-haired divorcee named Marge with a brusque and direct way of talking. "You won't find a man here, you know, so don't even think about that," she warned. "There aren't many that can string more than three words together, unless you want to hear about basketball or fishing, which means lobstering. But," she said, "you'll have peace and quiet, and the village is a good place to be for fall. We're so far out in the ocean that the water keeps us warmer, at least for awhile, so it will feel like Indian Summer. You can hole up here and people won't bother you unless you want to be bothered."

"It's all right," I told her. "I'm not looking for a man, just a quiet place to read and write."

"Are you thinking to rent or buy?"

"To rent, just for a couple of months probably," I answered, watching to see if Marge would be disappointed, relieved when she didn't seem to be. "Something with enough rooms so I can have my children here, and maybe some friends. Maybe we could have Thanksgiving here. A little place on the water would be lovely, with a couple of bedrooms, but just for a month or so."

"There aren't too many of the cottages that are winterized, but let me show you some photographs, and you can tell me what you like," Marge replied, pulling out several large blue binders filled with photographs and descriptions of cottages.

I found what looked like an old Cape with wings embracing the water of a cove. The interior was beautiful. Blue and white plaids covered the furniture in the living room, and throughout the house each room was a variation of blues on white. "Marge," I said, "I love this house. Do they rent it for the fall?"

"Well, they rent it in the summer, just for a couple of weeks. It's beautiful. They've never rented it later. It looks old but it was just built two years ago. I'll ask."

The owners were pleased if a bit puzzled that I wanted to rent their house for the fall. After they went home I moved into their cottage, thinking I would return to Boston well before winter.

It was hard to say good-bye to Sarah and Jeff when they left at the end of July, and it was even harder to lose Monica and Mary Barlow as I realized how much I'd relied on them. I met Monica for dinner at The Inn after Labor Day just before she headed home to Philadelphia. "I'm a little worried about you. I know you're a bit of a loner, and you'll sink back into your books and you'll think deep thoughts, but I don't know if you'll have any laughs." Monica looked at me and I knew she was right.

"Don't get me wrong, Becky, I know you have fun when you get going, but you're not really the social." and she searched for the right word. "The social, you know, Perle Mesta. Like Dottie. I don't see you crashing a dance on your own, and you need to do something. What are you going to do?" and she looked at me sympathetically.

"I'll be fine," I said, unconvincingly.

"You can always come to see me. You can come to Main Chance for a few weeks to get some pounds off, and then we could go down to South Carolina and later the Caribbean. I've rented a house in St. John again this year. We'd have a lot of fun.

"Maybe for some of it. I'm going to leave by November at least, but I'd like to stay for a bit first and see what it's like."

"So what ARE you going to do?" Monica asked me.

"I'm going to work hard at writing and learning about what it's like here, and I'm going to read and walk, and… I don't know, but something like that."

"Sounds like a drag," observed Monica, "so, I'll count on seeing you."

We parted with a big hug and I could feel the tears starting.

"Don't worry," Monica said, "You know where you can crash."

I enjoyed having more room in the rented cottage and set up an office in a small library off the living room because it had a view of the cove and a fireplace. I settled into a routine. Up by seven, breakfast at the dining room table overlooking the sound, waving through the window to the lobsterman when he hauled his traps just off the ledge in front of the house. Later I walked to town to get the newspaper and the mail, wrote until mid-afternoon, and then took another walk, most often along the sound, sometimes on the trails.

At Coffee Hour after church, I began to see that the village was a refuge for certain summer people, men who had been pensioned off by their families so they wouldn't work in a family business and women escaping a bad marriage or the death of a spouse. They all needed a haven, and I realized I was one of them. I thought about the times I felt safe—when my father was alive, and for a very short time with Ben—and I knew I hadn't felt safe like that in a very long time. That's when I liked myself best, when I was happiest, or at least that was before it all fell apart. As I thought about being a child, I felt as if I were trying to catch up the strands of my life and marry them like the frayed ends of a rope, as I'd tried to do in sailing class, clipping off the ragged, rotten bits with a sharp, curved knife, and re-weaving the solid fibers in an effort to make an almost invisible splice and whole rope.

❦

One afternoon at the end of September, when I was sure the owners of the summer houses had left, I drove to what had been my family's land. I knew that it was going to be difficult, so much had happened there. I turned my car into the driveway, a real road, I noted, not the rutted dirt track whose entrance we disguised with fallen branches, and drove slowly past two new houses. I rounded a curve and saw a house in the clearing where we picnicked so many years ago. It was hard to look at. Not that it was an ugly house, just that it was not ours.

I walked back along the path to the Green Place and stood next to the old apple tree. One huge branch lay dry and dead at its feet, the tree not much larger than I remembered, but thicker, and bent like an old man. I stood looking down the sound, seeing times I had watched the water, trying to let them pass through me: Ben and Captain Bunker bringing the float, sitting with Ben by the tide pools, walking with him to the cove. I walked over to the edge of the Green Place and sat on the rocks of the old granite pier.

I looked out over the water, letting the memories swirl around me like the tide through the few stubs of barnacled spars still jutting from the abandoned dock. As I watched the barnacles feeding, their feet undulating in the currents of the tide, I heard myself talking to Ben, "like apartment houses," and then as if I had opened a door, I saw us lying together on the pine needles near the cove. It was a scene that had so overwhelmed me when I was young I had only been able to deal with it by pushing it deep inside me. Now I saw myself rocking on the floor of my bedroom afterward, the pain searing up my legs, burning self-hatred knotting my muscles and gut.

When I undressed I found a little strip of pink flesh and a stain of dried blood on the crotch of my underpants and I sat on my bedroom floor and rocked myself back and forth hypnotically. There was no one I could tell, no friend, no other relative and not my mother or dead father so I sat and rocked silently. When my mother came home I heard her laughter, and the deep voice of a man, and then the front door closing and the jangle of the chain on the light switch in the bathroom. Throughout the night I sat rocking myself slowly back and forth, numbing the ache that intruded into my consciousness, and when the sun pierced the crack between the shade and window I got up from the floor and walked to the bureau where I kept my jewelry box. I took out the gold circle pin my mother and father gave me for my twelfth birthday and I threw it as hard as I could at the wall. I picked it up again and not satisfied with its destruction, I bent it with my bare hands, the metal cutting into my fingers. I didn't have a right to wear it anymore because I was no longer a virgin and I had violated everything I'd been taught to value. I knew again it was my fault, always all my fault.

My eyes were puffy and red, but on the trip back to New York, my mother didn't notice and seemed to have a secret as well, and I was relieved she didn't want to talk either. When we crossed the bridge from the island to the mainland, I moaned softly remembering the exaggerated groans Daddy had made the year before, but I was too numb to think about much else.

I stood up and followed the path that led to the cove, though the sensation felt more like being reeled in. Where the path turned to meet the sea, I looked for the tree that had sheltered me and Ben, but the spot confused me and for a moment I could not remember. When I did, I wished I had not. I could feel the desperate intensity, his skin as I bit against it, the smell of his neck, and the taste of salt. Disgust, disgust at my own body and loneliness, then and now surged through me and I collapsed on the pine needles. Again I cried deep wracking sobs that began to wash the pain out of me, until finally the mosquitoes interjected their torment into my thoughts and pulled me away from the past.

•

When I got back to the house I poured myself a glass of wine and called Monica. "I have to tell you something. I did something awful and I lied to you about it."

"What?" Monica asked.

"With Ben," I answered, my voice trembling.

"But that was so long ago, you said so yourself. Why could it matter?"

"Because it made me so ashamed of myself for so long."

"You went all the way," Monica said decisively.

"Yes, but…"

"That was a big deal then," Monica replied. She paused and then added, "You were just ahead of your time. I told you, you two had a lot of chemistry. So, he couldn't resist you."

After waiting for me to answer, Monica said, "There's something else. What is it?"

"I attacked him. I was so lonely, I needed him so much, I attacked him. I forced him to have sex with me. Monica, I raped him." Now I listened to Monica breathing, wondering how she would react, but she was silent.

"You realize, of course, that's every man's fantasy," Monica finally replied, "to have a beautiful woman want him so much she can't control herself. God, I bet he had some fantasies about you over the years."

The thought was startling, but I could only say, "It was so awful. I felt so ashamed. Then, now, all the time. It's haunted me."

"I can understand how strange that must have seemed, how difficult then, but I wouldn't let it ruin my life! " Monica continued.

"Ruin my life? I have, haven't I?" I answered myself. "I have let it ruin my life, well at least a lot of it, and what's past."

"Is past," Monica said firmly.

The next afternoon I made myself go back to what had been our land. I forced myself to walk to the picnic rocks and sit in my favorite place, cradled again by the folds of rock like a child in her grandmother's lap, and then to the tide pools and back to the edge of the Green Place. I stood looking at the rocks below, pitted with pools of water, glistening from the receding tide. It was a strange and uncomfortable thought that Ben might have fantasized about me as I had about him. It had always been safer to keep him in a box and let him out only when I wanted him, and I wanted to leave him there. I was beginning to understand that I must face the reality that he was married, but it was hard to let go of the dreams that had helped me survive for so many years.

I climbed slowly down the granite blocks, carefully finding toeholds and balancing before I put my full weight on each stone, and then I stood in a grassy place at the edge of the flat ledge and the tide pools, staring at the pools and the seaweed shifting in the water. I looked down at my feet and saw the faint image of a tooth, then another, and then the outline of a jaw. I bent down and cracked a dead branch from a puckerbrush, using the stick to poke at the ground. I picked away at the grass until I uncovered a huge jawbone, and then the remnants of old brown cloth and finally part of a hoof. When I picked up the cloth, I realized it was skin.

Skin and hair crumbled to dust in my hand. Oh God, I thought, it's a deer. But where's the skull, where are the antlers? And then I realized that they were probably nailed on someone's garage door or hung over a fireplace in a living room.

I sat on the rock in the fading light, watching the sun falling behind the mountains, looking at the colors of the bracelet on my arm, the bracelet my father gave my mother and that she had given me, feeling the past washing through me. I watched the dying light of the sunset reflecting through the stones of the bracelet until the keening of a loon startled me, pulling me back to the present. I live with ghosts so much of the time, I thought, as I drove back to my rented house. Why are they more real for me than reality?

Chapter Eight

I started to write an article about Jane Austen and the role of women in the twentieth century, but it felt stilted and purposeless, so I tried writing a short story about a young woman. I sat in front of my typewriter, an old Olivetti with arching little type bars that struck the platen like a woodpecker tapping against a tree. I plucked at the keyboard, trying to think of it as a musical instrument, my instrument, through which I was playing a complex melody. But the keys, with their shadowed pecking across the page, seemed to mock me. I stopped and decided to walk into town, past the yacht club, the maple trees fiery red against the blue sky and the oaks golden.

I walked past the pipe blowing warm steam from the cleaner's shop to the stationery store. Dot was standing behind the counter. "How you doin,' deah?" she asked.

"Oh fine, Dot," I answered. "I've been sitting in front of the fire trying to type, but spending more time looking at the leaves in the sun. Fall comes so late here."

"The ocean keeps us warm, but spring. It takes forever to get here, and by then, if you stay, you'll wish you hadn't left Boston."

"I need a new ribbon for the typewriter."

"That's good. Your writing must be going good, that you need a new ribbon, I mean."

"It has more to do with the ribbon being old than overused. I haven't made much progress at all. I sit down now in front of that old typewriter and I think it's just staring me down. It almost frightens me."

"You'll think of something. You'll take a long walk and you'll think of something. There's not much here that's frightening 'cept taxes."

As I walked back to the house, I thought about what Bob had said and wondered where my safe place was and where was the most frightening place, the place that took me into the darkness? The graveyard, I answered myself, when we buried Daddy—when I wanted to scream and stop time. When I first felt like an orphan.

I saw us standing at the grave on that dark October morning, the minister reading the Twenty-Third Psalm, and my mother dropping a white rose onto my father's casket and fainting back into Uncle Charlie's arms. Uncle Charlie asked me if I wanted to throw a shovel of dirt on my father's coffin, but I couldn't because I wanted him to jump out and tell us it was all right, or to lie next to him as the dirt covered us both. "Maybe that's the worst place," I thought, "my father's grave."

I sat in front of the dead fire thinking about burying my father, but the sadness that weighed me down finally grew intolerable and I knew I had to shake it physically as well as emotionally. I stood up, pulled on my jacket and started walking to the harbor. The early evening breeze off the ocean smelled of salt, and a few gulls still circled overhead. I sat on one of the green benches near the closed harbormaster's office and stared at the boats rocking at anchor, but again I heard Bob's advice and I knew I needed to identify the worst place and the safest. Daddy's grave—that was the awful place—the cold, damp earth, the darkness of the grave, and the person I loved most.

His death was an even greater loss than Rachel's, and maybe more of a shock because I wasn't with him. I was walking out of class my first year at Wilton. It was late in October and I already loved the school, though I worried that I didn't fit in. That first fall, before Daddy died, before I ruined everything.

I was scared when I applied to Wilton that I would disappoint my father by not getting into his school. When I was accepted, I felt excited and happy, until it occurred to me that they had probably sent the letter by accident, that they really meant to accept someone else.

I worried my clothes would be wrong, that I was too tall, too awkward, that my skin was breaking out, and I would fail my classes and never make friends. That first day of class I stood outside the wooden door of the classroom in the hall lined with photographs of the school's founders, and an older student came up to me and said, "Oh, you're the new girl with no ankles."

I wondered if that was the way everyone thought of me.

During the day, there was so much that was new, so many people to get used to, and so much new work that Ben was pushed to the back of my mind. Each night, however, as I lay in my bed waiting to fall asleep, when I was half waking, half sleeping, he would come to me in dreams in which I could fantasize the beginning but never see the ending. We would meet at the dock and walk along the harbor, holding hands and looking at the boats rocking in the waves. I thought of ways we would meet in secret, and how he would bend my head back and kiss me again.

I imagined a letter from Ben waiting for me on the hall table in the dorm where everyone got mail, a blue envelope addressed to Miss Rebecca Granger in strong masculine writing. I imagined opening the envelope, slitting it with a letter opener like the silver one on my mother's desk, and pulling the pages out. I imagined it would be many pages, a thick letter, full of words about how much he missed me, words that would make me feel loved and wanted, words so romantic I would blush like the girls in Baldwin House who got letters that made them scream, clasp the letters to their chests and run down the hall to tell their friends. But it didn't happen.

The house where we boarders lived was a handsome Georgian brick structure with a large formal living room, parlors, music rooms, and an oval, mahogany dining table that seated twenty-four. There was a study hall for first-year students and anyone who was doing poorly, filled with rows of right-handed wooden desks patterned with the aimless or desperate scrawling of generations of girls, erased every summer by custodians. I could still read the ghostly impressions on my desk: "Rosie and Todd" inside a heart pierced by an arrow, and more subtly, "GRB" entwined with "RCK." I wanted to carve into the wood, but instead I used the eraser on my pencil to draw a heart with the initials RG and BB inside, which I imagined only I could see.

As the first few weeks slipped past, I began to make friends and I loved going with them after study hall to the little wood-lined cubby where we picked up snacks and then to one of our rooms to drink milk and eat graham crackers and Macintosh apples while we talked about Holden Caulfield and Alcibiades and boys. I even loved Saturday sewing because it was just as Gretchen had described it.

When I first arrived at the school a heavy-set girl with cascading, ash blond curls and a huge smile walked into my room without knocking and said, "Hi, I'm Gretchen. I'm your Old Girl and I'm here to make you feel welcome. You can ask me anything about school, like who's the worst history teacher and where you meet boys," and before I could do anything but smile back at her, Gretchen plopped herself down on the bed and started helping me unpack. As Gretchen handed me stacks of new bras and slips, she said, "Seems your mother helped you pack! I bet you won't keep this stuff so nice for long. 'Course we have to go to sewing after we get laundry.

Mrs. Raagen, she's Danish. She has such a weird accent. She'll hold up some wretched pair of panties and bark, 'Whoz raggedy underpants are zees? Who has no name tag on her deerty underpantz?' I don't know how she got to be a Mrs. Don't worry, no one claims them, and we just put in a pair with holes and stains and no name tag to have her go through her speech. Then she tries to teach us to be young ladies and sew, but no one pays any attention." I laughed at the conspiracy.

But then, I lied about Ben, as if he hadn't been good enough for me just as he was.

"Now tell me about the man in your life," Gretchen commanded. "Who's your best beau?"

"Well," I said, stalling, "there's really no one."

"Come on," Gretchen replied, "you can't fool me, this is your Old Girl talking."

"Well," I said again, feeling the sweet-spot in the pit of my stomach glowing as it did whenever I thought of Ben, "there's a boy I met last summer, but..."

"I can tell," Gretchen said, grinning slyly, "You're sweet on him. Where's he from?"

"He's from Maine, from Islesford on Little Cranberry Island," I answered, but Gretchen said, "No, I don't mean in the summer, silly. I mean where's he from in the winter?"

"Oh, well, I don't really know, but somewhere near Philadelphia." I could feel the ugly secret sinking over me like a black cloud.

"I bet it's Bryn Mawr or Bala Cynwyd," Gretchen answered, "there's lots of really nice places around Philadelphia—of course no one lives in the city anymore. Where does he go to school?"

"He's at Saint Paul's," I answered shakily.

"That's the best," Gretchen replied, as I knew she would. I felt stupid and angry at myself for lying about Ben, but pleased that Gretchen was impressed.

Sunday evenings the boarders had to go to Chapel. We filed in first and then the boys trooped in and filled the remaining pews. They left the chapel before we did and formed lines on either side of the walkway. Sometimes a boy stepped out to take a girl's hand and walk her home, but most of the time they just stood there making remarks the rest of us were supposed to hear, "God, she looks worse than last week. That's the ugliest hat yet." The popular and friendly girls loved it, but the rest of us pretended to ignore the boys and stalked through the gauntlet, heads high, talking with feigned animation to our friends. Sometimes

I imagined Ben waiting for me in the line, and I could see him stepping forward, taking my arm and smiling at me as Diana's new beau smiled at her.

I wished Ben was there to walk me home and kiss me in the moonlight, I thought. Of course, I hadn't given him my address, but I thought somehow he would find it out. I was also sure he had forgotten me. I only kissed him once that first summer, but it meant so much to me. But he did write, after Daddy died. I was so grateful. It drew away some of the pain. I wrote him again. I worked hard on that letter. I almost went through a box of the thick cream stationery with the embossed crest of the school as I wrote different drafts. But he didn't write again.

❦

Only five weeks into the new term, after French class on Wednesday morning in mid-October, Miss T was waiting for me in the hall. "Becky," she said, her face very tight and almost angry looking, "I am so sorry, come with me, I am just so sorry to have to tell you this." I felt my heart shrivel. I could feel it sinking into my chest and I found refuge in trying to follow its descent. I wanted to say, "I'm sorry Miss T I really want to stay here. I love this place," but I didn't. I didn't know what to say, so I followed our headmistress silently down the main hall of the school, past people who looked at us curiously, and up the stairs to her office.

"Becky, sit down on the couch, please," Miss T said sternly. I walked over to the dark green couch and looked at the pattern of blue and yellow flowers twining over it while I heard Miss T say, "I have to tell you something very difficult." Here it comes, I thought, as I sat down and faced her. Miss T was looking at her hands, but she finally raised her eyes to mine.

I looked at her and started to say, "I love it here," hoping I could stop her from saying what I knew was coming next, that I had to leave. Instead, Miss T said, "Something awful has happened." I looked at her in fear and surprise, opening my eyes wide as Miss T added, "God will be with you and your family, Becky. Your father had a heart attack this morning."

I couldn't believe what she was saying. I wished that Miss T was just saying that I had to leave school. "But he's fine now," I said, willing it so.

"No," Miss T replied, looking at her hands again, "No, I'm so sorry," she paused, drew her breath in deeply and continued, "He didn't survive."

"No, no!" I repeated, as if I could make the ending different, make time stop as I had tried to do for Rachel. "No, that can't happen," I said defiantly. I felt my heart shatter. I thought of Daddy, losing the present in the past, standing with him as he held my hand on the float in Maine, helping me bait

the hook, showing me how to drop the line over the side and let it seek the bottom, then how to haul it up at little so it could entice a fish. But when I did, my father released it into the water, and I watched it tremble slightly before it swam deeper and we could no longer see it. Now I felt myself in that dark water, falling deeper and deeper into the blackness.

"Becky?" I looked up at Miss T again, tearing myself from the memories, "Oh no, not Daddy. Please, not Daddy," and then I sat very still and tried to hold in my tears, but they washed over my face. When Miss T handed me a tissue, I took it and blew my nose. Then I willed the pain inside and sat very still on the sofa. My chest felt so tight I could barely breathe but I knew that I would not cry again until I was alone.

"I am so very sorry. Your mother will need you now," Miss T said. "You'll go home now, of course, but when you come back, your teachers will help you make up your work. Now, let me call your mother, she's waiting for your call, and you can speak to her from here."

I thought, I don't want to talk to my mother, I wish she had died, not Daddy, but instead I mumbled, "Thank you." I could see myself sitting on Miss T's couch, waiting for the phone to ring in the apartment in New York, as if I were floating. I looked at Miss T's flowered dress shining in the shaft of sunlight through the window behind her, her white collar starched and immaculate, but it all seemed far away.

I was there but I wasn't. I was drifting around the room and out the door, floating up to Maine, circling over the island and coming to roost in my rock nest, looking down the sound, my knees pressed against my chest. Then in my mind I was scratching and bashing my hands against the rock and I cringed against the sofa. If I'd been home, I thought, he wouldn't have died. We would have gone to the park. I saw him running after the red-and-blue kite but falling, and then a policeman rescuing us. Again, I willed it so, but Miss T's voice intruded.

"Your mother is on the phone, Becky," Miss T said, standing up and holding the black phone. "Come sit here while I go in the other room." I walked over to the armchair across from the desk and sat down.

I held the phone for a moment and then raised it to my ear.

"Becky," my mother said, her voice quivering. I thought she would start crying, but she said, "I'm sorry, Becky, your father loved you very much and I know you'll miss him." She sounded stiff and formal. "I miss him too," and then she started to sob, and I could see her standing in the living room, see her hands go limp and her knees buckle as she slumped into the couch, but there was no Daddy to hold her.

Then another voice said, "Becky, this is Mrs. Peters. I'm here with your mother."

"I'm glad," I replied. "Thank you."

"Becky, I've gotten a ticket for you, and Miss Traworth has arranged for a driver to take you to the airport. You'll be home in a few hours. We must be strong for your mother. She needs all our help now to get through this. It was an awful shock."

"Yes."

"You knew he was going to Paris this week to work on a case?"

"Yes, I think so," I replied numbly. "When he came back he was coming for Parents' Weekend."

"He was waiting for the plane to take off, and he had a heart attack. There wasn't a doctor on board. He died before the ambulance got there. You know his father died of a heart attack when he was fifty-two, but, oh Becky, he was so young. Just forty-one. We're all devastated."

I could feel my mind drifting again and I pinched my arm hard. "Mrs. Peters," I asked, "will someone meet me at the airport?"

"Oh, I hadn't thought of that. Could you take a taxi? We need to stay with your mother," Mrs. Peters answered.

"Yes, thank you," I said like a wooden marionette as I pulled the phone away from my ear and put it back on the cradle. Miss T tried to put her arm around me, but I knew if I let her, I would cry and so I pulled away.

As I walked towards the harbor, I thought about my mother. She was aloof and cold, particularly after Rachel died. So hurt and angry. Then she found Taylor so quickly after Daddy died. It drove me further away from her, and I couldn't talk to her, she was always so disapproving. I wondered again what she would have done if she'd known there was really something to disapprove of? I picked my way along the stony path to sit on my favorite bench, watching the boats rocking gently, releasing a disquieting thought—perhaps my mother just wanted so much for me to be all right that she couldn't bear knowing I wasn't. I began to let memories of coming home after my father died creep out of the places where I had tried so hard to encapsulate them.

When I got home from Wilton after my father died and saw my mother standing in the living room, she seemed much older. Her face was gray, blotched with red, and her hair, usually so carefully washed and set, was stringy and lay flat against her face. She had no life in her, as if someone had cut the tendons and sinews that held her together; she moved only when someone forced her to. She held Robbie tightly, as if he could summon his father, but whenever Robbie got restless or cried, one of the other women took him away. Then she would sit wrapping her arms around herself and rocking until another friend went to sit next to her. I thought the doctor was giving her pills because she slept so much.

The next day, my mother's parents, Gaga and Gran, arrived from Chicago. Gran was always stiff and distant, but Gaga liked having me go for walks with him when we were at their farm, or to take pictures of me with his Polaroid camera, or just to sit and eat popcorn he made in the bright red metal popper he turned slowly in the fire. Now even Gaga was preoccupied with his daughter and didn't seem to notice me, so most of the time I stayed in my room, hugging my pillow and staring tearless out my window, too numb to feel or even think.

My father's mother, Grandee, arrived that night, but she and my mother had never been friends. Now she perched on an armless chair. Even after hours on the plane coming back from a vacation in Europe, Grandee looked as if she had walked out of a Chanel ad, her gray silk traveling suit unwrinkled, black alligator pumps and matching bag shining, the seams in her stockings straight, her hair elegantly coiffed to curl around her face and show off its fine bones. She sat absolutely erect, but looked drawn and pale. Everyone seemed about to explode—and afraid that if one of them did it would set off a chain reaction, terrified that by acknowledging their pain they would acknowledge the ways in which their lives were forever changed.

My mother didn't let me go to the funeral home, instead she went with Mrs. Thompson and when they got back, she had to lie down. Mrs. Thompson asked me to come into the living room with her and when we were seated, she looked at me, and her eyes started to water.

"It's best you didn't go, Becky. Your poor mother. It was horrible to see him lying there with the lights so bright, just horrible. They were playing dreadful music, and they'd put so much make-up on him...It was awful." I tried to picture my father laying on a table but all I could see was a clown with white pancake makeup like one we saw together at the circus. Then I could feel my father sitting next to me and remembered him handing me an enormous frothing stick of cotton candy, and the woman's voice faded into the sounds of the circus.

"Just awful. Remember him the way he was," Mrs. Thompson said again, "the way you last saw him." My mind slid back into focus and I saw my father waving good-bye as he got into the car and drove away from Wilton. "I wanted to tell him I loved him, but I didn't," I said so softly Mrs. Thompson didn't hear me.

The service was the worst part. I couldn't let go. I sat there trying not to hear or feel, trying not to let it all happen. I thought I was being buried, wished I was being buried with Daddy. Oh, dear God, that still hurts too much. I reached into my bag and pulled out sunglasses, hiding as best I could, and walked home. But memories were loose now. I had finally opened Pandora's Box.

I walked into the front pew of Saint Andrew's Episcopal behind my mother and Robbie. Robbie was holding her hand. I wished I was too young to understand what was happening. The only time I felt the tears rise was when we sang Hymn 608, "Oh, hear us when we cry to Thee, For those in peril on the sea!," because Daddy had been in the Navy. It made me think of Ben and his family, and that made me even more sad and scared. I'd never been to a funeral other than Rachel's, and when Daddy's friends carried in his coffin, I thought I would break into a thousand parts and disappear. I couldn't think of Daddy in that awful box and I tried to be anywhere else, at least in my mind. I remember feeling that I was flying out the window and up into the sky, as if I was looking down on the church service, removed from everyone and everything inside.

When the service was over, my mother got up to walk out behind the coffin, but then she grabbed Uncle Charlie's hand as she started to faint, so he led her out into a little room to the side of the altar, and we followed behind her. The room smelled sweet with incense, wine and flowers and I started to feel lightheaded. Then Uncle Charlie picked my mother up in his arms, carried her out into the sunshine, and held her until someone broke a little white vial of smelling salts under her nose, and she raised her head. Finally, he put her down, and he and his wife hugged her.

The next night my mother asked me if I wanted to stay home and not go back to school, but she seemed so far away and the little speech so perfunctory that I knew she didn't mean it. That was a relief really. I wanted to go back to Daddy's school, to be closer to him and to get away from my mother's sadness and from all her friends who seemed to think she was the person most hurt by Daddy's death.

I wanted to lose myself in books and studying. I wanted my father to be proud of me, and by being at his school, I knew I would be closer to him. The grief was always there, gnawing at me, draining me so I couldn't concentrate on anything else. When I returned, no one seemed to understand, not even my friends. I shriveled away from them, and they didn't know how to pull me back. I don't remember any of the faculty doing much either. Except for the teacher at the Boys' School. I wish I could have talked with him.

My roommate asked me to go to a basketball game one afternoon at the boys' school against their archrival, St. Matthew's. She seemed surprised when I said yes, but I only went to find Daddy's name on the plaque he had showed me in the study hall at the boys' school. I stood near one of the doors to the gym, and when everyone was cheering for the tie-breaking basket, I walked backwards into the hall. Then hugging the walls, I slipped through the darkened school and into the boys' study hall. I wasn't supposed to be there, but I was sure everyone was at the game. I walked slowly around the large room with high ceilings. A little light shown through the tall windows, enough for me to see the outlines of desks and chairs, the large wooden desk at the front, and the plaques along the paneled walls. I found the plaques for the years close to when Daddy graduated and then finally I found the one where I knew I would see his name. I closed my eyes for a few moments and then opened them; I could feel the tension straining my face. I reached out my fingers, touched his name and slowly traced the letters:

SAMUEL ASA GRANGER

Suddenly a man's voice broke the silence! "Young lady, what are you doing here?" he said and I spun around to face an old man with thin white hair, skin drooping from his chin like a bassett hound, and a cane in his right hand. He looked as surprised as I did. "I came to s…" but I started crying in the dark and I couldn't speak.

He walked over to me, handed me a handkerchief, and said, "You came here to?" I pointed to the plaque, and put my thumb on my father's name and then leaned against it. "I'm Mr. Anderson. I knew your father when he was here," the man said quietly. "I'm sorry. He must have been very proud of you." He paused and we both stood silently. "Do you want to stay here for a while?" he asked me. "I'll wait for you in the hall so no one will bother you. Take your time." I nodded, and he turned and walked to the door, and I could hear him pull a chair from somewhere and sit heavily into it.

I thought about how my father was never going to get old. I wanted to run into the hall and sit in the old man's lap and bury my head against his jacket, but I got up and stood beside the plaque stroking it with my hand until I heard a loud roar and knew the game was over and that we had won. I walked out of the study hall and found Mr. Anderson still sitting in the chair. "Thank you," I said quietly. "Thank you very much."

He nodded, and replied. "Any time. I mean that. Any time. I knew your father. Fine boy," and he handed me a piece of paper on which he had written his name and phone number. "Any time you want to come here and sit, just call. It will be all right. Or to talk," and together we walked out of the building. I left him without another word, merging into the crowd leaving the game and walked back to my dorm.

So many times over the long months that winter and spring and my final awful year there I thought of calling that kind old man, but it seemed like giving in and I thought I was stronger if I kept silent. I was so scared of losing control, but sometimes I lay in bed and I imagined curling up against his chest and crying.

Chapter Nine

It was late in the afternoon, but I wanted to go back to the harbor. I jammed some bread and cheese into a sandwich bag, poured merlot into a flask, and set off again. I reached the harbor as the golden streaks of the falling sun darted off the shining hulls of the sailboats, and sat down to enjoy my supper. The merlot gave me its fleeting sense of pleasure and warmth and I thought again, where is my safe place? It wasn't my old room at home or anywhere I had lived when I was married. I thought about places I had traveled to, mountains I had climbed, where I had sat on the little beach in Nantucket, and the hollow under the pine boughs where I had hidden as a young girl. But I could think of no safe place.

And then I realized, I was sitting near it, where I had sat once before with Ben. How strange I thought, I had forgotten, pushed it away but now the memory comes back. I stood and shook myself, trying to let in the good memories of Ben. I walked over to the granite wall separating the shore from the information center and the ticket shed and looked over the harbor to the dark shoreline on the other side. I stepped up onto the stone wall and balanced for a moment then stumbled over the edge and stood breathing deeply, pulling the salt air into my lungs and hearing the faint tapping of halyards on masts and water sloshing against the hulls of boats. I saw where Ben had held me years ago, sitting with me on the piece of driftwood wedged between two blocks of gray granite, the first time we met the summer after my father died.

I walked over to the granite blocks and looked for the piece of driftwood, but all I could find were a few remnants of rotted wood. I could feel Ben's arm warm around my shoulder. I sat down on one of the blocks and almost leaned against him, the memory was so vivid. I put my hand out to touch him. You stupid woman, I said to myself as I stared at the black water of the harbor. I was cold, and the damp salt spray covered my hair and dripped down my neck. "You stupid old woman," I repeated out loud and the sadness of losing Ben—losing both Ben and my father—closed around me.

I moved onto the gravel beach and leaned back sideways against the huge boulder of granite, a glacial erratic, dumped by the melting ice, and saw images of Ben that merged into images of my father—like snapshots in an album—always cheerful, always kind, always seeing the positive side of whatever happened. I wondered how he and my mother stayed together after Rachel drowned. Surely my mother must have realized he hadn't brought life preservers along. I wondered what they said to each other, if my mother ever talked about how angry she felt, or if he talked about his guilt. Were they too hurt or too well trained? Did people talk then about things that hurt, or did we only learn to do that later, and some of us not at all? Maybe that was what killed him? Maybe she was relieved when he died? Maybe her life with Taylor was better? I felt myself being pushed into the rock, turning into rock, standing forever by the water, looking out at nothing. Sadness and anger. Anger at my father and at myself. My father as a child, myself as a child, forever children. Forever oblivious and irresponsible, forever hiding from ourselves, seeing only ourselves.

I sat with my arms wrapped around my shoulders, hugging myself and thinking about my father, thinking he was holding me, confusing him, as I had so many times before with Ben, feeling their arms warm around me. I sat listening to the birds' muffled sounds of occasional quacking and squabbling as they settled in for the night in small gaggles on the beach and coveys floating close to shore. I felt the anger, like magma in a volcano, pushing up inside. I snatched a rock from the beach, threw it at the water, and watched as it bounced off the ledges, scattering the birds so the explosion of their wings sounded like shotgun blasts. I picked up another rock, stood for better leverage, hurled it at the ledge, and then another and another—at the birds, at the water, not caring what I hit, or didn't. Again and again I picked up rocks in both hands and threw them as hard as I could, listening to them shattering against the ledge. I screamed, "You stupid fucking birds," as they wheeled above me, crying and screaming until I was exhausted, my throat raspy and dry, and I fell back against the rocks.

As I rested, letting the thoughts and feelings seep into me, darkness settled around me and I could hear my father's voice, "I didn't want to die, you know—it's not as if I wanted to leave you."

"It's all your fault," I yelled out, "It's all your..." but I couldn't finish the sentence in anger. "Your fault..." I said quietly and in a little girl's voice continued. "It's your fault that I was so lonely and so scared. It's your fault I lost Ben, that I hid from myself. It's your fault, damn you, that I married Jordie. It's your fault I married Richard. It's your fault I fucked up. Oh God. It's all your fault," but I sounded unconvincing, even to myself. I sat for a long time looking out at the water, letting the harbor fade into shadows, and then I pulled my sweater tight around me, tucked my head under my arms like a sleeping bird, and stayed there until morning.

Before the sun slid over the gray horizon, the sounds of the ducks and gulls woke me and I moved, slowly, painfully, chilled deeply. I walked up the beach and down the path to my car and again sat looking at the harbor, seeing my father on the dock helping me fish, lighting the picnic fire with a long match, waving when he left me at school.

As I drove home, I thought about how hard I had tried over the years to block the pain of my father's death, and losing Ben. For the first time I knew what I wanted to do. I took a hot shower, ate a leftover bagel with cream cheese, and called Peter the minister at the church. "Peter," I said when he answered the phone, "This is Becky Evans, I need to talk to you. May I come over now? I know it's early."

"Yes, it's a good time now—I have a meeting at nine-thirty."

When I walked into his little office, I felt so full of purpose that the tinge of embarrassment and self-consciousness that usually colored my feelings receded and I felt a surge of surprising energy throughout my body. I sat down and smiled broadly, and with no preliminary small talk said, "Peter, I've come to bury my father. Sam Granger." He looked at me with surprise flicking at the edges of his eyes. He's heard everything, I thought, so he's not shocked.

"Bury your father," he answered slowly, but it was not a question.

"Yes," I replied, "I've made him into someone he couldn't be, that no one could be. I made him into the perfect father, but I also hated him for not being here to protect me. I've blamed him for all the stupid things I've done. Living on the edge when I was in college," and before, I remembered blushing slightly. "Getting married to someone who was crazy, and then burying the loneliness so I was just numb." Peter nodded, and I continued, "In some ways I'm no more grown up than I was when he died. It's like I went into suspended animation when he died," and I laughed apologetically. "I never let out the sadness, and it burns a hole in me that I can't fill—and I can't let anyone try to fill. I have to say goodbye to him," I added, then sat holding my breath so I wouldn't cry.

"What would you like to do, Becky?"

"I think, Peter, I think I'd like you to say the service for the dead, and I'd like to say goodbye to him. Not goodbye forever, but a goodbye, you don't have to run my life, I can."

"All right."

"And I'd like to let go of the sadness."

"I see. When you were a child you couldn't understand and perhaps you couldn't mourn. Perhaps you thought you had to be strong for your mother, or your brother, or just because everyone told you had to be. Maybe you never really mourned him. And you never knew him as a man, only as your hero, as a sort of magician, the man who controlled your life and made you happy." He stopped and then looked at me with such gentleness that I had to blink back tears. "And then that ended, but you couldn't let go. It makes a lot of sense to mark his passing, because this time you can let that happen, and he can pass to another place and let you make of your own life what you will."

"Thank you for understanding. Thank you, Peter, for not laughing at me."

He leaned forward and asked, "Do you want to have other people there?"

"No, just you and me. Could we do it now?"

"Yes."

We stood together and walked into the little winter chapel. The whiteness of the walls contrasted with the golden wood of the pews as the morning light cascaded through the clear glass. The plainness of the chapel appealed to me, and I felt more at home here than in the ornate summer church where I sang in the choir. Peter picked up two prayer books as we walked down the aisle and then he led me to the steps to the altar, where he turned and stood before me, motioning for me to kneel at the rail. He opened the small red book, found the page from which he would read, and handed it to me before opening the second book.

"I know that my Redeemer liveth, and that he shall stand at the latter day upon the earth; and though this body be destroyed, yet shall I see God," Peter said.

I heard his words and his voice, but I felt myself moving backwards to when my father died.

"Yet shall I see God whom I shall see for myself."

For myself, I thought and I tried to see an image, but all I could conjure was a halo of light around a blurred face.

Peter continued, "And mine eyes shall behold, and not as a stranger."

Not as a stranger, I echoed. A stranger. That's who I've been, even to myself.

"Blessed are the dead, who die in the Lord."

I don't know if he believed in God or not, I thought, and I don't know if I do either.

"Oh God, whose mercies cannot be numbered. Accept our prayers on behalf of thy servant Samuel Granger," Peter intoned, and I wondered if my father knew we were praying for him, and then I tried to quiet my mind and just accept the words and the peace they promised. "God is our hope and strength, a very present help in trouble," I heard, "Therefore will we not fear, though the earth be moved and though the hills be carried into the midst of the sea." I saw lava moving in ribbons of red, bursting against the blue of the ocean in plumes of steam. As I imagined water cooling the angry rock, I felt myself being cooled by the words, the heat and anger abating to something more solid that I could feel, if not comprehend.

"If I climb up into heaven, thou art there; if I go down to hell, thou art there also," and I wondered if I could erase the thought of my father's body in the grave. "Yea, the darkness is no darkness with thee," Peter said, and I saw light inside my father's coffin sweeping darkness away, "the night is as clear as day; the darkness and light to thee are both alike."

My mind drifted away again to a time we went to the circus. My father gave me a fountain of pink cotton candy, and thousands of flashlights flickered around the darkened tent, but then I heard, "Grant to all who mourn a sure confidence in thy fatherly care, that, casting all their grief on thee, they may know the consolation of thy love."

Fatherly care. No! I screamed silently, shocking myself with my own fear. That doesn't exist, I thought.

Peter opened his arms wide above me saying, "The Lord be with you," and I looked up at him, a feeling almost of resignation falling over me, and then I whispered automatically, "And with thy spirit."

"Let us pray," he continued. "Our Father, who art in heaven, hallowed be thy name." I said the words and felt a flock of Tree Swallows bursting out of my heart and flying free in the air, pirouetting and dancing, emerald green and white in the sun. I breathed deeply and let the air out of my lungs slowly. Peter put his hand on my shoulder and said, "Almighty God, Father of all mercies and giver of comfort: Deal graciously we pray, with all who mourn; that, casting all their care on you, they may know the consolation of your love, through Jesus Christ, our Lord. Amen."

Peter made the sign of the cross. I repeated the motions, and as I touched my forehead and breast I remembered my father's hands stroking my hair as we sat together on Sunday mornings reading the newspapers. Suddenly I saw him in front of me, bending down to kiss my cheek, and then standing up, waving and turning to walk away from me. The picture was so vivid that I gasped and clenched my hands tightly in my jacket pockets, hoping I would not lose my fragile command of myself. I breathed deeply again, and then stood up and together Peter and I walked silently out of the church.

"There's a time to mourn, Becky," he said, "mourn and let it wash through you, and time as the Psalmist said, "to walk before the Lord in the land of the living."

"The land of the living?" I repeated.

"Yes, that's what it's about," he replied. "'Thou hast delivered my soul from death, mine eyes from tears, and my feet from falling, I will walk before the Lord in the land of the living,'" he quoted and I knew that was the hard truth I had needed to hear: walk in the land of the living.

We walked down the aisle, wordless, until we stood outside the small church. "Thank you, " I said. "That helps, it really does."

"It's just a beginning," Peter replied, "but a brave new beginning, and one that you have chosen." Then he turned to face me and said, "Do you believe God loves you?"

The question always scared me because I was too insecure to accept that it was possible. "I don't know," I said, my voice stuck deep in my chest.

"Becky, you haven't had an earthly father for such a long time that it must be almost impossible for you to believe in our Heavenly Father. To really believe that he cares about you. But I'm telling you that he does and that you will grow to believe it and then to care about yourself."

"Thank you, Peter," was all I could say and I bowed my head and walked quickly away from him. I could feel tears churning up like waves rising to break against rock, but even through my sadness I could recognize that his words gave me permission to accept the brokenness of my relationship with both my earthly and heavenly fathers.

As I drove back to my house, I could feel myself changing, growing both larger and smaller at the same time, like Alice in Wonderland, but then I thought, no, more like a snake shedding an old skin and testing its tender new scales against the grass. I had a sense of weightlessness and purpose I hadn't experienced before that seemed to come from the realization that there were reasons I had distanced myself from my own self and from people and God who loved me.

I walked into the living room and decided to make a fire. I twisted the pages of the *New York Times* into pretzels, as Ernie, the caretaker, taught me to do. I piled three logs at angles and lit a match, pleased by the flame catching and the smoke turning upwards to the flue. I poured myself a glass of merlot and sat by the fire, looking out at the cove, seeing the moon glinting off the backs of Eider ducks, and, like so many times when I needed to talk to myself, I wrote a poem.

A PRAYER

Stretch my heart, Lord, like a tree
shading the water.
Its roots holding banks and
tunnels for voles, rabbits
garter snakes and worms;
with roots for kingfishers and young boys
to grip with toes and perch
waiting for sunfish to glisten the water.

Stretch my heart, Lord, like a river
bending its way through the earth,
Gracious and bountiful,
With places for children to run and jump, calling with joy
as water quickens their blood,
and banks for lovers, caressing with their eyes,
and old women remembering their men.

Stretch my heart Lord, like the sun,
unveiling your work as it draws back the darkness,
lighting the dance of children in playgrounds,
Sand Hill Cranes, and teenagers bobbing as they court,
lighting the path of miners and playwrights
soda jerks and florists
and women bending to hang wet sheets.

Stretch my heart, Lord,
until it encompasses with love
even itself.

Then I knew I needed to call my mother.

When she answered, I said immediately, "Hi, it's me. I've been thinking about a lot of things. There's a foolish question I'd like to ask you."

"Yes, dear."

"Why did you break the boat I got in Maine, the little boat with my name on it?"

"What dear?"

"You know, the one with the red sail and oars I got for my birthday?" I persisted.

"Oh darling, that's so long ago. I'm surprised you even remember it."

"Well, I know it's stupid, but I was angry with you for smashing it and I couldn't tell you. Now I can."

"But I didn't smash it," my mother answered. "I found it in your closet when we were packing up the apartment. I got the chair from your desk and stood on it to check the closet and I found the boat way in the back. I wrapped it in newspaper and put it on the top of a carton the men had packed. I'm so sorry. I guess I didn't do a good job if it got broken. It must have gotten broken when they closed the carton," and I knew she was sorry.

"You know all these years I've been angry at you for that. Maybe I just unpacked the carton upside down. Forgive me. Thank you. I love you," I told her, something I hadn't admitted to my mother or myself for many years.

"I love you too, dear."

I held the phone for a moment before I hung up, and then I sat thinking about our conversation, looking out at the cove, watching the moon rise and listening to the muffled sounds of the ducks. I couldn't put my feelings into thoughts, just feelings which, like the small red-and-blue plaid picnic blanket from when I was a child, without thinking, I had tucked around myself.

❧

The next evening I sat in my chair looking at the cove and realized Marge had been right. "There's not many men here for company. I'm lonely sometimes, but at least I'm enjoying my own company and my new friends. In fact, I prefer it." There was one man who had asked me out three times. But I could smell the sweet red wine, like fermenting strawberries, oozing from his pores and clothes, and I knew that as much as I would like to go somewhere, I couldn't go anywhere with him. The logs in the fireplace had burned to a glow of embers, and I thought about his ex-wife and children, wondering if they felt as I had—helpless, scared, disgusted, angry—when I watched Jordie drinking his way through his inherited money, destroying his body and trying desperately to control himself and us.

I finished the glass of wine but resisted pouring another one. Instead, I thought about being away at school after my father died and about how I created a world of fantasy, escaping the present by recreating the past, again and again. I forced myself to remember a time that had been so awful, and how I had disintegrated.

Winter term at Wilton, winter in New England. I watched the trees crust over with ice and the ponds freeze, and, like a small animal hiding from the cold, I drew into myself. My few remaining friends worried about me and they kept asking me to do things with them, but more and more I needed to be in a little burrow, wrapped tight into myself as small as I could be.

When I went home for spring vacation the year my father died, I just wanted to stay in my room and sleep. Sometimes, when my mother was out, I went into my parents' bedroom and lay on my father's side of their large bed, curled into the little depression that still held the shape of his body and tried to feel his arms around me.

❦

We're still so distant, and I haven't been very sympathetic. It must have been frightening for my mother to be on her own with two children and to lose Daddy and Rachel. It's hard to imagine how she must have felt. Even though it was late, I walked towards my desk, thought about what Bob told me about finding my safe place before I tried to write, and I imagined sitting on the driftwood with Ben. Then I lay down on the hooked rug in front of the fireplace and tried to imagine going down into my father's grave. I let myself down rung by rung until I was inside a dank crypt and could see the spiders and feel the shiny wood of his coffin. I forced myself to think about Jordie, to visualize what he looked like when he was drunk, when he was yelling at me, taunting me, and embarrassing me in front of our few remaining friends, or worst of all, our children. I got up as if in a daze, walked over to the typewriter again and started to write a story about a thin handled spoon with a tiny oddly shaped cup I had found between the cushion and side of an upholstered armchair Jordie sat in as he watched television. He slept there sometimes, where I would find him in the morning huddled against the chair, the screen pulsing black and white light. I left the spoon on the side table, and noticed later that he had moved it, but it wasn't until after I left him that I realized it was serving cocaine not sugar.

I sat back from the typewriter. I was shaking a little, but I remembered the other half of Bob's advice, to surface and find the safe place. I put my head on the desk and imagined I was standing next to Ben when we met after my father died. I saw us sitting next to each other on the driftwood bench, and I could feel his arm around me. Ben, who looked so much like my father. Ben, who reassured and accepted me, who let me be myself. I saw us now in the rowboat and felt his hands on mine again, and for a moment, the bubble around that memory held, until it broke and I slowly remembered where I was. The image of Ben was disturbing, and I didn't want to think how the story had ended. Images of Jordie washed over me again. How could I have believed him? I asked, but I couldn't answer my own question. "Ben," I said, clutching at the memory of him again and relishing the calm it gave me. But I can't, I thought, I can't go back there. And a gentle voice in my head replied, "Not to him, but with someone like him," which was a strangely comforting new thought.

❧

In the morning, I felt stronger and thought I could write about my father, so I went to the study and sat down on the large hooked rug with its design of a blue sailboat skimming the water. I felt self-conscious, but tried to trust Bob's advice, hoping it might work. I lay on the rug and thought about going down into my father's grave again, pulling back the matted grass and digging through the dirt until I found the lid, then prying it open with my hands and staring into the coffin.

I sat in front of the typewriter, but I saw myself back in the grave—cold, crouched like a rabbit, tasting the damp dirt and feeling the rotten blue satin material against my hands. I started to panic. The airlessness of the coffin was suffocating. "Becky," I said gently to myself out loud, like a parent to a child, "This is just in your mind. Close your eyes and open the lid." I took a deep breath and pushed against the heavy lid; slowly it creaked open, just like in a Boris Karloff movie. A little child. That's what I've been all these years. That's when I felt safe, but it doesn't work anymore. Maybe it didn't work then, at least not for very long. I'm still waiting for Daddy to come home and make everything right, but he isn't going to do that, is he? And neither is Ben.

I tried again to find a safe place, but all I could visualize was sitting with Ben on the driftwood. I fought thinking about it until I heard the voice in my mind saying again—that was then. Treasure what you felt like then. Find that with someone else. Or just with myself, I thought and I could feel the tight place in my neck begin to loosen.

Later that afternoon on a walk, I thought about the times I walked through Boston Garden or the Commons by myself after my divorce from Richard, pretending to watch the ducks and swans, but watching people. I watched them walking, pushing carriages, holding hands, stopping to kiss. I watched couples young and old leaning into each other as they stood on the bridge watching the ducks and swans on the artificial lake. Couples seemed drawn together by music only they could hear, but had been dancing to for years and watching them made me feel my loneliness in ways I didn't when I was by myself. Could I have had that with Ben, I wondered. Not with my mother lurking over my shoulder, not thinking he was good enough for me or, perhaps, for her.

"I've never lived with a man I loved," I said aloud, "except, of course, my father," and the bitter thought hung over me until I decided to go to the movie being shown at the Neighborhood House to shake it off.

❧

As Christmas approached, and the end of the extension of my lease drew near, I called Marge and said, "I'm not ready to leave. Do you suppose they would give me another three months?"

"I doubt they'd give it to you," Marge replied laughing, "but you could pay to stay."

"You know what I mean. Would you ask them about another six months? Do I remember that they don't usually come back until July?"

"That's right. I'm sure it will be fine," Marge said. "It would be a nice little windfall for them. I'll let you know."

After I signed the new lease at Marge's office on a gray afternoon, I drove the short distance back to the house through a fog of freezing rain and sploshed through puddles to the back door. My foot fell through a pocket of snow-skimmed ice, and as the freezing water swept into my low boots, I shivered and suddenly felt scared of being in the house alone through the winter. I took off my boots and turned the gas on to boil water, but I could feel the cold creeping into my bones. I sat huddled in front of a radiator, my knees drawn up against my chest, and then went into the living room and lit a fire that seemed only to draw in more cold air. Knowing tea wouldn't be enough to warm me, I poured a glass of ruby port and watched the flames shimmering through the glass.

I held the empty glass to my chest, wishing I had the warmth of a man, or at least a cat against me instead of cold drafts that fluttered papers piled on the floor. The loneliness of the house seemed ominous and the ice cracking in the cove sounded like women moaning and sometimes screaming. I began to feel scared, scared of the night, scared of being in a house with no other living creature. I don't even have neighbors, I said to myself because the houses nearby were shuttered for winter, their windows covered by heavy boards, the weathered numbers faintly marking the window they fit.

I dialed the number I had posted next to the phone, right after Fire, Police, and Hospital. "Hellooo," said the voice I needed.

"Monica?" I said, my voice quivering.

"Yes. Becky, what's wrong?"

"I don't feel so great. I'm sorry to bother you. I know it's late and, oh, Monica, I'm a mess."

"What's wrong, tell me," Monica replied.

"I was just sitting here and thinking that I don't know what I'm doing. I feel like a blank sheet of paper. I'm trying to write, I don't even know what about, and it seems so arrogant, so presumptuous. Why would anyone want to read this?"

"What's it about?" asked Monica not unsympathetically.

"It's about me," I replied starting to laugh self-consciously.

"So, are you going to read it?"

"Yes."

"Isn't that enough? Why does it matter if anyone else reads it? You said yourself that you need to figure out things. Now tell me what's really wrong." Monica asked seriously.

"What's really wrong? I don't know."

"How are you feeling?" Monica asked.

I paused, and when Monica didn't say anything, I thought more deeply and tried to sense what I was in fact feeling. "I'm lonely and I feel like a child. I feel like a silly lost little child," I answered finally.

"I know you're lonely. But you know, men aren't everything. You may not believe me, but it's something I figured out a while ago. What's really important is friends. And feeling loved, and I'm your friend and I love you. You've got me whenever you need me, like right now. There's nothing I'd rather be doing than talking with you."

I felt tears welling up and inhaled quickly before I tried to reply.

"Feeling loved, that gets you every time, doesn't it?" Monica said. "I love you, and your children love you and lots of people do. I know it's not the same because you want a man's love, but remember that it's a start."

"I feel empty. There are blank spaces where I should have been able to be a better person, a better mother, a better friend."

"I'm not so good at the serious shit as you are," Monica said. "But I care about you very much, and you can call me any time. Day time, night time, any time you're sitting there feeling alone. You're not alone. So remember that."

"All right. All right," and I breathed in deeply. "It's sort of like AA—or FA—Friends Anonymous. What you said, it makes me feel better. Thank you."

Then Monica said, "I'm not a shrink. All my friends go to shrinks, but I don't. I'm not smart enough for a shrink. But you are. Have you ever thought about getting..."

"Shrunk?"

"Yes. I bet a lot of what you're feeling now goes back to when you were a kid. Your dad. I can't imagine what it's like not to have your dad when you're a kid. I talk to Dumpie every week. He's an old Spitfire, funny as hell, and he makes me feel loved. Connected."

"Not in a long time. I did after I left Jordie, but I didn't make much of a commitment, and I didn't go for long. Someone told me I should go. But I didn't want to. It seemed like giving up," I answered.

"I don't think it's giving up to try to figure out what makes you happy or unhappy so you can figure out how to be happy."

"All right. I'll think about it."

"Call me, and I'll call you. Every Sunday, or in between, whenever you want."

When I hung up the phone, I realized the fire was dying, so I put on two more logs. The coarse bark felt strong in my hands, and as I watched the flames licking around the new logs, and felt their warmth, I found it oddly reassuring.

My father. How long ago? "Daddy, I hardly knew you," I said in a mocking voice and laughed, a bitter laugh, tight in my chest. I looked into the fire and watched the shadow of flames and dared just for a moment to remember the last time I had seen him driving away. Involuntarily, I thrust out my arm towards the fire as if to grab him, but pain blocked the memory as it had so many times. I could almost feel the barrier, and I tried to see around it to what might lay behind, but at first my mind was blank. This time, unlike so many others, I tried to see what I knew had happened after my mother and father left me at Wilton, and I walked myself backwards as if rewinding a movie. The girls hovering around the door to my room, my Old Girl coming in and helping me unpack. Before she came in, the other girls, and before them, I stood at the window and then I looked out at the circle and saw my mother getting into the car. I was angry and hurt because they were leaving. Because they seemed so eager to go. But that's not fair. They had a long drive and it was getting late. What else were they supposed to do?

Chapter Ten

The week before Christmas I drove to the little airport just off the island and flew to Boston. The trip was so quick, just a little bit over an hour in the air, that I was amazed I hadn't done it before. Because I had rented my house, I'd taken a small suite in a hotel on Commonwealth Avenue near Katherine and Mark's apartment. As I rode in the cab on the way from the airport, I thought about how different my life was in Maine than it had been in Boston, but how much I missed being near my children and grandchildren.

Stephen and his wife Maggie arrived from New York on Christmas Eve. As they sat around after dinner Stephen said, "We've got some news." I could tell from his beaming face that they were expecting a baby.

"We're having a baby," he exclaimed, "in June."

This time I was prepared. When Katherine and Mark told me they were expecting their first child I was so surprised, so excited, that I sat immobilized for several seconds until tears flooded my eyes, and I said, "I'm so happy I don't know what to say."

Now I got up from the sofa, put my arms around them and said, "There could be no better Christmas present than the promise of a new baby in the family. I'm thrilled. Congratulations."

As my grandchildren Nina and Sammy nestled against me, I soaked in the warmth of their little bodies and a sense of peace and contentment I rarely felt. Time seemed to have stopped in its track, suspended while the two children and I read together. I brought them a collection of books about Maine, including one of my favorites about a woman who travels the world and then retires to her island home and makes it more beautiful by scattering lupine seeds that begin to paint the land with plumes of purple, blue and white each spring. As I read the story of Miss Rumphius, I remembered that Dot had said, "Grandchildren are the great reward," and I knew she was right.

As I was leaving after the week, I said to Katherine, "I miss you all. It seems odd to go back to Maine, but I love it there. I hope you'll come up, and at least now I know the plane trip is so easy. The drive seems so long, but the plane makes it feel as if I'm still quite close by."

"Don't worry about us, Mom. Maybe we'll come up for Mud Season," Katherine replied laughing. "You really are going to stay all winter?"

"Yes, I think so. I may go down to visit Monica in St. John, and I can stop by and stay with you for a few days on the way back."

On the plane back to Maine, I daydreamed about coming home from school the second summer, after Daddy had died, after I'd been with Ben. "Been with Ben." What an archaic way to put it, I thought, but naming what had happened was worse.

I tried to calm myself by thinking about my children and grandchildren, but even that led me back. It was hard to be the warm, overtly loving mother I wanted to be when I had felt so distant from my own mother, but being alone now, really for the first time, made me think how difficult it must have been for my mother to lose a child and then her husband. We lived in our own shells, didn't we? I never really thought about her. I was just angry that she married so quickly. But what else could she do? I was scared of her—scared of her grief. It was so desperate, just like my own. When she told me she was going to marry Taylor, I was so angry. It made me feel even lonelier, but I couldn't tell her. She needed to marry didn't she, I thought. Just as I needed to marry Richard.

I didn't want to be alone with my mother during Christmas vacation, but I soon realized that she was going out with the Johnsons' friend Taylor, whom she had met on their last night in Maine. Taylor was a tall man, craggy and austere and almost ugly, I thought. His awkwardness made me nervous, but my mother seemed entranced.

One night when Taylor was in Washington, she asked me to come into her room after Robbie had gone to bed. "Becky," she said, "I know this is hard for you. I know you miss your father, but I have to talk to you about that. I, I don't know really what to say, but you're old enough to understand this. It costs a lot to send you to Wilton. It costs a lot to live the way we do," she added, looking around the elegant room. "Your father had some life insurance. He had some money. I don't mean to say that we are poor. But..." She looked down, and I could hear her voice trembling.

"What is it?" I asked.

"I'm scared Becky," she said in a child's voice, softly. "I'm scared, and I don't know how to take care of you and Robbie. Sam did everything. And ever since Rachel…" She was crying now, the sobs coming fast and blocking her breathing. I put out my hand, and my mother held it so tightly it hurt. "Ever since Rachel," she tried again, but I could see the tendons arch in her throat

as if she were choking. "Ever since Rachel died," she spat out, as if disgorging a bone, "I've been so scared." She dropped her head and repeated very softly, "So scared."

"I don't have to go to Wilton; I can come back here. We don't have to live in a fancy apartment in New York, and we don't have to have maids. Everyone doesn't have a maid and a cook."

I was relieved when she looked at me, surprise widening her eyes. "No, Becky. No, we do. People expect it." She stopped and took a deep breath before she continued, "I've been seeing Taylor. I don't think you like him, and he doesn't really know children. He hasn't had any, and I think really that he's just awkward and shy. It isn't that he doesn't like you and Robbie. He's just shy." She looked at me with such pleading in her eyes that I had to make this all right.

"But I do like him, Becky," my mother continued, "and he would give us," again I looked at her hands. I waited, sitting on the blue brocade covered chair she had been so proud of when it came back from the upholsterer because it matched the blues and reds of the Persian carpet she and my father had chosen carefully. "It isn't like with your father," she said, holding the needlepoint pillow she made the summer before he died. "We were young and we were in love, at least before…" She stopped, and then continued, "but this, this is for the future, and for you and for," and she sobbed again before finally she said, "and because I don't know what else to do."

"You don't have to do anything," I pleaded. "We can just go on the..."

"You don't understand," she interrupted. "It's too lonely for me. Before I was going out with Taylor, I missed your father too much. I could cope with it during the day. I have friends and they're very good to me. We go to lunch; sometimes we go to the theater. I hate thinking they just feel sorry for me, though I'm grateful to them. But I can't cope with the loneliness at night." She was holding her hands together so tightly that I could see the veins swelling with trapped blood. "Becky, before I was seeing Taylor, no one asked me anywhere. I was just a single woman, and no one wanted an extra woman at dinner. I think some of the wives were even scared to ask me. I sat here and waited for him, and sometimes I thought he was going to come right through that door. It's still true. I was hoping it would stop, but I can hear the key in the lock and I can hear him call out, "Darling, I'm home." She stared over at the hall and shuddered. "Sometimes I get up and go to look for him, but he isn't there. It's almost like someone is playing a trick on me. My heart jumps, and I go out in the hall, but he's not there." She looked at me, her eyes

so wide now I could see the irises, like marbles in a child's hand. "And he's never going to be there. You have your friends at school, and Robbie's too young to really know what has happened. He misses his Daddy, but…" And she stopped again.

"It's not as if I could get a job, I've never done anything but be a wife and mother. That's all I ever wanted to do," and again she started crying and twisting her handkerchief in her hands. After a moment, she continued, "I just wanted to make a nice home for him and you and...and keep the house and do my volunteer work. And Taylor, Taylor is a very good lawyer, and besides," she said, straightening up a little, light coming back into her eyes, "he has money. He has lots of important clients, and I think he wants to marry me, Becky." She stopped to look at me, and I tried not to reveal that I thought marrying Taylor was a terrible idea. "It's too early yet, but I think he does. And he treats me very well, Becky." She was talking more quickly now, excited, as if she were planning a party. "I could be a good wife for him. I love giving parties and entertaining, and I could make a good home for him—actually he has three houses—and it would be for all of us, for you and Robbie." She was almost smiling now, her eyes casting out the window as if for the horizon, and I realized, with shock, that my mother was seeing a new life ahead of her.

I looked at her hands. She was turning her wedding ring around and around, stroking it with the index finger of her right hand. I noticed that her rings were loose because she had lost weight since my father died. She was too vulnerable, I thought. I never want to be like her; I never want to be so dependent on someone else.

Three months later my mother and Robbie moved to Washington two weeks before she and Taylor married. They stayed in a hotel in Georgetown to be near his house, and when I left school for spring vacation, I flew to Washington instead of the apartment that had been our home in New York. Not saying good-bye to people I had known before I went away to school, not packing my own things, not sorting through what I wanted to keep or to leave, felt so strange that I sank even deeper into the cold space inside myself.

They married in the living room of his house on R Street in Washington. As I watched my mother walk into the room on Uncle Charlie's arm, anger and sadness poured into me. When a close friend of my father's came up to say how happy he was for my mother, I tried to smile, but when he held out his arms, I turned and walked away because I knew otherwise the sadness would break me apart.

Robbie and I lived in the unfamiliar house while my mother and Taylor honeymooned in Madrid for three weeks, but I spent most of the time in my room. They timed the wedding so I would be home on vacation to stay with Robbie and he wouldn't feel lonely, but I wished I was anywhere other than in Taylor's house. I began to wear the same pair of gray sweatpants and sweatshirt every day, stopped washing my hair and slept most of the time. I didn't do it on purpose, I just didn't feel like doing anything else. Mildred and Isabel worried about me, but they were also worried about their jobs because Taylor's staff of three made them feel useless.

When Taylor and my mother returned from their honeymoon, they seemed settled with each other in ways that surprised me. When I saw my mother sitting in bed, propped against lace-covered pillows while Sadie the cook stood nearby and they discussed the menus for the day, I realized that she was now really Taylor's wife and that he was her first priority.

I had a new room in Taylor's house, bigger than my old room and more elegant, but it didn't feel like my room. My mother had decorated it in a yellow and blue Pierre Deux print, but to me it seemed like a room in a fine hotel. All I could see as I walked into it was my old room, my real room in the apartment that had been home since I was born. I saw my childhood sitting in that room. First there was my teddy bear, a huge Steiff bear the color of butterscotch pudding that my father had bought for me at F.A.O. Schwarz. I called him Bandy because he was so big—bigger than I was when I got him—that I dropped him as I was taking him to my room and I knew he needed a Band-aid for his boo-boo. Now Bandy, I thought, I need a big Band-aid for my boo-boo, and again I felt tears rising to choke me. I looked away from Bandy and around the room to my books—Charlotte's Web, The Glory of Egypt, A Child's Book of Mythology, Mother Goose and the worn pink and blue cover of Pat the Bunny. I looked at the tiny brown china bunny sitting on the shelf and picked it up, rubbing my thumb along its cold shining back until it was warm again. My eye caught on Andersonville, and I wondered if Ben had read the copy I gave him.

That room held me like a warm nest through childhood, and I could hear my father's voice down the hall calling me to get ready for school, and his steps walking down the hall before going to bed when he went around the apartment checking that everything was safe for the night. I usually heard him just in time to shut off my flashlight, but sometimes the book I was reading transported me to a place without time, and he had to poke his head in the door and tell me I needed my beauty sleep.

Now I unpacked the few boxes with my treasures—Bandy, my other animals, and my books—hoping to recreate what was familiar. I found my red and white dingy, but it looked as if someone had thrown it in the box. It was wrapped in newspaper and it was broken, the hull flattened and one of the oars had snapped in half. I thought my mother must have broken it on purpose because she knew Ben gave it to me, but I didn't dare ask. Instead I cradled the broken boat in my hands and stared at the pieces, crying until the tears made it wet. I used the corner of my shirt to clean the dirt from my name, and then I wrapped it up again, this time in clean white paper, and put it in the farthest part of the shelf in my large new closet. I found my old jewelry box and dug under the lining for the mussel pearl Ben gave me that I'd hidden. It had lost its luster and it looked like a tiny piece of dried gray chewing gum, but I fondled it with the tip of my finger and then put it back into my jewelry box.

But then, I did something crazy. I picked the mussel pearl up and swallowed it. I thought something of Ben would be part of me forever. That seems so strange now, really sick. Yet, it makes me want to hug that little lost girl.

❧

I was relieved to go back to school for the final term of Second Form year and hide in my books and my room. When my mother called one evening to tell me we were going to Nantucket for the summer, I didn't react, and instead found a twisted satisfaction in denying to anyone including myself that I had ever wanted to go back to Maine.

❧

At the end of the school year, I flew home again to "his house" in Washington and was relieved when Lemuel the butler told me that the Mr. and Madam were out for dinner and Robbie had gone to bed, but his wife, Sadie, was holding dinner for me. After I ate, Sadie came in to the dining room while Lemuel cleared away the plates and stood in front of me. "Miss Becky," she started, and I was uncomfortable, not knowing what Sadie was going to say, but feeling it would be something formal and unwelcome. "Ah don't know if yu motha told you, Miss Mildred, she don gone back up to New York. She didn't like it here none at all. She wanted to go back to her folks, and tha's alright. But, I want to say, we're your folks now. We're gonna take care of you. You got ta put on some weight child, you lookin' poorly."

I was so surprised I buried my face in my hands and started sobbing.

"Oh you poor chile, you poor chile," Sadie said as she put her arms around me.

"I can't," I said almost defiantly. "I can't..." But the tears drowned my words and sobs heaved my chest as I clenched my hands together so the pain in my fingers took my mind away from the pain in my heart.

"You cry, chile. Good for you to cry," Sadie said.

"No," I said trying to stand up, but bumping against the mahogany table. Sadie loosened her grip and stepped away as I pushed my chair back from the table, grinding the legs into the floor. "I won't, I won't," I said as I ran from the dining room into the hall and up to the bedroom that still felt like the room of a stranger.

When I heard my mother and Taylor coming up the stairs, I quickly turned out my light. The next morning I walked down to the dining room for breakfast. He was eating a soft-boiled egg and reading The New York Times. He looked up at me, said, "Good morning, I hope you slept well. Welcome back." He stood up to give me a hug and I stood next to him while he put his arms around me.

"Yes, thank you," I replied.

"What do you want for breakfast? I'll get Lemuel and you can have whatever you want."

"I'll have whatever you're having," though looking at the gooey yolk that oozed over his plate made me gag. I tried to think of something to say to the severe man sitting stiffly at the end of the table, but all I could think to do was to pick up the first section of the Washington Post and pretend to read it. I felt Taylor's eyes on me, until finally he picked up his newspaper. When Robbie came in with Isabel, I looked up and smiled at them. Robbie was a handsome little boy, and when he smiled, I could see my father. Robbie threw open his arms and came running to my chair, "Hi, Becca," he said as I picked him up and hugged him.

I put him down and turned to Isabel, and, as we were hugging, I heard Robbie say, "Hi Daddy," as he ran over to Taylor, and the tall awkward man bent down to hug him. I cringed, but when I looked at Taylor, he was smiling and his face seemed softer. I could feel my face getting hot, and my stomach clenching, but I said nothing. Instead I listened to Robbie and Taylor as they talked about the toy sailboat they were going to race in the marble pool in the garden behind the house. I sat silently as I ate breakfast, and then left the room without saying anything to either of them.

❧

That summer we all went to Nantucket, where Taylor owned a large shingled cottage on the ocean. Each morning, I told my mother and Taylor that I was going to play tennis or swim at one of the clubs, but I only went when they invited me for lunch and I knew I had to go.

At these lunches, I answered their questions, or questions their friends asked me, though I never initiated a conversation and I imagined myself flying above them like a small bird. Several people asked me where I was applying to college, but if I paused they would tell me, almost immediately, about where they had gone. I soon realized that if I let them talk, I hardly had to say anything myself, but if they pushed, I said I was applying to Radcliffe, Wellesley and Pembroke, and that seemed to satisfy them.

As we drove home from one such lunch, Taylor said, "I think you've made good choices."

My mother added, "I'm so glad," but I sat in the back of the car and watched the sailboats racing away from Sankaty Head Lighthouse. I didn't have any idea what I wanted to do after graduation, because I didn't want to leave my father's school.

Whenever I could avoid being with my mother and Taylor, I went to a place I'd found in the woods behind their house where an old hemlock drooped its boughs to the ground in a circle, creating a dense shelter with light filtering through the green needles. I took a blanket and pillow out of the house and kept them in a black garbage bag inside the circle of branches, and when I could sneak away, I went there to read. At least I pretended to myself that I would read, but often I just lay on the pillow and stared at the patterns of the sun through the needles. I brought two photographs of my father and one of his old sweaters. I set the pictures up, put my ring between them, and held the sweater to my face, drinking in the lingering smell, looking into the photographs and trying to make fresh the pictures in my mind.

A fiction started to elaborate in my mind, a fiction that wove Ben and my father together, and erased the memories of my last night with Ben. I began to create one perfect man, younger than my father, older than Ben, and to braid stories about them that comforted me. I lay in bed and twisted my father's ring on my finger, thinking I would never forget what he looked like as long as I had his ring, but memories of him and of Ben began to merge and then to fade into little clips, like shorts before a feature. I felt myself losing the smell of the balsam and the sea, could hear only little snips of sound, and remember only moments—my father pointing out the Rose Breasted Grosbeak, Ben teaching me to row. By the end of summer, I was hearing only the clink of jewelry at my mother and stepfather's beach parties, the crack of ice as scotch poured over it, or the sounds of women talking in breathless staccato through pursed red lips as they sat around the club pool smoking filtered Parliaments.

I spent so much time alone that summer that I didn't want to return to Wilton, where I would be forced into contact with people and to be part of their community. I had few responsibilities even though I was a Senior, and I found I could drift through a day barely speaking to anyone. The more I turned away from people, the more time I spent in my dream world. The second semester I rarely ventured an opinion or raised my hand in classes, and I did my homework only superficially. As I sat at my desk in the large study hall, I felt a huge weight pressing on my shoulders but I didn't have the energy to move it.

Miss T asked me to come to her office to talk after Chapel one Sunday, but I dreaded the idea of listening to her. There was nothing Miss T could say that would make my father come back and that was all that mattered.

Miss T poured cups of tea for us and said, "You're going through an awful time, but you're making it worse for yourself. Your father would have been sad to see your grades slip. Your teachers are trying to help, but you've got to make an effort. You've got to pull yourself together and get back to work. It's been over two years and it's time to stop grieving and get on with your own life."

I felt as if I'd been slapped. I looked at Miss T and saw only the tight pinch to her face, her drab old-maidish dress with white polka dots on a navy blue background and the wide white collar. "Yes, Miss T," I replied mechanically.

"There's nothing anyone can do for you if you aren't going to help yourself, you know," Miss T said tartly. "You used to be such a good student. You contributed so much in class. Your father would be so disappointed."

"Yes, Miss T," I said again.

"College admissions offices are making their decisions now," Miss T continued, "and they'll make some allowances. I asked Miss Pratt to talk with them, but if your grades slip too far, there's nothing we can do to help. What's your back-up?" she asked.

"Boston University."

"Well, that should be safe," Miss T replied, looking relieved, "but even

that wouldn't be a sure thing if you slip any more. Come on, chin up," she added as she stood up.

In March when the letters from colleges arrived, the thin envelopes told me I hadn't been accepted anywhere. While other girls cheered, hugged and patted each other on the back, and others blushed and cried in disappointment, I picked the letters up from the front hall table and put them on my bureau. I had a single room that semester because I had chosen not to room with anyone, and sometimes at night I burned candles. It was against the rules, but I liked the flickering light and the smell of pine, and I liked disobeying.

I put the letters on my bed, lit the candles, and opened the envelopes. As I read, "We are sorry to inform you." I tore the letter and the envelope into small pieces and burned it. When I opened the envelope from Boston University, the letter was different. I was on the waiting list—the final humiliation. Wait-listed at my last choice.

The next day Miss T called me into the office and said, "Becky, your college results aren't what you or we had hoped for from you but, well, we'll just do the best we can. I'm sure if I call Mrs. Phelps at the Admissions Office at BU she'll understand that they are lucky to get you and that you'll do very well there. They're trying to make it a better place academically, and I'm sure by the time you graduate it will be a place to be proud of." I was relieved. I wouldn't be under any pressure to work hard, and I didn't know anyone at BU. No one from my class was going and I could keep to myself and not have to be polite or pretend to make friends. Now, as I looked at myself in the mirror, my pasty skin, disheveled oily hair, and ugly brown sweater made me laugh.

During graduation, I focused on the flag that hung over the auditorium and refused to look at anyone. I walked across the stage and received my diploma, then slipped away to stand in front of the plaque with my father's name. I almost cried, but even standing there I could not. I felt as if I were encased in stone, and that felt safe. Finally, I walked back to my room. My mother and Taylor were sitting together on my bed and Taylor was holding her hand, and patting her back.

"It's all right dear," my mother said to me, "It's going to be all right," but I knew that could never be true.

I walked over to the bags and the two cardboard boxes with my books. "It's time to leave," I said as I picked up one box and walked out the door to wait in the car. Everyone from the dorm was still at the reception after graduation, so I said goodbye to no one. During the long drive back to Washington, my mother and Taylor talked self-consciously and tried occasionally to include me. "Your room just got painted, dark green like you wanted," my mother said with a pleading tone. And I had the old rocking chair re-upholstered in a lovely print that goes beautifully with the paint. You'll love it, I'm sure you will."

They tried, didn't they? I was the step child from hell. Lonely, I guess I wasn't capable of doing anything else then. And are you now? the voice inside asked.

❦

When I returned to the village from seeing Katherine and her family, I got into the same habit as when they were at school or college of calling my children on Sundays. During the winter I made several trips to Boston and New York to see them. I also made myself write every day that winter. Sometimes, when I was reading my own words, the pain erupted with such suddenness that I was startled and frightened by my inability to control it as it coursed through me, leaving me sobbing and pounding the floor with my fists or clenching a pillow so tightly that my hands ached afterwards. But each time, I also felt cleansed of poison that had lived in my veins too long.

That winter I learned the beauties of shrouding snow, the bones of the earth gaunt against the gray sky, and the trees' dark branches shadowed on the snowdrifts. Ice coated everything and made walkways treacherous. Wisps of sea smoke rose from the cove, curling up from the warmer water into the freezing air. Dot told me that sea smoke, a freezing fog, relentlessly coated boats with ice, made them deceptively dazzling as gems, until their spars and halyards hung heavy and a sudden wind could heel them over. Dot said it was "wicked dangerous" for the men if they didn't chop or hose away the ice, and I began to see that was what I was trying to do with my own rime of loss and brokenness.

I learned to cross-country ski on the park carriage trails, to make a fire in the woodstove and to enjoy sitting by myself in the evening, sipping hot chocolate and reading. I learned to use snowshoes and to recognize the call of different owls, the tiny Saw-whet with its insistent "too-too-too," and the deep "who-who-he-whoo-ing" of the Great Horned Owl. I learned to read the tracks of coyotes and fox as they hunted. I found the tracks of otters and an icy slide they had made in a snow bank, and I pictured them like boisterous children wrestling and playing, and finally I bought a computer to replace the ancient Olivetti.

I learned the hunkered down mentality of a coastal village, a small world, intensified by the cold as winter deepened. I learned that high school basketball and church and bean suppers held the community together. I saw that there was sadness and joy for fishermen lost at sea with no life insurance, for engagements and weddings, thank-you notes in the paper for donations, for loving care in the hospital or nursing homes, a jar in the market collecting change for a child who needed medical attention, stories in the paper of drugs found, of a child or old person lost, of fiftieth anniversaries, and thirtieth birthdays. This was not a community in suspended animation, waiting for summer visitors to return. This was a world moving at its own pace, faster now than in the past. I was looking at the fine grains of a black-and-white photograph, the lines, blemishes, and wrinkles in high resolution, whereas before I had only known the airbrushed color postcards intended for tourists.

There was a side to this paradise that most summer visitors never got to see, perhaps no darker than that of other places, but impossible to hide among so few people. Everyone gossiped about everyone else, though I knew people in cities did the same thing. The difference was that in the city the stories were unattached to particular people and faded with the next such incident, while in a village they accreted steadily, ineluctably, to neighbors and family. I loved the quiet of the village, knowing everyone and being known, even if too often what we thought we knew wasn't true. I loved the rootedness of the place but no longer dismissed it as picturesque or simple. I knew I was fortunate to see both sides.

When I next saw Bob at the library, I said, "I'm glad I stayed this winter. It's quiet and cold, but I can see so many things I hadn't thought about before when I was just here for the summer. I can see them because the scale is smaller than in a city. People care about each other even if they don't like each other."

"Yup,' he replied nodding, "we put on a good show in the summer, but in winter the warts grow back."

❧

One afternoon as I was walking along the sound, I saw an eagle swooping down to snatch a fish and remembered the first time I saw an eagle catching its dinner. I felt like the fish then, but now I see them both, predator and prey. I thought about the birds I had watched with my father, and then without him, and I wondered about the birds we might have seen together and who I might have been had he lived. I pretended he was at my graduation from Wilton, that he came up to me as I waved my diploma at him, and that he hugged me and told me how proud he was of me. I saw him when I graduated from college, and then beaming when

I was hooded at the ceremony for my doctorate, taking pictures, standing on a precarious folding chair so he could see me more clearly. I saw him at my wedding and felt his arm supporting me as we walked down the aisle, but then the image faded and I could see neither my father nor the man waiting for me. I tried to conjure him again, like a child rubbing a lamp hoping a genie would burst out. I imagined him playing with my children, flying kites, sailing little leaf and walnut hull boats in streams, and rowing them out to the sailboat we kept in the harbor. I saw him playing tennis with them, throwing the balls gently and patiently over the net as he had done with me, and clapping when they hit one back. I began to welcome the bursts of memories and to let them flow through me rather than trying to clamp them off. And I began to appreciate what I had accomplished and to understand that because he hadn't been there to reflect his pride in me, I had not been able to see myself for who I was becoming. Against that emptiness, I had tried to define myself, but it had been a lonely struggle.

In late winter there was a dance at the Community Center. When I went to get the paper, I stood behind Bob at McKnight's as he and Dot talked about it. "Dancin' and bean supper. Should be a lively combination," observed Bob.

Dot added, "Alfred and I saw the Ramblin' Gents up to Ellsworth last year, and they were pretty good. Fiddler's real good. We wouldn't miss them. You goin' Becky?"

"Um, well, I hadn't thought about it," I admitted.

"You hav'ta go. Supports the Neighborhood House, and what else are you goin' to do?"

"You can sit with us," Bob said. "We'll pick you up and get you back, if you like."

As I walked into the darkened front hall of the large community center with Bob and Ethel, I was apprehensive. They chose a large table in the dining room, and we sat down in the metal chairs, and soon other people from the village joined us. "It's good to see you here, Mrs. Evans," said a man who worked in the gas station.

"Thank you, but please call me Becky."

"I guess that's okay. You're a year-round summer person now. In the summer I'll probably forget and call you Mrs. Evans," he said and I laughed.

"A year-round summer person! That's a real step up for me."

After the man walked to his table, I turned to Bob and Ethel and asked, "Year-round summer person? Is he serious?"

"Of course," Bob answered. "What else would you call yourself? You don't live here just in the summer now, but you're also not from here—never will be. But year-round summer person, now that gives you privileges."

When the band started playing, I sat quietly, but my foot was tapping in time with the strong Cajun rhythm and I loved the fast whiny sound of the lead singer and the fiddler. Couples started dancing, and I noticed pairs of women dancing, and wished I had the nerve to dance by myself. After awhile dancers formed a circle, and Ethel beckoned to me saying, "Come on. No excuses. You have to join." I was happy to be included, and when we sat down while the band took a break, I felt I had slipped past at least one of the seines that separated us.

Bob asked me to dance because, "Ethel's pooped," and we stomped our feet in a sort of polka clog dance, which made some people step back and clap along with the rhythm of our feet. When we sat down, one of the younger men from the market asked me if I wanted to dance, and I was thrilled. As I gave in to the music, I felt a glorious freedom. It seemed wonderful to feel no sin at being solitary, neither humiliation nor shame, and to enjoy my friends and my own company.

❧

When the phone rang one evening in early February, I knew it was Monica. Somehow she always knew when to call and there was an almost distinctive quality to the ring. Nothing Ma Bell had programmed in, but something that transmitted through the lines of Monica's cheerfulness and her almost playful acceptance of her self.

"Hi there."

"You sound good. Who were you expecting? Someone special?"

"Yes, you!" I replied. "I know your ring. You have nice cheerful ring, sort of perky."

"Did you really know it was me?"

"Yes. I'm so glad you called. The weather's turned cold, deep cold that blows through my wool coat when I walk from the car into the post office. I don't walk anywhere anymore."

"Sounds like you need silk underwear or some time in the sun. The underwear's cheaper but a trip would be more fun."

"You're right about both," I answered, thinking about getting some silk long johns but seeing myself lying on a chaise next to Monica the way we had so many times at the pool.

"I'm going to St. John in a few days. You want to come down for a while? I've got lots of room," Monica asked. Three weeks later I flew to Saint John. I spent a week with Monica doing nothing in particular but enjoying the sunshine and being with lots of people, doing whatever I felt like and being waited on. When I returned to Maine the slanted light seemed dim and shadowy, and I had to will myself to go for walks in the early afternoon, but my time away helped me see that I felt at home here, and that Monica's life would soon bore me.

Chapter Eleven

I could feel life quickening with the spring thaw and the peepers' tentative chorus. In mid-March, male Red-winged Blackbirds came to stake out territory with their oddly melodious squawking as they clung to swaying cattails. One unusually warm day in mid-May I walked out in the garden and little black flies dived like kamikazes into my hair and ears, down my shirt, and up my slacks. When I went to pick up my newspaper Dot laughed when I told her I'd been driven inside by a plague of flies and said, "Black flies. Maine state bird. They don't last but a few weeks, but yes, they're awful, and some people swell up real bad from the bites." I could feel the itchy lumps rising up around my neck as I listened. "Wear light clothes and a bandanna and put Skin So Soft all over you before you go out," Dot advised.

"It's different hearing about them, and experiencing them," I said.

As Memorial Day approached, I began to realize I was ambivalent about summer. "Dot," I said one morning. "I just was thinking about people coming back. I'm not sure I want them. I'm surprised."

"Some people say," Dot laughed, "they wish summer folks would just send their money and stay home. It's sort of a love-hate thing, you know. We have to have their money, and some of them are real nice, but some of them are like black flies."

Just after Memorial Day, Marge called me and said, "I think you've had a good winter. What are you going to do for summer? Do you want another rental, or do you want to look at something more permanent?"

"Marge, your timing is flawless. You're right, I've had a great winter. I love it here. I love being on the water. Is there anywhere I can buy so that I can be on the water?"

Marge asked me what I wanted to spend, and when I told her, she said, "Well, you aren't going to be in the village for that, but you might think of other parts of the island, or one of the outer islands. There's something on Sutton's I'll be listing soon. We can look around here and then go out there. Why don't I put some things together and we'll just take a day and poke around. It'll be fun, and it'll give you an idea. Then, if you want to get serious you can, or if you want to rent we can find something else, though there's not a lot left."

Some houses Marge showed me were too ugly to think about, like one with phony butcher-block kitchen counters and livid red cabinets. Others smelled of cats and litter boxes or were cut into cramped rooms, and though Marge tried to help me see that I could take down walls, paint and change cabinets, there was no house that I liked or could even imagine liking. Two weeks later we took the mail boat out to Sutton's Island to see the house Marge had just listed. As we walked along the worn footpath because cars were forbidden, Marge said, "The house we're going to belongs to two sisters. They haven't used it so it's a bit run down, but it has a view from some of the rooms. Of course, it's in much better shape than the house on Little Cranberry. That was a beauty, but my God, what they did to that place. You should see it."

"What house?" I asked.

"The old Captain's house." Marge answered. "It was a showplace when they sold it. They got top dollar for it, said they couldn't turn it down because one of the grandchildren needed surgery. The main house, the old house, well a hippie bought it, his father left him lots of money, and he did some weird things to that house," she said, dragging the corners of her mouth down in a deep frown. Upset the Bunkers, but there's nothing they can do about it."

"The Bunkers?" I stammered. "Is that house for sale?"

"Yes," Marge replied surprised, "do you know it?"

"I was there once," I said, instantly regretting my slip.

"When?"

"Oh, years ago," I replied breathing slowly to control my voice. "I was a kid, and someone asked me over for a picnic."

"I didn't set it up for you to see," Marge continued, "because it really would be a labor of love to bring it back and it's just that much farther out, but we can go over if you want. I can get the key from Bernie in the post office any time. There's no one living there now. You could buy it for a lot less than shore front on Mount Desert, but I don't know if you'd want to be way out there. Still, if you know them."

I could see curiosity sparking in Marge's eyes, and a little smile twisting her mouth. She was trying not to seem interested, but finally she asked, "Who did you know?"

I knew she would find out, and that it was best to be direct, so I said, "Ben, Ben Bunker, I met him the summer we were here. Do you know him?"

"Of course. How did you meet him?"

"His grandfather brought our float out, and then took us on a picnic to Baker's. How is he?" I asked, forcing myself to feel detached from the question and the answer.

"Oh, he lives on the island with his wife. They have one of his grandfather's houses. We'll probably see him if we're out there," Marge replied.

Then I wanted to be anywhere else. I felt a wave of sadness sweep over me, but I said, as evenly as I could, "Well, that would be fun. I loved the house. The library was beautiful."

"That's the worst now. Wait 'til you see it, you won't believe what they did. They turned it into a meditation room. Covered the maple floor with horrible lime-green shag carpet and ripped out the bookshelves." Marge stopped, drew in her breath and let it out slowly then said, "It's so strange what some people will do to a house."

The house on Sutton's was as grim as Marge had described. Piles of dead flies covered the floors near the windows, crunching under our feet, and the windows were small and faced away from the view, which surprised me. "Some people were on the water so much, they didn't want to look at it when they went home from fishing," Marge explained.

"The view's better at the other house," Marge said as we walked back. "The house is in rough shape, but the views are great. Do you want to go?"

"Not today," I answered. "I'm tired now, but maybe some other time."

When Marge ran into me at the market the next day, she asked, "What do you think? You want to see the house on Little Cranberry? I'd like to show it to you."

"I don't know," I replied and felt relieved when Marge said, "I can understand your reluctance. That island's farther out, and the house is a disaster. You seemed a bit put off by the Sutton house, but then the view there isn't much. The view from the Bunker house is amazing. The windows are small, it's an old house, but there are so many of them," and she looked at me expectantly. "You'd love the view," she reiterated.

"Yes," I answered, remembering when I stood in the doorway of the house looking towards the big island, oblivious that Ben's relatives were watching me. "All right," I said, "let's see it," though I wanted to drag the words back as I said them because I felt trapped by my curiosity and embarrassed to be thinking again about Ben.

I could feel my heart pounding as we took the mail boat over to Islesford dock on Little Cranberry. At the town dock I was sure no one would recognize me from so long ago and that Marge and I could walk unannounced over to the house. But as we walked down towards the road, I felt as if there were eyes all around me staring, wondering who I was. When the road turned left, I could see the house. The garden was overgrown, the shutters were awry, at least those that weren't missing, and I felt angry at people who had abused the house. We walked closer, and I could see that dirt and cobwebs covered the windows.

"I warned you," Marge said. "Just imagine it cleaned up."

"I know. It just makes me sad because I remember when the family lived here and it was so beautiful."

As I crossed the threshold, I instantly imagined settling into the house, cleaning it, repairing the broken windows and the cracked walls. As we walked into the kitchen I visualized pulling up the fake brick linoleum and the lime green Formica that covered the counters. I tried to stop myself, but the house pulled me in and I imagined tearing out the acid green carpet in the library that looked like a slime-covered pond, uncovering the wide pine boards I knew lay underneath, rebuilding the bookshelves and finding the rolling steps. I could feel the arms of the house around me, and even in the cold I felt warmed.

"Marge," I said as we walked out to the overgrown garden. "I love this house, but it scares me. The expense of renovating scares me, and being out here seems a bit like stepping off the edge of the world. I love this house and I can see the things I want to do to bring it back to life." I stopped myself and stood looking out at the ocean, then asked Marge, "What do you think the Bunkers would think about me living here?"

"You can ask them yourself. You can call Ben, or we can go over to his house and ask him. I think they'd be happy to have someone who loved the house and wanted to bring it back," she said thoughtfully. "They haven't been able to themselves. There's been sickness in the family the past several years, and none of them can buy it even here with shore front so pricey." She paused, and then said, "Let's go back in," and then let me walk around the rooms and look at the view of Mount Desert Island again.

"It is so beautiful here," I said quietly.

"Why don't you think about it and then we can call them together," Marge asked. "Or I can, if you want, and we could come back and look again. It's early in the season yet. There aren't many summer people looking, and they're the only ones who could afford it."

I thought, her timing is so good, she's just letting this house sell itself to me. I could look at that view forever.

"I don't know what to do," I said to Monica when we talked that night. "I love that house. I loved being there when I was a girl, and I love it now. But I don't know what to do about Ben."

"Why do you have to do anything about him?" Monica replied. "Seems to me you just have to do something about you."

"I think I'm over him. It's been good being here all winter. I've thought about how I'd like to have someone in my life like him, someone my age, to you know, be grandparents together." I could see us walking with a child, swinging her between us.

"Is it the house or the man you want?" Monica asked.

"I guess I want them both," I answered, surprised by my admission. "But I made him up," I continued. "I can't want him now. He's married. And I don't know who Ben is now. I didn't even really know who he was when we were kids. And I'm still so ashamed of how—what I did. That's burned me for years."

"I know. So what better way to extinguish it than to see him again?" Monica said simply. "Besides, he's probably got a pot belly and nose hair and you'll be totally turned off and become friends."

❧

All during the next week I thought about the house. It consumed me. I thought about rooms I had seen and loved, like the blue-and-white living room of my rental cottage, how I could turn the living room into an extension of sea and sky with shades of blue and green on furniture and in curtains, and about white cabinets with glass doors in the kitchen and a countertop of granite from the island. I planned an herb garden and a small orchard. I imagined the view looking at Mount Desert Island, set like an opal in the sea, the colors of its mountains changing with the light. I found myself agreeing with Monica. Ben had been a dream, an adolescent fantasy perpetuated by my loneliness. What better way to get over him, to grow up, than to live nearby, be friends perhaps. Besides, he probably did have a potbelly.

When Marge called she asked, "What are you thinking?"

"It's so hard. I love that house. I have since the moment I saw it when I was a kid. But it doesn't make any sense for me to buy it. To just pick up and move to an island where I don't know anyone." I knew I was lying. I did know someone. I knew him too well and not at all.

"Hey, sometimes you have to lead with your heart," Marge answered breezily, and I wondered if she had detected how deeply I wanted to be there. "Why don't we go back and you can talk to the family if you want."

The tension of wanting to flee and my attraction to Ben and his family's house twisted inside me, and I couldn't at first reply. Potbelly and nose hair, I reminded myself, and then I thought, perhaps by being near him, I would let go of the fantasies or they would let go of me. "All right," I answered giving in to what was becoming inevitable.

The next day we took the boat to Little Cranberry Island and walked from the town dock to Captain Bunker's house. This time I knew there were eyes on me, that people knew who I was, and that I had been there before. The man on the mail boat said, "Good to see you again, Mrs. Evans," before he swung into the wheelhouse. As we walked from the dock, Marge waved to some men fixing traps who waved back and nodded to each other in a way that made me feel they were talking about me and Marge, though not that they were unfriendly.

When I walked into the house, I felt as if it was mine already. I could see myself sitting in a rocking chair on the porch, looking out over the sea, learning to make chowder, or at least to boil a lobster. I stared out at the view, looking over the beach and what was left of a lawn, now gone to scrub grass and nettles. When I heard steps behind me, I turned and saw a man, but he turned into a boy with eyes like the sea, and then back into a man, his face lined, but handsome, the same face I had tried so hard to both remember and forget.

"Ben," I said, my voice deep in my chest.

"I knew it was you last time," he said. And for a moment I thought of him as mine, and then he added, "Why didn't you come to see us?" and the feeling drowned while surfacing.

He put out his hand. It felt warm and strong around mine, and I had to force myself to let it go. "We heard you were here." He stood back from me. "You look good. It's good to see you. I want you to come meet my wife, Abby. She'll be glad to meet you," and then he took off his cap. Before he put the cap back on I saw that there was a little patch above his ear where his hair was thin.

"I'd like to do that, Ben," I said, though I didn't think that was true. When he was in my fantasy world, I never thought of him as married, always as available for me. Even when Monica told me he was married, I hadn't really accepted what that meant. Now as I looked at him, I wished he had grown fat and bald. I could only push away the thoughts and speak from the masking civility I had learned as a child.

"Ben, I've loved this house since I first saw it. Would you mind if I bought it? Would you mind if I lived here?" I wanted him to mind, wanted him to be upset, to react in some way, but he just smiled at me.

"Becky, why would we mind?" he replied easily, and I wondered how he could be so calm and dispassionate. "We can't have it ourselves, and we would be honored to have you as a neighbor."

It was too easy—too simple—could that be all there was for him? His reaction, or lack of reaction, was a let-down, as if there had never been anything between us, and certainly not anything that could make him uncomfortable. I felt dismissed, diminished, but later I realized I also was freed from having to consider him or his feelings, and I made an offer on the house that the owners accepted immediately.

I didn't have to pay a lot because the house needed so much work, but bringing it back would more than offset my initial savings. Everyone agreed to a quick closing, and within six weeks of first seeing the house, it was mine. I decided to live there while it was being worked on, even though it was like camping out. A plumber wrestled with the pipes until I had water in a bathroom and the kitchen, and then I moved in.

I hired two women Marge recommended who lived on the island, Jane and Susan, to help me clean the house. Jane was a woman of robust proportions and rugged build. Her lips were always chapped, the little flecks of skin gathering around her mouth. Her hands were rough, but a smile and sparkling gray eyes made her handsome instead of intimidating and she could scrub a floor with more enthusiasm than most people brought to more enjoyable tasks. Susan was the wife of a young fisherman. She had moved to the island years ago from her home in northern Maine but was still "from away." In a week we had the kitchen, parlor, the bathroom and one bedroom sparkling clean.

I bought a bed and a chair and had them shipped over on the barge, and when I looked into the far reaches of the attic, I found old furniture coated in a grimy crust of cobwebs and dirt. Clay and Hubert, Susan and Jane's husbands, helped me haul it all out into the sun. Behind everything, tucked under the eaves, the last piece we found was the library steps. My throat clenched when I saw it because I was so happy. Though it was broken, it could be repaired, so I gave the lot to Clay to work on.

❦

One morning, while I was standing in line to pay for groceries, someone said, "Ayuh, you're the lady that bought the Bunker house. Too bad young Ben couldn't take care of it, but what with him being away, and Abby sick, it's too much."

"Abby sick?" I asked, bolts of conflicting concern and hope jabbing through me simultaneously.

"Ayuh, been doing' poorly for a while," but that was all I learned because I was afraid to probe. Ben had been on a fishing trip when I moved in to the house, and I was almost relieved. Since seeing him, I felt apprehensive whenever I walked to the little village to shop, and worried about how I would feel if we met.

Monica suggested I think of him as Paul Newman—someone to play with just in my mind.

"But Ben's not in Westport, Connecticut, Monica. He lives right here and I could run into him any time I leave my house," I told her.

The harshness of Monica's reply shocked me. "You knew that when you moved there, Becky. Do you want to bust up his marriage? Have you had any sign he feels anything for you?" I knew did not and I needed to get over it, and him, again.

Another day as I was buying bread, I saw Ben paying for a dozen eggs and a quart of milk. I watched him as he chatted with Ruthie the storekeeper, but I turned away. I stood staring at a row of ketchup bottles and then thought, this is just as dumb as when I couldn't talk to him at the dock, and I forced myself to pick up a bottle of ketchup and walk to the counter. As he turned, I put out my hand, and said, "Good morning. Nice to see you." I looked at my hand as he took it in his own, and I remembered when he had held my hand as we rowed his grandfather's dinghy. I could see us as we bumped into *The Sea Princess*—two kids and a lot of hormones, and I blushed deeply.

When I looked up at him he was smiling, but I could feel a darkness behind the smile. I wanted to tell him I was sorry for what had happened so long ago, but I didn't know how to start. "Who would have thought you'd end up here?" he said, but I couldn't tell what he was thinking.

"Not me," I agreed.

He took a deep breath and said, "How're you making out at the house? It was some mess all right."

"I'm okay, actually I'm doing very well. I love it there, and everyone's helping and making me feel welcome," I replied, listening to my own voice, thinking simultaneously of all the things I wanted to say to him.

"We haven't. I'm sorry about that. I've been away, and Abby's not feeling well. She said if I ever saw you I should ask you to tea, to be neighborly. Do you want to do that?"

"Of course," I answered flatly, trying to play the role he seemed to have assigned to me. "Is there anything I can bring?"

"No, nothing, just come around four o'clock and I'll make some tea for us. We're a little ways down North Wood Road from you, past the meadow and on the left."

When I went to the market the next day I bought his wife some flowers and ribbon to decorate a basket for lavender bath soap and hand cream I'd bought in Boston. I didn't know what was wrong with her. I'd been afraid to ask. When I told Ruthie who the flowers were for, she put them down and said, "Oh, it's too sad that. She's a wonderful woman, from Brant's Island. They have a lot of cancer there, people do. They get it from the rocks—radon they call it." She looked back at the flowers and wrapped them slowly in brown paper. "She has cancer, though I think it's in remission." When Ruthie finished, she looked at me again and added, "She's been sick a while. She's just marooned in that house now, but they're a loving couple, and he's doing the best he can for her," and then she sighed and gave me the bill.

Now the thoughts seeped through the dam against my feelings. Ben's wife was ill, seriously ill, and that raised possibilities I hadn't dared think about. I tried to staunch them, tried to argue with myself, but the emotion was too deep and the longing too great, though I had to acknowledge that Ben seemed oblivious. "Someone like him, someone like him," I reminded myself again.

Ruthie told me to take the path through the woods to Ben and Abby's house because it was shorter than the road. It wound through thick woods. Deep green moss carpeted the ground on either side of the path, and pines, firs and oaks laced their variegated greens in a complex pattern overhead. Here and there large mushrooms and toadstools interrupted the flow of the moss, and translucent Indian pipes stood silently next to rotting logs. There were circles of huge ostrich ferns, and smaller cinnamon ferns with brown spores lining their stems like buttons on a long kid glove.

At the end of this fairy tale path there was a grassy meadow. Theirs was the third house on the left, on the meadow side of North Woods Road. The houses were far enough apart so that there were big yards between them, but close enough so people knew they had neighbors. Ben's house was a white Cape with green shutters; there was a large vegetable garden, half unplanted, a flower bed overgrown with weeds, two wooden rockers on the front porch, and a bird feeder on the side of the house. I clutched the present and wondered what Abby would think of me, what Ben might have told her? I stopped in the middle of the field, looking at the house and thought again how strange and stupid it was to even be on the island let alone going to see Ben and meet his wife. "What else can I do?" I asked myself. "I'm here, what else can I do? Grow up," I said fiercely to myself.

I tapped the brass knocker, but no one came to open the door. I knocked again a little more loudly, wondering if I had the wrong day or time. Just then I heard fumbling with the latch, a key being turned, and a shove, against the door, and then there was Ben standing in the opening.

"Now that you're a year-round summer person, you'll have to learn that we never use the front door."

"Oh," I said, embarrassed, "I have a lot to learn."

"Ayuh, yes, you do. Come meet Abby," he added, "she's in the kitchen. She gets cold so easily now, and it's always warm there."

I walked through their house, breathing it in, thinking of Ben living there with Abby, raising their children. I saw some of the antique china from the Captain's House, some of the old leather-bound books, and lots of newer ones, books on gardening and quilting, biology and marine life, and many novels and children's books.

"I see you haven't given up reading, Ben. I remember your grandfather standing in his library."

"He's gone now. He died some years ago, and Grammie too, just last year. But we have some of their books and Abby's too," Ben said as he led me through the small dining room into the kitchen. "She loves to read. She's a school teacher."

Abby was sitting in a large rocking chair, her legs covered by a quilt, perhaps one she had made, I thought. She looked older than Ben. Her hair was wispy and her eyes sunken, but I could tell she had once been a pretty woman and her eyes were still bright. When she looked at Ben, I saw affection and humor. I envied what they shared, but simultaneously and surprisingly I felt happy for them both. Seeing them together made them seem almost ordinary, and the phantoms I had created began to melt away.

"Come in, I'm glad you're here, Becky," Abby said quietly. "Ben has told me about you, and I'm so pleased to have you as a neighbor." Her voice was tremulous, like a reed flute blown by a child, uneven but lovely, lilting but frail.

"I brought you a little present. I don't know what you might like, so I just brought something I like and hoped you would too." Abby's eyes seemed to shine even more brightly, and she reached her hands out to meet mine. They were thin and white, and I noticed bruises and the deep red pricks of needles blotching her forearms. Abby smiled, as if to say, "don't worry," and I smiled back.

"Well, this is a treat. What nice friends you have, Ben," Abby said. He was getting the pot of hot water off the stove, pouring a little into a large teapot and then pouring that out before putting in the tea. Abby watched him approvingly, and then said teasingly, "Isn't he well trained? Since I've been poorly he's taken such good care of me and now he can pour tea with the best of them."

When he sat down, Abby asked Ben if he would open the package. She was too weak to hold it, so he took the present. It looked small and feminine in his large hands, but he unwrapped it deftly, folded the tissue paper, then wound the ribbon around his fingers while she picked up the bath salts. Then he held the lavender for her to smell, and she said, "It's my favorite. I don't know how you knew, but I love lavender. I used to keep up the garden, but I haven't been able to and the lavender's 'peaked' this year. Thank you."

Ben put the pot of tea on the kitchen table, tested the cup against his own lips, and handed it to Abby.

"I'm so glad to meet you," I said turning to face Abby. "I'm sorry that you're ill. If there is anything I can do to help, I hope you'll let me know. I'm not far away and I don't have a regular job, so I can come if you need me or take you anywhere."

They looked at me, and then at each other and Abby said, "That's very kind of you, Becky. I'll take you up on that offer. It gets lonely for me here by myself. Neighbors drop in a lot, and family, but still, it gets too quiet."

"I worry when I have to be gone a long time," Ben added.

"You mean fishing?" I asked.

"Lobster mostly, so that keeps me close to home, but I also work for the university. I studied marine biology, and we're doing a study of the fisheries and also trying some aquaculture projects." He turned towards Abby and went on, "It's interesting work and it pays the bills, but sometimes I have to go out on the big fishing boats and I'm gone for weeks. I don't do that now—people understand. I go out, and then they transfer me to a boat coming home. Still, I don't like leaving, and sometimes we can't find enough people to check in."

"I've been this sick for just a few weeks," Abby apologized, "It hasn't been so bad. But I can't do much now, and I feel awful with Ben so busy and all the bills. I'm just so sorry," she said, turning first towards him and then to stare at her hands folded uselessly in her lap.

"Now Abby, you know that's not how it is, and I don't mind except to see you suffering," Ben said, looking tenderly at her. "Besides, you were the laborin' oar for too long," and they smiled at each other again.

We ate the store bought oatmeal cookies and I knew it was hard for Abby to serve something she hadn't made herself. After half an hour I thought Abby was getting tired so I said, "I should go now, but I'd like to come back. I want to see you again. Maybe when Ben has to go, if you want, I could bring a book and read to you, or just come and talk."

"I'd like that very much," Abby replied as she laid her head back on the chair. I stood up and put my hand over hers because she seemed too tired to shake hands and then I walked to the door and Ben followed me out.

"I'm so glad I met her, Ben. She's a wonderful person. It makes me happy to see you with her, really it does," I said, looking down and trying to control the quivering in my voice.

"Well, I could tell she likes you. You don't make her feel pressured. Some people want to talk and talk," he said sadly, turning to look through the screen door at Abby as she rested her head against the chair. "Don't know when to leave, but you see what she needs. I'd like it fine if you were with her."

I nodded and started to walk away but then he said, "God knows it's a free country. You can live where you want," and before I could answer he closed the door.

As I walked home through the woods I listened to the words again, "I'd like it fine if you were with her." But then he had added, "It's a free country," and I thought he meant I could do what I wanted, but that he wished I had not come to live on the island, his island as he had once called it. His reaction wasn't what I'd wanted, but somehow it had to be all right. He wasn't mine, but I was drawn to Abby, felt her wisdom and kindness. How very odd, I thought, I didn't expect this. I didn't expect to like her, so much and so easily. I wonder what she knows about me? The idea made me wince, but then I thought, she couldn't know about me. He wouldn't have told her. She was so welcoming. I wanted to see Abby again soon, but Ben was home for the next two weeks so I waited.

Chapter Twelve

As I settled into a routine, the world of what could have been in which I had lived so much of my life, began to dissipate in the realities of caring for my house. Where did all that angst and passion go? I asked myself sometimes. I thought it was like sand on a beach and that the tide and the wind and rain from storms leached it away. The thought made me flinch as I looked at myself in the mirror and saw a middle-aged woman with graying hair, sagging breasts and hopes, because I couldn't yet see that sand builds new dunes on other beaches.

As my house became more habitable, I thought about naming it. I'm going to call it Captain's House, I decided. That's what it was, and it's going to last a lot longer than I will. I asked a sign maker to carve a small wooden sign for the house that looked as if it could be on a ship. After I picked it up, I got out my toolbox and a short ladder so I could hang it over the door.

One morning Helen, my neighbor, brought me two kittens she said needed a home. She wondered if I could take them until someone else did. They were curled up in a tiny basket. Each had long gray fur and whiskers, a stunted little tail, and blue eyes.

When I went to buy them food and kitty litter, Ruthie said, "Helen gave you the kittens did she? She said she would, thought you might like the company, being by yourself and all."

"Oh, I thought she found them."

"Found them in her barn with her mother cat, she did!" Ruthie replied. "She's just being neighborly. Those are two Maine Coon cats; fetch a good price if she wanted to sell them, but she's given them to you as a present."

"I had no idea. What a kind thing to do. I guess she just told me she found them so I would feel all right if I didn't want to keep them, but I do. She's right about the company. I don't feel lonely here, but it would be good having something alive in the house besides myself and the plants."

They were mine and they were a present because someone was thinking of me and wanted me to be happy. I loved watching them playing with sunlight on the checked kitchen floor, chasing shadows or each other's runty tails, trying to clean themselves but falling over when they lost their balance, curling up on my lap when I was reading, and sleeping in the drawer of an old table that they could get into through a hole in the back.

❦

Stan Brown, Bernie's husband, did repairs that required more skill, but he taught me to paint and wallpaper. I liked stripping away the worn and soiled paper and finding names of the men who had put up the previous paper, signed and dated: "Elmer Stanley, June, 1976"; "George Bunker, 1873." I learned to clean well and efficiently and to do the things that women had done for centuries—things that I had always hired out. I was learning to take care of myself as well as the house—scrubbing floors and washing the windows, scouring the dirt from the old house, seeing rooms shine as the sun streamed in, and as I did, I also healed myself. One night I began to recognize this, discovering what I was feeling as I so often did by writing about it.

THIS OLD MIDDLE-AGED HOUSE

I started with the land.
Found the shadow of the barn in composted black earth.
The vegetable garden coughed up cows' teeth and halter buckles,
Nails and shards.

I found where farmers had thrown the season's crop of rocks
to the edges
and then the garbage.
I cleared away glass and garters, rusted skillets and milk pails;
planted trillium and trout lily
and wild azalea in the woods.

Then I tackled the house
Scraping layers of old paint off clapboards,
freeing gutters of clammy growth,
Digging out rot, daubing leaks.
I painted the doors hemlock green
and built the steps with granite blocks from an old foundation.

But now that it looks perfect to the outside eye,
I see the layers of interior
arteriosclerosis.

Now must I peel away what was
too deep to see,
or to be seen.

If I could have, I would have
started from inside out
not outside in.

At first Stan called me Mrs. Evans so I called him Mr. Brown. He was about my age, with a deeply tanned face and dark eyes, a circle of gray hair around his bald scalp, and the tips of two fingers missing on one hand. He knew how to caulk the sinks, check the sills, split and get in the wood, clean the gutters, and build whatever I could imagine. I wanted shutters because I remembered them from my first visit and to replace the wooden tracery missing from around the doors. I wanted to rebuild the bookshelves, and Stan suggested building wooden covers for the radiators. When he finished one it was so beautiful that we decided he would do several more, and after awhile we called each other Stan and Becky.

Everything we fixed led our eyes to a new project, and I knew Stan would be helping me for a long time. He came over almost every day, though he had other people he worked for, and slowly the house began to look beautiful again. Stan helped me figure out what had to be done immediately and what could wait, and together we planned a complete revival. Stan brought other men and women to work on the house, to re-putty all the windows, paint the larger rooms, re-sand the floors, and put in a new furnace, all of which gave me a chance to get to know people on the island.

❦

One day, as we were working on the guest bathroom, Jane said, "Timmy's marrying the Phillips girl." I was sitting in the claw foot tub trying to work out the stain with the paste of Zud and water that Jane had prescribed. I kept scrubbing diligently as the stain began to reward my efforts by fading. Funny, I thought, some where else it might even be pretty, a feather of blue and rust, like flame stitch on a chair seat.

"Wow. Angie and Timmy," Susan said.

"Ayuh, Angeline Susannah Bickford Phillips, that's a pile of names for a little sprig of a girl, but Timmy thinks she's some cute." Jane paused then said, "I don't know," under her breath. I wanted to ask what she didn't know, but I waited, hoping they would continue. After what seemed a long time Jane drew in her breath and said, "Don't seem quite right marrying a girl from away. I mean *we* never even thought about doing that."

"Well, remember, I'm not from here," Susan replied.

"That's different," Jane retorted. "Your people are from Maine, even if it was potato country. You knew pretty much what you were getting into."

"Where do you think they'll live?" Susan asked hesitantly.

"That's the bit... the trouble. Danged if I know," Jane replied, looking over at me.

"What's she like?" I asked.

"Fine girl," said Jane brightening for a moment. "We like her fine. Educated, going to college. Been there two years already. She went out a few times with Timmy last summer and she came up and stayed with us a couple of times during the year, and now she's come back early to their cottage. Nothing's ready," she added almost indignantly, "and now they're getting married!" Jane sighed and gave the sink faucet a hard rub with the old scrap of towel she used for polishing. "Hubert says he don't know what she sees in Timmy, but I do—same thing I saw in Hubert," and she and Susan both laughed.

"What do you mean?" I asked.

"Well, it's just hormones at their age. It don't make sense. I mean some summer girl falls in love with the stern man on a lobster boat. Kid doesn't have his own boat yet."

"Guess he will soon," Susan observed.

My mind spun back to my own first love, and I was grateful when Susan asked Jane about the wedding.

"When're they getting married?"

"Soon, they said, got me worried about if they had to, but we didn't ask. They say this summer. Here. I'm sure it's going to be some party. The Phillips' cottage. It's so big."

Susan laughed, and Jane continued, "I know they think we're good people, and we are. Hubert did some work for them. But I couldn't call them Jim and Barbara. Imagine calling Mrs. Phillips Barb or Babs!" and both women laughed, but a layer of fear in their laughter caught my ear.

"You don't have to have a big wedding. I didn't," I volunteered. When they both turned towards me and looked surprised again I added, "The man I married came from a family with a lot more money than my family, but he didn't want a big wedding." They looked even more surprised, which made me wonder if they thought all summer people were equally and impossibly wealthy.

The wind and rain lashed my face as we walked into the little department store in Clintwood, Virginia, to get married. When he proposed, Jordie told me he didn't want a big wedding. I thought we would marry in Washington, but my mother and Taylor preferred Nantucket. They made it all too fancy and big. My mother ordered 500 wedding invitations, and they rented most of a large hotel on the island, two tents, and a well-known band.

Thursday evening two weeks before the wedding, as I sat staring at the guest list of people I didn't know, I felt my skin itching and I was horrified to find raised welts covered my face, chest, and back with hives as purple as crushed grapes. My mother was already asleep, but when Taylor came out of his office, he gasped and rushed me to the hospital. In the emergency room, the young doctor asked me what I'd eaten and what I'd been doing. When I told him, "Getting married," he frowned and asked how I felt. He caught me off guard. "I'm really excited" I said, but my voice was flat and he raised his eyebrows. "No, really, really I am. It's just a little difficult now. My mother and stepfather..." But I couldn't explain so I just stared down at my sandals and studied my feet.

"Your mother and stepfather?"

"They want a big wedding, and his parents do too," I said and looked at the image of my blotched face in the mirror over the sink in the examination room. "What am I going to do?" I asked him plaintively.

"You're going to calm down or elope," the doctor said, "and I'm giving you a prescription to get rid of the hives. We got married last summer. It was hell. Just dealing with my wife's parents—it's like the one time they can outspend even themselves and put on a show to impress their friends and... So you need to deal with it. The hives are just a symptom of stress."

When I called Jordie to tell him about the hives, I said, "The doctor told me we should elope. It's making me a nervous wreck dealing with my mother and Taylor. They make me feel guilty because they're doing all these things I don't want them to do."

"That's cool with me," he said. "We'll talk about it tomorrow when I pick you up. It would serve all of them right," and then he laughed his icicle laugh and I imagined it twisting in my mother.

We drove to a small town in Virginia that made a side business of quick marriages. After the ceremony, I called my mother.

"We're in Virginia," I told her.

"Virginia!" But you missed the fitting for your dress."

"We got married," I replied. I could feel shock and anger coursing through

the line until the phone felt so hot in my hands that I dropped it.

"Jordie," I said, opening the phone booth door, "please talk to her."

"She's your mother; deal with it," he said with a sneer and turned away.

I picked up the dangling phone and said, "We just wanted to get married without the fuss," and I heard her stifled crying, low, thick, and muffled by her hands.

I remember unintelligible sounds of talking in the background and suddenly Taylor's voice loud in my ear, "What have you done to your mother now! After all the time and trouble, and not a little expense on our part, after all that your mother's done for you, you hurt her like this?"

"We just wanted..." I said, and I started to cry too.

"You're a spoiled, hurtful little girl, Becky, and you're going to regret this," he replied.

As I scrubbed the old bathtub in my new house, I knew Taylor had been right, I had wanted to hurt my mother, and I did regret it. I ran away instead of confronting what I wanted, or didn't. How different Katherine's wedding had been. We planned it together and she and Mark married in the garden at my house, well, Richard's house, in Boston. A small wedding, just the people they loved and who loved them. It seemed right, and I was glad we could help them have what they wanted. If only I had known myself and what I wanted when I married.

"So, it's Timmy and Angie's wedding," I said softly, "maybe they'll be able to have it the way they want. "Do they love each other?"

"Yes," Jane said. "Yes, they're young, and I know some of it's hormones like I said, but I think they do love each other."

"That's what counts," said Susan.

"If I can help in any way, you just let me know," I offered.

Jane grinned sheepishly and said, "Thank you. I thought I should get one of them etiquette books, but with you here maybe I won't have to!"

•

Ten days after I met Abby, I found a note in my mailbox from Ben. "I'm leaving tomorrow for a trip and I'll be gone for a week. Abby would like to have you stop by for tea any afternoon. Three o'clock is usually good. Just knock on the kitchen door."

The next morning I baked a dozen shortbread cookies and walked to Abby and Ben's house. After I knocked on the kitchen door, I heard Abby say, "Come in, deah," and I opened the door to the kitchen. Abby was sitting in the rocking chair, with a quilt tucked around her. "I'm so glad you came by. Ruthie walked over from the village on her lunch break and then I took a nap, so I'm eager for some company."

"I was hoping you'd be ready for tea and I brought some cookies."

Abby asked me to turn on the stove and told me where the teacups were. Her manner was gracious yet also matter-of-fact, as if we had been friends for years. She didn't apologize for asking for help, she just accepted it. After I poured two cups of tea and put the plate of cookies on the table, I sat in the chair near her.

"So how's the house coming along?" Abby asked.

"Well. I'm beginning to feel settled, and I've got two kittens that Helen gave me, and they're very good company."

"Do you miss your life in Boston?"

"No. Sometimes I miss people, but I don't miss the city."

"Do you get lonely?" Abby asked.

"No—not really. There's different kinds of lonely, I think."

"Different kinds of lonely?" The thought hung in the air for a moment before I added, "Yes, I miss people, but I don't feel as lonely as when I was married." Why did I say that, I wondered and I tried to read Abby's face, but she was just nodding in agreement.

I wasn't comfortable pursuing that conversation, so I asked Abby about her garden, and after Abby told me she missed caring for it, I volunteered to help. "I can bring over plants from the Captain's House that need to be divided. You tell me where you want them planted and I'll take care of them when I come over." Abby seemed to appreciate the offer, but I resisted slipping into the friendship she made so easy.

The next time I came to have tea with Abby, I brought divisions of delphinium and lavender from the Captain's House and Abby told me she would like to be able to see the blue stalks of delphinium from the kitchen window, and the lavender along the path to the house.

A few visits later as I settled into my now familiar seat, Abby asked, "So, who did you marry? You didn't tell me last time."

"Who plural. I married twice," I replied. "The first time to someone who drank too much and worked too little. I wanted to leave a long time before I did, but I was too scared."

"Scared?" Abby said, a look of concern darkening her pale face.

"Not that he would hurt me, though a couple of times he did. I just didn't want to be a divorced woman. I didn't want my children to have divorced parents. I wanted us to be good parents. Most of all I wanted my children to have a good father, but I felt like a single mother most of the time." I could feel the tears coming, and I picked up the teacup to steady myself. "I failed in that, Abby, I really failed."

"That's pretty harsh."

"Yes. But I know I did. He hardly ever saw them. He drifted away after I left him, after we left, just out of their lives. I think that's why I married again. I wanted the children to have a father. I wanted security. 'Social security.' Just like my mother, only it worked out better for her."

"How did you get out of your first marriage?" Abby asked.

"It's a story. I don't think you want to hear such a long story."

"Becky, what could be more interesting? You've come from another world and here you are willing to share it with me. What could be better?" Abby replied smiling.

"I married Jordie and hoped we'd live happily ever after." I laughed, a nervous titter I thought as I listened to myself and wondered what was making me so self-conscious.

"But you didn't?"

"No. At least not for very long. In the beginning it was okay, then I got pregnant. We had two children pretty fast, Stephen and Katherine, but then I didn't have time to do things when Jordie wanted. I couldn't just drop everything and go out with him, and I couldn't drink and smoke pot the way he did and the way we had before the kids were born."

I wondered if I was shocking Abby, but she turned to me and said softly, "Seems you were just a bit ahead of your time. At least you got married. Kids today—they don't even bother with that. And the drugs. The drugs are getting real bad here."

I could see Jordie lying on our bed, hear his words slurring as he yelled at me, hear the children crying. "When he was out, I wanted him home, and when he was home I wished he'd leave."

"So how did you get away?"

"I left a couple of times. Sometimes he'd disappear for days. And we'd go to stay with my mother and stepfather Taylor in Washington. I got to be pretty close to the couple who worked for them, because my mother and he were away often. Sadie cooked and Lemuel drove and did all the odd jobs. They looked after us."

I looked at Abby, wondering what she thought about having servants, but Abby was smiling. "It's all right, I know about servants. Some of my best friends are servants," she said and we both laughed. I loved hearing Abby laugh, but then I saw her wince and put a tissue to her mouth. "It's all right, really," Abby said. "I don't laugh enough, and some of my people were servants. It was the best way to make money in the summer. Did you go back?"

"I just felt so lonely, and like I wasn't good enough even for a drunk and I shouldn't leave him, not for him, not for the kids, not even for me."

"I don't understand why you didn't think you could do better. You were young and pretty and you had some money. I would have just walked out the door if a man treated me like that," Abby said almost angrily.

"Oh, Abby," I sighed, the guilt washing over me. "I see it differently now, a bit, but I thought at first he was handsome. He looked a little like my father, and he seemed so confident because he was always putting people down, always superior, and I mistook his sarcasm for confidence. It seems odd now, but I thought I would be safe, and that's what I wanted. I just didn't see the bad things. And then I was in the middle of them, and I didn't know how to get out. I think I didn't want to abandon him. It just seemed a terrible thing to do—to leave him—to leave anyone and it makes me sad now to think about it. I think he needed me, and I just left him." I could feel the tears welling up again, cramping my throat. "It doesn't make a lot of sense, I know that, but it was all the sense I could make then."

Abby sat quietly, and then said, "What persuaded you to go back that time?"

"He came down to Washington, and he was all cleaned up. He'd cut his hair, and he had on a suit. I learned later that his father told him he'd cut him out of his will if he didn't get us back, but at the time I was really touched. I thought it meant he loved us more than the booze or drugs. But it didn't last long."

"What happened?"

"It took me too long, but I began to see he wasn't funny, he was often cruel, he was selfish, and that the children, his children—my children—were anxious around him." I could see him roughhousing with Stephen, but there was no love, no fun in it and always it ended with Stephen fighting back tears and trying to be tough. "I began to see that Jordie was never going to work, never going back to college, never going to write the book he talked about writing. He was never going to do anything but drink and smoke pot and get angry and he was never going to care about me or even his kids. I see now that he left us a long time before I left him."

"How did you feel?" Abby asked.

"Feel? I didn't feel much of anything. I just seemed to get smaller and smaller, as if I was disappearing," I admitted. "He got worse. He'd do things like, well it was just gross." I stopped talking and stared at my hands. I could see him as he came home drunk and wanted to have sex. Not making love, just sex, rough, hard and ugly. I could see him walking around with his fly undone, a three-day grizzle on his chin, and clothes he hadn't changed. "I should have realized he was really depressed," I said, "but I was still so young myself. I didn't know what to do, so I cleaned up after him, and tried to stay out of his way." I saw his turds floating on the water in the toilet. "I felt as if I was trying to take care of three children, and I was exhausted," I said quietly.

"What made you leave for good?"

"For good. It was for good too. It got so I couldn't bear to look at him anymore. I can see him rolled up on the bed like a crushed beer can, and there was always a bottle of Harvey's Bristol Cream nearby. His pale blond hair—I'd liked it at first, but it was always so dirty, dirty and stringy and the sneer, always the sneer, etched across his mouth." I shivered from the memory. "I found out from his sister that the engagement ring had belonged to his alcoholic aunt who had fallen off a bridge on her estate and drowned. Then I noticed a flaw in the central stone. It was hidden before, but now I saw it and it kept getting worse, working its way across the emerald as if a tiny invisible hammer was hitting it." I stopped and looked at Abby. "Isn't that amazing really. The reason I left was that I saw the flaw and even the ring as a metaphor for the whole marriage. That's trite, but that was it. I knew I had to leave, so I called my mother, told her I had to get out, and she said to come home."

"I think we could use some more tea. That's quite a story. You were very brave Becky. Brave to stay, brave to leave."

"It didn't feel that way. I felt like a coward for staying so long. And I didn't know what I'd done to my kids. They were so young."

"You did the best you could. That's all any of us can do, even if we don't have any idea what that really is. What did you do next?" Abby asked.

"We went in a cab from the airport to my mother's house. Lemuel opened the door and he said, 'It's all right now. You come in. You home now, Miss Becky,' and then he picked up Stephen in one arm and Katherine in the other and walked into the front hallway and carried them down the long back hall to the kitchen. I can hear him. 'Look who I brought in from the rain," he said to Sadie. 'I just found these forlornsome folks on the steps and I thought they needed those warm chocolate chip cookies you just took from the oven.' I remember that word, 'forlornsome,' because it seemed so perfect. I started crying and Sadie came out of the kitchen and put her arms around me." Again, I felt the tears and I looked over at Abby. "I'm sorry. I guess it's still raw even after all these years. I hadn't thought about it in a long time."

"It's all right," Abby said. "Have some more tea."

"Sadie hugged me and then Stephen and Katherine. She said to me, 'It's about time, Miss Becky. It's about time you come home and brought my grandchildren back here.' My mother and stepfather came into the kitchen right then and we all just stood there and hugged and cried. It was wonderful really. They didn't ask me any questions; they didn't make me feel ashamed, and we settled into a routine for a while. Taylor played checkers with Stephen and taught him how to read the daily stock market numbers. My mother Anne got Katherine to work with her in the garden and showed her how to cut flowers and stand them in hot water to make them drink, and they even enjoyed collecting bugs and slugs together. It was quite wonderful, really quite remarkable. We lived there for a year, but they were gone a lot. Nantucket for the summer, Hobe Sound in the winter. We were by ourselves with Lemuel and Sadie, and the kids loved it. Taylor got me a good divorce lawyer and Jordie didn't bother us again. I think his parents were so fed up with him that they told him to leave us alone."

"And after the year?"

"I knew I had to have my own place. And I decided to finish college. I got into Georgetown University, which was great because I lived very near by and so it was easier with the kids, and I finished my degree," I replied.

"Well, drink to that," Abby said as she raised her teacup.

"Abby, I'm sorry. I've poured out my story, and I haven't learned a thing about you. I've tired you out." Abby was leaning back against the chair and she looked pale.

"Becky, I've enjoyed listening. I'm a little 'peak-ed' now, but we'll talk again. There's not so much to tell. Just stories from Brant's Island. They used to sew us up in our Long Johns in October and let us out again in April. Not sure you want to know much more about that!"

❦

Stan built the first two of four bunks in the children's guest room that folded out from the corners of the room on strong ropes. A ladder built of peeled tree branches latched onto the edge of the bunk when a child wanted to climb up or down. Stan brought me a sample of life-size tree trunks, branches and leaves as well as birds and animals that he cut from pine and plywood and painted.

"I was thinking of making a woods scene in the bunk room," he explained.

"What gave you the idea, Stan?" I asked.

"Thought of it when I saw the room. It's my favorite in your house," he replied. "Always liked the woods and the animals. Got sick of the sea. Dad faced our house into the woods 'cause he couldn't stand looking at the sea all day and all night too. Let the trees grow up all around us to block it out. Summer people, no offense, chopped 'em down. Too bad—good trees, and they kept us warm for the winter. These are just samples.

What do you think?" he asked earnestly.

"Yes, I like it," I answered, responding more to his excitement than my own conviction and not sure I could see his vision.

Stan made some trees with pegs for clothes, and he completed a few of the animals and birds that would soon be hopping and flying around the room. It was the only room besides bathrooms, the laundry and closets that didn't have a view of the sea. Instead, the windows faced the fields and woods and the room became their extension.

❧

Katherine and her children visited me for the last two weeks of August, while her husband was on a business trip. Sammy and Nina, now three and five, loved the bunkroom. The floor was painted grass green and the ceiling sky blue, and the circular hooked rug on the floor looked like a patch of grass and flowers. Nina and Sammy spent a lot of their time with Stan, drawing birds and animals they saw near the house. Nina asked Stan to make the toad that lived in the garden and Stan cut one out of pine and let her help him paint the base color, a rusty brown. Sammy wanted the Chickadees that lived in the bush outside his window to come inside, so Stan made a little wooden Chickadee and let Sammy help him paint it gray.

On the first Saturday after Katherine arrived, she and I went into the village to get food while we left the children playing with Stan and his wife, Bernie. As we walked, Katherine said, "I think I'm beginning to understand why you love it here, Mom. I feel as if I'm walking in slow motion and seeing things I haven't noticed for years. Like the colors of the flowers and the smell of the air. Everyone knows you and you seem to like everyone."

"The scale fits me," I said. "I think I can know people and myself more deeply here. Fewer distractions."

"I love seeing you working on the house—it's a project for sure."

"We have a long way to go, but it's fun," I replied smiling as I looked over the field towards the harbor below. "We really do have a long way to go with the house, but at least it's clean and habitable. I'm sorry your room isn't finished, but Stan got so excited about his forest room that we've neglected the guest room. It's a bit Spartan."

"But the forest room. That's really special. It's so much fun, Mom, it's not like anything you've done before," she observed.

"Well, I can't take credit. It was Stan's idea."

"But you let him do it," Katherine said, "and you're letting the kids enjoy helping."

"Thank you."

"And the guest room's great too. The bed's comfortable. The room is so pretty and sunny, and the view never seems to be the same. I watched someone taking in lobster pots this morning. I couldn't really see much in the fog except that it's a lot of work."

"Did you see the name of the boat?"

"Yes, it was the *Tea Kettle*. What a funny name!"

"Oh, that's Tinker's boat. His wife's always got a kettle boiling. His father's boat is *Kettle of Fish*, and his grandfather's was *Pot 'n Kettle* because his grandmother's maiden name was Kettle, and the old man's other grandson called him Pot instead of Pa."

"See, I told you. You know everyone and everything here," Katherine said.

"It seems so. It's rather satisfying, at least until you think about the rest of the world and how little we know about that."

"Do most people go lobstering?"

"Yes, they call it fishing. There's that and care-taking, and working on boats. Some people work on the big island or the mainland. I'm learning more about fishing," I replied. "I know a fisherman and I go to stay with his wife when he's away."

"Why does she need someone to stay with her?" Katherine asked. "Is she sick?"

"Yes, she's got cancer."

"I'm sorry."

"I think she's doing pretty well, but I'm not sure," I answered hesitantly.

"What kind is it?" Katherine asked.

"I'm not sure of that either. Either ovarian or uterine. We don't talk about it."

Katherine frowned and said, "I hope it's uterine. That's a lot easier to deal with than ovarian. I've got a friend whose mother has that and it's really a death sentence."

My stomach tightened at the words and I felt dizzy, then surprised at my visceral reaction.

"I'm sorry. I shouldn't have said that, but ovarian is really serious. Is she a good friend?"

"Yes, actually she is. It surprises me, but she's wise and funny and I like spending time with her. I've grown to care about her," I replied.

We walked on towards the village and I looked out over the harbor. "Let's walk over to the library. I want to show you where I spend so much of my time and I want you to meet Polly, she's the librarian."

"I'd like that," Katherine answered. "I'll be able to picture you there when I'm at home."

The thought of Katherine thinking about me made me smile. "That's a nice thought, you thinking about me. It's sort of a role reversal. I thought parents did all the thinking about their children, not the other way around."

"Mom. That's silly," Katherine exclaimed. "I think about you a lot. I used to think about Dad too, but now I don't so much."

Again I tensed, and I looked at Katherine, but couldn't read anything in her face. "I'm sorry," I said. "Have you seen him?"

"No, not since the last time I told you about when he showed up at our house drunk a few years ago. Nothing since then, though Papa sends me and his grandchildren a nice check every year at Christmas."

When we went into the library, Polly was sitting behind the large oak desk fitting protective covers on new books. Polly was a middle-aged grandmother with thick gray hair she usually wore in braids. She smiled when she saw us and said, "I was wondering when you'd get here. I've missed you the last few days but I knew you were busy. This must be your daughter Katherine, but where are the children?"

"Oh, they're with Stan and Bernie painting butterflies for their forest room."

Polly stood up and held out her hands. "So you're Katherine. You have your mother's eyes, and her smile. Do you love to read too?"

"Not so much. That's Stephen's job. He's the reader. But I like to read to my kids the way Mom used to read to us."

"Well, come over to the children's corner and maybe you'll see a book you'd like to take back with you. And your mother likes to read to children, does she?" Polly said, winking broadly at Katherine. "That's a job that needs doing here—maybe we can get her to read for Children's Hour some time."

Katherine and I walked over to the children's section and stood in front of a display Polly had put together from a contest she'd run the previous month asking people to take or make pictures illustrating Seuss books. There were photographs of several children jumping on their father's large stomach next to *Hop on Pop*, and a collage of an elephant and a nest next to *Horton Hatches an Egg*. Someone had taken a photograph of a large Maine coon cat wearing a red and white striped hat, with its paws up on a desk, and Polly had opened the *Cat in the Hat*, next to the framed picture.

I heard the heavy door open and shut and then Ben's voice as he said hello to Polly and told her he wanted to pick up the books Abby had requested. I turned around to face him, and he looked at me and nodded.

"Ben, this is Becky's daughter Katherine come to visit for a bit,"

Polly said, as she got up from behind her desk and walked him over to Katherine and me.

"Hello, Ben," I said as lightly as I could. "I'd like you to meet Katherine, my daughter. She's visiting for a couple of weeks with my grandchildren."

I watched Ben as he walked towards us and when he and Katherine shook hands. But another picture sliced through my mind. Ben holding Katherine against his chest when she had croup as a child, his arms around her and her small face with its blond curls tucked against his chest. The thought was so swift and so deep that I could feel blood rushing to my face, and I tried consciously to modulate my voice as evenly as I could.

I could hear him say, "It's so nice to meet you. You have your mother's eyes," but all I could think was that Katherine looked like Ben. The truth was that Jordie looked like Ben, and Ben looked like my father, and I saw them in that instant as one man, and I could feel my heart jump at the realization and the sense of loss and confusion that swept over me.

"We'd better be getting back," I said. "We've left the kids with Stan and Bernie and I don't want to impose on them too long."

As we walked back Katherine said, "So what's going on there?"

"What do you mean?"

"What I mean is what's going on between you two?"

"Nothing." I said, but it was more an admission than a denial.

"There's something there, Mom. I know it," Katherine said firmly, "What's going on?"

"There's nothing to tell. Really." I protested again.

"Mom, you don't get rattled that easily. You got nervous and your face looked like a cherry."

I walked in silence for a while trying to figure out what to say. As we rounded the turn in the road and saw the Captain's House Katherine said again, "Mom?"

"It was a long time ago. I knew him when I was a girl and we came here for the summer. He was my friend, but we couldn't be friends. Not really, so we lost touch. I guess there has always been some chemistry between us, but you can't build a life on chemistry."

"Is he why you're here?" Katherine asked bluntly.

"No," I said again, but this time I meant it. "He's married and Abby is his wife."

"You mean the woman you visit who's sick?"

"Yes."

"Isn't that a little strange?"

"Yes, I guess so, but I really care about his wife, and I didn't come here to be near him. I don't think I did. I just loved the house. I'd been there when I was younger."

"With him?" Katherine exclaimed, "Mom!"

"You don't understand," I replied, my voice rising. "The house was beautiful when I saw it. And his family. They were so happy and warm, and I thought that's what a family should be about. That's what I wanted for my family, but we weren't that way. That's what I wanted for you, for you and for Stephen. That's what I want for all of us now." There was such anguish in my voice that Katherine took my hand. I drew in my breath and continued, "That's what I thought the house could make possible. And, it's coming true. You're here; we're having a good time. So are the kids. Stephen will be here later in the summer, or maybe in the fall. Maybe you'll come back and we'll have Thanksgiving together."

Katherine let go of my hand and said, "Yes. But what about him? Do you see him? What about his wife?" and then she stopped walking and stared at me.

"I see Abby more than I see him. I did feel awkward at first, I'll admit. He meant something to me once, but that really was a long time ago, now. Now, he's married and I'm not going to intrude on that. Besides, he loves his wife, and she loves him, and that's all there is to that."

"That sounds nice, Mom," Katherine replied, "but I don't know."

We went into the house and walked into the bunkroom where Stan, Bernie and the two children sat on the floor together. Sam was painting a base coat on the butterflies while Stan put pipe cleaner whiskers on a rabbit they had painted the day before and he had over-painted with details that morning. Bernie was helping Nina mix purple paint for a butterfly's wings.

When Katherine and the children left ten days later, there were a lot more animals and birds on the walls and Stan had a list of others the children wanted him to make. Katherine whispered to me as we hugged before she and the children got on the mail boat, "Be careful, Mom. I know you love it here for many reasons. I just hope you can keep them all straight."

Chapter Thirteen

One morning when clouds were heavy over the harbor and the boats couldn't leave, I was sitting at one of the green wooden tables in the library reading a history of the island. Ben walked in and I felt him watching me from the door. Instead of nodding and walking to the desk to pick up books for Abby, this time he walked over to where I was sitting, and I clenched my hands on the book I was reading.

"How are you?" I managed to say.

"Well enough. Fishing's good. Abby really appreciates your visits. Says it's nice to have a new friend, one who knows books."

"I enjoy seeing her. She's a wonderful woman," and then I paused and said what I had been wanting to say for so many years. "Ben, I'm sorry," I murmured. "I'm so sorry. I was so sorry then and I'm so sorry now."

"All right," he said tersely. "Leave it be. I just wanted to thank you for all the time you're spending with Abby."

I started to reply, but he turned and walked away.

❦

I visited Abby on many afternoons when I had finished writing and my chores. Abby had good days and bad. On bad days she would look up when I knocked and walked into the kitchen and say, "Well, I can't be much company today, so I am glad you have a book. Thank you for being here," and then she would sink back into the chair and slip away for hours. When she woke, she always seemed surprised to find me still there, but I couldn't leave her now, not alone, because she was so weak and because I was growing to love her.

At times, Abby would slip into a short sleep and then wake up and continue a sentence where she had left off. When she drifted away, I read. When Abby was awake we talked and I got to know a little more about life on the island. Abby told me the history and gossip about people and sometimes I read the newspaper to her. She enjoyed the stories, like the one about a disturbance that prompted someone to call the police who found an inebriated young man singing to a herd of cows. When a man steered his boat onto a ledge he had skirted since he was a baby, she proclaimed him "Numb'r than a hake, or stupid drunk."

"Numb'r than a what?" I asked.

Abby explained, "a fish. It's just a way of saying dumb, like dumber than a truckload of rocks, or whale manure. So dumb he don't even suspect nothin' is what you use to say he's really dumb." I laughed, remembering that Ben had used the same expression years ago.

Abby talked about some of the summer people and the ways they were "uppity." "You know," she said one day, "My mother told me in the old days, if you were on the sidewalk in Bar Harbor or Northeast Harbor and you saw a summer person, you were supposed to step into the street to let them pass."

"That's awful," I replied, genuinely shocked.

"Well, there was so much money, so many 'millionists' they called 'em. There was a woman my grandmother worked for who put gold fixtures in the bathrooms of her cottage in Bar Harbor, said they were cheaper because they didn't need cleaning. They treated people like furniture. They still do that." She paused, looked at me, and continued, "You go into the newspaper store there at the beginning of the season and they're all in there greeting each other in those high-pitched baby voices they use, saying dahling this and dearie that, and oh you haven't aged a minute, and asking, 'Is anyone here yet; just no one's here yet.' All the time we're keeping the island going, but they don't think about that. So much money." She stopped again and sighed and then looked at me almost sternly, "Still do. Like you, you have the money to buy the house, to fix it up the way we would have liked to, but couldn't."

I couldn't find anger or envy in her eyes, so I asked, "What do you think of that, of me buying the house, Abby?"

"I wondered," she said, fixing me with her eyes, "If you were doing it because you still loved Ben, but..." stopping when she saw me wince. Abby looked at me directly, but gently, and with a forcefulness that drove its way into me like a nail. I thought that perhaps my eyes had given me away. "I know you loved him once, but it was a long time ago. There's no harm in loving someone, and I can't blame you, can I? I love him too!" and then she laughed. It was good to hear her laugh, a light tinkling in her throat, like a Chipping Sparrow, but then her eyes darkened and she said, "And I loved him even when we hurt each other."

"You loved him once," the phrase bumped against the corners of my mind and I thought, "Oh God, what did he say? What does she know?" but I said only, "What do you mean, Abby? You've hinted a couple of times, but I've been so caught up in my own self I haven't been a good listener."

"There were times we were cold to each other," Abby replied. I'd get so lonely and mad that he wasn't home with us. The kids and work. You know. I was just tired and lonely."

"What's the harm in that?"

"No harm, though I'd get cranky. He'd come home exhausted and he'd find a cranky wife. I'd be mean and cold. I didn't want to be, but I couldn't put it all into words."

I nodded, "The times when you should say what you mean, but you think they should just figure it out."

"I should have left it at that, but I got angry. And there was a man on the island then. He's not here now, but I hurt Ben, and I'm sorry. He knows that." We were quiet for a while and then Abby said, "And I always knew there was someone. Someone in his heart, someone deep down. I just didn't know who, and I was jealous of her. But that was so long ago. A lot of things become easier as I get older. Of course, a lot of other things have gotten harder."

"I don't know what to say, Abby," I answered truthfully, shocked back into numbness.

"Did you love him?" Abby asked.

"Not real love. It was more like puppy love, a summer love," I lied. "I didn't think I was supposed to love him, and so I didn't. But I know he's a good man." The words were stilted, what I was supposed to say, but I didn't want to admit to the years of fantasies I had woven around myself with Ben when I couldn't face my life, or how much I had wanted him to hold me.

"I can love the house now, though," I continued, feeling more comfortable walking on safer ground. "I loved the fullness of the house, full of people and family, and I thought I could fill it again. I loved the old Captain and his house and the view of the big island. The house seemed perfect when I saw it before. I loved the house when I saw it again because it was quiet and peaceful but I've worried that I hurt you because I could do these things and..."

"No, you haven't hurt us," Abby said thoughtfully. "And in some ways it's easier that you're here and not a ghost between us, and I think it's gone by. The people who hurt the house hurt us. They were so arrogant. They didn't even bother to find out who had owned the house and what the history was. They called it 'High Jinx.'" She grimaced. "What an awful name! They smoked a lot of pot. Just rich young hippies, and they tore out the library and put that horrible linoleum in the kitchen. We hated watching them make the changes. Ripping apart the library. Putting in that rancid carpet. It was plug ugly even when it was new. Worse actually."

She paused to catch her breath and sip some tea. "And we couldn't do anything about it, that hurt."

"It's different with you," she continued. "You treasure the house. We know that. And when you named it Captain's House we knew you cared about who had lived there before. Stan told us how happy you are there. He says, 'she's some worker that woman,' and around here that's the best compliment you can get." She stopped again, and then took a big breath and said, "And the other women, Jane and Susan, they're amazed to see you sitting in the old tub scrubbing until you work up a sweat. No, we don't mind. You're good for the house, and that house is good for you."

"Will you come to visit me?" I asked. "You could sit on the porch or kitchen and watch the sea? We'd bring you in the island's golf cart, and I'd set up a chair and a foot stool for you."

"I'd like to see it again, I would. Maybe when I feel a little better."

*

She didn't come, and I hadn't expected she could. I continued to visit her, but I stayed away when Ben was home from fishing. When we had tea together, she told me stories about what the islands were like when she was young, how the ice had crept out from the main island and their grandparents built tracks across it to the outer islands to bring supplies. Abby told me that she'd wanted her students to appreciate that Maine had been a thriving, self-sufficient economy exporting goods around the world and Maine sea captains had been revered as fair and skilled. She had talked, in her childhood, with some of them, and, like Captain Bunker, they were worldly, well read, and wise from having seen other places and other ways of living. "You know, we've shut down in some ways here. We're closer in than we used to be, and I don't think that's a good thing," she said sadly. "You'll notice, when there's a school bond, it's the older people who want to invest in education; the ones whose children are in school are frightened of it for fear the children will just go away to work, or they don't understand the importance of stretching your mind beyond the island, though this is changing."

She taught me tricks like putting out lemons in a basket to take away unpleasant odors and airing a bed in the morning to let the body's damp evaporate. She talked about growing up on Brant's Island, about going "tipping" for balsam boughs to make wreaths, gathering spruce pitch in a can to chew like gum, or how to dry codfish, the kind I saw at the market, shriveled and brown in little plastic bags.

Mostly we talked about things that pleased us. Abby was charmed by the antics of my kittens, like the time they worked together to drag in a huge dead fish off the seawall and onto my back stoop, and about our children. "It seems so odd," I said to Abby one afternoon. "We take care of children, we know them so intimately for so long, and then they grow into adults. Sometimes I feel as if I should still be running my life around theirs, organizing my schedule so I can pick them up from soccer and take them to a birthday party. Sometimes I miss that."

"That was the easy part," said Abby.

"What do you mean?"

"Well, you could set your day up so you never had to think about anything except what someone else wanted or you thought they needed from you. I think it's much harder to figure it all out when they're gone and you're on your own."

"You've got a point. I don't want to be in their way, and sometimes it seems as if everything I know is out of date. I never thought about peanut allergies or…"

"And cod liver oil solved everything then," Abby interjected.

"It's harder now, isn't it? The drugs and sex. Even here."

"We're usually a couple of years behind anything, but it does all get here eventually," Abby said. "And being alone together. Ben and I got along pretty well until the kids got older. They went to high school on the mainland in ninth grade, so it was just the two of us during the week, and then for a while we got on each other's nerves. We got bored." Then she closed her eyes until she fell asleep while I sat beside her wondering what had happened to them.

The next afternoon Abby talked about herself and Ben, about how he was now her best friend and she could talk with him about anything. "I could never do that," I said. "Not with the men I married, or any man, I think. I was afraid that they would find something unlovable in me, so I kept it hidden. I used to write scripts in my head, and then when I tried to talk with them, I would get mixed up because they never knew the script."

"You've told me, but I still don't see why you stayed with them?"

"Oh Abby, I don't know," I answered, the words tearing through me because it was the same question I had asked myself so many times. Why did I marry someone I didn't love, and not just once, but twice? Why had I stayed when I knew neither man really cared about me, when all I could do was give up pieces of myself and hope that by giving them up I could be loved? "I don't know, Abby, I really don't, and it haunts me. It makes me scared I'd do it all over again," I said finally, looking down at my hands and twisting them together back and forth, back and forth, until I realized with a jolt that I was doing the same thing I saw my mother do after my father died.

"Becky," Abby said, looking at me again with such directness that I could feel her eyes piercing through clothes and skin, through flesh and muscles, and right into my soul. "Becky, if you don't love yourself, how can you expect anyone else to?"

"What do you mean?"

"Well, forgive me, but you are a poor little, rich girl sometimes. You don't think much of yourself, which, personally speaking, makes no sense at all. Look at yourself. You're kind and smart, you work hard, you're good-looking, and sometimes you're even funny, and besides, you've got money and," she paused and said slowly, "your health."

"Abby, I don't ever feel like that," I said in a childlike voice.

Abby's voice was softer now, like a mother's, and she said, "I know that. Sometimes I think you see yourself as a little child walking down a long dark hallway with no one to hug you or hold you. I think you took that little girl and plopped her into the lap of those poor, pathetic men you thought you loved.

"What you loved was her—the little wounded child you found in them. The reason you stayed was that you were trying to heal her by healing them. You thought you could make it all better if you loved them enough. But you couldn't, could you?"

"No, I made it all worse," I whispered.

"Losing your father, that made you feel like an abandoned kitten. I think I'm right about you. You've started, I know you have, and once you figure that out you'll be fine because you'll accept yourself."

•

During the summer Abby tried to get me to go out with some of the single men who were in Northeast Harbor then. "Your friend Monica. Now she looks like a woman who'd know lots of men. She took you on that picnic, didn't she?"

"Yes, Abby, but I told you the guy was creepy. He's an ornithologist. I thought that would be really interesting, but all he could talk about was the dead birds in his collection at the museum. He told me he's got hundreds of Blue Jays lined up in drawers to study. Ugh. I could almost smell the chloroform."

Abby suggested that at church I sit near the one single man "from away" who came to the island for the summer. "Now, Aaron, he's really very nice," she said, then paused and smiled, "and he means well, though he's stiff as a church spire," and her eyes sparkled, "at least some of him." She chuckled and added, "and you would have to want to read together, lots. I don't think I've ever seen that man without a book in his hand. 'Course he wouldn't know what to do with a woman if he put the book down—you'd have no canoodlin' with him!" and this time she laughed harder. She was enjoying her joke, and I let her continue.

"Oh dear, there isn't much is there?" asked Abby.

"Abby, I'm fine by myself—I don't miss having a man around, really I don't."

"Well, you should. It isn't natural being by yourself all the time. Don't you ever think about it?" she asked, raising her bald eyebrows.

"It, Abby? You sound like a girl in high school talking that way."

"Well, I miss making love to Ben. I do," Abby said. "And I know he misses me too. I don't mean to be spleeny. I do feel awful, but I just can't now; I feel too sick."

I changed the subject as gracefully as I could, as if distracting a child, though I knew Abby saw right through me.

❧

Stephen and his wife, Maggie, visited in mid-September with their baby Max, and when I looked at my grandson snuggled in his basket, I could see Steven hunched against the end of his crib. "Do you suppose that's genetic," I wondered aloud.

"What?" Stephen asked.

"You used to scrunch up like that in your crib." I loved holding Max, remembering hours I had rocked Stephen to sleep. The curl of a baby against my chest made me feel warm and loved and I wished my mother had enjoyed being a grandmother as I did now. Why had the older generation kept children at a distance, or was it because they never took care of their own children that they were awkward when confronted by a baby? Or were they afraid of being old in ways that I was not? To live in the moment, I thought. It was a truism, a trite phrase but it made sense, and I realized that's what I was learning to do. Living in the moment, enjoying my own skin, my own place, and my own moment instead of living anywhere else than where I actually was. "I'm glad we've changed," I said.

"Changed what?" Stephen asked.

"Changed the way we think about getting older. Changed the way we think about our grandchildren. How lucky I am."

We went to the lobster pound at the end of the main dock for dinner one night. Stan and Bernie. Polly and Vince were sitting by the water. When Polly saw us, she waved, and said, "Please, come sit with us. We just got here so you aren't far behind."

Steven and Maggie seemed eager to join the group, so we asked the waitress if it would be all right if we pulled up another of the square wooden tables and when she said, "of course," we settled around it, propping Max in his little seat on a chair. Steven sat next to Polly, and I was delighted when I noticed during dinner that the two of them were in an intense discussion of a book they had both just read.

"Your mother's turning into an islander," Stan said.

"Well I haven't seen her look so happy or healthy in a long time," replied Steven. "Something good must be happening."

"It's the air. Blame it on the air, no matter what," laughed Polly. "That and good books."

As we walked home, Stephen said, "Katherine said you'd made a lot of friends. I'm glad, Mom. And I like the people I've met."

During the summer and fall I went to see Abby most afternoons for tea, always bringing cookies, shortbread, or muffins. One day Abby said, "I miss the children. I miss teaching in that one-room school. I miss their struggles and successes. I miss their funny little jokes and the flecks of peanut butter and jelly or dried cod on their faces after lunch. I miss being there for them."

I couldn't think of a response, but Abby continued, "You know in that little school the big ones help the little ones. We're like a big family. And we have kids from kindergarten to eighth graders, but they all get along. Well, most of the time. One kid, Alan Purdy, he'd stir things up some days, but he wasn't a terrible kid. Just an unhappy one. He tried to scare me one day by putting a snake in my desk drawer before class. When I opened it I was some surprised, and I guess he got a kick out of that. I knew there weren't any poisonous snakes here, so I just stuck it in an old aquarium and we went on a field trip and found rocks and branches and some dirt and made a home for it. I thanked Alan for giving us a school pet and he actually smiled that day."

"Do you see any of the kids now?" I asked.

"Oh sure, some of them are grown now and they come by. But it's scary for people to look at death. No one wants to think about dying."

I thought, "she said the word *dying*," but I just looked at Abby because again I couldn't think what to say.

"I am dying. You know that?" Abby asked.

"I didn't know, Abby," I said, not knowing if I had denied it. "I'm sorry."

"It's all right for me, I'll be gone, but I worry about Ben. With Ray moved to a job off-island, we don't see him much anymore. Just a week in summer and sometimes at Christmas. I never liked going to Portland where he lives, but I'm glad Chris moved back with her family. I hope they can make it fishing. It's a tough life. Tough on the men, and on the women and children." I could see her eyes cloud over and then redden, but she didn't cry. Instead she said, "You know Ben says we pay three times for our children here. We pay to clothe, feed them, and put a roof over their heads, then we pay taxes to send them to school and then college, and then we pay when they take all that somewhere else to live. But I think the worst... the worst is what we pay in missing them. Sometimes I wish I hadn't wanted them to go to college and that I could have kept them here.-

"Ben did that. He went to college and then more schooling after that, but he came back. There aren't enough jobs for everyone, and when the young people see the way other people live, they want some of those things. It's hard, Becky." She lay back on her chair, exhausted, and I could tell her speech had worn her out because her breathing was choppy and irregular.

"Would you like to rest now?" I asked. "I brought my book, and if you want to rest I can read to you, or just to myself until you feel like talking again."

"Yes, read to me, that would be nice," Abby said softly.

I read from *The Thorn Birds,* and Abby seemed to be paying attention, but soon she slipped into a deep sleep and I walked out to sit in the rocker on the porch, near enough to hear her. After a short while, another neighbor, Gertie, came by and we talked until we heard Abby stirring. I walked in to say good-bye as Gertie asked if Abby would like to hear the story in *The Bar Harbor Times* about a fisherman who had been lost at sea that week. "No, I'd just as soon skip it, Gertie. Well, no, I guess I should know, though it scares me to hear it," Abby answered, but then she smiled and added, "but that one always was wantin' for brains."

❧

As fall turned to winter, I continued visiting several days a week, and then when winter took hold and Abby weakened, I went every day. Ruthie was there before the store opened and just after Ben left, and then Helen came in before Bernie left the post office and brought her lunch over with Abby's mail. Polly left the library after lunch when she knew Bernie was walking back, driving the golf cart to Abby's because arthritis slowed her down. Margaret, a retired seamstress, was a nervous mouse-like spinster with darting hands and eyes. She didn't want the responsibility of caring for Abby for long periods of time, but was able to help for a half-hour. Gertie and I were there in the afternoons, and Susan walked over when Gertie had to leave to get her granddaughter from school. Sometimes Susan came over with her baby and little girl because Abby liked seeing them. Abby's sisters and brother came to see her, as did people in Ben's family, but his mother and father were both in a nursing home and the family had more than its share of visiting to do. A nurse stopped by every day to give Abby her medication and wash her, so she was well-cared for and loved.

❦

One gray day when the rain was blown hard by the wind into little darts that stung my face and hands as I walked to see Abby, I found her looking particularly cheerful as she sat in the warm kitchen. "You look terrific, Abby," I remarked as I shook the rainwater off.

"I feel good today. No special reason, I just feel good. Sit down," she suggested. "I asked Gert to get us some of this fancy tea. Hu Kwa. It's some smoky, and I like that."

We sat breathing in the intense odor of the tea, a smoky black brew that reminded me of fancier places where I had drunk it before. "You never told me about your second husband, Becky," Abby said. "I've wondered why you never talk about him, so tell me. This is a good day for you to tell me about him."

"I don't think of him much now. I guess he faded faster than Jordie. We never had children. That makes a difference."

"How did you meet him?" Abby asked.

"My mother. When I lived near them in Washington, a few years after my divorce from Jordie. She was always trying to match me up with the eligible sons of her friends by asking me to parties and concerts. It was really nice of her, I guess, but I wasn't ready and I sort of hid behind my children. Then one night, three years after I left Jordie, I went to a fundraiser for one of my mother's charities. She whispered in my ear as I walked in, 'I've found him. He's the most glorious man, just separated from his wife. He's going to adore you, and I've seated you next to him at dinner. Just don't get into any political arguments.' He was very handsome, tall with dark hair, and there was something familiar in the crinkling around his eyes when he smiled that I liked. He was smiling a lot as he talked to an elegant blond woman. I even felt a little jealous. I tried to ignore him because it made me mad."

"I thought Ben was so handsome when I first saw him," Abby said. "I didn't think he'd notice me because he was so handsome and I could see all the girls looking at him. We were all at a Grange Hall dance. Went over to the mainland specially. I figured the best strategy to get him to notice me was to ignore him."

"I was seated next to Richard at dinner, my mother arranged that. He was funny and smart, but very conservative. I remember he was impressed that I was finishing college even though I had two children. He said, 'That's pretty gutsy of you, Rebecca. It must be hard sometimes. I've wanted children, but never had any.' I wondered about that, but it was a relief really. He was a lot older than I was but that seemed okay—it made me feel comfortable and secure and I even got to like that he always called me Rebecca."

"Ben called me Abigail at first," Abby said. "But pretty soon we got past that. He told me he was really happy I was going to college. That wasn't something most girls did back then. And some of the men, they were scared off by it. Funny about men that way. You'd think they would be proud of having a woman who wanted to use her mind, but most of them aren't. Ben was different. He told me once he'd met a summer girl who did really well in school and who was going to college. I know now that was you. Funny that, isn't it?"

We stopped talking, and if we hadn't already spent a lot of time together, the break would have gaped before us, but it closed quickly and Abby said, "So you married him?"

"Yes, and I thought we were pretty happy. He liked my children. We lived in a beautiful brick house in Georgetown, and we sent them to the best schools. My mother was happy for us. Relieved too. Richard encouraged me to apply to graduate school. A few years later we moved to Brookline so he could be back home in Boston. I joined the garden club and got into the literature program at Boston University. It was a little odd being back there, but somehow also good. I was finishing something I'd started so long ago but quit. It took me six years to finish my doctorate. I didn't know what to do with it, but I was thrilled to have it."

"What went wrong?"

"We never really cared about each other. We grew into separate places."

"Lots of people do that," Abby said," and everyone does it some of the time. We had times like that."

"What kept you together?"

"My getting sick brought us together last time. Everything has a silver lining, I think. Sometimes it's hard to find, but it's always there. We get along better now than we have for quite a while and, well it's sad too, isn't it? We had some bad times, like I told you. Times I was too lonely with him being off fishing for long trips. I guess we have our regrets. Why did you split up?"

"I wouldn't have if something awful hadn't happened. I was okay with being married to Richard. I wasn't in love with him but I thought he was dependable and I thought he would take," and then my voice shook and I stopped.

"I think it hurts you more than you want to know," Abby observed.

"Yes, it makes me feel lost again. I should be grateful really." I tried to block the memories, but I felt them bursting out. "One day I came home unexpectedly and found him there with a woman. They were making love in our bedroom. They didn't notice me. I watched them. It seemed forever."

"What did Richard do?"

"He just said, 'Well, it's not as if we have been close. You must have guessed,' and I replied, 'Yes, I suppose I should have. I always believed you. I always made excuses for you. I didn't want to know.' We sat a few more minutes together, both of us very quiet. Then I remember saying to him, 'You know what is hardest for me is that I miss what you have. You have someone you want to touch, you want to love, and she wants you too. I could see that, just in the seconds I saw you together, there was something there we never had. I'm scared I've missed that.'"

"He said I married him too fast, that I never loved him, just the security of having a man to take care of me. Someone to blame things on. He was right. There wasn't any point pretending any more. Nine months later we were divorced and I moved to a house in the South End because the brownstones reminded me of Anne and Taylor's house in Georgetown."

"And why here? Why did you come to Maine?" Abby asked.

"I'm not sure, but part of it is that this is the last place I spent time with my father. And the best. We had the best times here. I shriveled up when he died. I just crept into a little cave and tried to feel safe, but I didn't. And here. Maybe that's all I'm trying to do. Grow up and feel safe," and I laughed nervously at myself.

"That's nothing to laugh at," said Abby. "If you don't do it when you're young, then the only time you can is when you get older. Most people don't get around to it even then. Give yourself some credit. At least you've got the guts to admit you've made mistakes and maybe even the time to learn from them." The idea of time disappearing cast its pall over both of us, and I left as soon as Gertie arrived.

❦

That night I rocked in a chair on the deck until I was drawn to the computer and words spun out of my mind almost of their own volition. There's still something inside me that's dead, that never lived, I thought and it seemed a sad mantra. "I can almost feel it inside me, like a tumor, a dark empty place where there are no feelings. Even when I thought I loved Jordie or Richard I felt the dead space inside me. As I sat in front of the fire, I fell asleep, and in the short nap I had a dream that startled me awake after a few minutes, or was it seconds, I didn't know. I tried to write down the dream because it seemed important, but I could remember very little. "I saw a ghostly wall, the brick encrusted with leaching mortar and bird droppings, the ivy snagging the walls, tearing into the mortar with little roots. I could see it but I couldn't get past it into the garden in my mind, the one I read about in the book, the one I saw in the movie. I knew it was there, but I couldn't get there. I remembered the black and white transforming magically into a mass of color and the robin's song leading me to the most beautiful garden I had ever seen. I could hear the robin, but he stayed hidden.

I stopped writing, suddenly exhausted, and sat looking out at the water, holding the crumpled paper in my hands. I thought about the words and wondered if they were about my father, Jordie, Richard, or maybe Ben. I knew the dream was connected to my memories of *The Secret Garden*, but I couldn't see why, or whose face was on the other side. And then I remembered reading that the dreamer is every character in a dream and unfulfilled wishes surface as the dream plays out. So I'm everyone, and every man I wanted is in the dream. Do I have to open the damn gate to the garden by myself?

I thought about what Abby had been trying to make me understand about pushing the wounded child in myself onto Richard and Jordie and the importance of loving myself. That seems such a lonely lesson. "To love myself first," I said out loud. I sat quietly, trying to remember what I had felt as a child, then married to men I didn't love. Remembering made me stop and ask why I was inviting the memories back, when before I had tried so hard to push them away, and I also realized that was the only way to let them out.

Chapter Fourteen

A few weeks later Polly stopped by to tell me they were going to Abby's house that afternoon to knit heads for old times' sake. When I looked confused, Polly explained that heads were the pockets the fishermen used to hold bait in the lobster traps, though they didn't use them much anymore as the factory-made plastic ones were so cheap. "Sometimes," she added, "we mean the net entrances to the parlors and kitchens of the traps, just to be confusing."

We gathered in Abby's kitchen, and the other women attached string to the doorknobs and the sink faucets, pulled out wooden needles and cotton twine, and showed me how to stitch around the mesh board, a little piece of wood the shape of a harmonica. Polly brought her father's old mesh board and showed me how he pulled the twine taut against pegs to make sure the openings were uniform. We laughed together, delighted as I caught on quickly because I'd crocheted a scarf when I was at boarding school. I smiled, remembering the puce and flamingo-pink stripes that had once seemed so fashionable. Susan and Jane explained how the 'parlor' invited the lobster into the traps, and the 'kitchen' kept it there and we talked about fishing and problems with the scallopers ruining the bottom of the ocean with the huge jaws of their drags.

When Abby grew tired and fell asleep, I walked to the harbor with a few of the women and we sat on the wooden benches looking at the setting sun. They told me that now they used the bait bags for decoration at Christmas and to hold suet for birds, but that only a few years ago the men would have taken them and dipped them in tar after slathering their hands with lard to keep the tar from sticking to their hands and soaking into their pores and to stop the heads from sticking together. They talked about Abby and what life would be like without her, which made me feel uncomfortable and sad. I didn't think any of the women suspected that a long time ago Ben and I had been... In fact I didn't even know how to describe what we had been to each other—something more than friends but less than lovers except in the intricate tapestries of my imagination.

❧

As soon as the excess moisture dried out of the dirt and I could turn it over that spring, I worked in Abby's garden, watering, weeding, spading in compost, and bringing over plants from my own garden: lavender, coreopsis like sunbeams, delphiniums with elegant stalks of blue and purple, and an apricot rose, Abby's Love, I had seen in a catalog. Helen said Stan had some "real good loom," and when I looked puzzled she said, "dirt, real good dirt." Stan brought over the loam a few days later, deep black-brown dirt, shining with humus. "Where did you get this?" I asked him.

"Liberated it," he replied, grinning, and I decided I'd better not ask any more questions. We mixed it into the vegetable bed, and then he looked back at the house. "We'll get something growing before she goes aft," he said.

"Before she goes where?"

"Yes," he said slowly, "before she goes."

Abby could see the garden from her chair and she told me once that sometimes it felt to her as if I was an extension of her. She said I was doing the things she wanted to do and that it gave her pleasure to see her garden come back to life, but I hated seeing her withering like a dying flower.

❧

One afternoon I stayed late with Abby because Susan couldn't come that day. In the late afternoon, as Ben walked in the door holding some lobsters, Abby suggested I stay for supper. Ben was quiet, but I felt I couldn't refuse. Abby was having one of her best days in weeks and she laughed and teased Ben. After supper, when I realized how late it was, I told them I had to go, and Abby, looking outside, said, "Ben will walk you home, the moon gives a lot of light, but, Becky, I don't want you wandering about in the woods by yourself." Turning towards Ben she asked, "Is that all right, dear? I'll be fine. You won't be gone long."

"All right, he said, smiling at her as she laid her head against the padded headrest of the chair. As we walked through the woods, along the trail I had come to know so well, we talked about Abby and how good it was to hear her laugh, but as we reached Captain's House Ben grew quiet.

I had managed to avoid Ben most of the time, though sometimes he came in the library when I was there, or into the market when I was shopping, but he was gone much of the time fishing, leaving very early and returning in the afternoon. Some Sundays I saw him in church, but I sat in the back of the church and Ben sat in the third pew from the front on the left side of the small granite building. We had not been alone before because there was always someone else in the library or store or on the roads around the island, and always Abby when I was at their house. Over the months—more than a year now—that I had lived on the island, I knew I had grown past the fantasies and congratulated myself that I had. I wondered if it was because I was just getting older, but it was in part because I had let my life thread more deeply around his wife and the present that the past was unwrapping its tentacles. It was at best a fragile truce, however.

As we walked on the granite stones leading to Captain's House, Ben reached for my arm. I could hear him breathing behind me, very close, and he pulled my arm, gently but firmly until I faced him. Suddenly I saw him again with the moon on his face as a boy, a boy who had kissed me in the moonlight. The man I had loved all my life. "Oh my God," I thought, "he's going to kiss me again," but he looked at me and grasped my arms. "I love her very much," he said. "She's been a good wife, a very good wife to me, and a fine mother to my children."

"I know that, Ben. It makes me happy to see you together, really it does."

He was quiet then, and I could feel some of the tension from his arms passing through mine, and I remembered the electricity I felt when we were together on the rock at the tide pools. I smiled at the thought, staring now at our joined arms. I heard him draw in his breath as if he were about to say something important.

"Look at me," he said fiercely. "Did you ever think even once about me, or what happened to me?" I blanched and my hands felt clammy. I stared at him, blood draining from my face, because I knew he was right. I had been so deeply in my own sadness that I had never thought about him, only about him as he was part of me.

"Dad knew something was wrong with me, and finally I told him, but Mumma never knew. Dad didn't want to scare her. But he was so scared you would tell, that you would be pregnant and what the hell would have happened then? Or someone would find out, and we would be in awful trouble. Summer people don't forgive, he told me, and I could have been sent to jail."

"Jail!" I exclaimed.

"For rape for Christ's sake," he yelled at me, "for rape, and a summer girl at that."

"Oh God, I'm so sorry," I replied, holding my hands over my face.

"Dammit, did you ever in your stinking rich life think about me again! Of course not. I was just some god-damn back side kid. I don't know why you're here. It doesn't make sense. Sometimes I've hated you. Really hated you." He glared at me fiercely and even in the moonlight I could see the veins on his neck bulging, and I saw the mark invisible before, reddening just above his collar.

"I'm sorry," I cried. "I'm so sorry," as he walked away from me back into the darkness.

I always knew he must hate me. Now he had confirmed my fears, but that I had never thought about him again, had dismissed him, thought he had never been important to me—that hurt more and forced me to realize he was right. I never thought about what happened to him, only about what had happened to me. I never thought about him as a person, only about him as I had molded him to fill my needs, and now I saw how selfish and childish I had been. The realization forced me, as if I was being pushed hard through a narrow aperture, to think about how he might have felt.

I continued visiting Abby but always in the very early afternoon when Ben wasn't there. I could avoid him most of the time, but the morning of a baptism at church he had to sit in a different pew and we walked out together. He seemed to steer me away from the people walking to the coffee hour in the parish hall, and said, "I need to say something to you. I'll walk you home," and I followed him silently.

"I'm sorry for what I said the other day."

"No!" I replied immediately, "It's all my fau…" but he interrupted.

"Be quiet. Please be quiet and let me talk. My father knew I'd fooled around with island girls, but it was different with you. A summer girl. You don't mess with summer people like that. He was furious. He grounded me, told me I couldn't play football that fall. That's part of why I started reading—a gift really. Shut up in the attic room night after night. But then nothing happened. For months he thought the police would knock on the door some night and haul me off, or your mother would call, or your new stepfather. But nothing happened. I don't think he ever completely forgave me, but after awhile he never mentioned it. And then I married Abby."

"Ben, I'm so sorry," I repeated. "I was so ashamed, so totally ashamed of myself. I still am."

He looked at me, but I could only hold his gaze for a moment before looking down. We had reached a place on the path where there were no houses, no one who could watch us, and he turned and stopped me, standing in front of me to block my path.

"You marked me," he said. "When that little baby was baptized, I heard Reverend Stephens say, 'You are marked as Christ's own forever,' but I thought of you, again I thought of you." He pulled back the collar of his shirt and I saw the mark—a tiny smudge against his skin, with two sharper lines embedded within it.

I felt nauseous and started to stammer my apologies, but he kissed his finger and put it over my mouth to silence me, and then again he walked away from me.

I didn't go back to their house to see Abby the next week. I felt as if I were wearing a straight jacket tied so tightly I could hardly breathe. "Marked," he'd said. My mark. But why, I asked myself, why would he say 'marked as Christ's own forever?' Had he carried me all these years in his heart and mind the way I had carried him? Had he thought of me when the rest of his life was too grim or boring or frightening or just sad? I didn't know and I didn't know how to find out, because I couldn't ask him. Running into him alone was now too dangerous, and I couldn't face him in the piercing light of day.

Then Polly called and said, "We thought you ought to know she's been taken to hospital again. Abby is doing real poorly. I thought you might want to go with us to see her."

"Oh, Polly, I'm so sorry. I haven't been able to see her this week; I've just been lost in writing," I lied.

"She's up to Memorial in Bangor. She's expected back in a few days, but a group of us are going in the morning, and you're welcome if you want to come," she said, and I could hear deep sadness in the gravity of her voice.

"I do, Polly. I'll be there. When are you going?"

"Six o'clock boat. Don't bring anything. She can't have flowers or anything with perfume. But she'll be able to see us. There's just four of us going, so's we don't tire her out."

The hospital was a gentler place than I expected it would be. The stark white of the halls and rooms was softened by the flowered uniforms the nurses wore and by paintings on loan from local artists. When we got to Abby's floor, we asked in hushed voices where we could find Mrs. Bunker. The charge nurse talked in a normal voice and I realized I had made my own unnaturally quiet and that to talk normally, if I could figure out what that was, would be more appropriate.

There was an elderly woman in the second bed in Abby's room with an oxygen hose in her nose whose head was wedged into a pillow and faced towards a TV, but I didn't think she was really watching it. The sound was turned way up because the woman was hard of hearing, so our conversation had to wind in and out of commercials and canned laughter.

But Abby couldn't talk much anyway, and we could only stay with her for a little while. Her skin was yellowish and mottled with age spots I hadn't noticed before, and with bruises. I couldn't understand how Abby could bruise lying in a hospital bed until I realized it was from the tests they were giving her, and, perhaps, as her body broke down, the veins were disintegrating.

As I watched the line from the intravenous sack going into Abby's pale arm, her small hand bloated with misdirected fluid, a flow of queasiness came over me and I had to leave the room. I stood outside the door, feeling sick and sad, holding myself erect by clinging to the wall and hoping I wouldn't faint. I heard one nurse saying to another, "Betsy, check 1212. I don't think she's doing good. You'd better tell the night nurses she's going to need tending tonight." When they saw me, they stopped talking, but one of them turned and said, "You look some 'peak-ed,' deah. Do you want to go sit down?" Without waiting for an answer, she led me to a chair and added, "You sit down and lean over for a minute and catch your breath. Just the blood went to your stomach, that's all." I thanked her and sat with my head down, feeling stupid and useless, and when my head cleared, I went back to Abby's room.

1212—Abby's room. Oh God, I thought, she's going to go tonight. I stood against the wall and I could feel myself trembling. Ben passed through my mind like a shadow, reminding me that if Abby died, he would be a widower. I can't think like that. That's awful, I whispered to myself, and the thoughts twisted inside me.

❦

Abby didn't die that night, and the next week Ben and his brother brought her in an ambulance to the dock on the main island to be put on the *Sunbeam*, the mission ship and floating ambulance, where they laid her on a gurney. As I watched the boat nearing Islesford, I thought of a dying princess being brought home on a royal barge attended by friends and courtiers. Most of the people on the island were waiting for her, and Ben, his family, and the visiting nurse were with her.

When the captain nestled the *Sunbeam* next to the town dock, men stood in two lines to help ease the stretcher off, and Ben and his brother guided it over the side of the boat. People started clapping and cheering, but one of the men turned and put his finger to his lips to quiet them and they hushed immediately. They hadn't seen her up close as he had, but when they did they knew that she had wanted to come home though she was barely with them. As she passed me, she raised her hand, just slightly, in greeting, and then she winked. The wink startled me as if there was a secret between us, but I didn't know then what it meant.

A visiting nurse lived with Ben and Abby for four days, and then another nurse stayed for three. A group, including me, set up a rotation so that there would always be someone to clean the house, cook, or spell the nurses when they needed to go for a walk. It went on for two weeks. The nurses said Abby's kidneys were failing and she was drowning in wastes her body could no longer process, but that she had a powerful will to live. Her daughter Chris and Ben sat with Abby, sometimes just holding her hand, sometimes talking with her about the times they had spent together and what her grandchildren were doing, and how much they loved her. Abby was in and out of consciousness, flowing from one state to another, and she slept much of the time.

One afternoon as I sat alone with Abby while she slept, only her shallow uneven breath told me that she was still alive. Suddenly she woke up and said, "Becky, I'm glad it's you. I was dreaming of you. I was dreaming of you and Ben. You will take good care of him for me, won't you?"

"Oh, Abby, we all will. The whole island will take good care of him," I answered, trying to deny what I knew she was saying.

"No, you know what I mean, you together," Abby replied and then she lay back on the pillows and drifted away. She died that night, with Ben, Chris, Ray and the nurse beside her. They said she smiled at them and then died.

Everyone from the island was at her funeral, as well as family and friends from Brant's Island, Great Cranberry and the mainland. We prayed, Reverend Stevens said the Twenty-Third Psalm, and we sang "'Tis a Gift to be Simple," because she had loved that hymn. We all went to her house afterwards. Everyone brought something to eat, and we sat for hours to fill the house for Ben and their children and to tell them how much we loved her. But finally we had to go, and I could feel the life going out of the house and sadness pouring in like fog through the boats in the harbor.

❧

It was hard for me to look at Ben after what Abby had said before she died, hard to acknowledge what he had told me himself, hard to think about what might have been, hard to realize that he had grown to love Abby instead of me, and hard now to know he was grieving for her in a way I could not have grieved for any man except him. But my grief over losing Abby was real, and I could feel the honesty of it and the relief of sadness expelled, sometimes in violent crying, sometimes just in walking alone along the beach. Grief I had held in for too long, thought about too much, and had tried too hard to control, was now uncontrollable. It was a grief combined of many griefs, compiled over my life, rarely purged, until now in grieving for my lost friend, I could grieve as well for my sister, my father, and my own lost self.

The summer waned like the moon. The nights were cooler, the angled sun almost as bright, but fading earlier. The blackbirds began to gather in large circles, wheeling overhead in preparation for flying south, and the Eider ducks and Scoters formed coveys near the shore. Katherine and Mark, Nina, Sammy, and Stephen and Maggie with Max, who was a year and a half, all visited at the same time. As I looked at my grandchildren playing together, the older ones taking Max for short walks on his stubby little legs, I realized that the house had fulfilled its promise to me and that it was a home for my family in ways no other house had been ever.

❦

When I sold my house in Boston I gave some of my furniture to Katherine and Stephen and brought up things I loved that seemed to fit—a brass bed warmer, more rocking chairs, a huge dining room table with ten chairs, an ogee mirror and my books. I bought old leather bound books, and Clay repaired the library ladder and re-set the track so we could push it along the shelves of books. Finally, everything seemed complete.

Well before Abby went to the hospital for the last time, I decided to give a picnic to celebrate completion of the house. I invited everyone on the island, including Ben and Abby, though I was worried that Abby wouldn't be able to come. Now that Abby was gone, I wondered if it would be appropriate to have the party, but Polly replied when I asked, "Of course. Abby wouldn't want to miss a good party, but even more than that, she wouldn't want any of the rest of us to miss it."

When I asked Helen she said, "I'd ask Ben and see what he says. I know everyone is really looking forward to it."

When I saw Ben in the market I said tentatively, "I need to ask you something."

"Yes?" he replied. His face look haggard and I noticed lines around his eyes that I hadn't seen before, and I wondered how he had been sleeping.

"You remember I was going to have a picnic at the house. I'm wondering now how you'd feel about that. How do you think Abby would feel?"

"Oh, you need to have the party. She'd hate to miss a party. Particularly if there was dancing."

"How are you, Ben?" I asked, worried by how he looked.

"I'm okay." But when our eyes met, he looked down. "I'm not doing so well, really. We were together a long time. I'm going out to sea for a while. Fishing. Won't be here the next few weeks, so I'll miss your party. She'd feel real bad if you called it off. Have it—and enjoy."

"Thank you, Ben. We'll miss you."

"It's good for me to go to sea. Make some money. The bills. I see best there anyhow," he replied.

I put up a reminder notice about the picnic in the library and post office. "Not much need for a reminder," Polly said. "It's the only thing people are talking about." When people called or stopped me to ask what they could bring I answered, "Your favorite dish," because I wanted them to share in the house's return to life. I was happy, content in a way I had never felt before, eased so that my skin softened; and people told me I looked pretty, which always surprised me.

On the day of the party, a bright shining day, Katherine, Maggie and I cut flowers and arranged them in vases we put throughout the house, set out borrowed picnic tables, and spread sea blue tablecloths on them. We arranged little wooden boats and buoys, rocks and moss, until each table looked like a scene from the island. Stephen and Katherine's husband Mark set the fires, and Stan came to help set up the enormous pots of water for steaming the corn, lobsters and clams. Soon people were arriving with pies, breads, blueberry chutney and salads. The tables were full of food, the beach full with people, and my heart was full of happiness.

We drank beer and wine, and then when we were having dessert, deep-dish blueberry pies and vanilla ice cream, I asked Sammy to bring out the champagne. I poured a little in clear plastic flutes for everyone and said, "I want to thank you all for helping me find my new life, my second chance. I want to thank this house for welcoming me, and I want to christen it "Captain's House." Stephen had made a CD of music about houses, and I said, "I know this is a little crazy, but would you all get up and follow me around the house," and everyone stood up while Beethoven's "Consecration of the House," and the original Payne and Bishop words and music to "Home Sweet Home" poured out the windows.

Then we went back to the door facing the water and I asked Reverend Stevens to say a blessing. When he was finished, I walked over to the doorway facing the water and slowly poured my cup of champagne over the large slab of granite at its base that Stan had told me was called the doorstone. Often in the summer afternoons I had found a large blacksnake curled up, the heat of the sun and the rock warming him from both sides. At first he scared me, but then I began to think of him as a neighbor and to use the other door. Now everyone cheered and they stayed until the children were sleeping, and some of the adults too, and then slowly people drifted away and I was left with my children, grandchildren and two cats, and I could think of no better company.

When it was time for my children and their families to leave, they did so knowing that I was happy, secure in the many friendships that bound me to the island. They knew I would visit, that I would write and call, but that I had found safe haven.

❧

During the late fall and early winter I rarely saw Ben because he spent so much time at sea. I tried to settle into a routine, but I missed Abby. Visiting her had made me feel useful and I had loved talking with my friend. Now the emptiness hit me, particularly in the afternoons, and many times I found myself sitting in the rocking chair thinking about our long conversations. I missed working on the house. Now that it was finished, there was only the work of minor repairs and the endless job of cleaning, which weren't nearly as satisfying as tackling a painting or renovation project. I began to feel bored with myself and to wonder what the long winter would be like.

The next time I went to the library Polly said to me, "You seem a bit out of sorts? How're you doing?"

"I miss Abby," I replied. "I miss going over there in the afternoons and sitting and talking. I feel a bit useless now. And you?"

"I miss her too. I used to love it when she was teaching and she'd bring the children over to the library. Of course, the kids still come, but Abby had such a knack of knowing what they'd like and how to get them involved in a book."

We were quiet as each of us wandered into her own memories and then Polly said, "I could really use some help here. Would you ever want to come read to the kids?"

"Me? I've never done that before."

"Of course you have," Polly replied with a laugh. "Katherine gave you away. Remember? She said you loved to read to them when they were kids, and I know you love to read to your grandchildren. It's the same thing, just a few more children, and there's only six on the island now anyhow so it's not exactly a crowd. Why don't you try it?"

"All right," I said hesitantly, wondering if I really wanted to make a commitment.

"Well, come over tomorrow around one? I'll tell the teacher and we'll see how it goes."

The next day I went to the library feeling worried the children wouldn't like my reading, but Polly told me to go to the children's corner and pick out my five favorite books and then sit in the large padded arm chair. She brought me a pitcher of water and a cup of tea and said, "Just read a few of your favorites and then ask the kids if they have some favorites. You can read them straight, or if you feel like it, you can use different voices. The younger ones love that."

When the children filed in, I was relieved that they seemed excited when Polly told them Mrs. Evans was there to read to them. Two of the younger ones brought blankets that the older children helped stretch out on the floor, and a third little girl went over to an older girl and sat on her lap. I wasn't sure what to read to a group that I guessed ranged in age from kindergarten through eighth grade, but the oldest said to me, "Usually we start with books for the little ones, and sometimes they go to sleep. Then you can tell us a story of something we don't know about. Maybe about a place you've been?"

"Thank you. That helps. I'd like to start with two of my favorites. I'm sure you know them, *Blueberries for Sal* and *Miss Rumphius*?"

One of the littlest children said, "I love Sal," so I knew I'd started well. I read, and as I warmed to the stories and delighted in the children's wide eyed looks and clapping when I finished a book, I began to try reading the different characters in different voices.

When it was time for everyone to leave, several of the children thanked me. I felt as if I should be thanking them, and after they left I said to Polly, "Well that was the best therapy for the blues I've ever had! You knew they'd hook me, didn't you?"

"Ayuh," Polly replied, laughing. "So you want to do it again? I could use you every Tuesday and Thursday."

I read to the children twice a week and began to think about ways in which I could bring the best things I had known in the world outside the island to these children and to create themes for each session. When I realized that some of them didn't have a place to go after school because their parents worked on the mainland, I started an informal after-school program every day at the library. I invited people who could teach crafts or painting to come, and sometimes Polly and the teacher and I took the children on field trips to draw or collect flowers and shells or to sit and write about what they were seeing or feeling.

❧

I had escaped my life for too many years by fantasizing about Ben, and I didn't want to do that again, but sometimes I dared to think about him and to wonder if we could grow to be friends or more than friends. At first I was sure it would happen. Even the other women knew it was what Abby had wanted for Ben and for me, because they knew Abby had loved me too. Polly would say, "there's going to be a church suppa' on Sunday. Why don't you make a picnic? Ben's home so you can come over together. He can pick you up. It's on his way." Helen suggested the women should go mushroom picking in early fall and then have a party. "Ben loves the chanterelles that grow in the woods behind the Higgins place." In late fall Jane said that she was going to get a party together to look for brush tips in the woods for wreaths and that Ben had a good stout sleigh they could put behind the golf cart and then she giggled like a teenager. The attention made us feel awkward, and the few times Ben and I saw each other in the market or walking into church we kept our distance.

One day, however, when I was in the library getting ready for the children, Ben walked in, came over to the table where I was sitting, and stood by my chair. "I don't like the way things are between us," he said. "Will you go for a walk with me?"

"I can't now because the children will be here in a minute. But after? Yes, I'd like to."

"I'll come back."

After the children left, I started packing my books in my leather satchel, and Ben walked into the library. I looked at him, and my heart stopped still for a fraction of a moment. I walked towards him, grabbed my coat off the hook, and then turned to face him. "Thank you for coming back."

"It's a little dark for a walk, but the moon is coming up full. Let's just walk around the shore path for a bit. Are you going to be warm enough?"

"Yes, and the exercise and fresh air will be good."

"We were friends once," he said.

"I know what you mean. I feel as if I know you and don't know you all at the same time. Like I should know you better, but I know you as a child, and now you're a man. Like I lived with you in my head for many years, and now we're friends again, and Abby…"

"I didn't ask for a psychological evaluation," he said, grinning, "just a walk." We walked in silence for a while, and then he said, "There's lots of talk about us now, so I figure we'll just go for a walk and let everyone see there's nothing going on."

I replied a little nervously, "Did someone dare you this time?"

"No, just me," he said, smiling again, and then continued, "I'm a very ordinary man, you know. Sometimes I think you're just slumming by living here. Like we're so ordinary we make you feel like Queen for a Day, and we're your serfs in the village around your castle."

"Ouch. That's harsh," I answered, though I knew there was truth in it. I looked out over the harbor and wondered why I had always felt more comfortable in the servants' wing than in the living room. Had I always been too insecure to want to live in my parents' world? I knew that was part of it, but I smiled because I knew that I liked being with people who weren't pretentious and didn't think they were entitled. Though there was truth in what he said, I knew the island was now my home as well as his, and that I felt loved and secure in ways I never had before.

"Can you ever forgive me?"

"For what?"

"Ben, you know. For the way I acted when we were kids. For the trouble I made for you. I've felt so sorry, so sad I ruined everything. So ashamed of myself. All these years."

"God, woman, you're clueless sometimes. I was angry. Angry at myself that I didn't know how to make love to you. Angry at you because I knew you weren't after me—even then I knew that. You were such a hurting puppy, Becky. But I loved you then. Love and forgiveness. Abby taught me that. Of course, I forgive you and I hope you forgive me."

I looked at him again and saw a handsome man, a good man, and a good friend. I saw him as a boy and as a man all at once. "I don't know who you were to me, or even who I was then, or who we might be to each other, but I'd like to be friends. You're a good man, Ben. A good person, and you make me feel as if I am too."

We walked along the path around the harbor. The smells of the sea, the lobster, and the bait had become so familiar that I hardly noticed them. Instead, I watched the moonlight playing on the waves in the cove and enjoyed walking with him. "I need to thank you for something," he said.

"What?" I asked, again surprised.

"When we were young. You made me think about my life in a different way, as if I could do some of the things you took for granted."

"How do you mean?"

"I thought about you a lot after that first summer. I knew I should get you out of my mind, but I thought about you and I wanted something more than dropping out of school and working on the back of a lobster boat for the rest of my life. I started to work harder in school. That was some surprise for my teachers, but I stayed, I did well and then I got a scholarship to UMO."

"I never thought about that. I never thought you thought about me like that."

"That's just foolish. Of course I thought about you, you and where you came from, and your mother and father. I tried not to. After awhile I didn't so much. And the year after—well after what happened, when

I couldn't go out, couldn't play football. I hated you, because I couldn't see you, couldn't hold you, couldn't even talk to you. I hated what had happened and I wanted you to come back. I wanted to see you the next summer, but you didn't come back, and I started putting all that energy into my studies. That was really a gift."

We walked in silence for a few minutes. I listened to our feet as each step crunched against the gravel path. Then he said, "My parents didn't want me to go to college. Didn't think it was necessary. Thought I'd never come back here if I went to college. Grampie, he knew. The older people have traveled more, on the ships and to wars, so they know. Grampie pushed Mumma and Dad. Then I went to UMO and I met a professor. He saw I had some talent, and I was on his boat every weekend and I helped him with his research."

We got into a habit of taking long walks in the late afternoons when he came back from fishing and I was finished at the library. We looked for places to take the school children and we went to church suppers. He took me fishing and taught me about lobstering, showing me how to measure the carapace and which lobsters to toss back and how to avoid getting nipped. But he never went into the Captain's House, and I never asked him. Somehow we both knew it was too close, too personal and that it was, at least for then, out of bounds, just as touching each other would be.

When my granddaughter Nina caught pneumonia and almost died, Ben sat with me through the night in the shed at the lobster pound while we waited to see if the winter storm would abate and he could take me in his boat to the main island. The next day the ocean was still too rough but he took me to the dock to catch the ferry. When I sat with Katherine in the hospital in Boston, she asked me about the island. She said, "You look so peaceful Mom, relaxed and happier than I've seen you ever look. Must be a man, Mom."

"Don't assume," I replied.

"I bet it's a man," Katherine added, but she didn't push me with more questions.

❦

Ben called me one blustery Saturday afternoon in the late winter. His voice sounded distant and strained, and I wondered what he had to tell me. "I want to come to talk with you. Would that be all right?"

"Of course, Ben, I've finished working for the day. I'm just puttering around. I'll make some tea," I said, trying not to sound nervous.

When he came to the door, he had a day or two of stubble on his chin and his face looked older.

"Come in Ben," I said, breaking our unspoken agreement. "Come into the library. I've got some tea there, and scones, and we can sit and talk," I added, leading him into my favorite part of the house.

As he walked down the hall, he looked at everything carefully. "That's a beautiful photograph of the house, Becky. Did Curly give you that one?"

"Yes. I had a copy made of his. It must be from about 1910, at least that's what he thought."

When we walked into the library, his eyes widened and then he walked over to the wooden library step and stood stroking it slowly with his hand as if he were patting a beloved dog. He pushed it gently so it moved along its track towards me, and when I caught it, I could feel the warmth of his hand. Then he turned to look at the old books that filled the shelves, pulled one down and opened it. "Aristotle," he said with surprise. "Becky, it's the one my grandfather had. How did you get this?"

"I went to the Chicken Barn near Orland and looked through the old books there. I bought quite a few. I found that one, and also this book," and I pulled down another, *Poems by Edgar Allen Poe*, and showed him the inscription from his great-great-grandfather, "To my Annabel, from her Captain, for our kingdom by the sea."

"My God, they were some romantic those old guys," Ben exclaimed smiling, the back of his neck reddening slightly. He walked over to the chairs and couch in front of the table where I had set the tea and sat on the edge of the large wing chair. I poured the tea and gave him his cup, then offered him a scone. We sat stiffly while I tried to think of something to say, but before I could speak he looked at me, put down his cup, and said in a rush, "Becky, I have to go away. I'm going to be away for four or five months. I found a research project on the banks and I'm going to be the second in command, sort of a combination researcher and boat captain."

"Oh, Ben, that's perfect," I managed to say.

He looked at me with a little smile in his eyes and said, "Well, you could be just a little sad."

That broke the awkwardness, and I could answer him honestly. "Ben, I will miss you terribly. I'm glad we're friends again, but it's hard when people seem to think we're..." and then I stopped and stared at the tea leaves strained against the side of my cup, wondering what I could read in them.

"I know," he said, "they thought we've been having an affair for the past year, and now they wish we would."

I looked at him, and we both laughed. Then I said seriously, "Well, sometimes I've wished we had been."

He grew silent again, and then said, "Not yet, Becky, not yet. I have some growing to do. I did love Abby and I don't want to dishonor her memory. She loved us both. The greatest gift is to be able to let the people you love be happy, even if it's not with you. She said that to me once. She knew about us—or most of it—about how I'd felt and now I need some time with her by myself."

"She told me she wanted me to take care of you after she was gone, but I didn't want to talk to her about it. She was a very good friend to me, Ben, and I loved her for that."

"I know that, Becky. I do know that," he said then paused. "I have to let this out of my mind, have to just give it time and then come back when I'm ready."

I sat looking out the window at the sea, thinking about Ben in a ship traveling beyond my sight, beyond the horizon where I would have no idea what he was doing or thinking.

"I started one time to tell you that I'd married her because she reminded me of you," he said.

"What do you mean?" I replied, startled.

"When I walked you home from our house. It was so close, too close to memories of when we were kids, and I couldn't then."

"I didn't know," I said softly, my heart jumping in my chest.

"I can now, though," he stopped and took a long drink of tea. "I think a man can love two women," he said, and then he grinned at me. "Hey it works for Mormons and Muslims, why not us Mainers?"

"I'm glad I didn't know that," I said. "I think it would have made me… It would have gotten in my way of knowing Abby."

I looked at him again, afraid my eyes would betray my fear of missing him, or perhaps even losing him. "You made me think what it might be like to care about someone you could talk to and enjoy being with, not just boast about. At first there was just the dare," he said.

"What?" I asked worried again.

"Well the dare. It was just about boasting rights. Who could get a summer girl to come to Islesford. I may have been the first man ever. It was good for boasting at first, and Jason and the other guys were some envious. Then I got to know you. I saw you as a real person, not just some summer girl. Not just a trophy."

"I'm glad I didn't end up over the garage door."

"Oh, you've seen the new antlers Jason's put up?"

"No, thank God, but I've seen others."

"So you know. Do girls do that?" Ben asked.

"Of course. But I didn't have any boyfriends to boast about," I said remembering the times I had pretended Ben went to St. Paul's or lived on the Main Line, and how each time I lied, I knew I was betraying him. "You're right. It wouldn't have worked back then. I didn't know myself or who I wanted to be."

"And would *it* work now?" he asked, emphasizing the word "it" in a way that reminded me of the time Abby had used a similar inflection. I blushed at the thought, but Ben leaned over and took my hand in both of his. "That's not what I meant. I'm more worried that you'd get bored with me, get bored living here."

"No," I replied thoughtfully. "I'm not bored here. I'm not angry with myself or anyone else any more. I like being where I am and there's lots of things I enjoy doing here. And lots of people I love to be with." Then I turned my head to look at him squarely and said, "I'm never going to get tired of feeling cared about. That's what I feel here, and it frees me to do so many other things."

"All right then," Ben said, letting out a long breath. We sat quietly for another moment and then he squeezed my hand and let go of it. "I'm going now. You know I probably won't be able to get word back to you. I'm not sure I want to. I just need to be by myself for a while."

"I know," I said, and then more slowly, "I know."

When we turned to face each other underneath the light at the front door, he held out his arms, and I slid next to him and buried my head against his brown corduroy jacket. It was soft, worn with age, and I breathed in the smell of him. We stood for moments and I wondered if he was thinking of the last time we had held our arms around each other. I knew I had to step away from him, to let him have the time he needed, and to hope that at the end of it he would come back to me. "Good-bye. Take care of yourself. God be with you."

"Good bye," he said. "Thank you for waiting."

But after I shut the front door, I said, "I love you, Ben Bunker."

Chapter Fifteen

Many times I wished we had made love that afternoon. I wished I had held him and told him with my body how much I loved him. But he left the next day and for the next five months he was gone. Like an adolescent girl again, I thought of him when I was waking up and going to sleep, and often when something happened and I wanted to tell him about it. I had learned the danger of living in fantasies, and now I could laugh at myself. Because I mooned around, so lost in my own thoughts, Polly told me I was "drifty as a dinghy in a storm tide," and I worried, of course, about storms and accidents, imagining all the ways he could be taken from me again.

Late one day in early February I walked into the post office and Bernie looked at me with a sly smile and said, "I've been counting the number of times you come in here now, Becky. Wouldn't be still waiting for a letter from some special man now would you? You come in here at least three times a day, and you know the mail boat only comes but once."

I blushed and smiled at her, saying, "Bernie, never more than two. Besides, I just want to see your kind face and see you smile. I'm just trying to entertain you."

"Well, I think today you got something in your box that will entertain you," Bernie laughed, arching her eyebrows.

My heart thudded in my chest, and I felt as if I was going to explode. I tried to walk slowly over to my mailbox and steady my shaking hand as I twirled the dials, but I fumbled the combination and blushed harder as Bernie laughed at me again. "Now, I'm enjoying watching you make a fool of yourself, Becky, but would you like some help?"

I threw my hands up over my head in frustration, and exclaimed, "Bernie, I miss him, what can I say. I miss him a whole lot, like I never missed anyone before."

Bernie moved behind the boxes, and I saw her hand inside the box wiggling the latch and then waving a letter out my side of the box. "It's got the best perfume on it," Bernie said, the metal box giving her voice a tinny echo, "perfume of the sea. I think they've been into the cod. Keeps 'em out of worse trouble."

His handwriting hadn't changed so much over the years, I thought. The envelope did smell of fish, and I laughed and thought I'd send him something more romantic back if I only knew where he was. The letter was very short.

"My dearest Becky," he wrote, "You are in my thoughts now all the time. I know now I want to come home, to love you and live with you, to grow old with you, to see our children and our grandchildren and, if we are so lucky, our great-grandchildren, growing up. I want to sit with you looking at the ocean and hold your hand. With all my love, Ben. PS: It sure will beat counting cod." And that made it all right because he loved me and I loved him. I didn't know where he was, but I could picture him lying on a bunk staring at the ceiling and thinking about me as I lay on my bed thinking about him. Now I could make love to him and hold him any time I wanted to because I knew he wanted me and he loved me.

❧

I worried about all storms along the east coast because I did not know where Ben was. I got in the habit of having a mug of tea early in the morning at Ruthie's store where people gathered to listen to the Coast Guard weather reports. Sometimes they sounded frightening—20-foot seas, high winds—but people told me not to worry, and that helped. One morning, however, a deep red sky loomed ominously around the harbor. As I walked into the store, I saw people huddled together near the radio on the counter. "What's going on?" I asked.

Ruthie turned down the volume, and people put their heads down as they walked past me muttering 'mornin.' I felt confused and hurt, but Ruthie wouldn't tell me what was going on. When I went to get the mail, I asked Bernie if there was something wrong, and a slight catch in her voice made me even more concerned.

When I got home, I turned on the radio, searching for a weather channel, and finally heard the nasal intonation of the Coast Guard announcer. "Officer Jones with the latest NOAA weather report. North'easter approaching with 60 mile an hour winds, gusts up to 80 miles per hour affecting the Georges Bank. All vessels advised to seek shelter between 2400 hours Friday and 800 hours Sunday. Expect 50 foot seas in a wide area. Ranging from..." I could see the huge waves clawing at Ben's ship and dragging it down, the ship a tiny dot in an enormous angry ocean. I ran to the post office and almost screamed at Bernie, "Why wouldn't you tell me! You should have told me!"

"You haven't been through a big storm before, Becky. You can't do anything but wait."

"But I need to know how he is, where he is!"

"There's nothing you can do but wait, and that's the hardest. The not knowing and the waiting. He's in a big ship. Chances are good—he'll be all right. Worry about the little boats—the fishing fleet. This storm was a surprise. We thought it was going to turn inland to the south of us, but it's heading northeast."

The next day I couldn't stand being by myself. I went to the library and tried to read, but the wind got louder and finally Polly said, "Becky, I'm sorry, but we need to close up. I'm going to put up the shutters, and we must go home and get ready. It's going to blow hard."

When I got home, I found Stan who had already put up many plywood storm shutters over the windows. I didn't even know we had them. Together we screwed in the last ones, and he said, "Becky, it is going to blow hard, but we'll be all right. You'll lose power. Fill a bathtub with water and get your candles and flashlights ready. Put one in your pocket so's you have it with you. We just have to hunker down. You can come stay with us if you'd rather."

"I'm okay," I said, holding the kitchen counter to steady myself. "This house has been here a long time, and I want to be here with it. If it gets too rough, I'll go down cellar."

I filled a bathtub with water, got in some wood for the stove, boiled hot water and got the flashlights and candles ready. I made soup and tried to read, but my mind kept searching for Ben. I tried to sense where he was, but I could only feel the desperate climb of the ship against the waves, the sickening pitch and fall as it crashed into the trough. Dear God, we are closer to you than we know, I thought. I can't bear to lose Ben again, I pleaded and I would have struck a bargain with the Devil himself, if I believed that could save him.

The power went out about two o'clock that morning, and it was almost a relief—a way to share in what was happening, and escape the relentless media coverage of the storm. I did not sleep—and in the morning the sky and ocean were still quivering in the wind. When the rain and wind had almost stopped, I went to the docks. The fishermen gathered around the radio looked grim, their hands in their pockets. "Rough night," one of them told me. "Our fleet's in, but there's a ship in trouble on the Banks. Don't know the name yet."

The *Sarah Ann,* I begged silently, please don't let it be the *Sarah Ann.* For two days we waited. People came to my house—their kindness unwelcome, emphasizing the need to worry. But finally we heard that a ship out of Castine had lost an engine, foundered in the wind and waves, and that two men were still missing. That brought guilty relief, but it was a long winter of storms.

❧

He did come home. On a warm afternoon when the lupine were just beginning to cover the island with their purple blue plumes, my phone rang and a deep voice said, "Do you want to marry me?" I was so startled I froze. All the excuses to say no flew through my head like a flight of sparrows, but I said, "Yes Ben, more than anything in my entire life. I want to marry you."

"Well now, that's a relief," he replied. "You were taking so long I thought you'd changed your mind!"

"No," I countered, "once I figured out who was doing the asking. I wasn't going to give you a chance to change your mind."

"I love you, Becky. I loved you then and I love you now. I've loved you ever since we were kids." He could hear me crying now, just softly, as I thought about how much I wanted his arms around me, to have my safe place be home with him. "Now, woman, don't get gormy on me. Hush up and look out your window for me."

"Where are you, Ben?" I asked, breathless.

"Right down here in the harbor, next to the lobster shack. I'll be there in five minutes, but," he hesitated, "I smell like a man who's been on a cod ship for five months, so maybe I'd better go get cleaned up."

"No, you come right here."

"Well, my love, that's exactly what I had in mind," he said, laughing at me.

"Oh, Ben," I replied, blushing, and then threw down the phone and ran out the door, across the field of lupine and down the hill overlooking the harbor. When I saw him, I ran faster, and then he was swinging me around in his arms and I was kissing him, hugging him so hard I thought I would burst. I was crying and laughing at the same time, and hugging him as he hugged me back. Our neighbors Polly and Sam, Bernie and Stan, Susan and Clay, Jane and Hubert, Ruthie, Helen and Dan, Clem, Tom and then Chris and many others, gathered around us as we stood in the field next to the docks, and they started clapping.

The men slapped Ben on the back, and some of the women came to give him a hug and welcome him back. I stood watching them, tears of joy trickling down my face. I had to use my hands to wipe them off until Polly gave me a handkerchief, saying, "Just give it a good blow." I laughed and stared at Ben. He turned towards me and grinned his wonderful wide grin, the dimples crinkling his cheeks and his blue eyes clear, and then he said, looking at his friends and raising our hands over our heads, "We're getting married!" Everyone cheered, and the men threw their hats in the air as the women laughed and clapped and then came over one by one and kissed me. The children ran around us and some did cartwheels, dogs barked, and the whole village seemed to be welcoming Ben back and congratulating us.

Chris came over to me and said, "I miss my mother, Becky, I do. But if she can't be here for my father, I want to tell you that I'm glad you are."

"Thank you, Chris. That means a great deal to me. I miss your mother too. I don't know what else to say," and we put our arms around each other and tried not to cry.

"Let's have a dinner to celebrate," one of the women interrupted, and at first I didn't want to share Ben, but then I realized he belonged to them too, so I was quiet. Polly grinned at me and said, "We'll make it a short one," and everyone laughed at me, but I didn't care. "As long as it isn't fish," Ben said, and his cousin Tom said he had good steaks he'd just bought on the mainland to freeze, others offered salad, and potatoes and we agreed to meet in the parish hall in an hour.

As people drifted away, Ben and I stood looking at each other. Then Ben bent down to pick up his sea bag, hoisted it over his shoulder, put his arm around my neck and tickled it until I laughed. "Your place or mine?"

"Well, really they're both your places, so I think you should come to the Captain's House."

"I accept," he said. "I'm wicked dirty."

"You smell like fish, grease and dirty laundry, and I love it." We walked holding hands up to the door of the old house and suddenly he dropped his bag, picked me up, and carried me over the threshold. "Oh Ben," I said, kissing him, his beard scratching my face, "no one ever did that before."

"Well, that's good, at least there's one thing you haven't done before."

"There's lots, Ben," I replied, "I never really loved a man."

"Well, my deah, now's your chance," he said, as he put me down and stood looking at me.

He walked into the hall, took my hand, and led me to the master bedroom. He walked in saying, "I need a shower," so I turned to the new bathroom, and Ben followed me. "My God, woman, what've you done to this old bathroom!" he exclaimed. I looked around the white-and-blue Mexican tile floor, the sunken tub with a Jacuzzi, the separate tiled shower, the huge marble counter and the deep sink.

"Guess I did go a little nuts, but I wanted a soaking tub so I could sit and relax after writing, and it's really wonderful just to sit there and..." My voice trailed off because I could see us then, sitting in the tub, soaking and washing each other, though I had never wanted to do that before. "Here," I said, "I'll get you a towel and you can take a bath, or a shower, and just soak."

"And you," he said, "where do you think you're going?" I was walking away, striding really, feeling his eyes on me, and feeling awkward. "Don't go anywhere," he said, and he walked towards me, holding out his arms, and then he held me against him. "Just stay here and talk and we'll pretend we're an old married couple and sit in the tub and soak together."

I looked up at him, my voice dropping into my throat, and I said huskily, "Maybe we should pre-wash you first, like a dirty pair of jeans."

He laughed and bent to turn on the water and then started unbuttoning his shirt while I looked at him in surprise. "Oh you think I should be unbuttoning your shirt, do you?" he said laughing. "I told you we're playing old married people, but here, I'll help," as he reached for me. "But no kissing," he added, "until I shave, and no playing until I get clean."

I went out to get two big towels, and when I came back he was in the tub lying back so his chest was above the water and his eyes were closed. "Becky, this is wonderful," he said dreamily. I put on the whirlpool, and the water swirled around him. He laughed, "It's making my di... Well, it does feel some good," he laughed again. "You'd better not come in here. I've been away much too long and I don't feel like an old married man right now."

"Well, you aren't one," I replied.

He sat up and looked around for soap and started scrubbing himself, but I bent down by the tub, took the washcloth and the soap, and washed his back and then his arms. "Like washing a big baby," I said, taking his leg in my hands and rubbing the washcloth over him.

I scrubbed down to the little circle of hair that made a tonsure in the small of his back, and then he said," You can do the rest you know."

"No, not yet."

"Well, get yourself in here then."

I looked at the blue-and-white clock over the door and said, not without some relief, "No. We've got to get to dinner and there's not enough time."

"Spoken like a wife," he replied, grinning at me. "Watch out, I'm getting out and I'm going to get you all wet," he added, starting to stand up. I threw a towel at him and ran out the door, laughing and thinking that life was going to be fun.

We walked to the church hall, swinging our arms as he told me stories about the cod, the weather and the long journey. Just before we got to the hall, he drew me to him and kissed me, a deep kiss that made me dizzy, a kiss gentle and passionate, tender and loving, a kiss of old married people and of young lovers, of a man and woman who had loved each other for so long, but from far away, joined now under the moonlight, oblivious to the stars and the washing of waves against the rocks, the sounds of owls and nighthawks, oblivious to the bats and moths swooping around us, to the wind whispering through the firs and the smell of dew on the lupine, entwined only in each other for what could have been the thousandth time or the first.

As we walked through the door, we saw the circle of our friends and family gathered in the main room of the parish hall, now decorated with candles, flowers and pink and lilac crepe paper in a huge bow over the center table. Everyone threw confetti and rose petals at us, and I laughed and delighted in the shower filtering down through the light like colored snow. "Now where did you get all that in an hour?" Ben asked.

Polly replied, "We had it from the last church social when Auntie Harriet celebrated her ninetieth birthday and we hauled it up from down cellar." Polly had made her famous American fries; Susan brought arugula and spinach salad from her garden. There were Tom's steaks; John had asparagus from his garden, and Bernie had made a cake that said, "Welcome Home Ben and Congratulations!!" in huge letters.

"How did you do that so fast?" I asked.

"I've always got them in the freezer. Never know when you're going to need a cake, so I zap them in the micro and decorate 'em up." We drank toasts of homemade hard cider that Bill stored in his cellar. As we sat in a circle of neighbors and friends, Ben had his hand on my knee and he rubbed it slowly.

After dinner Polly asked me to join her as the other women formed a circle, and the men made a separate circle around Ben. Polly was wearing a flowered pink and white dress with a white collar, her cheeks red as the roses in the dress, and her white hair plaited in thick braids around her face. Jane was, as always, dressed in a blue denim jumper and a turtleneck; and she towered above Susan who was standing next to her. Susan, the youngest of the group, had her baby suspended in a shawl from her neck, and Helen, Margaret, Ruthie, Chris and Bernie completed the circle, friends and allies, together. Polly stepped towards me and said, "We just want to say a few things to you. This comes from all of us. We talked about it before you got here. We want you to know we're so happy for you. You're a good woman and our neighbor, and if Abby were here she would say the same thing. You'll be good to Ben, and he'll be good to you. And, well, we know this isn't your wedding night, but maybe it sort of is," and she giggled, "so here's something old from me." She pulled out a piece of lace in the shape of a crescent moon and said, "It's just an old piece of lace, not much use for anything, but I've had it a good long time."

And then Polly turned to Jane, who blushed a little and took a step towards me. "And this is something new," she said, looking at her hands. "It's a handkerchief I made for the church fair, but it's got a Bee on it, and that's your initial, so I think you should have it."

"And you obviously need it," Polly added.

Then Susan stepped forward and said, "this is something to borrow," and she handed me a thin book titled *How to Speak Yankee*. "I found it really helpful for learning a foreign language when I moved here. There's expressions from the coast I never heard in the County, and I guess there's words I used in potato country that don't make much sense here, though I can still grow a great spud."

Helen and Bernie held out a jar of blueberry jam and a bag of lupine seeds, and Helen said, "And this is something blue from the island for you. Once you eat the jam and plant the seeds, you'll never leave."

Jane walked over to me holding out a balsam pillow she had made and said, "And this will remind you of the woods even in the midst of a Nor'easter when you've hunkered down."

Ruthie gave me two scented candles from the gift section of the store, and she held one in each hand as she gave me a hug and said, "I checked, these are made in Maine, not China."

Chris walked over to me very slowly and gave me a set of index cards. "These are mother's recipes. I haven't given you all of them, but I've made copies of Dad's favorites so you'll have a good chance of keeping him well fed."

I held the gifts on a tray that Polly had handed me, and tears were trickling down my face. I put the tray down on the table behind me and went to each of them, hugging them for a moment and breathing deeply until I had come around the circle. "Thank you, thank you for being my friends and for caring about me. Thank you for being so generous and for being with me and making this the happiest time in my life."

Polly handed me a tissue and said, "That hankie won't be enough. You'd better start keeping a pack of these if you're going to go on so," and we laughed as I saw Ben walking towards me. I could tell the men had been teasing him and making him know how much they loved him because his eyes were red around the rims and he looked at me like a sheepish little boy.

"All right, off you go," said Polly. "We're cleaning up and we'll see you in the morning," and she shooed us out the door back into the moonlight. Some of the awkwardness and strangeness came over me again, but Ben took my hand and we walked into our house together.

"I've got a split of champagne in the ice box and some beer. Would you like something to drink?" I asked him.

"No, let's just go out on the porch for a minute. I want to sit there like Grammie and Grampie." He held the door for me and we sat down in the faded green wicker rocking chairs and rocked back and forth, listening to the tide coming in and the sounds of night, the scurrying of mice and the sawing of crickets. Then Ben said, "Now let's go soak in that big tub of yours. If you'd told me about that, I'd have been back months ago."

The cider, or something, had gone to my head, and I felt silly and excited. I went to the little chest of drawers in the bathroom and pulled out a packet of bath bubbles Monica had given me. I turned the water on, poured the whole packet in, and watched as the foam built up quickly like banks of clouds. Ben turned around and laughed, "You think you can hide in that, huh? No way."

"Ben, I wish I were young and beautiful for you, not an old woman with wrinkles and cellulite."

"So, you're old and beautiful. I'm no fingerling, let's just be happy we can still even think about loving each other."

"I'm glad I put dimmers on all the lights," I said as I dialed the wattage down.

Then he walked the few steps over to me and put his arms around me; I started to say something, but he put his finger on my mouth and moved it back and forth, caressing and quieting me. He was undoing the buttons of my shirt and his hand slipped over my breast. I almost swooned into him. I started kissing his other hand as it played over my mouth, and then his hands were cupping both my breasts and he was stepping back and letting the moonlight through the window bathe me. "You're as beautiful as you were when you were sixteen."

He knelt down in front of me and pulled off my clothes, and then I was standing naked and he was kissing me. I felt wet and then I jumped, realizing the bubbles were flowing over the tub and onto the tiled floor. Ben jumped too, and I picked up a cloud of bubbles and threw it at him. He unbuttoned his shirt and pulled it off, and I threw more bubbles. Then he stepped out of his pants and I said, "Well I guess you're young at heart, or at least somewhere," picked up another big clump of foam and hung it on him, then slipped into the tub and grinned at him. "Looks like I hung a wreath on your door."

He laughed again at me and replied, "You're some bawdy old lady," and he slid into the tub next to me, picked up a pile of bubbles, and dropped them on my head. We lay there together, feeling the warm water coursing around our bodies and exploring each other. I found a scar on his arm, and he told me a hook had dug deep into him and that Clem had cut it out. He found where I had cut my thumb in Girl Scouts because I wasn't paying attention. We stroked each other and kissed, then let the soapy water run out, ran fresh water to clean the bubbles off, and dried each other. I put on a filmy nightgown, but Ben said he didn't have anything clean so he would just have to go to bed with nothing on, which I told him was just fine. We slid between the covers, and he put his arm around me as I curled against him, my head on his shoulder. He put his hand on my chest, and I waited for him to start making love to me, but instead he started breathing deeply and in a minute or two he was asleep, breathing rhythmically, and I laughed, "Yes, just like old married people," and fell asleep myself.

❦

In the morning, I heard him get up before the birds were chirping, then rolled over and went back to sleep. A while later he opened the door, came in carrying a tray, set it on the bed next to me, and said, "This is the first course. I'm the second," and grinned.

"You look like a Satyr prancing around in the woods," I said, a bit groggy. "Oh, that smells good. Sausage?"

"And French toast, with blueberries and fresh-squeezed orange juice," he said proudly.

"Just a minute." I went to the bathroom and cleaned up. My hair curled in odd ways from sleep and I wasn't sure he had ever seen me by the cruel light of morning without mascara. 'I guess that's the test,' I said to myself as I went back into the bedroom.

"Look at you. Look at you. I'm a lucky man, Becky, a very lucky man." I bent down to kiss him and got into bed next to him, then we ate the breakfast he had cooked. "You're not much for coffee, I could see when I looked for some, so I made tea the way Abby taught me, in the pot."

"Do you miss her?" I asked.

"Yes," he answered, "sometimes, but being on the ship was good for me. I made my peace with her. And I thanked her. We had some hard times. You probably didn't guess that, but she always knew part of me was lost in you and what that might have been, and then I was gone so long, so many times. Everyone knew about the man, the school teacher that she—well, you know, except me, of course for a long time. I felt so foolish—'cold as a dog and the wind northeast,' Grampie would have said."

"What's that mean?"

"There's nothing as cold as a short-haired dog sitting on the ice and the wind blowing, and he's waiting while his master's fishing, or drinking in the ice house, but he won't give up. She shut me out, and I got colder and colder. Finally, I felt like I was dying and I did give up. I turned around and did the same thing to her—started seeing someone on the sly. It was a pretty ugly time for us. Did she ever talk about it?"

"Yes, she told me a bit. But I know she loved you."

"I don't feel good about those times. But I loved her and I took good care of her when she was ill. I don't know if the worrying made her sick, they say stress can do that to a person, but I don't know. We got along most of the time, but in some ways best towards the end. We always lived in the same house, but that can be some grim. You come back from the boat and she's there, but she won't talk, and just going in the house made me feel like I was going to lose supper. But then several years ago, about six now, she started having the pains and they put her through chemo and an operation. We thought she was all right. They said if she made it through five years she was going to be all right, and she did. But then it came back, and when it did it was like a flood tide it came through so fast. I did love her and I took care of her the best I could these last years," he paused, and looked out the window.

"Sometimes the kids are still mad at me. They think I wasn't good to her when they were young, but they don't understand how hard I had to work, and we never talked with them about the school teacher. People tried to protect them from the rumors, but I'm sure they knew. We never talked about it, though. No, the kids, they just thought I went out and... Well, it's over now, but sometimes Ray, he still carries a grudge. He can be sour, and I'm scared he'll do the same thing, but Christine… Well, I think she's forgiven me." He stopped, and looked at me. "We've always got to talk, Becky," he said seriously. "I don't want to live with a woman who's got secrets and things she can't say—or she's scared to say because she thinks I'll be mad."

"It's hard, Ben. I haven't had much practice at that."

Then he took my plate and mug and put them down on the floor beside the bed, saying loudly, "Ready or not!" He rolled over and blew a loud rhubarb in my neck, nuzzling and tickling me until I was giggling uncontrollably. And then we began to make love and we were moving along an undulating trail through woods and beside ponds, discovering landscapes neither had known existed. It was wilder, gentler, and more loving and exciting than anything I had ever imagined.

When we were finished, and I lay on top of his chest looking down at him, he opened one eye, said, "Well that was worth waiting for," and laughed.

"Forty years?"

"I'm glad it wasn't any longer." We lay listening to each other's breathing, until he said, "I think I need to buy you a ring. What sort of ring do you want, one of those fancy cut diamonds or rocks surrounded with diamonds women like to wave in your face? Or maybe Kashmiri Sapphires. I'll have to go to sea again to afford that, but as long as you promise the same kind of welcome, it'll be worth it." He rolled over on his belly and I lay next to him stroking his back.

"Ben, I've actually thought about this. I don't want that kind of ring at all. I know exactly what I want. I want to go with you to the Rock Shop and get someone to help us pick out some stones and make me a ring. I don't want diamonds. I think they're cold and ugly," and in my mind I saw my mother's hand with the huge diamond marquis ring Taylor had given her. "I want my own ring, one that makes me think of you and of places I love," I said.

Three days later we took the ferry to the mainland and went to Bar Harbor. We walked down Main Street, past a new shop that sold pottery painted with the mountains and ocean, quilted wall hangings in vibrant colors, and stained glass that cast a spectrum of lights around the shop. We walked past new restaurants and the old pharmacy with its soda counter and apothecary bottles lining the upper shelves until we stood in front of the Rock Shop, holding hands and looking at the windows. Ben teased me that it would be appropriate, and much less expensive, if I would just choose a ring set with a polished pink granite pebble like the pair of earrings in the window. I replied, "Maybe for my birthday. See, you have lots of presents for many years just lined up right here. Makes it easier for you."

"Oh, come on, let's get it over with," he sighed with exaggerated pain as he opened the door for me. I stood in the doorway looking over the shelves lined with chunks of semi-precious stones and at the glass vitrines displaying inexpensive jewelry from manufacturers all over the world. Then I led Ben to the back of the store and stood next to him as I had stood next to my father so many years before. But now it was my time to choose what I wanted. A woman with red hair and freckled skin like cinnamon on toast, came out and said, "Good morning, can I help you?"

I looked at her and said, "I wonder if you're related to Mr. Willis?"

"Yes, I'm his daughter, Sandy."

"I used to come here with my father, years ago, when he was buying things for my mother."

"That's wonderful," Sandy replied, "wonderful that you've come back."

"Yes," I answered, looking at Ben, "it is."

"So, what are you thinking about?"

"She's thinking of marrying me, and she wants to pick out her own ring. Some persnickety—persnickety and uppity, I say," Ben said in his deepest accent. "These women from away," he added, sighing. "But she's a keepah." He looked at me, "you ah, deah, you ah," and made a silly face, crossing his eyes.

"Well you asked me what I wanted, and I told you," I answered, laughing, "So stop complaining. I might have said, "Dahling, I only wear jewelry from Tiffany or Harry Winston."

"Ayup, but I wouldn't be marrying you if you talked like that."

"So you want a ring?" Sandy said to get us back on course.

"Yes," Ben answered.

"And what kind of ring?" Sandy asked, pulling some out of the glass cabinet. There was a large one, yellow as a gleaming scoop of sherbet, one with tiny stones set in concentric circles, and another of deep purple amethyst.

I looked at them and said, "I want stones like the sea and the air, like the green of the firs and the purple of lupine. I want to think of Ben and things that I love when I look at it."

Sandy turned to the shelves behind her and pulled out boxes of stones. The green stones were tourmalines, the blues the deepest aquamarines, and the purples were amethysts. We spread them out in the boxes and I shuffled them around, remembering the sounds of the pebbles in the seawall in front of the Captain's House when the tide ran through them. I looked at the aquamarines, letting them trickle between my fingers, and saw the water of the ocean following a boat in a wake. I saw the cloudless sky arching over me and the branches of evergreens. I saw the paths through the woods to the Green Place, the smell of rhodora and crushed sweet fern, and the fields of purple lupine swaying in the wind. I saw places I had loved since I was a child, and I turned to Ben as I dug my hand into his shirt. He held me until I could let the moment pass, and then I turned and pulled out the handkerchief with the embroidered bee and wiped my eyes.

We picked six stones of each color and set them on a velvet cushion on the counter. Sandy said, "You've made good choices. There are lots of rings here, but maybe this and this, set with this one in the middle would work well." She lined them up, a deep aquamarine, a domed amethyst in rich lavender purple, and a round, green tourmaline.

"That's perfect," I said, "that's what I could see in my mind."

I turned to Ben and hugged him, and he said, "Okay. Now go look at the big chunks of rock over there," and he pointed out the citrine and malachite on the other side of the store. I walked obediently to the malachite and closely inspected the swirls of green and black in the stone while I tried to hear what he and Sandy were saying. They talked in whispers for a few moments, and then Ben said, "All right now, you can come back," and I walked over to him and took his hand.

"Thank you so much," I said to Sandy. "How long will it take to get the ring?"

"Aren't you some nosy now," Ben said laughing at me again.

"Well, if I'm going to be engaged, I want everyone to know it."

"You know it does take awhile, and we've got lots of orders ahead of yours. We'll just do the best we can," Sandy answered.

"I know. I'm just impatient."

We spent the afternoon walking around Jordan Pond and then had tea and popovers as the sun disappeared behind Penobscot Mountain. Ben suggested we stay for dinner in town before taking the last boat back to the island. He needed to go down to the docks—something about the overboard discharge system and getting a new Loran—and hoped I wouldn't mind going to the market and buying some of the hard cider he liked so much.

We agreed to meet at an elegant restaurant we'd read about in the newspaper. I ordered salmon and Hollandaise with a glass of my favorite wine, Chassagne Montrachet, and Ben had steak with garlic potatoes and his favorite draft beer. We sat and talked about when we might get married, who we wanted to have there, and whether we should wait until the fall or even next spring or just elope. After dessert—my favorite, crème brulee, and Ben's, strawberry shortcake and whipped cream—Ben said, "Well I've got something for you," and pulled a gray, velvet box from his pocket.

I saw the name inscribed on the box, the Rock Shop, Willis & Sons, and, puzzled, said, "Ben, what's this?"

"You could open it and find out."

I did, and saw my engagement ring sitting in the black velvet, held by a little ribbon, as beautiful as it had been in my mind. "How? How did you do that?" I asked.

"There's advantages to not being from away, you know," he said. "Sandy's boss is Clem's wife's brother. I told her it would mean a lot to me to get it today, and I promised her some lobsters."

Ben picked the ring out of the box, and I held out my hand as he slipped it over my ring finger. It felt as if it had been there forever. I kissed it, and then I leaned over the table to kiss him.

❦

I called Katherine, and then Stephen, to tell them I was getting married. I felt badly that I had shared so little with them that they were surprised.

"Isn't this kind of sudden?" Katherine asked.

"Well, yes and no, it's Ben, Ben Bunker. I met him years ago up here and then again after I moved here," I explained.

"The man on the island, Mom?" Katherine asked. "That's amazing, Mom. I had no idea you were even seeing someone. No wonder you looked so happy. But what about his wife?"

"Yes, he's lived here all his life," I answered, the secret finally airing in the breeze like an unfurled sail. "She was my friend who died."

"Last year?"

"Yes, she was sick for the past couple of years."

"Isn't that a bit quick?" Katherine said bluntly.

"Yes, it is. But we're getting too old to wait around. And Katherine, I know it's hard to understand, but his wife loved us both enough to want us to be together if she couldn't be here. It's a huge gift of friendship and I will love her forever for it because it means I can love him without feeling guilty. I can love him and miss her at the same time."

"That's beautiful, Mom," Katherine answered.

"That's great," Stephen replied when I told him about Ben. "You love it there; he loves it there. That's great, Mom." I could detect nothing but happiness in his voice.

I thought it would be harder to tell my mother. When I called, she said she had been in her garden clipping roses and was a little out of breath. "Let me just sit down dear and drink some water." I could see her, immaculately dressed even to work in the garden, using an Irish linen handkerchief to pat her face and sitting down in the Queen Anne chair. "You sound excited dear, so tell me what's going on."

"Well, I'm going to get married."

"Again!" my mother said with surprise. "Well, you just don't give up! Who is it this time?"

"It's Ben, Ben Bunker, the man who gave me the little red and white boat." There was a long silence in which I could hear her breathing, until I finally said, "Are you all right?"

"Of course, dear," she replied. "I think that's the most romantic thing I've ever heard. I was just sitting here thinking how wonderful that you found your lost love. He was your first love, wasn't he, and I almost made you lose him forever. I'm so sorry."

"What?" I said, incredulous.

"Just let me go on. I knew there was a chemistry between you, like there was between your father and me. But I worried that was all there was, that there was so much distance between you that you couldn't grow together, and, besides, I was young then dear and I didn't know any better."

"I thought you would be mad at me, mad because I want to be with someone who comes from, well..."

"That's just silly," she said. "You have more money than you need, what you need is someone to love and to love you, to grow old with and be your friend. If that's who you've found, I wish you and Ben all the happiness you've missed before—and then some," she said, and then asked, "When is the wedding?"

"Next month."

I worried again that she wouldn't think that was proper, but instead she said, "Good. Don't waste time. Now dear, I really must rest. I love you."

We married in late July. Katherine was my matron of honor. She sat me down in the living room the night before the wedding and asked, "Do you think you know what you're doing?"

"No, of course not, and it was a stupid question for me to have asked you when you and Mark were getting married. I don't have a clue what we're in for." And then a moment later I added, "I just know I love being with him. He makes me laugh and he makes me feel safe, and those are two things I treasure. He seems like the best things I remember about my father rolled into one with my best friend and best lover, and that's more than enough."

Katherine smiled at me and said, "You know you had a lot of guts to make another chance for yourself. Most people don't see that they can have a second chance at being happy if they try. You remind me of Anne in Jane Austen's *Persuasion*."

"That's a great compliment," I replied. "She's one of the nicer women. Some of them are awful."

"And she finally married the man she loved, that Lady What's-Her-Name had told her wasn't good enough for her when she was younger," Katherine said firmly. "But he was good enough. He was a good man and he loved her, and he had a sense of humor and irony. So many of them seem like worthless fops and such incredible snobs. He was all she needed and by the time they got together again, they were old enough to appreciate that."

"And it only took them eight and a half years to figure it out," I replied. "It took me, my God, I can't believe it took me so long." Sadness and awareness of the enormity of wasted time washed over me and I stood looking almost vacantly at my daughter, thinking about the years that had vanished. Finally I said, "I guess I wouldn't have been able to get to the present if I hadn't been through the past. Maybe there was no other way to get here than to wander around for so long."

"So here's to you, Mom, to you and Ben and second chances," Katherine said, holding her arm up so we could clap hands, "Here's to you and Ben, no matter how long it took."

Just before the ceremony, Stephen took my arm and led me out the library into the doorway where we stood for an instant, and I remembered standing in the same place so many years before at Ben's birthday picnic, looking out at the ocean and the other islands. I saw my mother and Taylor, Robbie and his wife, my friends, Monica and her friend Chuck, Sarah and Jeff, Ben's children, brothers, their wives and their children, and my children and grandchildren and my friends from the island, and their smiles filled me with happiness. Then Stephen said, "Is this what you really want, Mom? If not, we can turn around."

"No, but thank you for asking. This is what I want. I'm sure."

"Then let's skip, skip for joy." I gathered my aquamarine silk skirt in one hand and together we skipped out the door and across the boughs of balsam and rhodora we had strewn that morning from the house as an aisle, laughing and smiling at everyone. People stared in surprise and then laughed and clapped as well.

We skipped along the aisle, and then I saw Ben laughing with us and standing next to the white wooden arch through which we had woven pink rugosa roses the night before. I smiled at him and thought, "He looks so happy. How wonderful that he looks so happy." I went up to him and hugged him, and then we stood together under the arch, facing Reverend Stevens and the sea. After Reverend Stevens married us, we kissed, and then I looked up and saw a pair of eagles circling over us, the sun reflecting off their white feathers, and I laughed at such a wonderful omen.

Epilogue Fall 2012

Islesford, Little Cranberry Island, Maine

As we sat close together on the green wicker rocking chairs looking at the dark ocean, I moved my hand to the armrest just as Ben did, and our fingers twined. He turned to me and smiled, but we didn't speak; instead we rocked slowly, adjusting our rhythm without thinking until we were moving in time both with each other and the waves swishing below us, like taffeta, against the rocks. I felt the motion of the chair and wondered if he missed being on his boat now that he had given it to Chris for her husband's growing fleet. I thought about the children I read to that day at the library. Little Sue Coombs, grape jelly staining her mouth, who stared at me from under uneven bangs, transfixed by the story of Miss Rumphius. When I finished the story, Sue exclaimed, "Ooh, Mrs. B., you're just like Miss Rumphius. You're old, you're from Maine, you're a librarian, and you have lots of lupine in your field!" I wanted to protest, "But I'm not an old lady," but instead I just smiled at the little girl who was so excited by her discovery.

When I walked home from the library that afternoon, I thought about the ways in which Sue was right—I was old, I did have a gray bun of hair knotted at the back of my neck, and I always threw on an apron with lupine stenciled on the front when I worked at the library so that I could keep a handkerchief, a stick of lip balm, and a pen and pencil in its deep pockets. "I'm just a frumpy old librarian," I muttered to myself.

Now, as I sat rocking next to Ben, I thought about how sometimes he looked like an old turkey gobbler, with a little fold of skin suspended from his chin that shadowed his profile. Well, I thought, if he could forgive my age spots and bad knees, wrinkled thighs and the little red veins that criss-crossed my ankles so thickly that they looked like permanent bruises, then I could forgive him his wattle and the fact that his butt seemed to have migrated to his belly. I laughed out loud at the thought and he turned to look at me, inquiring with raised eyebrows what I was thinking. "I was just thinking how handsome you are."

"Oh sure," he replied laughing. "I'm just a wrinkled old man."

"But you're my old man, and I love you," I said as he raised my hand to his lips.

"Do you ever wish we had the same children, the same history? Do you ever wish we'd gotten married when we were young?" I asked.

He sat for a while quietly and then said, "No. It wouldn't have worked. You'd have still been mad at everyone, and I'd have been trying to prove I was as good as you and your family in all the wrong ways. Better to save the best for last."

"Forgiveness and love. The best for last," I said raising my glass.

❧ ❧ ❧